SOUTH OF THE SKYWAY

NOMADIC RHODES
BOOK 1

SYDNE BARNETT

FLAME & FICTION LLC

AUTHOR'S NOTE

Well hello there, darling. Thank you for joining Rhyett and Brexley on their journey, and I hope you love them as much as I do—which is *a lot*. These two came to me while I sat across the table from my first ever Booktok-turned-real-life friend, discussing all things romance books and life in Florida. I didn't expect to fall as deeply in love with them as I have.

Overall, the *Nomadic Rhodes* series will be light and spicy, with a dash of dry humor, lots of love and big family dynamics. The content should stay fairly lighthearted.

That being said, there are a few elements I want to draw to your attention, because—as always—***mental health matters***!

<u>**Here are *South of The Skyway*'s content disclosures:**</u>

Mention of domestic violence (no on-page content, not one of the main characters), after effects of domestic violence, survivor of childhood neglect, mention of a stillbirth/infant death (no on-page content, not one of the main characters), extensive open-door explicit sexual content including but not limited to fellatio, cunnilingus, and anal play.

I do take these lists seriously, so if I missed anything, please feel free to reach out via my website: sydnebarnett.com

Happy reading! Xoxo

ONE
BREXLEY

"With all due respect, give me the goddamned penis."

I cackled, hiding my face behind the frilly pink book as Noel slammed another copy onto the shelf. After twenty-four years of friendship, you'd think her antics would have lost their touch, but she never failed to make me laugh.

"We get it, we get it. Delay, trauma, *delay*. But it's been *three* books. We all know where this is ending up." She slid another thick paperback onto the shelf before turning for the box of character-scented candles. "Get it on already."

"It's called a *slow burn*," I pointed out playfully. Dusky, blush light filled our little bookshop as the hands on my watch kissed closing time. The ironic part of this conversation was that Noel was the one who helped our customers find said slow burns, whilst I scuttled away and tracked the inventory.

"It's called *boring*."

"To each their own."

"People actually buy this stuff?"

"All day, every day," I said. The soft hiss of the last copy sliding into place made me smile right as the bell rang. I pushed the empty box aside as Noel sighed, turning for the door with her signature grin.

"Milly!" she exclaimed, as though she hadn't just been berating an internationally bestselling romantasy author. Wiping her palms off on her jeans, my best friend made a beeline for the little blonde beaming back at her. "You're here for the new Lucy Score!"

"Absolutely, I am! Do you have it?" *Like clockwork.* Milly memorized release dates like our baristas memorized latte orders.

"Of course, I do," Noel said playfully, making her way to the romantic comedy shelf. "I read it in one sitting. It's so good to see you! How are you?"

Milly grinned, following her lead. "Better than I deserve, darling. Thanks for asking. How 'bout yourself?"

The remainder of their interaction faded to a distant blur of sound as I moved to take over stacking ruby glass candles into a tidy pyramid. I loved this one the most with its sandalwood, balsam, and cedar scent. Personally, the idea of bathing in a fragrance that was curated in an ode to fictional book boyfriends struck me as a little odd. But women went haywire for the things, swiping them from our shelves faster than the artists could ship in more. I had to admit, this one took me right back to one of my favorite series, and sneaking sniffs was officially part of the job description.

The evening light was fading behind towering buildings, condensation still gathered in the corners of our picture window, the cars beyond idling at the intersection. When Milly made her way out the door, a handful of chattering women entered, my throat instantly constricting. *My cue to leave.*

With a personality as colorful as her wardrobe and coppery auburn hair, Noel was the people person of the two of us. She was always quick to strike up a conversation and find commonalities to relate to. Whereas I preferred to avoid small talk with more dedication than I'd likely give to the bubonic plague.

It worked—our little arrangement—I squirreled away, taking inventory and running the backend of the entire operation, while Noel tackled...well, the peopling. The dream of The Cracked Corset had been in my heart since we graduated high school, and I couldn't imagine opening it with anyone other than my designated extrovert. With my general distaste for human interaction, I certainly wouldn't have opened it alone, that was for sure. Our all-romance bookstore and whimsical coffee shop was nestled among other quaint businesses in downtown St. Pete, and took the vast majority of our time, tenacity and determination in our early twenties.

Royal, my cheery little retriever, perked her head up as I absconded into the office like someone had released a hive of bees rather than our sweet regular clientele. Her tail was flicking as though she couldn't be bothered but was happy to see me, nonetheless. She settled back onto her bed as I turned on my laptop, the machine making a jovial little chime as it came back to life.

This was my forte. The web work, social media schedules, coordinating with authors for signings and events, booking live musicians, profit and loss—pretty much all things data analysis that made Noel's brown eyes go glossy a beat before she'd blink and start a new task that kept her moving and her hands preoccupied. I sighed when my email about the space across the street still appeared unopened. The Corset had grown, the niched business thriving in the bustle of the city, and desperately needed more room to expand. The building was antique perfection just begging for someone to see the beauty in its bones and breathe some life back into the brick and mortar that time and vacancy had allowed to crumble. Yet again, I was chasing a vision I wasn't quite sure I could bring to fruition, but the space kept calling to me. Every day I passed those enormous picture windows, my mind filled with what could be—where I'd put the shelving, or the cute and cozy couches we'd been drooling over online. I'd been sending emails almost daily ever since the sign went up in the window. Either we'd unintentionally stolen the owner's parking spot, or she just never checked her email, because that little envelope still showed up as sealed. Noel would be just as disappointed as me if we couldn't scoop it up.

My thoughts easily drowned out the women's chattering voices, blurring them into the background as my music played softly on the little record player in the corner. Impractical as it might have been for small spaces, there was nothing—and I mean nothing—like hearing it on vinyl. An old habit I'd inherited from my grandpapa.

When the chatter wandered into a tunnel of a quick exit, I leaned back in my chair to peek out, curious if the coast was clear. Tote bags encouragingly stretched full of merchandise, the gaggle made its way onto the noisy street. The briefly open door filled our space with the noise of engines, horns, and the whirr of passing cyclists. Noel returned to the table, unpacking and positioning the stack of character art in a skillful little display. They were the last customers for the evening. Our coffee shop had already closed with their side work done, baristas having long-since headed home for the night.

"You're coming to The Three Leaf tonight, right?" Noel called over a shoulder, well aware of my eyes on her. The Three Leaf was our favorite bar, and played host to the vast majority of our girls' night gatherings.

I sighed, glowering and wandering to her side, only to find unyielding eyes beneath those chic, choppy red curls. She ran her fair, freckled fingers through the copper highlights before tucking a nearly limp strand behind her ear. End-of-the-day hair was never in its finest form in this climate.

"I don't wanna hear it, Brex. We promised the girls."

The girls were comprised of a handful of women we'd met in high school and college, all of whom Noel stayed intimately in touch with, memorizing each facet of their life and compiling more facts with each phone call or coffee date, while I was content to simply observe.

"Yeah, yeah." I waved her away, making my way to the espresso bar and fishing my keys off the hook below it. "I'm coming. I promised I would."

"Mhmm, like I haven't heard that before."

It wasn't that bad. Really, I wasn't a flake—always studious about my commitments—but I loved socializing as much as I enjoyed contracting pneumonia. I whistled, summoning Royal as I twirled the ring.

"Must I pinky-promise for you to believe me?"

"I'll settle for an escort."

I rolled my eyes and released an airy laugh, catching her drift. "If you wanted to pregame, you just had to ask."

"But where's the fun in that?" Noel grinned, mischief in her eyes as she settled the final print, standing as Royal proudly pranced to my side.

"You're impossible."

Noel flicked the leash off the hook on the wall, bending to clip it on Royal's collar before ruffling her golden coat. The bell clanged as she opened the glass door and stepped onto the sidewalk. Thick Florida heat slicked my skin, abrasive enough that I practically felt my hair frizzing out. Winter was comparatively mild, but summers in this humidified swampland felt like gradually suffocating with a wet rag strapped to your face.

Oblivious to the sweat immediately dripping down my back, Noel turned her face to the sun like she worshiped the thing, unwilling to acknowledge her freckled skin still refused to adapt to her unfortunate environment. Our walks to the park had become tradition a few years back when we first opened The Cracked Corset.

Royal was practically salivating, her head tall as she led the way to the park against the bay, enthusiasm intensifying with every yard we closed. She was something of a local favorite. Her promise of cuddles and a wagging tail were as much an enticement as the curated selection and collector's edition covers.

"If Nick is there tonight, you should say hi," Noel encouraged.

"Eh, too eager."

"*Too eager?* Do you hear yourself? I'm not sure any woman has ever said a man begging to date her was too eager."

"Honestly, have at him. He's not my type, and I don't know…I'd like to decide for myself if I'm interested before someone's propositioning me."

"What? Did he—"

"Figuratively speaking."

"Jesus, woman. Give me a heart attack."

"Like you'd expect me to say yes?" I balked, tugging on Royal's leash as she buried her face deeper into the shrub, likely for discarded food from the cafe we were passing. Or attempting to pass. Pulling again, she finally budged.

"No, but I need to know these things."

"Obviously, I'll keep you apprised in the dating department."

"You better."

"Albeit, it's been so long, I think I've forgotten how."

"It's like riding a bike. You'll hop right back on, promise," she said with a wink.

We stepped out into the road, Royal now happily trotting a step in front of us as I complained, "There are freaking cobwebs down there."

She snorted, shaking her head and sending her soft hair swaying. "So, stop putting so much pressure on things. Lighten up a little. Have some fun."

"Fun—because tolerating idiots until you find your soulmate is fun?"

"It's supposed to be, but we might need to surgically remove the stick up your ass."

"It's just, nothing's been the same since Robby."

Every girl has to fall for one bad boy, right? Robby was mine. Maybe it had been the fact that one look at his grungy band t-shirts, leather cuffs, and loose-laced skater shoes would have had my dad turning twelve shades of crimson, and that *Top Gun* mustache of his quivering. Of course, that assumed the man had come around to lay witness.

Spoiler: *he didn't.*

Maybe it was just the fact that after a few short flings, he was the first guy to pay me any consistent attention. But after a year of cleaning up after the lazy ass, paying both our bills for the sake of his 'music', and putting up with his stoner buddies pissing on my bathroom floor, I determined flying solo was infinitely more freeing. The Cracked Corset had been taking up my time and energy ever since. And our numbers freaking showed it.

But so did my dating life, or pathetic lack thereof.

Stopping just outside the black gate, Noel leveled me with a glare. "I know."

"It's probably best to just give up. There's nothing to miss unless you bring it up."

Noel bent down to unclip the leash when we stepped inside the dog park's gate. "You're thinking too hard again. It doesn't have to mean anything. You just need a fling. A very belated rebound."

"Maybe," I admitted, taking a deep breath as the blessing of thick foliage shade blocked off the sunset. End of day or not, the heat was everywhere. Palm trees bordered the entire dog park enclosure, towering along the walkways beyond and marking the perimeter of the grassed-in space. The telltale buzz of a mosquito cut my relief short. Yep, that was par for the course.

"You *do*!"

"I guess," I grumbled, throwing the neon tennis ball and smiling as my girl sprinted straight for the far side of the enclosure.

"Well, I *know*, and as your best friend, you're obligated to trust me." She knelt to accept the ball when Royal returned it, throwing the slobbery thing and wiping her hands on her jeans as she rose, glaring at me. "Starting tonight."

"Yeah," I muttered. "Fine."

TWO
RHYETT

"I swear to God, man, if one more contractor tells me it's the supply chain problem, not their lazy asses to blame, I'll can every single one of them and build the damn thing myself."

Broderick sighed at my frustrations. "It's not that bad."

"Oh, but it is. One delay after another. There's a reason I'm down here and not out on the boat with Jameson. They're freaking raking it in this season."

"Of course. It's Murphy's law, Rhy."

"Yeah, yeah." At that, Broderick's smooth laugh cracked through the speaker, and I smiled. I didn't believe in any of that pessimistic bullshit he clung to, but something about him falling back to it was familiar in a way I needed during all the upheaval. He'd been in my life nearly as long as I could remember–my younger brother, Jameson, picked a fight when we were four and five, and we'd all been best friends since. "Miss you, man. How're things up there?" By *up there*, I meant with his witch of a woman. Broderick was the kind of guy that had never struggled to get a girl but struggled to keep one worth hanging on to. We had that in common. However, where I relished loving freely, Broderick had wanted to settle down since we were in college. Now, he taught at the damn place and was settling for the girlfriend from hell.

"Miss you too. Same old, same old. Nothing to report here."

Like he'd get away with that shit. I was just waiting for the phone call that he'd finally freed himself from those shackles.

"How's Sarah?" I pressed. His hesitation spoke volumes.

"Fine. Great, she's working a lot."

"Good, hope that's going well. How are you?"

"You know. Just hanging in there. Work's been great. Some truly promising students this semester. I'll enjoy these last few months with them."

"Well, there's always that."

"Yeah," he agreed, a beat too quickly. "Hey, Rhy, I gotta run. But keep me posted on things down there, will you? And do your research before signing any out-on-his-luck, Joe-blow with a clipboard onto the legacy house, alright?"

"Like I'd do something like that."

"Totally would. Talk soon."

"Yeah, man, talk soon." The phone disconnected, my truck speakers flipping back to Pink Floyd. I rolled down my window, setting my arm on the edge and savoring how the warmth wrapped around my bones here, the breeze kicking up as "Money" started blaring on the speakers. I chuckled at the irony. That's about what the family account sounded like with this project finally up and rolling. My mother had dreamed of retiring in south Florida for as long as I could remember, starting a little mini homestead somewhere her bones didn't ache for half the year.

We'd gone a few times growing up, although traveling with your own freaking football team-worth of children certainly posed its challenges. Last year she'd found the perfect property, not too far inland, still within range of that coastal breeze, and a quick jaunt to the beach. Just enough land to keep a handful of animals and grow her own garden. The quest to build the first family home on the land consumed enough mental energy that she'd finally asked if I'd be willing to oversee it.

Maybe it was being the oldest son, or perhaps it was that I'd dabbled in construction between commercial fishing seasons, but either way, I'd agreed. Which brought me here. Basking in eighty-degree sunlight as rubber met pavement, climbing up the four-mile bridge between the central city and southern retirement communities. They might be ready to settle down on the sleepy stretch of the coast, but I thrived under pressure. My bar back in Mistyvale was thriving, despite the challenge of a limited demographic. Working from fifteen on had its benefits: like saving up enough to start businesses in my twenties, and push them to thrive by thirty. It started with The Grizzly Grind, a coffee shop on the harbor. My next venture was a grungy, industrial bar called The Birch Barrel, and both businesses had grown to be local favorites. If I could embrace a tiny, cold rock in the middle of the ocean and make magic on it, a thriving metro like this would be freaking epic.

Where my siblings saw endless competition, I saw the infinite potential and a culture ready and teeming with patrons who would delight in the character we'd intentionally build into the space. This shit was my catnip. Planting businesses, feeding them as they grew until they flourished. And today was day one. Ground zero. My first attempt at recon in my new city—checking out the cool parts of town and dropping in on the nightlife to get a feel for the local vibe, and my soon-to-be competition. It would be a much-needed reprieve from the chaos of the build job, endless meetings with architects and engineers, soil tests, and tracking down permits.

First on my list? A little pub that commanded live music and raving reviews, not three blocks off the bay. Five minutes on foot would drop me at my second, a bougie little sushi joint with an exclusive list of guests that—to me—indicated I'd have the perfect clientele. An odd combination? Hell yeah. But there was studying to be done everywhere, if only I remembered to slow down and look.

Speaking of which...*damn*. The view from the top of this thing was ridiculous. Ripples of white-capped waves to either side, the teeth of urban skylines ahead and behind. Enormous barges drifted calmly through the bay as boats tore trails through the water. It wasn't particularly windy, though I'd bet there would be windsurfers on a good day. And that *glorious sun*. After spending my first three decades as a consistent companion to fog and rain, there was something so satisfying about knowing I'd see it every day. My sisters were going to lose it. If anyone wore anything besides bathing suits for the first six months, I'd be flabbergasted. And was that—*holy shit, yeah*— that was a fishing pier in the water, lined with car after car, spots of colored shirts and buckets littering the side of it as people milled about. The thing must've been miles long. Jameson, Axel, and Broderick would never leave. They'd just camp out right there in the middle of the bay.

Laughing, I soaked up the last rays of sunshine and wind in my hair, keeping the beat with my palm against the side of my truck as the bridge was swallowed by the city. This was going to work. Everything would work in our favor as long as we trusted our intuition. My intuition? It couldn't wait to order a pint and a plate of cheesy potatoes and see what kind of local flavor I could find.

I finally arrived at the pub just as another truck pulled away from the curb, opening a valet-worthy space for me. Grinning, I swooped in, turning up The Beatles and allowing my eyes to rest as the last trace of sunshine dipped below the horizon. I stepped out, grateful the parking was free this late, and grinned at the sound of a drum solo and raucous laughter pouring from the black front doors.

This was going to work.

THREE

BREXLEY

If an Irish pub and a cigar lounge did the nasty, the resulting love child would likely look a lot like The Three Leaf. Aged brick walls kissed weathered wood floors, long tables took the place of individual gathering spaces, and the barstools lining them were always full of bystanders waiting for their turn. The booths were full to the brim with laughing patrons. Honestly, the whole ruckus was just a bit overwhelming while somehow maintaining a semblance of calm.

Noel's obligatory *girls' nights* had become expected about once a month, maybe every other during the busy season. I appreciated their company as much as I could when they insisted on gathering in establishments with more semi-contained percussion solos than places for soul-deep conversation.

"So, how's business?" Josie was most empathetic and likely to abscond from the chaos and talk about shit that mattered. I liked her, although I could never remember to actually instigate a get-together to bask in her brilliance, despite perpetually promising myself I would. She had a way of making everything look fashionable, and tonight was no different. Josie elegantly emphasized her glittering hazel eyes with an understated lilac shadow that caught the low lamplight. Her onyx curls were dramatically swept to one side, fingers consistently running through her shiny mane again as she looked between us expectantly.

"It's been great," Noel chirped happily, dipping a fry in her left-over tartar sauce.

"Staying busy?"

"Sold out of four authors before Wednesday this week," I said with a smile, absently stirring the straw between ice cubes.

"Of course, business is good," Vallie said pointedly. If every group had a ringleader and a cheerleader, Noel was the latter and Vallie was the former. She and Josie were two years ahead of us at university, and took Noel and I under their wings. I'd tried to resist–stay in my little bubble–but good luck arguing with the captain of the debate team. It was no shock to anyone when she kicked law school's ass. She rolled her deep brown eyes, muttering, "Your barista is as hot as the coffee she's serving."

Noel cackled into her cup, setting it down with a little more force than was strictly safe as her face cracked into a grin. "You could finally say something, you know? Wrenly is newly single, not psychic." Wren managed the coffee shop side of The Cracked Corset, and had been Noel's right hand woman for the last two years.

Rocking her drink around its rim, Vallie shrugged. "The timing just wasn't ever right, you know?" She fluttered a defensive hand, shooing us away. "And she's too good for a 'scraps after the firm' kind of life. We're busier than ever." The duo had danced around flirtations at the shop since we opened, both in and out of relationships, always with the wrong person at the wrong time. But Wren had dumped her most recent boyfriend a few months ago, and the posse had been joking about taking bets on who would finally say something. When she shot me a desperate gaze in a rare plea for assistance, I smirked but changed the subject, turning to Josie as she slipped her phone back into her pocket. Checking on the kids, inevitably.

"How about you? How's the agency?"

"Boss still a bitch?" Vallie quirked a brow, sipping pointedly as her shoulders relaxed. Josie snorted, nodding. The two had been inseparable since their freshman year in high school, adding Noel and me on like designer bags they couldn't leave behind when our dynamics collided. Where Josie was all quiet contemplation, Vallie had been born to lead. She was so freaking clever, always a dozen steps ahead, so by the time someone had thought to ask a question, the answer was already on her tongue. It's what made her such a formidable opponent in the courtroom.

"That won't change," Josie admitted. "But honestly, as long as I work from home, it's not so bad."

"Psst," Noel hissed, nudging me in the ribs.

"*Ow*," I complained, scowling at her as she jerked her chin towards the door.

She snickered, smirking but keeping her eyes on the entrance. When I followed her gaze, I spotted the cause of the distraction.

"Hot damn," Vallie murmured. She quickly threaded her fingers through her black and purple goddess braids, running her tongue across her teeth to check for stowaways. "Found me a tall glass of water."

"As if," Josie said, chuckling into her cocktail, eyes flicking up. She lurched like she was trying not to choke. "Dibs."

"Nah-nah, Brexley has birthday month dibs. End of." Noel grinned, quirking her head sideways like she was assessing an asset.

"In my dreams, maybe," I scoffed, using the back of my chair to twist around for a view, craning my neck to get a peek past the table in front of us. I immediately wished I hadn't, as the air leaking out of my lungs dried out my mouth. We all studied the mountain of muscle poured into fitted jeans and a sexy as fuck Henley, top button undone. "Even then, he'd probably say no," I muttered to no one in particular.

"I hate birthday months," Vallie said under her breath, earning chuckles around the table.

The six-foot-two dreamboat boasted a crown of luscious golden waves above sun-bronzed skin, dark ink peeking out of one rolled sleeve. When his eyes landed on our stretch of the table, we all shifted, returning stiffly to stilted conversation as heat crept up my cheeks.

"Oh. My. God," I mouthed breathlessly as I turned back to the table, finding Vallie's gaze on me, a flush beneath her warm sepia skin. We both broke into nervous laughs, ducking our heads and sucking down alcohol like our lives depended on it.

The man's smile had been as blinding as the Florida sun. *Good lord, did he burn my eyeballs?* Might as well have for all the clarity I could gain from my new surroundings. Josie was the first to recover, clearing her throat.

"Anybody tune into the game last night?" she asked as the others readjusted their drinks, everyone shifting as we brought our attention away from the newcomer. "Rhodes made the game-winning drive."

"You and freaking Paxton Rhodes," I muttered, rolling my eyes. She'd been fangirling over the Chicago quarterback for three freaking years, her enthusiasm not dwindling as the novelty wore off. "He walk on water again this week?"

"Might as well have. God, the man can *move*."

Vallie laughed, twirling the pink straw in her drink, which she appeared to be focusing on with all she had. "That's literally the name of the job. He does it for work."

"Welp, he's welcome to *work me* whenever he likes."

The table transferred a round of giggles, my cheeks warm with liquor, and let's be honest, probably some semblance of lingering flush. That would be my last round if I was wise. "Final score?"

"Twenty to seventeen."

"Lame," Noel laughed into her drink, earning an eye roll. Noel knew as much about football as I did astrophysics, which was a little less than nothing. "Any new dates on the horizon?"

"Zip," Josie shook her head, stabbing at her ice cubes again.

"Zero," Stacey said, leaning back and pulling her hair into a sleek mahogany ponytail. She was the quietest of us, rarely speaking up unless the subject was immensely valuable to her. One too many hours poolside the day before tinted her pale skin pink, and she looked more likely to fall asleep on Vallie's shoulder than make it another hour here.

"Zilch," Vallie muttered, shaking her head and prompting her braids to bob.

"I mean, studies show the happiest people in our country are unmarried women without children," Josie stated matter-of-factly. She almost always brought this up when one of us pointed out the hopeless situation that was dating with our thirties around the corner. By this point in life, all the good men seemed to be taken, and those strewn about looking for body warmth were carrying baggage none of us had the capacity to take on. We'd all prioritized our careers in our early twenties, building reputations and businesses. Although, as those damn biological clocks started ticking, it seemed less and less likely we'd meet an adequate match. Only Noel had a suitor—a slick-talking corporate ladder climber I didn't particularly care for. As long as he kept her happy, I'd leave it alone. But Eric had slimy schmoozer written from the gel in his hair to the overpriced watch on his wrist.

I ran my finger through the water ring abandoned by my martini and said, "Honestly, I don't even miss the chase."

"And what about *the hunt*?" The resonant timber wracked shivers up my spine, skin needling with anticipation as a warm, spicy scent invaded my senses, rounding my eyes. The girls all snapped their heads up, wide gazes locking behind me.

"Oh my god," Vallie murmured with no attempt at subtlety as she nearly choked on an ice cube. I rotated to see a cocky smile laced with expectation below gray-blue eyes set in an ungodly beautiful face.

It should be illegal to look that good and have a voice that could liquify a chastity belt, but he managed, drawling, "I was going to offer a drink, but since that's off the table, could I persuade you to join me for a game of darts?"

My throat bobbed, anxiety settling where the air should go. Dear God, the man was delicious. The skin beside those intense eyes wrinkled in deep laugh lines. He was probably thirty, every inch of exposed skin kissed by the sun, his Henley and jeans advertising each swell of his toned physique. Sporting a smattering of short, scruffy stubble that just begged to be touched, he kept that cocky smile on as he waited for my answer.

I raised my hand, about to wave him off, when Noel blurted out, "She would love that. But you better put money in the game, hotshot. She doesn't play for free."

If I'd had two fewer drinks in my system, I would've been mad. Hell, I would've been enraged. But drunk Brex and sober Brex were entirely different beasts. And drunk Brex was acutely aware of the fact that her lady parts were dusty enough to put the Sahara to shame and intrigued enough to size up the outsider flashing a panty-melting grin.

"You make it sound like I've stumbled on a shark in heels?"

Swallowing down the wave of attraction, I turned to face him head-on, tracing his frame from foot to face.

Um. Yes, please.

God, this place was always the same incestual crowd of regulars, save for the occasional stray looking for a home. But this newcomer was absolutely delectable, earning a sincere smile as I locked on bottomless blues.

"I guess you're about to find out."

FOUR
RHYETT

Women confident enough to wear an outfit like that, with an ass capable of making a priest pause to reconsider his life choices, rarely bothered to be seen at little dive bars in the heart of the city. They certainly didn't throw darts like some undercover assassin. This one was something worth slowing down for. I'd known it the moment her eyes found mine. I was supposed to be studying the business, not its patrons. But dear God, I'm just a man, and spotting her was better than basking in the sunlight.

Blonde hair cascaded in precise waves to her waist, a rich purple top draped across her breasts, the deep v-neck disappearing in her beige, curve-hugging skirt. Grey thigh-high boots gave her an extra couple of inches, making her lean physique tantalizingly long. I was supposed to be beyond lusting after a tight body at thirty-five years old. Still, she had me fighting to focus on her baby blues instead of lingering on the gold body jewelry sparkling across her sternum and draping under her breasts.

The woman wasn't just mouthwatering; she held herself with that self-assured confidence that said she knew exactly who the fuck she was and where she was going. It was hot as hell. As her final toss knocked a pre-existing contender from the bullseye only to replace it, I blew out a low whistle.

"Jesus. Your friend wasn't kidding."

"Noel?" she said, beaming as she tossed those golden waves. "We never kid about high stakes."

"Competitive?"

"Absolutely."

"Got siblings?" I asked, curious.

"None worth mentioning."

Straight to the point. I could appreciate that.

"You?" she questioned, blowing a soft blonde curl off her face. Taking a second to study her before answering, I noted the precise blade of eyeliner, her cosmetics sheer but applied intentionally, a light shimmer over each lid.

"Twelve of us," I finally replied. The double take was precisely as expected, as was her next question.

"Good lord, are you, like, Mormon or super Christian or something?"

"Nope."

She blinked, before delivering the classic follow up question. "All one set of parents?"

"Yep."

"Your poor mother."

Chuckling, I quipped, "I'll tell her you say so."

She giggled before choking on the sound and covering her mouth. "You know what I mean."

"Honestly, your concern is warranted. I'm not sure how she's retained any semblance of sanity." It was true. We'd certainly given her a run for her money, especially the younger boys.

"Mine lost her shit with one, so I don't have a clue." She marched forward, plucking out our darts as she asked, "Where you from?"

"How do you know I'm not from around here?"

Bright eyes flicked to me as she popped her hip. "We own this bar."

Well, that was interesting. It would be a little inconvenient if she didn't believe in community over competition, now, wouldn't it? "Literally or figuratively?"

"*Socially*. And believe me, if we had seen you before, we'd remember."

"It's an awfully big city," I pointed out. Some part of me was deeply satisfied when she immediately countered.

"And an awfully small bar."

"Play," I said over a smile, jerking my chin towards the board. She complied, the sharp point sticking just to the left of the center. She spun one between her fingers before handing it to me. It was such a chaste graze of skin, it shouldn't have caught my attention, but it did. Something electric sparked up my spine. "I'm Rhyett," I offered as I tossed it, landing just to the right. I certainly wasn't as practiced as my opponent, but it wasn't too shabby. At least good enough to keep my balls intact.

"Brexley," she said as her next shot hit the red.

"How about you?"

"Just told you, didn't I?"

I chuckled, shaking my head, and making a point of handing over her drink, lingering for just a beat too long to see if our chemistry was as electric as anticipated. It was. Of course, it fucking was. Heat shot through my spine, yanking tight beneath the zing of her touch.

"You from around here?"

"Born and raised. You can't tell from the exhaustion under my eyes? You *are* new around here."

"Not a fan of Tampa Bay?"

"Not a fan of Florida in general."

"Seems a shame to live in the sunshine capital of the country and loathe to be here."

"The tourists get the good stuff. They leave the scraps for the rest of us to fight over."

Yikes. My parents had their hearts set on somewhere their joints could thaw out once my dad handed over the wheel to my younger brother. Hell, it was all my mother could talk about, shy of preparations for the upcoming season.

"Oh, come on, it can't be that bad, can it? You guys have how many thousands moving in every month? That's gotta mean something."

"That's the problem."

"Sorry to add to it."

She flashed a cheeky smile, rolling the dart between her fingers before sending it flying with a quick flick of her wrist. "For you, I suppose we can make an exception."

"Glad to hear it."

"So, do you always challenge strange women to a game?"

"You looked like you could handle yourself."

"Excellent judge in character."

I lined up my next shot before returning to my studies. The dipping fabric revealed a quote scrawled just below her collarbone in dark ink, skilled fingers adorned with a handful of delicate designs. A woman after my own heart; she had opted for a decorated temple. Her skirt clung to the subtle curve of her toned legs, and I didn't bother to keep my eyes from wandering as she rotated, stepping wide to steady her stance before her final toss.

Brexley nonchalantly brought the glass bottle to her lips. Martinis, dark beer, scary accurate darts all wrapped in a gorgeous little frame?

Fuck me, who is this girl?

"I never thought I'd get this lucky, though." When her brows arched, I knew the words had come out of my mouth rather than staying in my mind where they belonged. *To backtrack or run with it?* Obviously, I'd run with it. What the hell else was a man to do?

"I've always dreamt of getting my ass kicked by a five-foot-five blonde."

The heat of her body had just caressed my skin when some jack-off wearing a dark baseball cap stumbled into her shoulder, dumping both her beer and his down her side and earning a round of expletives so flavorful I nearly lost it laughing. She had a freaking mouth on her. I'd never been prouder. I stepped between them, partially in her defense and partially so she didn't break his freaking face with the bottle now clutched in her manicured fist.

Steadying the idiot, I sent him on his way with a curt, "Get lost," before turning back for her. Brexley eyed the back of his head like she still might seek retribution, so I snatched a pile of napkins from the nearest table. Then I stepped into her space, blotting down the line of her arm up to her shoulder. I didn't miss the way her breathing sped up, although I'd tuck that away for another time.

"Thanks," she muttered, leaning over to set down her bottle. "Fucking prick."

I put my hands up in surrender, "My bad, just trying to help."

The diffusion did precisely what I'd wanted; that cheeky smile appeared, replacing her momentary scowl as she accepted my outstretched offering, commencing the recovery process.

A deep breath later, she offered me a shaky smile. "Thanks, Rhyett. God, this is why I hate coming out. This shit always happens."

"Might I suggest playing at a different bar, then? This one clearly has some shit juju."

"You know what I mean. Some drunk asshole gets in the way, or won't stop hitting on us, or starts swearing at the bartender or—"

"Dumps his brewski down your favorite outfit."

"Yeah, that." She sighed, setting the sopping towels on the table before motioning for the bathroom. "I'll be right back."

"I'll walk you."

For a beat, I thought she'd say no and bark to stay put. So when she gave me an anxious nod, my heart leapt in its cage. Broderick would never fucking believe this, even if I held her for validation. The man was one hell of a wingman, but this whole evening was next fucking level. If I walked out of here with her phone number, I'd be happy as a clam.

I grabbed Brexley's hand, relishing that the attraction translated to heat that flicked up my arm and around my low spine. Weaving between bodies in a stilted dance, I led her toward the back, carving my way toward the green neon sign for *the loo*.

"Take your time."

"Don't go anywhere," she bit back. Even as the shadow in her eyes told me she didn't believe I'd stick around.

"Wouldn't dream of it." To prove my point, I leaned against the opposing wall in the hallway, sliding my fingers into my pockets. The space smelled of cheap booze and piss and a faintly detectable lingering trace of vomit. Live music played from the center of the tables, the band actually not half bad, and the bustling servers seemed sincerely content in their space. I just leaned back to 'people watch' as I waited. Couples danced, groups of men played pool, and some poor bloke turned away from Brexley's table, looking dejected as the petite Latina crossed her arms, glowering pointedly. I chuckled to myself. Maybe I was the odd one out, after all.

"Hey, I'm sorry, there's no salvaging this."

I turned back as she emerged from the ladies' room, seemingly frustrated and somehow still hot as hell as the damp fabric clung to her frame.

"Do you want me to take you home?"

Her laughter erupted in a manic explosion. "Rhyett, you're a peach and all, but if you think for a second that I'm walking out that door with you without those four chasing me down, probably tasing you, or bludgeoning you to death, you're high."

That's freaking cute. "Good. As it should be."

Brexley quirked her head, brows dipping before she demanded, "Come again."

"Look, I'm all for chasing karmic connections, but I've got six sisters, and I'd hope to God their friends would threaten some rando at a bar with imminent violence if he was pushing one of them."

Blatant skepticism pinched her features as she asked, "What's your sign?"

"As in, zodiac?"

"No, what's your top-secret hand sign? Yes, your zodiac, Rhyett."

"Sagittarius."

Her eyes narrowed. "For real?"

"Yeah. Let me guess, you only date Aquarius."

"Hell no, too freaking emotional. Plus, water signs smother my fire."

Fighting the urge to laugh while digging through the useless mental files of star signs my sisters had long ago planted, I guessed, "Aries."

Those blue eyes narrowed again, yet she shifted closer to me as another woman squeezed by for the bathroom. The band transitioned to a new song. "How'd you know?"

"Kinda obvious."

"Oh, it is not." She tucked another step tighter, though I couldn't tell if she'd intended the movement or if her feet just did it for her.

"Feisty, competitive, direct. Yeah, you remind me of Jeanne."

"Ex-wife?"

I snorted, shaking my head. "Older sister."

"You know," Brexley said as she wrinkled her nose, "you could just say you're not interested."

Oh, hell no.

I closed the gap, sliding my hands around to cup her face, savoring the little hitch in her breath. When she didn't pull away, I threaded a hand through her silky hair, loving the parting of her pink lips. The way she refused to drop my gaze even as that slender throat bobbed. Heat climbed through my chest, wrapping around my spine as our exhales hung heady and heavy between us. The taste of her laced the air, anticipation sending my free palm down her side, grazing her breast and the exposed skin along her ribs where the halter dipped in the back, before grabbing her tapered waist and pulling her into me. Brexley raised onto her toes when I finally grazed her lips with my own, her eagerness sending my blood thrumming. Euphoria swept through my veins. I needed to taste her, feel more of her. Her lips parted as though in invitation, and with the compliant way her body immediately melted into mine, I certainly wasn't about to tell her no. Our tongues clashed like they fucking belonged together, need sparking hotter, muscles coiling as drive demanded I give her more.

Women weren't generally complicated. Most needed a friendly reminder of their radiance, and they'd turn to putty below a practiced touch and a whispered compliment. But not Brexley. She moved with me. Each flutter and shift was symbiotic, as though we'd synchronized it. As if she anticipated each advance.

Goddamn.

I wrapped my hand in her hair, sliding the other down to grab her ass and pull her closer up against me. Needing her body closer as the blood rushed to my cock. She shifted too, climbing up on her tiptoes, fingers cupping my jaw as she kissed me back. When my movements became more dominant, she moaned against me. Fuck, what I would give to know what sounds she made when she was full and satiated.

Hands sliding to her waist, I turned her back to the wall, rotating to cage her in as the woman left the bathroom, rushing past us. Brexley certainly didn't seem to mind, her fingers finding their way to my hair, pulling our mouths tighter together.

"Rhyett?" she breathed against my lips.

"Huh?"

"Your place or mine?"

FIVE

BREXLEY

Rhyett's chuckle was like Christmas freaking morning, his breath hot against my lips as he cradled my face in his calloused palms. This was so not what I expected when Noel dragged me out tonight. But who the hell was I to look a gift horse in the mouth? The impossible was suddenly a *reality*. The most gorgeous guy to ever grace The Three Leaf with his presence had only just pulled his tongue from my mouth because, like an idiot, I moved to talk. He grazed his lips over mine in a heady caress, our breath one enormous cloud of lust between us. Fuck, even his laugh was sexy.

"I'd like to avoid being bludgeoned."

"Chicken."

He shrugged nonchalantly. "Too much left to do, Ace."

Ace. Why the fuck did that moniker make me want to puke less than the others I've had thrown at me over the years? *Sweetheart, princess, baby*—yuck. Maybe it was the fact that his cock was rock hard where it pressed against my belly; that detail alone was intensely intimate. Perhaps it was some dumb subconscious part of me that was painfully aware I had never, ever, under any circumstance, thought about hooking up with some hot mountain of muscle I didn't know from Adam in the back of a pub. However, as my hand slid down to cup his erection and satisfaction rumbled in his chest, I realized the number of fucks I had left to give was precisely zero.

I was sick of trying so hard, worrying so much, clinging to my life like I had an inkling of say in anything in the world. Rhyett was cute, fun to play with, and took zero offense to my foul mouth. And—let's be real—he was sexy as fuck.

We all know where this is ending up. Noel's words rang in my mind as he brought his lips back down, more urgent, more demanding. God, my entire life had been a slow-burn. But, like, the kind where I was the side character. The smart best friend that never sat at center stage. And maybe it was the hormones, or maybe it was the margarita-martini-Guinness combo currently assaulting my bloodstream. But for one night, I just wanted to be the badass main character that saw what she wanted and freaking took it. So, I sucked down a breath, peeling away from his perfect, hot lips.

"You wanna start with me?"

"Are you kidding?"

Fear spiked through me for a beat, worried he was insulted, but as his mouth came down, hands roaming freely, leaving an unbearable fervor in their wake, my excitement and arousal intensified.

"Fuck, yes."

I settled my hands on his solid chest as the words buried into my belly, wanting desperately to peel the fabric from between us, and gave him a shove towards the bathroom. He didn't budge, instead looking around, making sure the coast was clear before snatching my wrists between his fingers and plowing through the swinging door backwards. The moment it closed behind us, he moved for me, hands gripping my ass and hoisting me into his arms, wrapping my legs around his waist.

"Well, hello, sailor." His responding chuckle sounded so familiar that I narrowed my eyes, demanding, "What?"

"I'm a commercial fisherman."

I blinked back at him, wanting to ask questions, but acutely aware of the ache now throbbing between us. "Tell me about it later?"

"Deal," he breathed, backing me into the wall as his mouth descended, stealing my air and forcing my eyes closed. God, the taste of him was incredible. Below the beer, there was spice and something salty. He slid his long fingers around to cup my inner thighs, inching towards where I suddenly needed him more desperately than oxygen. Fuck, Noel was right. I had missed this, had needed it desperately. The feel of his calloused skin against mine, the way he ground his body into me, pinning me against the brick wall.

My eyes snapped open, and I glanced around the abandoned room, wrinkling my nose. He sensed it, the sudden apprehension, peeling apart to pepper my neck with kisses that made my resolve teeter like a cheap bowling pin.

"I can stop," he breathed against my skin, sending tingles firing down my neck and arm.

"Don't you dare," I hissed, tightening my legs around his waist. Rhyett shifted into me, pressing us impossibly closer together. His hot palm cupped my sex, pressing against the apex with deliberate and delicious intent as he found the wet spot in the lace, a groan forming in his chest. My damn brain...

"It's just..."

"Just what, Brexley? Talk to me, pretty girl."

"Wash your hands."

"What?" He spluttered, leaning away from me, mirth written across his face.

"I'd prefer not to regret this moment because my vagina is an inferno in a day or two. Wash your hands, Rhyett."

"You are a particular kind of keeper." He snickered but brought his mouth back to mine, hands slipping away from my pussy and chuckling when I whimpered. Twisting towards the sinks, he growled, "Make up your mind, Ace."

"Go. *Yes*, go. Me too."

He shook his head, settling me on my feet to turn, and pointedly dumped an exorbitant amount of foaming soap into his palm as I jammed the deadbolt closed and lunged for the sink beside him. Smirk growing across that tan face, Rhyett seemed at war with his amusement. As I scrubbed my own palms, he shifted, slipping beneath my skirt in a smooth motion as the opposite hand gripped my waist, pulling the arch of my ass against him.

"Are you wet for *me*, Ace?"

"Find out, hotshot."

"Yes, ma'am." His fingers dove beneath the lace, slipping into my soaked entrance with a soft, satisfied groan. "Oh fuck, you're a good girl, aren't you?"

A little thrill shot through me, and then he was moving, my spine arching as he shifted against my walls with practiced curls that sent pleasure into my body. Rhyett had a way with his fucking hands, the movements applying just enough pressure to drive me wild. As he hit that elusive spot in the back, another finger deftly slid between my lips to put pressure against my clit.

Holy fuck, holy fuck, holy fuck.

His chuckle faded into a breathy demand. "Quiet, Brexley. They can hear you."

"Fuck, that was out loud?"

"Yeah, baby, now shush, or we'll get caught."

"I'm not anyone's baby," I grumbled. Only Rhyett just slid a palm up my side, gripping my neck and turning my face back to his as the other worked inside me. His lips put an end to that concern, all synapses firing simultaneously as he stroked my G-spot with expert motions. I tried not to think of why he was so damn good at that. When my knees buckled, he hummed appreciatively, sliding a thigh between my legs and pinning me against the counter as I grappled for purchase.

Oh God, I'm hooking up with a total stranger in The Three Leaf's bathroom. Adrenaline shot through me as it battled arousal for dominance.

"Condom?" It was somewhere between a demand and a question as he traced the edge of my jaw with his lips. His hand fell away from my neck as he rummaged in his back pocket. My head was swimming. Spinning as he called forth pleasure that was utterly world-rocking. He handed me the condom, moving to my breast, working the sensitive bud through the fabric. Some judgey corner of my mind winced that he was the kind of man who carried one.

I wanted to eat him alive as he tugged aside my top, making me only kiss him harder, dipping below to wrap a hot palm around my breast.

"Fucking hell, Ace. You feel too good."

"Show me."

He dropped his hold, straightening the elastic before the zip of his fly reached my ears. "I'm clean," he said as I felt his fist stroke his smooth cock against my ass.

"Same," I hissed back, needing to feel him fill me, though I wasn't about to tell him that.

"You're perfect," he whispered so softly it was almost as if to himself. He grabbed one of my hands, guiding me down to feel his impressive length. "You want me, pretty girl?" I gripped him in answer, a bit intimidated by his size, if I was honest, yet I nodded, nonetheless. God, I hoped he could use that thing. Nothing would be as disappointing as throwing myself into the deep end only to come up with some idiot who couldn't use his equipment. Judging by those hands, though…

He slipped my fingers away, the crinkle of the condom wrapper telling me he'd swiped it as I braced against the counter.

When Rhyett sheathed himself, he was entirely uninhibited, a thick finger holding my panties out of his way as he slid into place. His cock so swollen it hit all my walls, painting stars in my vision. On a groan, he stilled, waiting for a solitary pulse before wrapping his arm around to rub against my clit in steady motions, timed with each glorious thrust.

"You're so close. I can feel you, Brexley."

The air left my lungs as he set the pace of a starving man, free hand roaming up and down my side like he couldn't get enough of me either, lighting every nerve ending on fire.

"That's it, baby, give it to me."

Fucking hell, what was it about this man's mouth? Robby definitely hadn't ever used his words to his advantage. Not like this, anyway. Tauter and tauter, pleasure wound me up until his pace became demanding. Rhyett showered me in affirmations, a constant stream of words like 'so beautiful', and 'fucking perfect'. Hot palms caressed my sides, my ass, gripping my hips as his thrusts came harder, his body coaxing mine into submission. My walls fluttered and gripped him until my release slammed through me with Rhyett tight on my heels, as he leaned his body over mine, pressing kisses to my cheek, my neck, and jaw as he panted against me.

SIX

RHYETT

We'd straightened ourselves, exchanging breathless laughs and nervous smiles, when I slid my palms up to cradle her face, pulling her back to me for a kiss. She returned it with a delicious fervor before slipping out of my arms and making for the door on the tail end of a smirk.

"Very pleased to meet you, Rhyett."

The laugh burst from me as I lunged forward and snatched her wrist. "Nice to *meet you*?" I questioned. "I think we did a little more than meet, don't you?"

She shrugged nonchalantly. "You could say that."

"Can I have your number?"

"I don't do booty calls."

"Like I would assume such a thing."

She giggled, returning to straighten my belt, untuck the side of my shirt, and run her fingers through my hair. The woman's touch was a fix I was already craving, and we hadn't even left yet. I needed to see her sprawled out and needy on my bed. On all fours. Screams muffled in my pillow.

Brexley teased, "What could possibly give me that impression?"

I slid my fingers through that silky blonde hair, tugging her lower lip between my teeth. "I'm not in the habit of being a fast fuck when I stumble upon a dream girl."

"And what about luck?"

"Luck?"

"Do you believe in it? Luck? Fate?"

"Feeling pretty lucky right this moment."

"Then count to fifteen, and if you're meant to have my number, fate will see that it happens."

"That's insane. Brexley, that was incredible. You can't tell me you didn't feel that."

"Oh, I felt it," she said breathily, shooting me a wink before straightening her skirt again, pulling her hair up only to drop it down again. "And if we were meant to meet, we'll see each other again."

She giggled when I just kissed her harder.

"Come on, hotshot, let the fates decide."

"Fuck," I grumbled, rubbing at my jaw. "This is insane. You know this is crazy, right?"

"Maybe."

"As long as you're aware," I tossed back, fighting the smile as I ran a hand over my hair. "Jesus, I can't believe I'm saying this, but fine. We'll let fate decide."

"Good boy," she said, slinking for the door as I shook my head.

"See you soon, Brexley."

The mischief in her smile sent anticipation yanking my spine. "We'll see."

My heart stuttered when Brexley walked out the door, every inch of my body rebelling against those fifteen damned seconds before I rushed to follow. The room was full of the same level of chaos as earlier, although my gaze went directly to the now-empty table I'd fished her away from, and despite myself, my heart sank. I bolted through the room and out the front door, scanning both sides of the sidewalk before raising a hand to my jaw, trying to decide if I was desperate enough to sprint off in hopes of catching her. If I'd only known which direction she'd gone.

<hr>

NOT UP FOR THE DRIVE, and secretly hoping I'd run into my Ace, I stayed in a boutique inn a few blocks from the pub. The sushi place was as cool as the reviews claimed, but every little blonde that walked in the door made me perk up, only to be disappointed.

Jesus Rhy, man up.

Brexley wasn't my first sneaky link and likely wouldn't be the last, yet none of them had left me wishing I'd pushed harder for a number or a freaking social media handle. Not that she could learn much from the three photos I'd ever bothered to post. Hell, why hadn't I thought to invite her to the exclusive restaurant everyone—and I mean everyone—wanted a chance to try?

The bed was comfortable enough, but sleep was being an evasive bastard, and by about two in the morning, I'd given up. Should have just made the drive home. I rolled over, shoving aside the fluffy white duvet so I could reach my phone on the bedside table. My younger brother, Jameson, answered on the second ring. We were a polar pair, the two of us, but growing up less than a year apart, all that push and pull came with an unparalleled camaraderie.

"It's two a.m. your time. Are you drunk or on fire?"

I chuckled. "You're in port?"

"Yeah, I freaking reek. Was about to hop into the shower. What's up?"

"I fucked up."

The faint click of a lamp switch accompanied a groan before a distant thud. I imagined him dropping his duffle onto the hardwood. "Alright, I'm listening."

"I met a girl."

"That was fast."

"But she told me to let the fates decide if we're meant to meet."

"What the fuck does that mean?"

"That I'm an idiot." There'd never been a truer statement. Fuck, I should have fought for her, pushed her on it. But everything about her felt like the fire sign she so proudly claimed. Wild. Uninhibited. Like she'd smother if I put too much pressure on her.

"I'm afraid that's well established, so what's new?"

"Piss off."

He chuckled, and suddenly the audio was tunneled. I assumed he was putting me on speaker. "For real though, fill me in, man."

"Met her while doing some market research—"

"Is that what we're calling it now?"

"—and we just, I dunno, clicked. But when everything was done—"

"Christ Rhy, *in* the bar?"

Like he could talk. Jameson was hands-down the wild-card in our family, next only to our youngest brother, Maverick. "—and I asked for her number. She told me if we were meant to connect, we'd see each other again."

"Welp. Clearly, you're both crazy, and it's a perfect match."

"Come on, be real."

"I am being real." He cleared his throat as I heard the shower flip on. "I love you, man, but you're a hopeless romantic if you think that was anything short of a dismissal."

"Fuck."

"I mean, didn't you *just*?"

"Shove off."

Jameson's laugh had always sounded like home to me. It was no different when he was serving me a steaming pile of tough love. I ran my hand over my hair, wishing I could see his face, and had been smart enough to drag Paxton into the conversation. Five years Jameson's junior, Pax was likely the most level-headed of our brothers. He was direct like Jameson, without being quite as cut and dry. The siblings between us were both far too optimistic to construct proper feedback, so we'd loop him in whenever we needed a mediator and an actionable game plan.

"You get a picture?"

"Between zipping my pants, and her skirting out the door under the guise of fate?"

Jameson hesitated for a beat–a telltale of him actually bothering to think before speaking. "Nothing before?"

"No."

"Dark and tan?"

I countered, "Blonder than me."

"Damn," he chuckled. "That's new."

"Long, gorgeous hair, tan, tattooed, sexy as sin."

"So, long story short, you're screwed."

"Yup," I said, sighing in resignation.

"Welp. We all have at least one that got away. I gotta shower and pass out, man."

"Yeah, alright. Love you."

"You too. Keep me posted."

I scoffed. "The odds aren't particularly in my favor."

"They flip that way more often than not."

"True. If fate's on my side, the Brexley saga shall continue."

"Brexley?"

"Yeah."

"Cool name," he noted.

"Cool chick."

"Lame."

Huffing a discouraged breath, I said, "I know."

"Don't fuck it up next time."

A CALL from the contractor woke me hours before checkout, giving me plenty of time to stretch and meditate before heading back into the city. I had an hour until the next showing, so I followed my feet. In the process, the white chocolate creamer had swallowed the temperature and flavor of my coffee, and I'd been able to check out a handful of cozy cafes and opening shops along the way. Breakfast consisted of a chocolate croissant that would make my trainer break out in hives, except this was kind of a vacation. A *staycation*, if you will. And it was damn good.

My phone buzzed for the seventh time in as many minutes as I crossed the street into a shaded park brimming with blooms that would make my sisters melt. Speaking of...

ELORA

Have you found our new empire yet?

HADLEE

Seriously, it's been a week. Shouldn't you be reporting back?

PAXTON

I still don't get why you guys don't come here. I've got years before I can bounce.

MAVERICK

Because it's colder than a witch's tit on Halloween. That's why. Hell, we have that here.

AXEL

Love you Pax, but yeah, no thanks, man.

JAMESON

Rhy got a little...distracted.

ELORA

Jesus, this is why I should have gone.

HADLEE

Am I going to be an auntie?!

RHYETT

Oh piss off Jameson. You've got a fat mouth, you know that?

JAMESON'S only response was a series of laughing emojis.

LEIGHTON

So? What's the consensus? How's the sunshine state? Find any promising LOCATIONS?

RHYETT

On my way to a showing now.

HADLEE

I expect a report back tonight.

MAVERICK

I can't wait to get off this rock.

RHYETT

Yeah, yeah. Talk soon.

I SLID my phone into its designated pocket, shaking my head as I glanced around the bustling park. Tossing my now-empty coffee cup into the trash, I looked up when panicked shouting filled the air. A rogue golden retriever was full-throttle sprinting after what appeared to be a petrified squirrel. I burst out laughing, deciding against my better judgement to jog forward until the dog spotted me, the momentary distraction enough to send the squirrel flying up a tree. Prey forsaken, I squatted down to the ground with open arms, pleased when it came bounding forward. There was a reason these fluff balls were called man's best friend, and I ruffled layers of copper fur as the tiny beast buried its face in my chest.

"Hey, buddy, what are you doing off on your own?"

The dog quirked its head and, as though it understood, turned over its shoulder like I'd be able to spot the owner.

Two women came stuttering to a stop, the redhead's mouth popping open before curling into a coy smile. Then I met round, bright blue eyes set into tan skin, disbelief rushing through my veins.

Well, I'll be damned.

SEVEN

BREXLEY

"You have got to be kidding me."

Rhyett's satisfied smile was radiant enough to knock me on my ass, the joy permeating that delicious timbre as he asked, "How's *that* for fate, Ace?"

"I think fate had the treasonous assistance of a canine companion."

"Royal can assist me any day of the week," Noel muttered. She didn't bother to hide her assessment of his frame as he stood from Royal's side. Fuck, I was shocked she didn't liquify when he turned that grin in her direction, reaching out with an eager hand.

With a sigh, I motioned to her and said, "Noel—Rhyett. Rhyett—this is my best friend and business partner, Noel." When the two of them released their handshake, he immediately moved for me, pulling me into an unexpected hug. I awkwardly patted him on the back as Noel stifled a smirk, snatching the leash from my hand and bending down to hook it on Royal's collar. As he pulled away, Rhyett tucked a strand of hair behind my ear, the gesture strangely intimate after our salacious encounter, before freeing that sunshine smile down like my personal freaking star.

"How was your morning, Ace?"

"Fine, thanks. Yours?"

"Better now."

Heat crept up my cheeks, the accompanying eye roll big enough to knock over a building. "Shameless."

"Are you working today?" He nonchalantly pulled his shoulders back, ignoring my quip and straightening despite the incessant begging of my suddenly needy dog as she nuzzled into his limp hand. For pity's sake, the traitor was straining against her leash to get to him. Rhyett complied contentedly, absently rubbing up and down her jaw without dropping his gaze, sending her tail into a frantic fan.

"Uh—yes, yeah, I am. I'm heading in now, actually."

Did the fucker just swallow a laugh?

"When are you off?"

Oh, hell no.

Noel, the nosey-nancy-turned-mind-reader, was quick to interject, "We close at seven."

"Excellent. Let me take you to dinner." The demand should have been aggravating. That machismo bullshit never worked on either of us. Only, my belly ended up clenching as his eyes drifted down my face, lingering on my lips until I nervously bit the lower one. He jerked his gaze up, satisfaction lining his eyes. When he brought a hand up to brace his jaw, heat rushed through me at remembering exactly what those fingers had felt like on my neck, my breast, down the line of my waist...buried inside me. Thighs clenching, I cleared my throat.

"I've got plans afterwards."

Noel, grinning maniacally like the meddlesome psychopath she was, went to open her mouth before I could glare pointedly enough to keep her quiet. *Freaking twatwaffle.* She was going to throw me under the bus for the fib. Instead, Noel cleared her throat.

"I better get the place open. See you in ten, Brex?"

"Right behind you."

She patted a palm on his broad chest as she passed him by, taking my traitorous wretch of a dog with her. Rhyett's chuckle only partially distracted me as she turned over her shoulder, pointing two fingers to her eyes and then back to me. I couldn't help but laugh.

"Brex?" He quirked his head. When I nodded, anxiously tucking my hair behind my ears, he mirrored the motion, face saying that was right on par. "Nothing serious. I'm checking out some commercial spaces today, but then I'm just doing recon all afternoon. There's a Brazilian bar a few blocks east of Three Leaf with rave reviews, cocktails on fire, smoked whiskey, skewers of meat served however you like it."

"I don't know, Rhyett. I think I had my fill last night."

"Come on, Ace," he said, shifting forward and cupping either side of my jaw in his warm palms. A trail of sweat dripped down my spine, settling on my low back. I wanted to say something sassy, wanted to push back for all the reasons I'd decided I was done dating. For all the reasons Robby had ripped my heart out in the first place. I was *distant*, flighty, and scared of grabbing life by the horns. I wasn't entirely sure I was mother material, and even if I was, did my life need to be consumed by a ruckus group of crotch goblins?

If not, was there even a point in compromising my finally content little bubble to make room for someone else?

But something in Rhyett's touch made me feel likely to turn into a puddle of puree, the words freezing somewhere between my mind and mouth. He lowered his face until he was an inch away, resting his forehead on mine as the heat of his breath parted my lips.

"You and I both know I haven't even gotten started with you." A chill snaked down my spine as everything went hot. But when his lips should have taken mine, should have liquified me into a puddle seeping into the cracks of the sidewalk, the fucker pulled back. Cocky smile twisting his expression, he obviously knew exactly what he'd just done. "I was dumb enough to let you slip through my fingers last night, Brexley. I'll be damned if I do it again."

Putty. My bones had turned to putty. It was a fight to not clear my throat. "Cheesy line, Rhyett."

"Did it work?" He chuckled.

"No," I said, too quickly. The slant of his mouth told me he knew it. "Maybe," I admitted, trying to will my body to reclaim its faculties. Sucking down a breath, I peeled away from him, needing a few feet between us to screw my spinning head back into place.

"You feeling lucky?" He parroted my challenge, laughing when my eyes narrowed.

"The deal was that you get my number, not that I'd come out with you."

"The number is a good start." He slid his phone from his back pocket, handing it to me. "How else could I text you the address?"

"You're a cocky little thing, aren't you?"

"You know as well as I do there's nothing *little* about me, Ace." If it hadn't been so goddamned sexy, that smile laced with pure masculine satisfaction would've had me seething. But the man was not wrong. Our scandalous tryst in the bathroom had been the best damn sex I'd ever had. I'd seen stars. *Twice.* Once when he fucked me breathless and once when I remembered it, alone back in my apartment.

Maybe it was the fact that it had been months since anyone

touched me or the heightened adrenaline at the premise of being caught bent over the counter with a stranger in the back of Three Leaf, but a growing suspicion in the back of my mind said it had just been...*Rhyett*. At the end of a long-suffered sigh, I lifted his phone, entered my name and number, and slid it back into his hand.

"Happy?"

His smirk turned wolfish as he hit the call button, melting into something milder when my own cell began ringing. "Very," he said. "I'm texting you my name."

As if I would ever forget it. This man would be forever seared into my retinas—his grip on my hip, palm to my breast, scent on my skin—for the rest of my days, whether or not I saw him again. "Sounds good."

"And the name and address of the restaurant, the reservation is under my name. Seven pm."

The deep inhale did very little to calm the stampede of anxiety in my belly, but I nodded and said, "Don't get your hopes up. I don't really do dating."

"Lucky for you, neither do I. Would you prefer to meet there, or should I pick you up?"

"Rhyett. I wouldn't even have time to go home and get ready."

"You're perfect like this. Why would you bother?"

"Do me a favor?"

"Yeah."

"I haven't even told you what the favor is, and you're just agreeing?"

"No less responsible than letting your dog run off on you."

"She recalls just fine, normally. Usually, not even the damn squirrels—" I bit my lip as he started chuckling. The beautiful bastard was messing with me. "If—and I cannot stress how big of an 'if' that is—I ever agree to a date, just leave the cheese at home."

"Fine, no cheese. So...I'll see you there?"

When I narrowed my eyes, he stepped forward, wrapping one palm around my neck and the other around my waist, leaning and creating an infectious cocktail of mingled breath. *Christ, get it together Brex.*

"Keeping me on my toes here, Ace."

Just as I made to rise up to taste him one more time, he smiled. The arrogance permeated the air between us as he straightened out of reach. Again. He flashed a wink, swaggering backwards. *Cocky son of a bitch. Did he withhold his lips to prove a point? Did he just tease me?*

"Welp. You better get used to it. Like I said, I've got plans tonight." I thanked every star in the sky my voice came out steady. Oh god, I wanted him. Here. Now. And the worst part was, he freaking knew it. I shook my head, chewing on my bottom lip and starting down the trail Noel had taken a few minutes before. But when Rhyett turned on a heel, striding in the same direction, I stopped in my tracks, scowling at him.

"Are you stalking me?"

"Hey," he said, raising his hands in mock defense. "I just allowed fate to decide, since that was your rule."

"No. *Right now*. What are you doing?"

"Heading to my showing."

"No."

"*No?*"

"You're walking this way?"

"I mean, I haven't figured out levitation yet, so yeah, that was the plan."

"Dammit."

"We're doing it."

"Doing what?" I balked.

"That awkward thing when you say goodbye but have to walk in the same direction."

"It would seem so."

"So?"

"No. We *just* parted ways."

"Fine. How long am I waiting today? Fifteen seconds?"

I smirked up at him, shaking my head at the amusement written over his features while some kind of desperate humiliation rodent burrowed into my belly. "Make it thirty."

"Seems excessive."

"To each their own."

His chuckle sent flames up my neck. "Alright, Ace. You've got thirty seconds. Better make 'em count."

I MADE it back to The Cracked Corset before glancing at my phone to see a smiley emoji and "Rhyett Rhodes."

Well, that was interesting.

EIGHT

RHYETT

The three little dots indicating Jameson's forming response were amputated by the flash of his face as my phone buzzed in my palm. I'd texted him that fate was swift, and the moment I answered his call, he barked, "No way, man." Disbelieving laughter ensued.

"Get this, her dog—which is a gorgeous mini golden retriever, by the way—wouldn't listen when called and ran right into my arms after the squirrel fled up a tree." Jameson had always been absolutely obsessed with Goldens and naturally loved those that kept them happy.

"That's some chick-flick level shit."

"I know. She's joining me tonight at The Pint."

"If she didn't just tell you what you wanted to hear."

"You're a terrible wingman," I muttered, shaking my head.

"Yes, well, you left Alaska, not the other way around."

"Hey, probably temporary. Plant a few businesses, come home at least for the summers."

"I'll believe it when I see it. So, what time are you meeting up?"

My feet came to a halt outside the crumbling facade. This place had been beautiful in its day. I could just see it in the architecture, behind the peeling coral paint and dented plaster. The wide-open windows would let in a ton of light during the day. Jeanne and Elora would lose their freaking shit over the intact cornices in the doorway. A few months of restoration, and a less unfortunate color palette, and we'd be in business.

"Well, I mean... technically, she said no, but I have a good feeling."

"It's official. You're pathetic."

"Seven. Reservation is at seven."

"Six, five, four, three—"

I snorted indignantly. Shook my head. "What in the hell are you doing?"

"That's three pm here."

"Did you just count on your fingers?"

"So what if I did?"

"This is why I handle the real estate."

"Don't judge a fish climbing a tree."

I chuckled even as I glanced at my watch and up to the address for the third time, just to confirm my feet had led me to the correct location. Yep. This was it. "The fish can eyeball an entire catch plus or minus a pound. He's doing just fine."

"Alright, well, we'll be up here prepping on the boat when you go in. Slacker." I could just picture him rolling those gray eyes. "However, keep me posted on the Brex-a-nator."

"*Brex-a-nator?* Alright, dingus. How was yesterday's haul?"

"You know Milo."

"*Nice.*" We had the pleasure of being raised and trained by the infamous Captain Milo Rhodes. He trusted intuition over projections, and the movements of aquatic friends over human statistics. Usually tiptoeing on this side of the law, he'd become a local legend before his twenty-first birthday. He'd just follow his gut to the weirdest locations and pull up enough fish to weigh the ship down, nearly scraping bottom as he came into the cannery. He held more records than anyone on the island. They were wrapping up cod before heading down to see the progress on the new homestead, only to return home to prep for salmon season.

If I weren't so excited about not having icicles currently hanging off my beard, I'd be bitter about missing the summer. Salmon had been my forte since I was a teenager, and there was nothing as satisfying as the sea in the summer.

"Well, enjoy the day off. I'll update you after the showings."

"You always have the best luck. You'll find a spot, don't worry."

I chuckled. It was true, I'd become a master manifester in high school. Odds were, that's why I'd been sent down here. "Talk soon."

"Love you."

"You too."

Phone returned to my pocket, I grabbed the brass handle and pushed open the door to the clatter of metal tools and a loud thud. "Hello?" I hollered. "Everything okay?"

A muffled, "Back here," was the response. Quirking, I followed her voice down the wide hallway. God, the history in this place had to be fantastic. A few cracks in the plaster and dents in the drywall were the only signs of wear on the interior. The stretching honey hardwood was full of character, mottled with marks and dings the wealthy paid to have artificially created. A stain and a seal would bring her back to life in no time.

"Marco," I called out, chuckling at the immediate response.

"Polo!"

I glanced at my smart watch, double-checking the woman's name before saying, "I'm supposed to meet Clementine."

"Yap."

There was another crash, followed by a muffled curse, a shift of metal across hardwood, and then the swinging door at the end of the hall flew open. My heart suddenly ached for my mother; the similarity in their energy was uncanny. Clementine's thick silver curls were swept back into a claw clip, loose spirals hanging beside her face. A pair of round bronze glasses—more of a steampunk costume than a day-to-day accessory—were set on her nose, with a tiny notch at the center. Sparkling amber eyes sat above rouged, light umber cheeks.

"Here," she pressed a paintbrush into my hand, scowling at the mess below the old ladder. "Hold that." She quirked her head, evidently considering what to do with the spill of black paint. I grimaced, shrugging.

"I mean, I wanted to restore these beauties, except black paint has a certain grungy, dark academia vibe to it. Pair it with some original wood accents and gold accessories. It'd work."

Mischief sparked in her eyes, full lips curling. Plucking the brush from my fingers, she dropped into a crouch and happily spread the spill out over the sanded floor before rising back to her feet, crossing one arm under the other as she surveyed the fresh coat of color.

"S'pose that'll do it. Mr. Rhodes, I assume?"

I mirrored her positioning, leaning back to observe the coat of drying paint. "At your service."

"Evidently so."

"Happy to be put to work if the terms are agreeable."

"Happy to get back in my garden and far, far away from that

contraption." She jerked her chin at the ladder, still teetering uneasily.

"Why don't you show me around? We can talk terms as we tour."

Clementine tucked a strand of peppered hair behind her ear, stepping over a bucket of supplies and reaching a handout to steady herself on my shoulder. There was something enchanting about people who assumed a familiarity before it had been established. My mother had the same effect. She gave an exasperated sigh, wiping her other hand on a pair of faded overalls to rid it of shiny charcoal paint.

"What's a young buck like you gonna plant in my building?"

"First up, I'm thirty-five—"

"*Youth.*"

"And I'm sitting on a few plans, although for this place, I'd like to utilize what I learned building my bar in Mistyvale and design a speakeasy. Embrace the roaring twenties. Create a space for vintage artists to play their music." As I explained, the woman's face gave away nothing, so I just soldiered on. "Spoken word. Community events. Truly bring together a space that celebrates where we came from. Classic vinyl when we don't have live music."

"And you're qualified for this venture? Lemme show you around while we discuss. This is the third room." Clementine stepped around me, motioning back to the hallway. I pressed myself into the wall to make space as she maneuvered, then followed in her wake. The blur of cars rushing by the front windows was a momentary distraction, and I swallowed, trying to stay focused.

"I'm a born entrepreneur, ma'am. Grew up on the water, third-generation commercial fishing. Stashed my income until I could invest in my first business."

"Which was?"

"A coffee shop on the harbor."

"And?" She pointed to a beautiful room full of natural sunlight. Elora would lose her mind at the wainscoting, let alone the warm afternoon glow. I cleared my throat as we approached the front, trying to follow her lead.

"We've since expanded."

"Well done. Are your people happy?"

"Customers or employees?"

"Either? Both?"

"Based on the reviews and the fact that I've had the same handful of leads for the last five years straight, I'd say it's been well received."

"Why a speakeasy?"

"My next venture was a bar and became a local staple." It was true. Back home, the bars leaned more towards 'dive' than the atmosphere, so it hadn't taken a lot to set us apart and create a space people wanted to hang out in for more than piss beer and good company. Leaning into a theme would make that all the easier. "I figure if we're contending with widespread civil unrest and infectious diseases, we might as well embrace the more entertaining aspects of the twenties. Party in plain sight but create a clever requirement for entry—secret passage, mystery lever, code on the old school payphone. Eventually, be reservations-only and a waitlist. Niche down and deliver a one-of-a-kind experience."

"I like it, Rhyett—can I call you Rhyett?"

"I'd certainly prefer it to Mr. Rhodes."

"Well then, Rhyett, I think you're in the right district. You've obviously done your research. And I like your moxie. That being said, Tampa is not some rocky outpost in the Bering Sea. Bars are a dime a dozen down here, and your competition is tight." Mistyvale wasn't anywhere near the Bering Sea, but I squashed the desire to correct her. Irrelevant anyway.

Instead, I offered, "There's more than enough business to go around."

"Cutthroats down here will beg to differ."

"A rising tide raises all ships. If we elevate the expectation of a memorable experience, the businesses that follow that lead will rise with us."

The smile lines around her eyes and mouth crinkled before her lips fully curved. She extended a paint-flecked hand for a shake. "Well, welcome to the sunshine state, Rhyett. I look forward to seeing what you bring to the community."

NINE

BREXLEY

"You know the best thing about America?"

I snorted. "Soul-sucking commercialization and toxic hustle culture?"

"Someone's particularly stabby today."

"I need a bucket-sized margarita for the amount of salt I currently possess."

Noel ruffled her short auburn hair, rolling her eyes. "Mr. Tall, blonde and shredded didn't put you in a better mood?"

"Rhyett's easy on the eyes. Yes."

"But?"

"Noel, I know you and Eric are listening to wedding bells to the beat of your steps, but not everyone sees heart eyes all day."

Her gaze fell to the shipment of books by her feet, and something in my gut twisted as she laughed, the sound somehow hollow. "Yeah, but daaayuum." Her expression slipped back into a cocky smile. "As if his face wasn't good enough, I glimpsed that ass, and you could really sink your teeth into that thing."

Why hadn't I thought of that? I mean, between the nerves, arousal, and screaming self-doubt, I guess I hadn't made it that far. "Don't get me wrong. Best sex ever. I'd love to see what the man can do on a bed."

"Or a shower."

"Ugh, yes. Shower sex is nice."

"But just-showered-together sex is better."

"I'll have to find that out for myself. But is it messed up that I kind of want to preserve that memory?"

"What do you mean?"

"You know. Just preserve that one perfect night together? Laughing, sneaking off to a freaking bathroom."

"Never took you as an exhibitionist."

"Certainly fucking not."

"Wouldn't have thought you had it in you."

"Welp. Certainly had *him* in me." I laughed. "But come on, I'm not crazy. I like my life. I've worked really, really hard to say that. I love our shop, and I have friends, and things are finally moving the right way. A man like Rhyett...he'd be a distraction. One I certainly can't afford. And frantic, feverish, can't-wait, gotta-have-you sex in a bar. It can't get better than that, right?"

"Jesus, Brex. Of course, it can get better than a fast fuck in The Three Leaf bathroom. Super sexy man, let's you self-sabotage with some bullshit line about *letting fate decide*, and still wants to take you out when *fate* herself brings him back to you? Did he hit your head on the mirror or something?"

Hands raised in surrender, I shrugged. "Ugh. Fine, okay, it can get better. I'm just not...in the place for something steady."

"You act like it's torture."

"I just don't want to ruin hot Rhyett that bent me over the counter."

"I have a sneaking suspicion he'd happily agree to a reenactment."

Glaring at her, I turned to lean against our display table and tucked my hands in my front pockets to avoid peeling my nails. "Relationships are freaking complicated. How can I want someone and be totally content single at the same time?"

"Everything good takes work, Brex. Hell, you taught *me* that. I don't know. You two had sparks bouncing the instant he waltzed up to you. Don't you think that means something?"

"It means the chemicals in my body liked the chemicals in his body and demanded a taste." My attempt to stay quippy wasn't erasing my anxiety. Her response to my ribbing was still riddling holes in my resolve, best friend radar in full alert mode. "Hey," I said, nudging her in the ribs. "What about you? Everything okay in the House of Commons?"

"What?" She smiled, tucking her hair behind her ear. "Oh yeah, I was just going to say the best thing about this country is that no matter where you are or what time of day it is, you can always find a channel playing reruns of *Friends*." Before I could respond to the apparent deflection, the bell rang, jerking our attention to the front door and Noel to her feet. "Hi there! Welcome! Please come in. I'm Noel. What can I help you find?"

The customer was a petite mid-twenties Latina with Disney princess eyes above a button nose. Dark, sleek hair that fell to her waist framed sun-kissed skin. She smiled tentatively at Noel, who giggled sweetly, motioning her forward. Everything about my best friend was disarming. She could lure people in just with her energy and then keep them indefinitely with that endless golden retriever charm.

"We've read everything we stock, so there's no judgment here if you have questions."

"Well," the woman said with uncertainty, shifting on her feet and dropping her purse from her shoulder into her hand. It wasn't an uncommon reaction. Women were generationally programmed to deny and resist their own sexuality, shoving desire and curiosity into a corner instead of embracing it. "I think I'm in a dark romance mood."

Noel wiggled with excitement—she should have had a tail. "Oooh, do tell. Are we looking for villains that get the girl? Morally gray hotties? Stalkers? How deep are we going?"

The trill of laughter would've thawed out even the most frozen of hearts. The duo moved together, now shifting in synchronicity as Noel led her over to the proper shelves, expertly color-coded with our custom covers. Some bibliophiles would shudder at the mere idea of anything beyond Dewy Decimal. Noel and I? We wanted this place to be personal. Easy to navigate for mood and niched readers alike.

"Is there a word for someone who gets excited by frisson?"

"Ohhh yes. Oh, man." Noel snapped her fingers, saying, "I know this. I swear I know this." The espresso machine let off a cloud of steam as our manager, Wrenly, popped her grinning, freckled face around the bar. Dark chocolate curtain bangs framed her baby face, long hair in a frizzy braid down her back.

"Oooh! Oooh! Um. It's like a fear-kink?"

The customer's face flushed, her throat bobbing, but she bit her lower lip, shrugging. "Maybe?"

"How dark are we talking here?" The sing-song phantom voice

carried from the back room as Holland carried out her lilac laptop, looking inquisitive. "Any triggers?"

"Not that I've found." It was somewhere between a statement and a question.

"Mmm, I'd say Penelope Douglas." Holland shut her laptop, moving towards the coffee shop as Noel turned to the left, rising on her tiptoes.

"You thinking *Devil's Night* series?" she clarified, glancing at Holland's navy-blue eyes as she stepped under the archway between the coffee shop and our bookstore. Where Wrenly boasted full, soft curves, our bookstore manager was almost gangly, her chestnut hair tucked behind both ears giving her the endearing eternal air of youth.

"I mean, it's kind of jumping in the deep end. Have you read any bully romance?"

The chuckle shimmered in the air, and I smiled, turning back to my office as their conversation spiraled into favorite reads and more recommendations. Whether she'd known it or not, she'd unwittingly found her people when she wandered through those front doors, subconsciously summoning our top dark romance readers like a beacon. If she wanted them, there were friends-a-plenty and themed book club nights pinned all over the bulletin board beside the bathroom. That had always been the vision—a community for the quiet, bookish girls otherwise on the outskirts of society. Watching it thrive was...well, it elicited this uncomfortable warm thing in my gut that usually sent me fleeing.

Retreating to the cubby I called an office, I slunk into my seat, wiggling a finger on the mouse to wake up my computer.

Clicking keys filled the space until I'd penned out the last of my emails just as another came in.

"Fuck," I breathed, closing my eyes and rubbing a thumb between them where my perpetual frustration began to show my years. Well, Noel would be disappointed with that piece of news. The space we'd been bidding on across the street had been scooped up. No doubt, another out-of-state investor swiping the profitable real estate out from under good locals. The bookstore had overflowed into the cafe, shelves now lining walls and duplicating as decor. It was time to expand, and in our effort to be the Florida version of *Powell's*, we thought swiping up more of this block was the way to go.

With a huff, I leaned back, crossing my arms as I bobbed in my chair.

The gift basket from a new roaster glared up at me from my desk, a little miffed I'd yet to sample anything. I sighed as I peeled the crinkling plastic open, pulling a bag of beans out and sucking down a long whiff. *Damn.* It smelled amazing. I unfolded the top, rocking the bag back and forth to survey the beans. Perfectly dry. Well, if they could get past Wrenly, they might stand a chance.

When I strode past our newcomer, now happily settled in with an espresso, coffee cake, and a stack of romance books that would make even *my* toes curl, she smiled up at me, nodding as Holland settled in beside her, laptop again open. I'm sure she'd get the rundown on all of our upcoming events before she escaped, her bag ten pounds heavier.

"Wren?"

"Right here!" she hollered back, emerging from the kitchen with a towel over her shoulder.

I leaned over the bar, stretching across it on my belly to extend the bag still held between my hands. "Free sample bag! You wanna give it a test run? See if it's up to par?"

"On it!" She flashed me a cheeky smile, turning for the main pot and pulling out the filter bin with a subtle clunk. "It's been extra busy," she noted happily as she swiped the bag from me. I braced my chin on my hands, kicking a foot up.

"Good. We had that influencer post last week, and it's been chaos in here since."

"You both deserve it." She turned back, carafe in hand, and her eyes went wide. Wrenly blew out a long breath, jerking her chin over her shoulder as she clumsily lowered the carafe onto the counter with a skittering thud. When I turned to follow her attention, I found blue eyes and a mile-wide grin.

No way. There was no freaking way. I was suddenly acutely aware of how short the hem on these shorts was and the provocative way the bar positioned my backside.

"Well, hello." That warm timbre snaked up my spine as his eyes pointedly flicked to my ass and back. "Happy to see me?"

TEN

RHYETT

Contract in hand, Clementine assured me she'd pull the listing on the building immediately. She'd looked through the mood board and business plan, then had chomped at the bit to be a part of the project. Something about the old bones there just felt...right.

Always an encourager of following intuition, I canceled the remaining showings after the tour. I could see it. Every room brought to life a vision of what we'd craft within it. I knew where the bar and lounge would go. There was already the skeleton of a kitchen in the back, and two bathrooms plumbed and in need of a build-out. This was my fucking catnip. Nestled in a location that couldn't be beaten, it was perfect. Precisely what I was looking for when it came to my own personal project.

Sun beat down against my skin as I opened the door, and I turned up to face it, basking in the warmth. Rearranging the afternoon would be about twenty minutes of phone calls and emails. For a moment, I thought I might be an idiot committing to the third property I toured, but then I opened my eyes to a smiling Clementine as she straightened the sign out front, traffic buzzing and voices chattering, and I grinned right back. Breathing life into old buildings was an art all on its own, and I'd been dying to tackle a project. We had eight months to renovate and be up and going before the snowbirds came flooding down to fill the seats.

Which would fit perfectly under the bar...Which I'd stick in the back corner sharing a wall with the kitchen adjacent to that glorious window—maybe add an arch, since the pane and rotted frame both needed to be replaced, anyway—plenty of room for a bench seat. Imagination already in full swing, I cleared my throat as Clementine fished her keys from her bag.

"Thanks again, ma'am. I appreciate your time."

"Ma'am?" She barked a laugh. "After all our chatting, do I seem like a *ma'am* to you? It's Clem, handsome, just Clem."

The laugh was involuntary, and I stifled it when I could. "Alright, *Clem*. Where can a man get a good cup of black tea around here?"

I could have told her pigs ran the moon, and her face might have been less sardonic. She scoffed, "Your eyes work alright, Rhyett?" She pointed across the bustling street to a sprawling shopfront painted black, bearing a gold sign that said The Cracked Corset. The subheading read: *a literary cafe*. "Beginning to worry about you, son."

"Ahh, I was just too excited about meeting you to look around much."

"Sure you were." She gave a husky laugh, looking all too pleased with her ribbing.

"Have a good day, Clem."

"You too, kid."

I turned to stroll towards the nearest crosswalk when my future landlord hollered my name. Turning back as she opened the cherry-red door to her little coupe, I quirked my head. Offered a smile.

"Stay alert down here. You're not in Kansas anymore, kid."

When she received my nod and smile, Clementine-*Clem*-climbed into her sporty little car and had the engine purring before I even got to the nearest light. A sixty-something woman looking out for a thirty-five-year-old man. That was oddly heartwarming.

The concept of wandering into a literary cafe named after women's lingerie wasn't particularly up my alley. But as I peered into the window, I spotted mile-long legs and a denim-clad ass partially concealed by a sheet of shiny blonde hair. For a big city, this little stretch of coast was feeling ironically intimate.

Chuckling, I opened the door and wandered inside, struggling to pay attention to anything else with Brexley so casually draped over the bar top. In my defense, this was the angle I'd gotten to touch her in, and fuck if I wouldn't beg for a repeat.

I'd never been one for romance, always down for quick and dirty. Always enjoyed company and connection while it lasted and was the first to move on before anyone could get their hopes up. But fuck, this was different. Everything about this girl was different. I forced my eyes away from the endless, lean legs and perky ass to check out the shop.

Espresso machines hissed, billowing steam out into the space as patrons chattered. A pretty little lady with long dark hair was contentedly flipping a silky strand between her fingers with a stack of paperbacks piled precariously on the table before her. Bookshelves were artistically mounted directly into the exposed brick walls and lined with color-coded spines. Pinks and purples, reds and blues, grays and blacks. There were floral arrangements everywhere, mini vases on every table.

Another step forward, and I could glance through the open archway to the second room. There was no sign of the cafe, but over-flowing shelves filled every available wall space. Greenery cascaded down from hanging plants, dotted with splashes of color. A pink neon sign flashed *good vibes only*. Smiling, I turned back to Brexley to find she had company behind the bar. Curvy and freckled, the brunette hesitated when she spotted me approaching the woman laying across the counter.

When she jerked her chin my way, I got the distinct impression that customers of the male variety were far and few between inside the floral-heavy shop.

Turning, Brexley didn't bother to hide her surprise when those baby blues landed on me. Damn, she was younger than I thought she was. How hadn't I noticed that in the park this morning? Had I truly been that smitten? Maybe it was just the lighting, but the noticeable absence of makeup and girlish doe eyes made me question whether I'd still been sober the first time I saw her. Nerves bristled, but I couldn't deny the attraction pulling me toward her.

"Well, hello," I said as my cheeks ached with the smile stretching them. "Happy to see me?"

She gaped for a moment before catching herself and finding her feet. "What are you—you *are stalking* me?"

"I mean, could you blame me?"

"Yes," she balked. "Yes, I could."

"Fortunately for us both, I'm just here for a pick-me-up, beautiful."

"Twenty coffee shops in a ten-mile radius, you just so happen to wander into mine?" Feet now firmly planted, she turned to face me as her companion quirked her head, leaning against the bar as the coffee maker made happy percolating noises.

"Fate must've thought you might need a nudge. Haven't been thinking about me, have ya' Ace?"

Her narrowed eyes confirmed more than denied my suspicion. I laughed, jerking my chin at the menu mounted above the coffee counter.

"What's good?"

"I'm a little biased, don't you think?"

"This is your place?"

She sucked down a breath, face relaxing a bit as she assessed me before the tension fled her shoulders. "Yeah. Mine and Noel's."

"Your friend from the park."

"And the bar," she corrected.

"That's right."

The woman was magnetic, that electric charge between us drawing me forward, closing the distance. She ran her fingers through her hair, straightening the pieces around her face. A delicious shade of pink caressed her cheeks. Some carnal corner in my mind wondered what other colors I could draw out of her, how many effects I could have on that perfect little body.

Aiming for casual, Brexley quipped, "Forgot her that fast?"

"I was a bit preoccupied staring at you."

"I bet you say that to every short skirt you meet."

"Nah, I usually assess my options pretty thoroughly."

"Gross." Her lips twitched.

Not my best comeback, but as long as she was smiling, I hadn't fucked anything up too badly. "You were the standout from the minute I stepped in the door."

"You flatter, Mr. Rhodes."

"I'm authentic, Ms—"

"Snows," she supplied, evidently amused.

"Brexley *Snows?*"

"If you crack a joke, I'm changing my number."

"It's a fine last name," I assured her, trying not to laugh.

"For the love of God, don't tell me you'll change it."

"Not yet." What the fuck was I doing? She was obviously too young for me, that fact painfully obvious now that the layers of makeup had been peeled away.

"You're a shameless flirt, aren't you?"

"For you? Absolutely." Okay, my mouth adamantly insisted on not staying closed. "Can you blame me? You bewitched me, *Brex.* No shame in that."

On a long-suffered sigh, she turned to her friend behind the bar and introduced me to Wrenly, keeper of the coffee and queen of the baristas. After a string of pleasantries, I learned Wren had been with Brexley and Noel from the beginning, almost five years ago. She'd come along for every step of the road and, should they expand, would manage the current branch through the transition. Brex wasn't just the most electric physical connection I could remember. She was freaking sharp. Wren said so too.

"Wren, can we sample the new roast? You like coffee, I assume?"

"Uh—" No. I mean, perhaps with my body weight in sugar and covered in whipped cream. But like an imbecile, eager to make her happy, I said, "Yeah, of course. What do you got?"

"New roasters trying to get us to stock their stuff."

"Put me to work."

"Careful what you wish for."

I grinned, eyeing her up and down, drinking in those endless legs, lean waist, and drop-dead baby blues. Fuck, had anyone ever said no to those? "What do you have in mind?"

ELEVEN

BREXLEY

The subtle jangle of her metal tags preceded Royal's unceremonious arrival on the scene. As if Rhyett's last question summoned her like a beacon for voluntary pets. She skidded to a clumsy halt by his feet, tongue lolling as she looked up at him, brimming with expectation.

Traitor.

The man was a freaking sunbeam. He grinned down at me, husky timbre light as he ruffled fluffy golden ears. "Hey, sweetheart, you're just my little guardian angel, aren't you?" While she panted in response, I could practically hear every set of ovaries in the building self-combust. *Ffffs.*

Wrenly's brows merged with her hairline, her fair cheeks reddened, eyes full of sinful insinuation that earned my no-shit glower. She shook her head as she turned back to the percolating godsend.

"Seriously, do you bathe in peanut butter or something?"

Even his *chuckle* overflowed with warmth. "What?" he balked.

"She never leaves my office. Not unless Noel or I bribe her with treats or a regular comes in, promising pets."

"Knows good people when she sees them," Rhyett supplied.

"How humble."

His laugh was entirely unruffled. "How old is she?"

"Four."

"So, just getting out of her puppy stage. Such a fun age."

I scoffed. The affection in his tone was equivalent to a mother of five, not a bachelor loving on a nosy attention whore. "Big dog guy?"

"Hell yeah. We always had a brood of them running around."

"Because a dozen children weren't busy enough."

"Including cousins? Never."

"Jeez," I mumbled. "I dunno how you deal." Who the hell was this man? So endearingly crooning about his siblings, his cousins, like growing up in a zoo had been a damn good time, rather than the absolute chaos I imagined in my head. Life felt overwhelming as an only child. I couldn't imagine being surrounded by people all the time, with nowhere to go to be alone.

"Eh," he shrugged, straightening like an idiot, not expecting the immediate nose pressed into his palm. He absently petted her jawline. "It's all we know."

There was some merit to that, I supposed. Although, who in their right mind would intentionally clone a dozen crotch goblins when the world was going to hell in a handbasket, I couldn't understand. Wren cleared her throat, drawing my relieved attention her way.

Proudly boasting two cups of black coffee, she set them on the counter, stifling the smirk curling her lips as she glanced between me and Rhyett. *This is the problem with befriending your employees...*

To her credit, she swallowed her glee until she was in the back hallway, tucking into the kitchen.

"Coffee," I said, lifting one of the cups and nodding to an empty table as the bookstore door rang again. Noel certainly had her hands full. I spotted Holland glancing over her shoulder, ruling in favor of supplying reinforcements before shutting her laptop and waving goodbye to Ms. Dark Romance. They'd handle the gaggle of girls, no problem.

By the time I'd turned back for him, Rhyett was beaming with his mug in his hand, thick fingers dwarfing the handle.

"Does your face have a lower wattage setting?"

His suppressed laughter rippled through the dark liquid as he led the way and set the mugs down on the light wood, sliding aside the bowl of hibiscus. Noel brought them fresh each morning, her parents' property lined in rich greens, pinks, and purples. Royal happily collapsed onto the floor beneath the table as though he'd presented her with an engraved invitation.

"Just the one, I'm afraid. Do you need sunglasses?"

The fucking audacity of the man. The fucking audacity of *my face* mirroring his gleeful expression. Before I could process the quick movement, Rhyett had crossed and pulled the chair out, motioning for me to sit. Scowling, while equal parts confused and turned-on, I accepted. He smoothly lowered into the one across from me, sliding his mug back in one big hand.

"So, how long have you owned the shop?"

"Five years, give or take."

"So you've been running this place since you were, what, a zygote? Impressive."

My mouth fell open, gaping as he grinned. "What is that supposed to mean? We signed on this space our senior year in college."

"Oh man. I spent my senior year perfecting my beer-pong skills. You're making me feel like I wasted my time. Good on you, Brex. That's a hell of a head start. I'm all for young entrepreneurs."

Scowling, I indignantly insisted, "We're not that young."

"I—uh—not gonna lie, at Three Leaf, I figured you were my age, maybe a few years younger. But if you signed here your senior year, you're...what? Twenty-four?"

"Twenty-*five*."

I couldn't help but laugh when Rhyett winced, palming his face dramatically. "You're killing me here, Brex."

"What?" I squeaked defensively. *Good job, Brexley, squeak again. That will help.* He rested his forehead against his fingers, looking at me through a set of dark lashes. Feeling the need to reassure him for some damned reason, I added, "Don't worry, I've been legal for quite some time now. How the hell old are you? Can't be over thirty."

"Pretty girl, I was starting middle school the year you were born."

"Oh, you were not."

He nodded solemnly, "As certain as the sunrise."

Sucking down a breath, I glanced sidelong, looking for the girls. They would be positively feral when they found out I'd slept with an older man. The bronze of his skin and lack of wrinkles had me permanently suspended in disbelief. Hell, I had smile lines deeper than he did. "There's no way you're thirty-five."

He chuckled, shrugging his shoulders as he said, "Fate is a cruel bastard."

"You have a rule against doing a younger woman?"

"Younger? Nah. But there's gotta be a line somewhere."

Laughing despite myself, I shook my head. "Too little too late, Alaska. I think we crossed it."

"This doesn't bother you?"

"Why would it? Age is just a number, and lucky for you, I've always been good at math." When he only sucked on a tooth, some strange tangle of lust and guilt in his eyes, I insisted, "I wanted you, you wanted me. And I'm a woman that enjoys getting what I want. Ipso facto."

Rhyett studied me for a long moment, eyes uncharacteristically serious before they finally softened. "Alright. I think you're letting me off the hook too easily, but I'll allow it."

"Not prone to flagellating yourself, I hope?"

"Haven't given myself much reason to before," he gestured vaguely at the space between us. On the tail end of a sigh, he pointedly changed the subject. "So, what inspired the literary cafe?"

"We're proud smut sluts and—"

Rhyett practically choked on his first sip of coffee, his eyes watering. I wasn't sure if he'd scalded himself or attempted to inhale it when I'd said —

"I'm sorry," he muttered. "*Smut slut?*"

I grinned. "We read spicy books."

"Spicy...books?"

"You know—romance, with flavor."

Confusion drew a V between his brows before understanding dawned. His lips parted in surprise for only a beat before he grinned again. "Ahh, okay, I'm with you. Jeanne and Elora both love those stories."

"Sisters?"

"Yeah. Jeanne's the leader of the rat pack, Elora's four years younger than me."

"How do you keep track?" I took a sip, savoring the dark blend, admiring the hint of cocoa undertones.

He shrugged as his phone audibly vibrated for the third time in as many minutes. "Jeanne travels—mission work, Doctors Without Borders, that kind of stuff—Elora is like the designated family know-it-all," he said, chuckling before adding, "She's actually a life coach." His face softened noticeably, little smile lines pinching the skin by his eyes affectionately. "She's a peach. They both love to read. I mean. Most of the girls do." He took another sip and grimaced before he seemed to catch himself. I stuffed down the laugh, trying to climb up my windpipe.

"You don't drink coffee," I stated flatly, trying my best not to smirk at his obvious repulsion. "Do you?"

He grimaced outright. "That obvious?"

"Your face is loud." It was. His joy, humor, and revulsion all painted across those chiseled features, not concealed by the thin coat of blonde stubble.

"Always been an open book." He shrugged. "Not a problem except for situations like this."

"Where you lie whilst wooing a woman?"

"Is that what I'm doing?"

"Aren't you?"

"Apparently pretty pitifully if it's this obvious." He attempted another sample of black coffee, barely concealing his nose wrinkle. I laughed, tossing my hair over a shoulder and waving at Wren, miming holding one of our little trays of condiments. She grinned, turning for the cabinet.

"What do you usually drink?"

"Tea, mostly." He shrugged nonchalantly. "I like my coffee in the 'counts as dessert', combined with the 'drink your calories' variety."

"Ahh, a frilly beverage man."

"Guilty as charged," he said, raising his hands in self-defense as Wren arrived with a petite gold tray engraved with flowers and vines. She settled it on the table with a gentle clink.

"Can I snag anything else for you two?"

"That will do, thanks, Wren."

I motioned to the assortment of goodies. "Oat creamer on the right, local dairy on the left. Raw sugar, stevia, and Splenda if you're more of the *Atkins* variety."

"How's that for a throwback Thursday?"

"Seems like everyone was on that thing."

"Same back home." He opted for the oat milk creamer and a packet of Raw sugar, mixing both in and taking a tentative sip before smiling. You could tell a lot about a person by how they took their coffee. I suppose, whilst Rhyett probably opted out more often than not, his choices screamed *health freak*. Not that I'd needed much confirmation beyond the definition in those biceps. The most unfair thing about our little rendezvous was that I still had no clue what his tattoo was, just the edges peeking out of his t-shirt.

"Much better."

"A for effort, hotshot."

"So. You're smut sluts. Why coffee?"

"Coffee, pastries, breakfast potatoes. We eat like a *Hobbit* clan here."

"Anywhere I'm allowed to consume two breakfasts is good by me."

"Three, some days."

"I like a girl that knows how to eat."

It was entirely illogical, but my stomach did a loop-de-loop, heat flushing my face. I shouldn't care. It *shouldn't* matter. And it shouldn't be embarrassing that he now thought I binged like a deprived animal whenever my emotions got the better of me.

"Hypothetically speaking, who would a man talk to about getting some of those breakfast potatoes?"

"Hypothetically speaking?" I parroted back, smirking despite myself. "Wren is the keeper of the POS."

"Excellent, excellent. I'll have to hit her up after." He motioned vaguely to the coffee. Not a coffee drinker: if I was considering an honest-to-god dating scenario—which I was absolutely not—that might be a deal breaker, even though the distressed twist to his features threatened to crack the case I'd shoved my sense of humor into.

"You do not have to finish that," I teased. Well, partially teased. Partially stated out of moral obligation as I remembered the distaste carved into his face.

"What do you mean?" Rhyett asked with mock innocence. "I love this stuff."

"Hey, Brex?" *Saved by the barista.* I twisted in my seat to find Wrenly with her phone squeezed between her ear and shoulder, eyes expectant as she juggled a plate in one hand—a second wedged against her forearm—and the coffee carafe in the other. "There's someone on the phone for you."

"If you'll excuse me, I gotta get back to it."

I startled when Rhyett stood as I did, swallowing as he extended a hand. It was a mistake to accept it. I knew it before our skin connected like a freaking jumper cable, sending energy up my bones and tingling down to the base of my spine. His scent was warm and clean and somehow distinctly...male. It was overwhelming, and I snapped my mouth shut for fear of salivating over him. Too many synapses fired simultaneously. Calloused and warm, his palm encompassed mine entirely, and no sane woman could feel the subtle give of his skin and not remember what he'd felt like wrapped around a breast, a hip, squeezing my—

Clearing my throat, I did my best impression of a smile, working to extricate my limb while frantically digging through the useless compilations of files in my brain where somewhere, in the very depths of the chaos, I would locate instructions on how the fuck to *inhale.* It wasn't until he'd released me, putting space back between our bodies, that intoxicating scent no longer wrapped around my windpipe, that air worked its way into my lungs. Vaguely, I recognized Wren had said my name again in an apologetic plea.

"See you around, Ace."

TWELVE
RHYETT

Appointments canceled, honorary coffee forced down, tea cooling, I fired off my dozenth email of the day. It was a cruel game, trying to focus with Brexley buzzing about like a busy little bee. She was in her element here. Checking on tables, helping patrons find books, and restocking supplies. Royal was in her element, too, happily sprawled below my table where I could rub along her ribs with a shin from time to time. But Brexley...

Fuck. I'd known she'd bewitched me in that bar, but this was ridiculous. KaiL Baxley's soulful sound filled the space with "Boy Got It Bad", and I blew out a long breath. Forcing my eyes away from the blonde that soaked the air out of the building, I ran through some numbers for the Alaska businesses, approved a handful of change orders on the house, and sent an update to Milo and Juniper.

My parents were...I wanted to say lucky, but perhaps *blessed* was the appropriate term. They had that one-in-a-million kind of love story. High school sweethearts that survived hell and high water in pursuit of a dream life for their family. Jeanne had surprised them with a wedding night present when they were only nineteen. The two of us were Irish twins, making them exhausted parents to two under one by the following Christmas.

But they'd freaking made it. Against all odds, in the harshest conditions, spending more time separated by sea than united, they'd clung to each other like a life raft. Maybe that's why so many of us were so stubbornly single. We'd set impossible standards, their priceless love story set the bar by which we judged everyone.

Jameson and I had decided that nobody ever could live up to it. So the fact that one night in a grungy bar bathroom had me staring after a twenty-something businesswoman wearing stylish little shorts, a too-tight crop top, and a black blazer, more accessory than attire, was enough to send my stomach down a rollercoaster. What in the hell was in the water down here? Could brackish water actually strip a man of common sense?

Now and then, fate gives you a wire to follow—as likely to trip you as guide you if you ignored it—and everything about Brexley Snows felt like a wire. She'd brushed off my invitation, but I couldn't help but think I should keep tugging back. I shut my laptop and slid it into the messenger bag, startling Royal with the movement. She jerked upright, one ear flopping backwards as she cocked her head—a silent demand for answers.

"Come on, girl, help me out." Her tail gave a heavy, pathetic string of thumps against the floor. "Really? Nothing? You've got no ideas?" *Thump, thump, thump.* I sighed, scratching her silky ear to distract myself, muttering, "Me either."

"Are you conspiring with a dog?" Noel's sudden appearance resulted in me smacking my head on the table as I righted myself. Grimacing, I rubbed at the spot as she swallowed a laugh. She slid the opposite chair out, twirling it around so she could straddle it.

"Maybe," I admitted. "She's been brilliant so far. Why stop now?"

"You might have better luck with a humanoid alliance."

"Promising theory."

"Might I suggest a *best friend?*" she asked, batting her lashes playfully.

"Got any ideas?"

Her conspiratorial smirk spelled mischief, and I wasn't sure if it was promising or discouraging. "On forcing the hermit out of the house?"

I laughed, turning to survey the powerhouse in question as she arranged a display in the window, hanging up three-leaf clovers for St. Patrick's Day. "She didn't strike me as a loner."

"She's...subject to routine."

Sipping on my tea, I glanced between them, weighing my options. Noel had eyes only for me. Which I was quick to point out. "You're staring."

"Yep."

"Why?"

Her delicate brows flicked up as she said, "Because *you're* staring."

"Not at you."

"First, *rude*. Second, my best friend is more important to me than I would ever be. If you're interested in Brex, you've become my business. Understand?"

"Yes, ma'am."

Those amused brown eyes narrowed. "You sure you're not from the South?"

"Alaska is a misplaced Southern state. Kinda like Idaho."

She snickered. "Look, charmer, Brex is...her own person. She likes it that way. But she's the best friend a girl could ever ask for, and if you get her to let you in, she's loyal to the death."

"What are you saying?"

"Don't fuck it up."

A laugh lodged in my throat. "Well, I'd have to win her over first. But, honestly, I'm more worried about the whole age thing."

"Age thing?" Noel said, hiking up her brows.

"I've got a decade on her."

"Oh jeez, hotshot." Her eye roll was colossal. "Like Brex would give a shit. That girl has always been an old soul trapped in a young body. An older guy is inevitable."

"And you think I stand a chance?" Flashing my best smile, I leaned back in my chair. Noel studied me for a minute, letting the silence linger before she answered.

"Her being safe and healthy and happy is all I want."

"But...?" I hedged.

"She's sick of being let down. And I'm sick of seeing her let down. Her family is...shitty. And going it alone is better than forcing yourself to be around people who make you *feel* alone. Brex, unfortunately, also applies that ideology to men."

"You're telling me she's got walls up?"

"Fortified in stone and mortar."

"Seemed pretty friendly to me."

"That's why I'm sitting here." Wrenly materialized beside her, a French press of tea in her hands. She set it on the table between us, proudly presenting two cups and wordlessly escaping. Noel called after her, "Thanks, Wren!"

The exchange earned Brexley's attention. Golden brows dipped before the slender woman with the laptop re-emerged, happily presenting something to the future Mrs. Rhodes. Her answering beam was priceless. They scurried through the bookstore and vanished into the dark hallway beyond.

"Eyes over here, buddy." Noel's smirk said enough about my dumbass, open book of a face, her fingers snapping. "What are your plans, Rhyett?"

"Today, or in the grand scheme of things?"

"Ahh, wit. I like it. Both. Start with today."

"Uh, I just wrapped my workday. Don't have to be back at the property until tomorrow. So, A—convince your friend to come to dinner. B—convince your business partner to join me for dinner. And C—"

"Convince Brexley to go out to dinner?"

"Bingo."

"And the latter?"

"We're building a mini-farm for my parents to retire on, complete with guesthouse and bunk rooms, so the litter can visit."

Her laughter was infectious, her smile more so. I could see why Brexley kept her in proximity. "The *litter?*"

"We weren't technically duodecaplets, but we certainly move in teams."

"So, where's the second half of your pair?" She narrowed her eyes at the wording, and I lost my very brief fight with the responding chuckle.

"My sister—I *think*—is in Malawi at the moment. Last I heard, they were tackling an outbreak of Cholera. Our younger brother, Jameson, is on the island."

"And you're here."

"And I'm here."

"Staring at my platonic soulmate like she's a snack."

I smirked, leaning forward and lowering the plunger on the French press. "I plead the fifth, Red."

She tried to narrow her eyes, even though a smile broke through instead. "What are your intentions, Mr. Rhodes?"

Noting that they'd undoubtedly exchanged a decent amount of information, I offered her a smile she readily returned. I decided I liked Noel. So honesty, it was. "I'm ready to settle down. Plant some roots. I'm tight with my parents, and I don't know how long I have them for, so I'll go where they go. Which happens to be Florida."

"You're not a serial killer?"

The tea practically splashed as I shook with mirth. Once both cups were poured, I lifted my gaze, meeting delighted hazels. "No, ma'am."

"But if you were an axe murderer, would you tell me?"

"Somehow, I think you'd just know."

"I would," she agreed quickly, lifting her chin. "I know all things when it comes to Brex."

"Oddly enough, I believe that."

"Good. So you'll believe it when I tell you that if you hurt her, I'll kill you myself and won't think twice about it while I sleep at night."

The smile was involuntary. "I've always wanted a woman worth killing for."

"Well, you might've found one. If you can get her to let you—*ahh, Brex*, that looked like it went well."

Heart picking up, I turned over my shoulder to see the little badass closing in on us, eyes a mixture of curiosity and caution.

"Intend to abscond with my dog and my partner, Rhodes?"

Before I could answer, Noel said, "I was just telling Rhyett that I had something come up and need to cancel our plans tonight."

If looks could kill, Noel would've ignited right then and there. Only a fool would've laughed, though I was downright tempted.

"Leaves you two free to check out that bar."

Yeah, the consensus was final. I definitely liked Noel.

"Noel," Brexley said, evidently speaking in laser vision. "We have that thing tonight."

"I know," Noel sighed pointedly, standing and returning her chair in one smooth motion. "So sorry, Brex. I couldn't get out of it. You know, stuff with Eric. Already rescheduled the appointment, so you don't have to worry about it."

The fact that there was clearly no appointment did little to deter me. I had somehow earned the blessing of a best friend's stamp of approval. There were few things more sacred when it came to women. Or at least, that's what I'd learned from my sisters.

Jumping at the opportunity, I offered, "I'm happy to pick you up, if that's easiest. We can drop Royal off at home before we head that way?"

"That's unnecessary, Rhyett. I don't think this is a good idea."

I certainly wasn't about to beg. Not yet, at least. "Well. How about this, Ace? You've got the name and address. You drop Royal back home, and if you change your mind, you'll have a chair at my table." I stood, gathering my things. "In the meantime, I just wanted to tell you, you have an amazing place. I'm out of here for the week, starting tomorrow."

That seemed to catch her attention, her pretty little face shifting to what I could only describe as concern. "What do you mean?"

"Our property is outside of Venice."

She blinked, brow furrowing again. Jesus, she had a jawline women would die for. Like some sort of sentient sculpture. "You live south of the Skyway?"

"The what?" My backpack shifted against my shoulders as I adjusted the weight of it.

"The terrifying, four-mile bridge over the bay?!"

"Oh!" I laughed. St. Pete and the lower cities were separated by a solid five-minute drive over the Tampa Bay, connected only by an enormous, towering testament to modern architecture. Great columns erected from the water, propping the roadway high enough that the tallest of barges could glide right under it with plenty of room to spare. Without it, the drive into the city would have been double or triple the time. Although where she said 'terrifying', I said 'breathtaking'. You could see for miles in both directions. Shrugging, I added, "Hell of a view up there. Loved the pelicans."

Her eye roll was legendary as she sighed, "*That's* the Skyway."

"Fitting moniker."

"What in the hell are you doing up here?"

"Looking for commercial real estate."

"I know. But why? You live *south* of the *Skyway*."

My grin earned a bemused expression, those glossed lips twisting in a smirk. I wanted to lick it off her. Taste each inch. Fuck, to feel them wrapped around my dick...

Reminding myself I wasn't a freaking animal, I stated, "You're gonna have to translate for me here, Brex."

"Nobody really goes south of the Skyway," Noel offered. "And people down there don't really come up here."

"What?" I laughed. "That's ridiculous. It's a bridge."

"Why fight traffic on a four-mile bridge when we have everything we need on our side of the damn thing?"

"For one, I had the best sushi of my life last night."

"There's sushi in Sarasota."

"Second, the demographics in St. Pete are better for my business."

The glare she shot me was nearly conspiratorial. "Plenty of patrons in your neck of the woods."

"Is this, like, a west side, east side kind of thing?"

Noel shook her head, grinning. "There aren't any rules or anything, we just..."

"Don't do it," Brexley supplied, finishing her sentence. She leaned over to steal Noel's mug, sipping her tea.

"Well, there's a first for everything."

"Where's this bar, hotshot?"

I was suddenly aware they outnumbered me, and they looked infinitely amused. "This side of the bridge, I swear."

"Fine," Brexley said, huffing a breath.

"What?" I scoffed.

"Text me the address."

My cheeks were aching; I was smiling so much. In an effort to not sound too damn pathetic, I kept the response short. "Yeah?"

"No promises," she warned.

THIRTEEN

BREXLEY

"I'm not going." It was a bit of a relief when the hot iron didn't break with the force I put into slamming it onto the counter. Royal quirked her head, big doe eyes staring up at me, perplexed by the sloppy flopping pancake that was my emotional state. "Don't look at me like that. He lives an hour away—*two*, once the snowbirds invade. And he's so damn presumptuous." The furry freeloader harrumphed, turning and leaving the bathroom, likely in pursuit of more dignified company. *Great.* Not even an actual golden retriever could tolerate my miserable lamenting.

"I'm not going," I muttered again as the sound of water lapping told me there was an incremental chance that my canine companion had simply been dehydrated, not abandoning me in my time of need. With a huff, I raised the curling wand. The playlist swapped to "Here Comes the Sun" by The Beatles, and I glared at the Bluetooth speaker.

"Hilarious," I hissed, looking around for my phone. I'd put on a more fitting sound—Cigarettes After Sex or Billie Eilish—and keep curling my hair for the not-date with the Alaskan fisherman turned entrepreneur-homestead-hottie that lived South of the most terrifying bridge in history. Seriously. When the wind blew, it would just shove my car around up there. That little concrete barrier did jack shit to convince me I wasn't moments from plunging to my death every time I'd been forced to cross it. It was definitely *not* so I could check to see if Rhyett had texted me. Since it didn't really matter, because I wasn't even going.

I loosened the now-steaming curl.

When the cosmetics bag relocation successfully revealed its whereabouts, I snatched the damn thing off the counter, sighing at the line of unopened messages from Noel. I wasn't dealing with her yet. She knew what she did. *Punk.*

I did not need any help securing dates or deciding to extend them to men who'd yet to earn them. Thank you very much. Releasing the next strand, my fingers worked on autopilot to snag another.

Rhyett hadn't sent any updates, but I opened the thread just in case, staring at the address for at least the dozenth time. Brasilia Bites, near the bay. The name brought to mind a flaming logo and a long waiting line. *Of course.* Of course, Rhyett would have a hookup to get into the swanky little hipster spots in town.

There was something about Rhyett Rhodes that screamed *charmed my way through life* like a neon sign. That cheeky smile, bright blue eyes and blonde hair. The man was a freaking walking Henley commercial. And what the hell was it with gorgeous men and freaking Henley-clad muscles? Some fucked up bro-code conspiracy to liquify the female population in one swoop.

The jingle of Royal's collar hit me as I swapped for another curl, hissing as the steam bit at my fingers. She sat expectantly at my feet, looking up at me like a crazy person. I *was* a crazy person. What was I doing, scalding my fingerprints off in the name of a not-date that I wasn't going on?

BREXLEY

I hate you

NOEL

No, you don't.

You love me and you know it.

Now go have fun.

BREXLEY

You go have fun.

NOEL

I plan to. Now move your ass, or you'll be late.

BREXLEY

I'm not going

NOEL

Sure you're not. Takes fifteen minutes with traffic.

MY MIDDLE FINGER emoji earned her favorite laughing GIF, but I slid my cell into its appointed pouch in my bag, scowling as though it had offended me. Royal nudged my leg.

"Fine," I said on a long-suffering sigh. "But only because he offered tequila. And grilled pineapple."

BRASILIA WAS, unsurprisingly, packed—the line of people out the door was a testament to both marketing and reputation. I was a sucker for a good business plan. There was something perpetually addictive about it once you'd taken up the mantle yourself. Every expedition became a matter of studying what was working well and what wasn't. I even developed a habit of taking notes as I was out and about, jotting down the things that stood out to me as customer experience wins.

The hostess had one of those bodies women paid five figures and a long series of painful needle pricks to achieve, and I tried to decide whether I could in good conscience hate her or not. Although when she turned that bright smile my way, immediately motioning for the entrance when I gave her Rhyett's name, my mouth filled with saliva at the aroma that greeted me. I decided then that she was best kept an ally, if not a friend. Her name tag read Priscilla, and she led me back to the swanky corner of the place.

It was impossible to miss him, looking dapper in a white button-down in the back of the restaurant, his blonde hair windswept in that laid-back chic thing he had going. My blood heated. My heart pounded a little faster, just a bit harder, demanding I perk up and pay attention.

Rhyett was...nothing, if not satisfying to look at. Then again, so was art. And art came with no complications and zero chance of accidentally incubating a human after admiring it closely.

The space was gorgeous and modern. Red lights illuminated the underside of the bar, in the otherwise low-key room. Stunning vases with otherworldly floral displays sat on every table as bustling servers moved from one to another, enormous kabobs of sizzling meat in their hands. The culprit of the tantalizing aroma, no doubt. When we reached the far corner, Rhyett slid out of his little booth, standing in greeting. Before I knew it, he'd reached forward, slinking a long arm around my waist and pulling me in for a hug that felt way more familiar than it had a right to. His lips against my forehead had a disproportionate impact on my ability to regulate my breathing.

As he released me, he admitted, "Gotta say, Brex, I'm pretty relieved to see you."

"You invited me, didn't you?"

"Didn't think you'd actually show."

"Disappointed?"

"In your company? Never."

I diverted my eyes to the deep reds and oranges of the flower arrangement. But the momentary distraction did nothing to alleviate the feeling of his eyes on me as swanky jazz music trailed over the air. Priscilla, the life-size doll, motioned to the opposite side of the table. She turned to leave, politely telling us our server would be right over in a voice that belonged on airline speakers.

"Beautiful," I said stupidly, motioning to the arrangement. If I wasn't positive the man was human; I would've been fairly convinced he had X-ray vision, the lingering gaze stripping every inch of clothing between us.

"Not as beautiful as my view," Rhyett said softly, his hand settling at the low of my back as he guided me to my seat, sending heat flushing through my body like a shockwave. Breathless, and cursing myself for it, I glanced up to where I knew he was still staring at me.

"Thank you."

"I mean it."

"I know. Thank you."

I'd no sooner hit the upholstered bench than our waiter stepped up, eyes on me as Rhyett returned to his place across the table. "Can I get you something to drink?"

We both glanced down to see a mostly full glass of scotch.

"Martini, please."

"Yes, ma'am. Anything else for you two, or do you need a moment?"

"That'll do for now, Scotty. Thanks," Rhyett said, oozing confidence as if he had it in spades. And he knew the server on a first-name basis. What was that about?

"Scotty?" I questioned when he'd vanished into the sea of chaotic choreography.

"Good kid. Going to school here. Family over in Palm Beach."

"I should've known you couldn't be left unattended for even a moment before befriending the staff."

"Best to have friends in all places."

"Your philosophy sounds like more fun."

"What's yours?" He laughed, replacing the napkin on his lap and casually snagging the glass off the table.

"I have a habit of avoiding humans, pretty much at all costs."

"You run a thriving shop," he pointed out.

"At all costs, after work. I dunno. It's different when I have a job to do—something to keep my hands occupied—and an automatic common interest."

"Smutty books."

I laughed aloud before slapping a hand across my mouth. "Yeah," I muttered. "You paid attention."

"I have a habit of doing that when something is important to me." If eyes could leave holes, his would've drilled right through me. Holy shit, he was intense. Meeting that piercing blue gaze, I had the sneaking suspicion that everything Rhyett did would be with the same caliber of focus.

Brexley Snows held my attention on the shortest chain I'd ever seen. Tugged me around. Rapt with her story and vision for The Cracked Corset, I was content to listen as she shared. She had a business mind, rival perhaps only to Milo, and the idea of presenting my father with a contender for his cleverness set warmth through my blood.

"Anyway," she continued, "I have this vision of a two-story bookstore with spiral stairs, where we could make the interior feel like some secret clubhouse. Everyone except Noel thinks I'm crazy."

"And Noel?" I questioned, plucking a leftover corn chip out of the bowl and scraping up the quickly disappearing guac. Brexley had eaten herself silly, happily leaning back and setting her hand on her belly. I freaking loved that she could eat. She hadn't exactly kept up with my enormous appetite, but it had undoubtedly been a respectable selection of options.

"Is my ride-or-die."

"So, she's on board?" I asked, wanting clarification. "Or she just backs your play?" Her laughter did something to my circulatory system, sending more blood south than was strictly necessary.

"A fair translation request. She's on board. I'm...the numbers person of the two of us. Noel is quick to take a picture and turn it into a cinematic experience. She took my idea for a coffee shop bookstore and turned it into The Corset. So naturally—"

"The idea of something on a larger scale is right up her alley."

"Right. She's always been so...fearless." She eyed the last bite of guac, chewing on her bottom lip as though in a great debate about continuing or exerting self-control. I snagged a chip and scraped the last layer from the stone bowl, leaning forward to give it to her. She surprised me when she darted forward with an open mouth to accept. The woman's lips on my fingers snapped any ounce of restraint still buried in my bones. Trying to anchor myself back in the present was suddenly fucking impossible. The urge to have her on her knees, to feel those beautiful lips wrapped around my cock, was instantly overbearing. *Easy, Rhyett. Jesus.*

Clearing my throat, I said, "You seem pretty fearless to me." Her answering laugh was more scoff than humor.

"I'm...analytical."

"Do tell," I prompted, snagging the napkin from my lap to clean my hands of salt and oil.

"I don't know..." she hedged. "I hide in my office and let Noel face the people."

"Sure didn't hide in The Three Leaf."

"Ahh, yes, *alcohol*, my old friend."

When I laughed, her cheeks lifted, flushing with color as her eyes darted to her lap. Mine lingered on her soft breasts, my newfound fantasy still blazing in my mind. I forced them up. Whether she didn't notice my lusting or was kind enough not to acknowledge it, I wasn't sure.

"Any regrets?"

That damn little nervous lip bite. It was like she didn't know how tempting she was. "Not so far. Please don't change my mind."

"My goal is certainly a direct contradiction."

"What is your goal, Mr. Rhodes?"

Throat suddenly thick, I snatched up my scotch—my third, and last—using the hot liquid to soothe my anxiety. Keep me steady. "How about we start where I should have."

"And where, pray-tell, is that?" Brexley steepled her fingers, bracing her elbows on the table like she'd just asked for diplomatic immunity.

"Spend some time together, play twenty questions. I'm not usually one to...what do the kids call it these days? Date?"

Expression thoughtful, she studied me for a long moment before asking, "You hardly know me. What could be so compelling to break your habit?"

"Well, I think we got pretty familiar last night," I countered with a wink. "I don't believe it was a coincidence, our meeting, bumping into each other *twice* since. Wouldn't fate tell us that's our sign to see what this could be? If you can honestly tell me you don't feel this thing between us, I'll let it lie. But I think you do. And I'm fascinated by you, Miss Snows."

The wrinkle in her nose was the cutest damn thing I'd ever seen. "*Brex*, Brexley, anything except for that."

"Ace?"

"Even that's a step up." My phone buzzed in my pocket, and while I was used to the constant bombardment, her eyes narrowed. "Don't you need to get that?"

I shook my head.

"So confident you can just neglect your responsibilities?"

Laughter forced up my windpipe as I shook my head. "Nothing is more important than being present at the moment. And I'm not neglecting anything but a needy pack of siblings."

"That's *all* your siblings?" she balked in blatant disbelief.

"The family text thread has been erupting all day. Mom and Dad are booking tickets to come down two weeks before Salmon Fest, right before the season starts, and the sibs are debating who's coming with, who's meeting up, and who's holding down the fort—or, dry dock, rather."

After two pointed blinks, Brexley asked, "You're close?"

"For the most part. We have our...scuffles. But we show up when it actually matters."

"You've mentioned the doctor—"

"Jeanne," I supplied, earning a nod as she continued.

"—and Jameson. He's a fisherman, too, right?"

"Right. He'll be captain when Dad retires."

"And Elora."

"Designated know-it-all." That earned an endearing slant of her mouth. On the rare occasion I earned a full-tooth smile, she had a pearly-white set that would make dentists pop open champagne. But I was learning to appreciate any indication she found joy in something. Even if it was big, nosy family trivia. "She lives in Portland, but I don't think she'll last much longer. Too chaotic."

"Who else is there? Are any of them at home?"

"The youngest four are eighteen, twenty-one, and twenty-three—Maverick, our twins Leighton and Kaia, and Finn. Mav graduates high school in May, and I assume he'll hightail it off the island the second he possesses his diploma. The twins are dominating the local Honors College. Finn is about as hard to keep track of as Jeanne, always off on some adventure. I think he said Philly or New York was up next. We'll see. He works remotely. So, the plan changes weekly." I chuckled, that endearing fondness growing in my chest as I worked down the list. "Alessandra goes by Alice. She just wrapped up her *second* bachelor's degree and came home to figure out her next step. But she's self-contained. They're almost empty nesters."

"Hence the move?"

"Hence, the move."

"Okay, so Jeanne, Jameson, Elora, Alice, Finn, Leighton, Kaia, Maverick, and you. That leaves *three*?"

"Hadlee's in Idaho at the moment, though it's hard to keep track. She likes to travel. Van life—social media, travel blog, something or other. Paxton is in Chicago until his contract is up. Not sure where he'll go, but my money's on him heading back home. Axel is home and has his own place down the street from me and Jameson. Works the boat every summer, but he takes off to travel for the winters. And then there's Broderick."

She held up a hand in protest. "I thought you said twelve. Now there's *thirteen*?"

"I mean, if we count all the people that we pseudo-adopted, you're looking at more like sixteen." Broderick had been a bonus brother since we were practically in diapers and Elora and Hadlee adopted Max as one of our own, his omnipresent chatter as much a part of the house as the rest of us. Between best friends and cousins, our house had always been filled well beyond capacity.

A genuine grin dawned on her stunning face. "Pseudo-adopted?"

"Juniper has a habit of collecting strays."

"Now wait, who's Juniper?"

"Mama bird," I said simply.

"Ahh, so who's Broderick?" She questioned, humor tugging at her lips. Well aware we sounded like a freaking circus attraction, I soldiered on.

"My best friend since we could toddle."

"Nice."

"You don't stay in touch with your siblings?"

"Never met them."

She said it so simply my heart seemed to stutter. My loud, obnoxiously nosy brood of crazy siblings were as much a part of me as any other aspect of my upbringing. I couldn't fathom not even knowing them. Keeping my tone light, I asked, "What?"

It was my first time seeing her shoulders curl, and I immediately regretted asking the question. Fidgeted in my seat. "My parents bought one-way tickets on the hot mess express, both looking for a way off the crazy train when they got pregnant with me. They were the textbook example of a duo who shouldn't procreate." Brexley sighed, grabbing the straw wrapper off the table and leaning back as her fingers began shredding the paper into tiny pieces of glum confetti.

"Mom took off when I was too little to remember much. And Dad...he tried but wasn't cut out for living life as Mr. Mom. His career came first. And I—was *there*." She shrugged again, the motion almost compulsive as she tore more paper pieces off the end. It took a massive internal battle to keep from reaching out to comfort her, silence her fidgeting. "When I was in high school, I decided to find my mom—what I expected would happen when I did...I still don't know."

It was like a car wreck. Miserable and messy, I still couldn't stop myself from asking, "And, did you?"

"Yeah," she said, expression flat and eyes hollow. Now I definitely regretted my prying. The sinking feeling in my gut told me whatever haunted her wasn't something I could fix. "Married with two daughters. She started her own perfect family in Maryland. And left us with nothing."

It wouldn't help to tell her a chemically balanced mother couldn't have left her child. Wouldn't help to rationalize. So, at last, I stopped her ceaseless shredding, looping her hand around mine and running a thumb over her knuckles as her throat bobbed, eyes darting between our joined hands and my face.

"Thank you," I said softly. I meant it. She'd opened up in a way I couldn't fully reciprocate. Trusted me with that piece of her so willingly. That pretty little face flushed again.

"For sharing my pathetic story?"

"It's not pathetic, Brex. You became a badass all on your own. That's noble."

"I—" Her mouth popped open before closing again, like she'd thought better of what she was about to say.

"What?" I squeezed her fingers between mine. Gave a little nudge.

"I'm sorry, I—that was—I tend to overshare. That was too much info and not even what you asked."

"It was exactly what I asked, Brex. I appreciate not being tossed the *Cliff Notes* version." I squeezed her fingers again, hoping the contact was reassuring. "Are you in touch with your dad, now?"

"When he remembers he has a daughter, we do alright. Postcards, mostly. The occasional airport terminal phone call or picture."

"I'd give Juniper approximately ninety seconds before she calls you her own."

"Your mother won't like me." She rolled her eyes.

"What on earth makes you say that?"

"Tattooed smut dealer who slunk into a shady bathroom and seduced her perfect son?"

"She'd congratulate you for the efficient catch."

To my utter delight, she actually laughed.

"You know what sucks about this whole situation, Rhyett?"

"The fact that they're closing before we can make room for a second dessert?"

Her laugh turned into a snort. "That," she agreed. "And the fact that you don't live north of the Skyway."

FIFTEEN
BREXLEY

BREXLEY

Damn you.

NOEL

LOL, I KNEW IT!!

BREXLEY

What the hell is in the water in Alaska?

NOEL

That good, huh?

BREXLEY

He's perfect. And I'm sure by now he's regretting
asking me out in the first place.

NOEL

Oh, please.

He's thanking his lucky stars he waltzed into our bar.

BREXLEY

I babbled like a moron.

NOEL

I'm sure that's an exaggeration.

BREXLEY

Straight-up trauma dumped on him.

NOEL

It probably wasn't that bad.

. . .

Oh, but it was. For pity's sake, I never talked about my dumpster fire of a family life. What in the hell was it about Rhyett Rhodes that made my brain pour words out like I'd been slipped a dose of mental Ipecac?

Laid bare, scrambling internally for my loathsome habit of over-sharing, I'd wrestled with the distant memory of being capable of swallowing while he stroked soothing lines down my hand. Like I hadn't just dumped way too much info on him on our not-a-first-date.

BREXLEY

Even if I didn't scare him off with my parental problems, he lives over an hour away. He's intelligent and beautiful and successful and has vision and has the cock of Eros himself, and I'll never see him again.

NOEL

Listen. If the god of love and sex wanted to bend me over a counter and court me like a proper lady, I'd drop Eric like a hot rock and call Eros daddy.

LAUGHING, I tossed my phone to the bed a moment before I collapsed beside it, covering my face with a hand and wishing the mattress would swallow me up. This is why I didn't go out. Going out led to emotions and emotions led to expectations, and there was only one ending expectations could bring about. Disappointment.

Because one of two things was bound to happen. Option one, and this was the most likely of the two: Rhyett would associate with me just long enough to come to his senses and lose interest. Option two: Rhyett was a secret axe murderer. And if I didn't die, I'd escape by the skin of my teeth, because he couldn't really be real with all his reassuring tones and ridiculous understanding, and enthusiasm for business strategy.

Royal bounded onto the bed in a fluffy cloud of lick-filled enthusiasm. She slathered my bare calf with her affection in the form of doggy kisses, and I wrinkled my nose until she collapsed over top of me in much the same manner as her owner. Her big, clunky head rested across my chest, doe eyes wide with expectation. Appeasing her desire for scratches, I let out a long-harbored sigh.

"I shouldn't have gone," I whispered. Nothing good could come out of a free fuck and fast feelings.

———

RHYETT

Good morning beautiful! Meet me this morning? I've got to head back to the property by ten. I'll bring the coffee. Bring Royal. She'll love it.

STARING at the partially cracked screen didn't actually transform the words into some semblance of sense. Nor did it rally the courage required for me to respond to the dang thing or soothe the fact that I still wasn't sure what I wanted. The soft white spot on her chest shivered as my pup stretched out on her back, warming up her joints with a yawn, tail thumping.

"Morning, baby," I cooed, scratching her exposed belly and earning a more rapid tempo of tail wagging.

The heels of my palms pressed into my aching eyes as I forced myself to inhale. Rhyett Rhodes had texted me at six forty-five a.m. Which meant, like me, he was a morning person. And he had the good sense to supply stimulants if he expected me to hold a conversation before the sun was hot. Third, he'd called me beautiful...which should not have immediately impacted my body chemistry, yet somehow sent my blood humming.

Robby never woke me up with a 'Good morning, beautiful'. And there had been no men between the two to clean up the pitiful mess he made where a relationship should've been.

Fourth, and finally, he included my dog in the invitation.

BREXLEY

You up?

IT HADN'T BEEN thirty seconds before Noel's face flashed on my screen. Her hair was askew, like a neglected bale of dark red hay, and her freckles were smattered with pillow lines.

"This better be good, Brex." She was hoarse, her voice dry with sleep.

"Rhyett texted me this morning."

"Great," she said sardonically before being attacked by a yawn. "There are two of you to drag my butt out of bed at the ass crack of dawn." Noel's zest for life mainly arrived after about eleven forty-five, following three cups of coffee. Before that point, she was as good as a trash gremlin. "Why?"

"He wants me to meet him before he heads down to their property."

She sleepily raised an intrigued brow, the corner of her parted lips curving before being overtaken by another yawn. "Wants to meet up? That's what we're calling it now."

My eye roll was firmly planted in the camp of epic proportions. "He invited Royal and promised me coffee."

"Mmm, coffee," she mumbled, palming at her face on the screen, which bobbled as she stood and meandered through her apartment. "We draw the line at dogs in the bed, though."

"Eww, don't be gross."

"You're the one that brought Royal into my fantasy about the hotshot."

Shaking my head as my nerves picked up, I said, "There's no fantasy. It doesn't seem like a booty call. He said *good morning beautiful*—"

Her sigh was a huff as she breathed, "God, it's sexy when they do that." The heavy clunk of her pulling the filter bin from her coffee machine reached my speaker.

"—and asked me to meet him."

"Okay."

"So?" I demanded. This girl had been my go-to for all things social situation, of the male variety or otherwise, since we were surviving pre-pubescent drama.

Noel set the phone on the counter, giving me a prime view of the bottom of her cabinets, the sound of pouring water competing with her voice as she barked, "So?!"

"What do I do?"

"With the successful, sinfully sexy man who's bribing you with caffeine and quality canine time? I dunno, Brex. Sounds complicated." The clumsy crash of the carafe enhanced her sarcastic tone as she set it back in place and jammed the button before picking me back up to give me a one-eyed glare.

"So, you think I should go see him?"

"Did he do something atrocious at dinner last night?"

"No," I whined, running a palm over my face. "The fucker."

She snickered, phone bobbing again as the sound of the sliding door caught my attention a beat before blinding sunlight white-washed her screen. When the lens compensated for the sudden flood of sunshine, she was blinking up at the sky like it had personally offended her with its golden enthusiasm for a new day.

"Walk me through it. Why are you hesitating?"

"Well, the annoying twat of a hostess—"

"Annoying twat because she's actually annoying, or because—"

"She's more plastic than Kammi Barrow's tits." Kammi was one of those talentless, tasteless soap opera stars masquerading as a 'reality tv' show. She had a body more silicone than flesh and didn't bother to hide it.

"Very good. Carry on. What did the twat do?"

"So she led me to the back where he was already in a booth and *God*, Noel, he's so beautiful."

"I do hope you've at least fantasized about sitting on that face."

It was my turn to cackle. "Obviously," I added on a wistful sigh.

"So, he's annoyingly handsome. Continue." Noel sat down in her egg chair, and I wandered to my balcony, squinting against the assault of morning light.

"And when we got there, he stood up to greet me and did that thing where he set his hand against my low back."

"*Ugh*," she sighed. "How do they know how sexy that is?"

"God, so sexy."

"Seriously, where they just casually slide down as precariously close as they can get to your ass and then linger."

"Right. So, he *lingered* and guided me to the booth before sitting on the opposite side. Polite to the waitstaff. Open to try anything on the menu—"

"So, no stick up his ass."

"Exactly."

"Did you try the jumbo shrimp? I hear amazing things about the—"

"Noel."

"Right, sorry, not the point. Dreamboat did what next?"

"We talked. But, like, really talked. Not about dumb, shallow shit, either. There was no discussion of pop culture, no drama. I mean a little drama, although that was my fault. Trauma dumping. However, Rhyett never made me feel like it was drama."

"There's nothing as sexy as a good listener," she said, ironically a bit absently, as she wandered back inside. "Was he intentional about that with you?"

"So much so that I couldn't shut up."

"Oooh," she said, biting her lip. "I dunno, Brex. I think if our situations were reversed, I'd be applying lip plumper, not talking to you right about now."

"Thanks, asshole," I said, rolling my eyes and wandering over to my espresso machine. It was cheating, really, the tiny box programmed with so many different drinks. It kept my creamer chilled and everything. With the press of a few buttons, the machine was humming as it heated water for a flat white. Noel poured her first cup, juggling the phone as she swapped hands and headed back out to her balcony.

"I thought for sure I ran him off with my trainwreck of a genetic code."

"Eh," she shrugged, coffee edging precariously close to the rim of her mug. "Genes are solid. There was just a malfunction in the dynamic. Good people. Not made for each other. Oil and water."

"Regardless."

"He didn't run off."

"Right."

"But...?" Noel hedged, sipping what had to be scalding liquid.

"But should I even be dating? Everything is good right now. You and I are good, business is good, life is good. I don't want to fuck it all up."

"There's always room for more love, Brex."

"Woah, now, you're skipping ahead."

"Fine. The *pursuit* of love."

"Maybe."

"Definitely." She took a long drag on her mug before making a happy little noise. "The girls have the shop this morning, so don't worry if you want to go."

"Should I?"

"Do you want to?"

"That's a trick question."

"Pretty damn straightforward, actually."

I chewed on my bottom lip as the machine buzzed and clicked

and the last of the froth settled in the cup. "Yeah," I breathed. "Yeah, I do."

"So, go. You're a badass, Brex. You've got this."

SIXTEEN
RHYETT

Not entirely sure whether she'd actually come, Brexley Snows had surprised me for the second time in a twelve-hour period. Yes, she'd said she was coming, though I hadn't fully believed her. Shock turned my palms sweaty when both my beautiful girls appeared at the edge of the parking lot, scanning through the jungle flora. Royal went on alert, tail manic, as her posture pointed my way, leading Brex to her target. God, I needed to buy my body weight in antlers for that retriever.

I thought Brexley's eyes held my attention, but, dear lord, that *smile*. Everything in my body went on alert. And I mean everything.

Down, boy. I attempted to discreetly adjust myself, yet it did little in the way of providing any relief at the sight of all that tan skin on display. She'd worn a pair of cutoff Daisy Dukes and a black bikini top beneath a chic mesh cover. Her long blonde hair was braided back into two cute, chunky rows—Elora and Hadlee both wore theirs like that, so I should have known the name. It wasn't French.

The two of them sauntered over with pep in their steps, and I had no choice but to greet our furry friend first as she all but lunged in my direction.

"She freaking loves you. It's ridiculous." Brexley muttered, curiously scowling at her dog like she'd committed some kind of betrayal.

"Morning, beautiful," I said, straightening back to my full height, tentatively wrapping a palm around her tight waist to pull her in for a quick hug, trying not to preen when she returned it. She had to be a runner, her body long and lean.

"You said that already," she said breathlessly as we released each other. God, the sound of her winded, just because my skin was on hers. I wanted to hear her heady and panting, begging me for more. Pulling her in until our hips met, I smiled down at her.

"And I'll say it again. Good morning, beautiful." I wanted to kiss her, to slide my rough palm up her hot skin. To touch and feel as I had that first night. But if I started now, with no one around, there was no chance I'd be able to stop myself.

And I meant what I said on our date. I wanted to get to know her. Beyond that mouthwatering body I'd been dreaming of for days, I needed to know *her*. Which meant clothes had to stay on, at least for the time being. Brushing flyaways from her face, I ran my fingers down the length of a braid. Pinched the end between them.

"I like your hair like this—what are these called? Not French braids..."

"Dutch," she supplied, still breathy as her eyes darted between mine, lingering on my mouth. Oh hell, this was going to be so much harder than I thought it would be. Reluctantly, I slid my hand down and stepped away, putting distance between us and directing her to the shore in one forced motion.

"Well, the Dutch knew what they were doing."

"Thanks."

Surprise number two of the morning? She said nothing as she accepted my hand, stepping into the canoe with a look of utter dread carved into her brow. "Royal!" With a click of her tongue, Brexley summoned her dog into the boat in one long leap, nails screeching against the plastic bottom. "Who's a good girl?"

Said good girl's tail smacked loudly against the plastic.

"You come out here often?" I asked, pushing it off the sand and following into the water. The maneuver-in was always a little sketchy, but it went off without a hitch as I positioned myself in the back. I was a grown-ass man; I should not have been relishing the graze of our legs as I grabbed the paddle between us.

"As kids, it's pretty much all there is to do around here. Beach. Books. Boys. Boats."

"Four B's?"

She snickered. "Bang."

"Five," I laughed.

"Wasn't too keen on the last one, so it stayed off my agenda."

"And now?"

"When he knows what he's doing?" Brexley glanced over her shoulder, stifling a smile with fire in her eyes. "It's not too bad."

Squeezing her hips between my calves, I grumbled, "Oh man, I'm in trouble."

"The bar is high, Hotshot." Brexley took up her paddle and rowed, and I smiled at the subtle jolt forward, shifting to do the same. It took a couple of minutes to get into a good rhythm together, but after a few clumsy splashes, our movements synchronized, both naturally compensating for Royal's happy shuffling from one side of the nose to the other as she stretched out to sniff at the water rushing by.

"You don't seem to have lost much," I said with a smile, watching her defined arms and ripple of lean muscle down her back. My hands buzzed with the need to run rough palms across that smooth stretch of tan skin.

"Like riding a bike," she offered as she swapped sides and I wordlessly did the same. The crystal water of the creek flowed silently beneath us, the only sound a subtle splash of our paddles. Up ahead, the creek narrowed, thick tropical flora stretching together like arms made to grasp. Birds chirped high above us as the roar of city traffic faded behind.

"I forget," she breathed, "that we can actually find pockets of quiet out here. The city is so...*much*, all the time."

"Has a pulse of its own."

"Yeah, it's exhausting. Never ceases."

"I'm just enamored with the ability to find any kind of food whenever I want."

She snickered before asking, "Not a lot of selection on the island?"

"I mean an abundance of fish. Burgers. Greasy spoons."

"Charming."

"It is, in its own way. Quiet, friendly."

"Good sense of community?" she asked, and I wished I could see her face. Was she intrigued? Appalled at the idea of a tiny fishing village on a North Pacific island? I might've been planning to live near my parents, but Mistyvale would always be home. Even with the never-ending gossip of a small town.

"Nosy, meddling gawkers is more like it. Still, yeah, they rally when it counts." A small fish leapt directly in front of us, marring the glassy surface as the ripples worked their way out towards the banks.

"Why Florida?"

"You can only see gray for so many months a year. Back when we were kids, we'd plan trips to the lower forty-eight at least twice a winter, longer stretches if the warm seasons were good."

"You sound like a fairytale."

I chuckled, turning my face up to the sun peeking through the dense greenery above us and reveling in the warmth. "More like a brood of rugrats shoved into an RV for months on end."

"A stressful fairy tale," she acquiesced. Royal laid down with a clumsy thud, setting her muzzle on the nose of the boat. Sighed dramatically. "I can't wait to get out of here."

"Why?" She couldn't see it, but I quirked my head on instinct, returning to a casual paddle as she set hers across her lap. The shade of the canopy grew denser as the banks narrowed on either side of us.

"Are you kidding?" Brexley scoffed, shaking her head. "It's a freaking swamp. There's nothing good here if you're not a beach bum. And even then, there's nothing to do except roast in the sun. We don't get a big enough surf to ride. Red tide spoils half the year. I've been here my whole life, and half of it has been spent inhaling fumes in traffic."

"Paints a pretty bleak picture for my parents."

"Yeah, well, at least you can prepare them."

"Where to?"

"What?" she asked, sneakily slipping her paddle between the edge of the boat to push off a gnarled root reaching from the bank.

"Where to? If not here, where would you go?"

"Mmm," she sighed. "Somewhere with seasons. This place is a mind fuck. Never changing. Always the same day, day in and day out. I want to experience the seasons. And mountains!"

"No shortage of those where I come from. The seasons are in short supply, it's pretty much sunny and cold, or rainy and cold."

"At least something changes. Here we have hot and humid and hot and dry."

"Grass really is always greener somewhere else?"

"Turf."

"What?" I chuckled.

"The turf is greener. If it's green down here, it's fake. We have swamp and sand, and that's it."

The light spread wide up ahead, a clearing in the path as the water grew shallower below us, paddles pushing off sand instead of slicing through the water. "I hear the springs don't suck."

"No," she agreed. "They don't." As the words left her mouth, we pushed our way into the wide-open clearing of crystal and turquoise water. Palms and green blades fenced the perimeter, a few fellow visitors floating aimlessly around great grey blobs at the surface. If I hadn't come here to see them, I would've thought enormous stones were bobbing in the water. Manatee season was in full swing, the pods coming in with their calves to escape the cold. Peaceful and majestic, they slowly drifted along without a care in the world, enjoying the balmy spring water. Enamored, I set my paddle over my lap as I watched them munching on the greens along the bank. My low laugh caught Brexley's attention, a smile on her face as she glanced back at me.

"What?"

"I've never seen one before. At least, not that I remember. They really are sea cows."

"Ocean potatoes."

"That might be better," I agreed with a grin. Never in my life had I seen water so clear with this kind of foliage around it. If it weren't for the dozens of gentle giants so happily minding their business, I would've insisted on slipping into the water myself.

"Rhyett, look."

I did, following her outstretched finger to a couple of turtles happily gliding along below a school of metallic fish. "Now this—this I could get used to."

"Haven't been in years. Honestly, I avoid the tourist traps like the plague."

"We lucked out today?"

Brexley shrugged, braid shifting over her shoulder as she leaned over the edge to get a better view. "It's still early. They'll flood in and crowd everything. Give them an hour or two."

Glancing at my watch, I grinned. This girl had met me on the water before eight in the morning. Who was crazy now, Jameson? The big baby. I knew my habits would pay off, eventually.

My heart stuttered. Because Brexley was beaming back at me, and the woman stole the breath from my chest. Fuck, she made my heart race, cheeks mirroring her expression without my permission. I'd needed today. Needed to confirm that I wasn't crazy. Okay, I was definitely crazy. But the thing between us was real. Beyond the chemistry that had dragged us into a women's room, there was a spark I couldn't deny, even if I wanted to. I ached to touch her again, ached for her lips to open below mine, for her body to accept me as needily as she had before.

She ran those straight teeth over her lower lip, eyes flashing. "Do you trust me?"

SEVENTEEN
BREXLEY

The fact that the man hadn't hesitated to nod had glued my heart to the upper ring of my throat. Instantly, he'd agreed to follow my lead. No questions, no fishing out information. Just a confident nod. Did I trust anyone in my life enough to agree so quickly? Noel. But beyond her? Maybe—*maybe*—Josie, but even then, I'd have reservations.

Silently we paddled, careful to avoid the manatees as they bobbed along silently. He followed my lead, paddling around the bend in the stream. Finally, he hesitated at the sight of the low overhang and knotted branches arching over the water.

"Lay back, Hotshot."

"Uhh, Brex, you got a plan here?" Royal hunkered down more into the canoe, as if *she* had over six feet of body to conceal below the limbs.

"Duck."

"Very funny," he grumbled, but I felt as the boat rocked, his bare feet and long, lean legs sliding further around my hips. I slunk down low, feet wrapping around my furry friend like a little anchor. I stowed my paddle down the length of the boat, hearing the subtle clunk of Rhyett mimicking the strategy.

From one branch to another, I stretched up a hand and shoved before jerking it back to my chest, nose nearly skimming the mossy underside and trying not to focus on the crabs and spiderwebs precariously close to my face.

Abs aching, the motion grew steady until I felt Rhyett's powerful shove slide us forward faster. God, the man was built. Nearly setting my fingers directly in a web, my breath hitched. Our momentum slowed as we both waited for a clear spot to shove off of. Core shaking, I exhaled when I could finally swing us forward again, Rhyett using the same grip to increase our momentum.

When we were finally free of the tunnel, wide-open blue skies greeted us as the second spring sprawled ahead, and I sucked down my first full breath, abs screaming their relief.

"Do I wanna know how many snakes we just passed?"

"Don't ask questions you won't like the answer to."

"Jesus," he muttered, but the sound was equally spooked and amused. "You've been here before."

"Yeah, my dad used to bring me as a kid."

"Not so excited about having to go back," he admitted, and I laughed.

"Big bad fisherman afraid of the swamp?"

"Absolutely, I am." His lack of hesitation jerked more laughter from my chest. "I've enjoyed thirty-five years of snake-less freedom."

"Most of them are little," I said, teasing.

"It's the *most of* in that sentence that bothers me." His smoky voice trailed off on a deep breath as we floated into the center of the pool, silent save for the subtle song of the birds. Our signature crystal clear spring water stretched out below us, gradually darkening to turquoise towards the bottom. Not even the manatees had braved the tunnel back here, leaving the water uninhabited save for silver fish that glinted in the sunlight.

"No gators back here?" he questioned.

"If there's water, there's a gator. Rule of thumb in Florida."

"Yikes."

"But I don't see anything." Albeit, the far side of the spring was mostly in the early morning shadow. "They rarely bug someone your size, at least not in clear water. Murky water? Keep a wide berth."

There was no warning before his tank top landed in my lap. The boat rocked, and a happy splash splattered me. Royal barked, lunging to her feet on alert as though her new friend had fallen in. When Rhyett's head broke the surface, he whooped, shaking out his hair before motioning me forward.

"Get in!"

"What?" I balked, shaking my head.

"Get. In!"

"I think I'll stay out here."

"Water's amazing!"

"I've been before, thanks."

There was a flash of mischief across blue eyes that sent me lunging for my paddle to push him away. Rhyett was faster. His broad, chilled hands clamped down on my arm, Royal yelping as the little boat rocked and we both spilled into the water. Warmer than the ocean, but startlingly cold, I broke into the air muttering curses to the roar of his laughter.

"Asshole," I spluttered, shoving a wave vaguely in his direction as Royal's soft splashes told me she was heading for shore. I'd no sooner cleared the spring water from my eyes than Rhyett's breath hit my cheek, his body heat only a beat behind.

His arms wrapped around me, pulling me in tight to him and sending warmth across my spine. We both stilled, save for our treading feet. My vision cleared up to see him grinning back at me, dirty blonde hair mussed, after he'd shaken the water from it. The rigid muscles of his body pressed down the length of my torso and I wrapped my legs around his waist. It was *his* idea, so *he* could keep us afloat. His smile widened, like he knew why I'd just done it. But the feel of him between my legs, warm in the cool water, unraveled my resolve.

Damn it, what is it about this man?

Without dropping that satisfied swagger, he brought his forehead to mine, halting my breath.

"You look stunning this morning," he whispered softly, tapping my nose with his.

"Just had to r-ruin it?" I chattered, glaring at the sun and, for once, wishing it was warmer.

"Had to take advantage of it," he corrected, arms tightening around me. His lips came down in a crushing kiss; nothing about the man before me exhibited hesitance or concern. Powerful legs kept us upright as Rhyett devoured me, heat singing in my blood as my body reacted, begging for more. One chilled, rough palm caressed my side, cupped a breast, slid up to my neck, and then he sucked my lower lip between his teeth.

My answering moan egged him on, his hand flattening against my back, sliding down to grab a handful of my ass. Rhyett moved like he'd memorized my body that first night. Like he was rehearsing a performance he'd thought through a thousand times as he kissed and nipped, feet kicking, friction building between us as desire unspooled inside my low belly. When his firm erection pressed against the slip of fabric between us, my breath hitched.

"Easy, stallion," I breathed, earning a chuckle before he claimed my mouth again. When his tongue danced the length of my lips, I opened, feeling the sun against my face, the cool water down my skin, soaking my hair, delighting in his hands as they roamed where he pleased. Mine had made it as far as his hard pec and shoulder, locking in place as if I'd anchored myself to him.

When Rhyett peeled us apart, it was with enough restraint his breath hardened. "I get you on a bed next time."

My laughter seemed to drift away on the gentle breeze, palm trees hissing as they shifted. Chest heaving, blood pounding, arousal demanding, I leaned away, finally peeking at his ink. The man was a masterpiece of sculpted, lean muscle and sun-kissed skin painted in a dark mural across one pec and down his arm, cutting off at his elbow. Shaking, I traced my fingers over the globe on his chest, the white sails of a ship, prominent anchor, and the arc of a compass. He'd inked his years on the sea across his skin.

"This is beautiful work, Rhyett."

"I can say the same." He ran a gentle thumb up my sternum, fingering the Unalome, then the floral wreath around a stack of books on the inside of my bicep. Craving the taste of him, it was me to close the gap this time, licking over his lip and then pinching it between my teeth. He ground his erection against me, the movement providing just enough friction to leave me wanting more intensity as my clit throbbed with need. His fresh, summery scent saturated my senses, next only to the salty water coating our skin, our lips.

The frantic whines and splashes of Royal approaching split us apart in a fit of laughter as the soggy dog placed herself between us, looking for the security I'd been enjoying in Rhyett's arms. She climbed up onto his shoulder and he grinned, shaking his head as she trembled against him, fur coating him in a fresh layer of silt.

That smile made me want to kiss it off his face, but he shook his head as Royal's claws dug into his shoulder, like she knew he could keep her safe. Ironically, I had to agree with her.

"Okay, okay. I'll get you home, princess."

EIGHTEEN
RHYETT

It was beautiful, but it had very little to do with sun and sand and everything to do with the enamoring blonde I'd left in the city. Comical satisfaction wrapped through my ribs as I crested the peak of the bridge Brexley was so petrified of, the unspoken divide between cities. You'd think it was the River Styx, not the Tampa Bay flying beneath asphalt and rubber. The sprawling wings of a pelican caught my attention, and I watched as the feathered beast dove and scooped up his breakfast before flying away.

My phone buzzed, and I tapped the screen so it would read it to me.

RHYETT

Fair. New location?

PAXTON

Haven't decided. Tell me what you think.

RHYETT

Rodger. I'll let you know.

I SET a reminder to call him in another couple of days in hopes I'd have a better feeling for the local flavor. Eventually, the stretching bridge gave way to the city streets of Bradenton and Sarasota. Still, the buildings and endless traffic flew by as my mind stayed firmly planted on the slick feel of Brexley's legs wrapped around my waist, her silky skin beneath my hands, the perfect handful of her breast and peaked nipple, hard with cold and what I prayed was desire as aggravating as mine.

There was no forgetting the taste of that woman. Sweet beneath the lingering caress of coffee. Or the feeling of her lean body against mine, breasts heaving against my chest as she clung to me. It had been a gamble, deciding to play in the water like that, but one worth taking. The Rhodes worked hard, but we played even harder, and if she was going to survive even the prospect of being initiated as an honorary member of the tribe, she'd have to know how to deal. She had willingly wrapped around me, opening her lips as I grazed across the center...so that was a delightful bonus.

Even as I pulled down the private dirt lane leading to the new Rhodes estate, all my mind could think about was how she'd cry out my name when I finally got her under my hands again.

So it was a bit of a shock when I rounded the corner to find trucks parked outside the skeleton of the main house. Pulling my attention to the actual task at hand, I glanced at the clock, confirming that no contractors were due for another ninety minutes. The plan had been to swing down to the fifth wheel, shower off the salt of the spring, eat breakfast, set my intention, and arrive before the meeting time.

With a sigh, I rolled with the punches, pulling a tank top on a beat before swiping my Windy City Wolves cap from the front dash.

Stepping out of the truck onto crunching gravel, I started with, "Morning, gentlemen."

"I'M TELLING YOU, until you've watched a thunderstorm roll into southern Florida, you haven't really lived."

"Storm's a storm," Broderick argued as the telltale sound of his aluminum desk drawer rang in the background.

"Nah, man, they're different down here."

His low laugh rumbled over the line. "Glad you're enjoying the little things."

"I believe you mean the enormous things." I snapped a quick photo of the dark towering mountain of cotton as it rippled and flashed with lightning that arched and popped. Nature's strobe light. Fired it off to him. "It's not even storm season yet," I noted, doing my damndest not to gape as I stared up at the looming threat, drawing out a long, awed whistle. "Couldn't pay me enough to sail in that."

"I'm sure Milo would be thrilled to hear his big bad son is cowering about a little bit of—" I heard as his phone vibrated and smirked, picturing the way those brown eyes would widen and round as he took in the wall of doom barreling my direction. I turned back to enjoy the sunset over the gulf. "Damn. Alright, a *lot* of rain."

"Sounds like I'm rolling down a mountain in a tin can when it hits the RV roof."

"Christ, isn't it March?"

"It's just the beginning."

"You gonna stick around and see the actual monsters?"

"It'll depend on the progress on the house and bar. If I'm making headway, no point in breaking the momentum."

"Wild, man." He cleared his throat. The sound of the computer powering on could be heard as I watched the wall of black swallow the Florida sunshine. "How's everybody else? Haven't had many updates with Jameson so focused on the season."

Broderick had been in our life for as long as I could remember. Sandwiched directly between Jameson and me, the three of us had grown up like hell on wheels, causing trouble and adding a four-teenth mouth to most family dinners. His mother had been the Mistyvale mayor for most of our childhood, and while she worked her ass off to be present, some mayoral duties just couldn't be avoided. Broderick would crash at our place after studying his evening away while Jameson and I skated by, filling our time with video games rather than academics.

"Haven't heard from Jeanne in a few weeks; she's probably out of service. Elora's still in Portland. No update on getting out of there, but she likes her clients. Paxton's got two more years in Chicago before he can head God knows where. Had's still in Boise and seems to like it. You have better tabs on Alice and Mav than I likely do."

He chuckled, agreeing, "Yeah, I guess I do. Is that weird?"

"A little," I admitted. I'd never been away this long. Nothing brought out the childlike longing for home like suddenly being five thousand miles away.

"So, Elora's still not sold on Oregon?"

"Not her vibe, I don't know. You know El, once she gets it in her head, there's no changing her mind." There were few forces of nature more determined than my younger sister. If she decided a mountain needed to move, the damn thing would be smart to pick up its skirt and shuffle away.

Broderick gave a raspy laugh. I could practically see him shifting in his seat. "Oh, I know."

"I met someone."

"Like, a contractor worth mentioning? Or a woman?"

I scoffed, "A woman, smart ass." I smiled fondly as images of Brexley filled my mind. Her laughing as the candle between us flickered, her in that bikini top with her face upturned to the sun. I needed to see her, touch her, taste her.

"Hey, man, no judgment."

"Her name's Brexley."

"*Ahh*, the Brex-a-nator."

If I'd had a liquid in my mouth, it would've been airborne. I brought him up to speed on my girl, the woman who'd pulled me into a complete infatuation in ten seconds or less. Broderick let out a low whistle.

"Well, well, well, Florida has its perks."

"Indeed it does," I agreed.

"What are you gonna do, man?"

"What do you mean? Obviously forget about her."

"Cold, bro."

I laughed. "Jesus, Broderick. I'm gonna convince her to let me chase her down and never let go." Ever. For any reason. She sunk her claws so deep into my flesh there was no going back.

"I'm not sure which I'd prefer."

"Not ready to share?"

He chuckled. "Obviously not. I can't picture you settling down. You're so...you."

"Yeah, well, *me* wants to plant some roots." My phone beeped, another call coming in, and I lifted it to glance at the screen. Brexley was calling me. "Ho-ly shit," I breathed.

"What? You get struck by lightning?"

"Yeah, 'cause that would be the response."

His laugh warmed my chest, as if we were home joking around together. "Hey, I saw you sever a chunk of your finger, strap some tape on it and call it a day."

"Nah, Brex is calling."

"Hell, say *that*. Talk soon." He amputated the call before I could respond.

Sucking down a steadying breath, I said, "Hey, beautiful. Miss me already?"

"What would you say if I did?"

My cheeks ached, and it took me a second to realize my grin had stretched them wide. I leaned forward, planting my feet more firmly in the sand and eyeing the impending storm, its dark promise draining the color from the surrounding beach.

"I'd say I miss you, too. Then I'd tell you I have the perfect spot to watch this storm roll through, with a bottle of brandy and a fireplace."

"Sounds idyllic."

"I mean, as picture-perfect as an RV can be."

Her laughter glittered in the air as I stood, dusting the granules from my cargo shorts. "Surprisingly, unopposed to that."

"But?" I clarified, heading back for the parking lot as the warm sand slid beneath my bare feet. Thunder growled ominously in the distance.

"I like you, Rhyett. But I'm still not sure the distance is workable."

"I'll be in the city three days a week. Won't even make you drive where pelicans fly."

"I'm not...a relationship kind of girl, Rhy."

Rhy. I about crumpled, my steps faltering at the sound of the affectionate moniker on her perfect pink lips. "Come see me."

"You can't change that. Are you okay with that?"

"Baby, if it's the difference between getting to enjoy your company, and not, you can call us whatever you want."

NINETEEN

BREXLEY

Thunder rolled, and my windows rattled, the flash striking through the space like a blade. I swirled the merlot in a steady circle, snuggling tighter into my chunky knit cardigan. What I would give to have an entire quarter of the year to wear my cozy clothes, not just the occasional storm that fought a cold front into submission. Muscles sore from my daily run, I stretched and twisted, wishing my mind would take a break. Hell, my mind was why I was sore in the first place–its persistent bunny trail back to Rhyett was why I'd done twice my usual distance.

I'd tried to sleep, but every time my eyes closed, they were painted with an image of blue eyes and sun-kissed skin coated with beads of fresh spring water. Warm, hard muscles tucked between my legs, the heady taste of summer and—

A clap of thunder jerked me present. Rhyett. The phone call had been a mistake. I knew it before his voice had even cracked across the speaker. Not entirely sure of what I'd been doing, my breath hitched when he answered.

Companionship on my terms. That's the offer he'd left on the table.

Who the hell was this man? Rhyett said we could take it slow—get to know each other—or pick up where we'd left off in the spring. Either way, it was up to me. Never in my life had I heard of an offer like that. Friends with benefits? I guess, sure: Vallie had one of those in college. But friends with benefits with a lease-to-buy option?

Another flash of lightning filled the night, and I took a sip of the smooth liquid. A monsoon-level downpour crashed against the earth, and I thanked my lucky stars that I wasn't trapped on the road. As much as his proposal to watch the storm in his RV on a quiet property beside a fireplace sounded idyllic, that damn bridge was terrifying enough in pleasant weather. This was anything but.

Nevertheless, I wanted more of him. More to taste and touch. More of his laugh in my ribs and hands on my skin.

Jesus, Brex. Pull it together.

I glanced at the clock, realizing it was later than Noel usually called, and quickly texted to check on her. The response bubble appeared and vanished twice, for good the second time. That was weird. Something was going on with her, and so help me, if Eric was anything less than princely, I'd happily dig a six-foot hole. Hell, I'd just see if Rhyett had hogs on that little farm of his. The only reason I tolerated Mr. Ostentatious was that he made her smile.

Robby had never made me smile like Noel did. But Rhyett...the man had me beaming and laughing in the first twenty-four hours. My brain couldn't decide if that was acceptable or not. Nerves in my throat, I checked my phone only to decide I was pathetic, entering the spiral of self-loathing when disappointment greeted the empty screen. I tossed the damn thing onto the couch with a roll of my eyes, stood, closed the curtains and retrieved my book off the coffee table before heading to bed.

The male main character was twelve kinds of dreamy. But as I drifted off to sleep, it was Rhyett that I thought of.

"YOU KNOW WHAT'S HIGHLY IMPRACTICAL?"

"Hmm?" Noel said from one stall over.

"Tarzan."

Her laugh burst out like it snuck up on her. "What?"

"I mean, I'm all for unlikely love stories, but what woman in her right mind would willingly leave indoor plumbing and running water to live in the jungle?" I wiggled the dress over my head as I shifted it into place.

"Agreed," Josie said from my opposite side.

"No abs are worth that," Vallie's voice trailed from across the aisle. "You know what else is impractical? This freaking outfit."

We'd all had high hopes for the new spring line, yet as I turned this way and that, studying the unflattering fabric that somehow gathered across my belly, I scowled. Evidently we were all striking out.

"Seriously, there's a fine line between prison jumpsuit and fashion jumper. Ugh–this one gives me camel toe. Damn Viking genetics." Noel sighed pointedly. For a woman of average height, she had an abnormally long torso, and it posed problems any time we were hunting for one-piece outfits. Swimsuits were worse. "Whyyyy did we need extra ribs in the North? Everything fits me in width, except they're way too short."

"Shut up, I'd pay for your waist," Vallie said, a bit out of breath like her garment was wrestling her. I slipped out of the dress, frowning as I re-hung it.

"And I'd kill for your curves," Noel shot back with a laugh. "Some of us are freaking rectangles. Slap a cap on and I'd pass as a boy. Pull a *Mulan*."

Vallie's retort was cut off by Josie's squeal of excitement. "Oooh! Can I wear this color?" The sound of four sets of creaking hinges in synchronized motion filled the space as we all popped our heads out, Josie stepping into the aisle in a lavender wrap top with a plunging v-neckline.

"Dayyum," Noel said, eyes going wide.

"Yeah?!" Josie asked, rising on her tiptoes excitedly.

Vallie grinned, "Um, *yeah*. You look gorgeous."

"Makes your eyes pop," I agreed.

"Hair up or down?"

"Down," the three of us answered at once, swapping laughs like currency. I suppose they were these days. We all worked our asses off in our respective fields, so these stolen moments were farther and fewer between. Twice in a month was the best it could get, and only upon Noel's insistence that we all splurge on some clothes and hit up happy-hour in celebration of Vallie's promotion.

Half an hour later, all with at least a few winners in branded totes, we headed into the city to find food. The obnoxious traffic noise, chattering, and the never-ending herd of humans slammed through my senses.

"You hear from Rhyett?" Noel asked, linking our arms as Josie took the lead, swinging her bag happily as she looked around at the chaos.

"We talked a few nights ago."

"That hottie from Three Leaf?" Vallie leaned forward to lock eyes. When I nodded, she tossed her braids over a shoulder and indignantly added, "And you're just bringing that up *because?*"

"It's your night, Val."

"Yes, and as my nether regions are drier than a fast-food biscuit, I'd like to hear about yours."

Our round of laughter was loud enough to draw several sets of eyes, one woman smiling as a handsome twenty-something guy raised his brows.

"Nothing else has happened," I insisted when we caught our breath.

"But...?" Josie hedged as she reached for the front door to a little wine bar with killer hors d'oeuvres. When I didn't immediately supply a story, she rolled her eyes, demanding, "What was said the other night?"

"We both enjoy each other—"

"How could you not? We all saw the man," Noel interjected as we stepped into the lobby.

"But we know the distance is a hurdle. And I don't have the time to dedicate to dating right now."

"What the hell does that mean?" Josie said with a scowl. Genevieve, a curvy bombshell with onyx skin and a halo of natural curls, smiled from the back of the restaurant, waving off the hostess as she made her way to the front. She'd started as a busser fresh out of high school, working her way up the ranks until they made her a manager. We'd been regulars since before her time, so she always made sure to get us the best tables.

"It means my plate is too full with the bookstore and finding somewhere to expand. We didn't get the shop across the street, so I need to find a new location, and I'd like to host more author events. Evening, Gen."

"Evening, Brexley!" Genevieve pulled me in for a hug before moving down the line, greeting everyone by name before she set us up in a back booth away from the racket and promised our favorite server would be by soon.

"Well," Vallie sighed. "That's bullshit."

"What?" I laughed, hoping we'd moved to a new topic.

"You're making excuses. You're here with us; you have the time."

"Are you telling me to cut out girls' night so I can fool around with a guy a decade older than us?"

"No, I'm saying you'd find the time if you decided to. Work isn't everything, Brex."

"Ten years isn't even that big of a gap," Noel added.

"Of course not, although like tonight, for example—I have to go wrap up after we're done here. Anything else I add to my plate takes away from something already on it. I've never even found the time to write my book, even though I've always wanted to."

"Hire help," Josie chirped, placing her napkin on her lap.

"We have help."

"I mean…" Noel bit her lip. "We have the budget to outsource some stuff, Brex. Social media, blogging, running ads. All things you don't technically have to do."

"Hiring someone means I'd have to train them."

"So?" Vallie said, smiling as one of the new servers brought by our regular drinks—courtesy of Gen, no doubt. "It'll pay off in the long run."

"But it would take longer than just doing it myself. And then I'm even shorter on time." Of course, I'd thought about it. Becoming a business owner essentially traded a boring nine-to-five with someone else's name on it for a twenty-four-seven with your own. Only by the time I slowed down and showed someone the ropes, I could have put that time into something more productive—finishing the task in a third of the time and moving on to the next. There just hadn't been a moment where I could afford to make that initial sacrifice. Especially with every jerk off in our generation twiddling their thumbs for a week before they abandoned the post. It was easier to just keep things with me. My plate was organized. Chaotic and overloaded, but organized.

"Temporarily," Noel allowed with a shrug. "Except Val is right. It's time, Brex."

"Hey, tonight is about Vallie's promotion, not ganging up on Brexley night," I said as anxiety surged between my ribs. I loathed being the center of attention.

"We just don't want to see you miss out on something good in the name of your career, okay? Just think about it," Josie said softly before mercifully redirecting the conversation. "Has anyone heard from Stacey?"

I was vaguely aware that Vallie and Noel dove into discussing her whereabouts, but my mind stayed on books and a particularly mouth-watering blonde for the rest of the night.

Seeing as I was still sitting in my closet of an office, scheduling blog posts when my timer chirped that it was nearly midnight, drawing my focus up and out of the computer, maybe they weren't so far off base.

City uncharacteristically quiet with the late hour, my eyes drifted to the vacant space across the street when I spotted the light on. The front door was open, releasing the soulful melody of "If Only" by Teeks. That twinge of regret twisted my gut, full of the long list of my if only's. If only I'd had the guts to knock on the door; if only I'd gotten a realtor to reach out on my behalf.

It didn't matter. I was used to disappointing myself. At least the new tenant had good taste in music.

Would it be pathetic to sleep on a plastic tarp? It was the cleanest surface in the future speakeasy. I'd just worked up the courage to walk over and see if it was Brexley or Noel still working at ungodly hours when the pipe started leaking. I've always been damn good with my hands, however, plumbing is an entirely different debacle.

By the time I had the damn thing fixed, the window at The Cracked Corset was dark. *Dumb.* I should've taken the time to pop in sooner.

Maybe it was better this way. If she wanted me in her life, she would've invited me in when I offered. Right?

With a sigh, I rolled over and pushed off the dusty tarp, brushing debris from my skin. Okay, so maybe Brexley and Noel had a point about the commute, because the idea of a forty-minute drive back home was suddenly daunting. Not as daunting as having to wake up early enough to drive the ninety minutes it took with traffic to be there in time for the eight am meeting with the general contractor, Eddy. With a long-suffering sigh, I cleaned up the space, not sure if Clementine would continue to pop in for progress reports or not, but wanting her to see I was respecting the building if she did. The stereo was the last thing to be turned off. Couldn't think without music.

The drive home was nearly abandoned, and I soaked up the oddity that was a silent city. Still, as my lids grew heavy, I cranked up the music, running through the to-do list for tomorrow.

Meet with Eddy.

Finalize tile selection.

Order custom glass garage doors for the shop.

On and on, I ticked them off on my fingers until I was safely planted on Rhodes property. It took all my remaining willpower to strip off the drywall-coated clothing and step into the too-short shower, ducking to wash my hair under the spray.

MY MORNING RUN started when the horizon was just beginning to turn blue. There was something invigorating about getting started while the world slumbered. Sun hovering over the horizon, skin slicked with sweat, I finished mile five turning down our dirt road, and smiled. Slowed to a trot, panting. My smart watch buzzed to announce the victory.

Good man, Rhyett. That's what Milo always said when we finished strong. Rhodes were finishers—end of discussion. I intended to attack the house with the same level of tenacity they had trained us to bring to any table we sat at.

After a deep stretch, a cool shower, and an hour of meditation, I looked up to see the two pickups kicking up dust through the broad picture window at the back of the rig. It was a monster of a fifth wheel, about four hundred square feet, complete with a second bedroom in the middle, a loft, and a pull-out sofa. We could almost fit all of us on the selection of beds. Almost. But my favorite thing was the amount of windows they'd built into the damn thing. Made it feel more like a tiny house than an RV.

Packing away the rest of the fruit bowl, I made my way outside. My boots clomped down the stairs as Ed's red pickup shifted into park beside the house, looking more like the drawings and less like a skeleton of one.

"Morning, Ed," I hollered as he stepped out. When his right-hand man did the same, I added, "Morning, Joey."

The men both waved back, turning to retrieve blueprints and coffee before heading in my direction. And with one last sigh, the day was off.

AS SOON AS my parents declared themselves residents of Florida, I would get my ass into an apartment in the heart of the city. At least, that's what I promised myself as I made the drive for the fourth time that week. Doubling down on a family project and business venture might not have been my brightest idea, though Rhodes had done more with less.

It would all work out. It always did. It would just require more black tea and dirty chai than I wanted to admit. I'd pray for my adrenal glands and call it a day.

A sixteen-passenger van pulled away from my store space right as I came around the corner, chugging my Vitamin B energy drink like my life depended on it. But his vacancy opened the perfect spot to unload all of my finds from the week. Turns out, Florida had an impressive selection of salvage yards. Hidden under mountains of clutter sat a plethora of perfect finds to bring vintage back to life in the bar.

Light spilled onto the sidewalk from The Cracked Corset. I glanced at my watch, confirming what I already knew. It was after eleven. They'd been closed for hours. If the lights were still on when I got this truck bed empty, I'd head over and say hello to whoever was burning the midnight oil with me. I was praying it was a certain sexy blonde with a propensity for igniting my blood. Blood that rushed south the moment I pictured that face, the little dimple on her chin.

Fucking temptress.

I plugged the Bluetooth headphones in and hit play on my watch. "Shrike" by Hozier set a peppy pace, and I dropped the tailgate to unload. Trip after trip, I hauled in treasures. Crates of reclaimed wood. A chandelier I could restore for the back hallway. Old frames for the mirrors if I painted them first. A coat rack that would double as vintage decor. It took a good lift and focused breathing to haul in the cast iron sinks on my own, but I did the damn thing, panting as I turned back to the truck for the last load— an old cruiser bike we could put up on the plant shelves.

Hands aching and arms a little shaky from too much exertion and not enough calories, I stepped outside to catch my breath, only for it to halt when I spotted the now-dark storefront across from me. Whipping my head to the side, I spotted a black jeep as it rolled through the intersection, the light just turning green.

My palms seemed to buzz.

"Rhyett?" A smooth, feminine voice pulled my attention back as Noel waved me down. I crossed the empty street, pulling her in for a hug. She bounced back with a smile, shaking her head as she happily demanded, "What in the hell are you doing here?" Her eyes flicked from mine to the lit, soon-to-be bar behind me. Those freckled cheeks fell. "Oh, man. Don't tell me."

"What?" I asked, confused by the reaction.

"*You're* the new tenant?"

"Oh yeah—that dumpster fire will be my bar by the end of the year."

"Don't tell Brexley," she said on a nervous-sounding giggle.

"What?" I balked again. "Why not?"

"She had her heart set on that building for years. When the for-rent sign went up, she sent them emails daily for months."

"Oh man," I said with a grimace. "I had no idea."

"How could you?"

"Man, I just—that's what I was doing, the day I came into the shop."

"Signing the lease?"

"Yeah, I just...had a good feeling about Clem."

"Clem?"

"Landlord," I supplied, running a palm over my hair. Noel offered me what was clearly meant to be a reassuring smile.

"Don't worry about it, Rhyett. Wasn't meant to be. We didn't have the renovation budget, anyway."

"It's not going to win me any brownie points, though, is it?"

Noel looked like she was wrestling a smile into submission. "You still hoping to win brownie points, Hotshot?"

"Obviously," I admitted. "You know Brex."

"Yeah," she said, glancing down to her hand as her phone lit up. Her brow furrowed, jaw tightening. A picture of her with a brunette guy in a suit popped up. "I should take this."

I raised my hand in farewell. "Goodnight, Noel. Will you let Brex know we're neighbors?"

She chuckled, shaking her head with unearned fondness in her eyes. "Chicken shit."

"I plead the fifth," I said, retreating across the road. I turned off the lights, locked the shop up, and headed on home, thinking of Brexley.

Four miles beneath my tennis shoes, four shots of espresso, and four new inquiries for author signings into my morning, I finally packed up Royal's belongings, and we headed out the door. Mornings were my favorite. Not just because I could be productive, but because the city was mostly silent. Still anticipating the tumult of the day but not yet descended into the melee of urban hustle culture. For a moment, I could pretend I was anywhere else. A quiet small town like my romcom authors wrote about. Not the enormous petri dish where we all piled on top of each other like sardines in a can.

Blocks between my townhouse and shop were always eager to dissolve that optimism. Littered with trash and lined with poverty, the streets quickly reminded me of how harsh the world could be. Of why I had to fight like hell to make something of myself.

I stopped by a homeless man who didn't know his own name, dropping off his morning muffin and banana and wishing him well as he nodded his thanks. We'd affectionately named him Nick, but he didn't respond to that, either. His words were a jumble of nonsense, only his body language conveying that he was still in there as he bowed his head in gratitude or waved hello each day. But "Nick" was a daily reminder of the countless families struggling to make ends meet or unable to make them meet at all. And all I could provide was a meal for one. Few things were as effective at making me aware of my insignificance.

With a sigh, we kept cruising, despite the foreboding sense of anxiety that had peeled my eyes open before my alarm even went off.

Not even my run had been able to shake it. As we got closer to The Cracked Corset, my heart rate seemed to increase, my mind swimming as it pounded against my skull. I'd chalked it up to an impending headache until Royal sat down expectantly beside our front door.

The bronze handle jammed into my palm, not turning, and I scowled. It had been a week since I'd made the idiotic mistake of calling Rhyett Rhodes, and aside from a handful of texts checking in on each other, we hadn't talked since. Naturally, my mood progressively worsened, coming to a climax as my hand stung where the metal had nearly broken the skin when it refused to budge. More important than the ache was the fact that I never beat Noel to the shop. Most mornings, we walked together, and even Royal had looked gradually more and more dejected as the journey went on without our companion, tail drooping. On the rare occasion when she woke up early or couldn't sleep, she always headed in first. The shop would be lit with her enthusiasm, and she'd be writing or reading happily in a corner booth.

But the energy was vacant as I slid my key into the lock and turned. I fought the desire to call out for her, well aware that Noel's presence was as formidable as a storm cloud. I would've known.

"Shit," I muttered, guiding Royal inside and flipping on the lights. In the next movement, I had her on speed dial and pinned my cell between my ear and shoulder, digging through the motions of opening operations. My first two calls went to voicemail, as I turned on the lights and walked to the coffee bar to get a pot going. That was rule number one of opening at Corset. We loved our espresso, but when it came time to set the vibe, a full pot was required.

Grumbling, Royal standing guard at the front door, I walked through the motions of bringing the place to life. As the cooks came in, we all exchanged greetings and pleasantries, but it was Wrenly ringing the front door, looking befuddled as she found me behind the bar sipping coffee and answering emails that made me reach for my cell again, only to circle back to her voicemail.

"Okay, this is freaking me out. Tell me you're okay, please. Love you." With a huff, I slid it into my pocket, shaking my head as Wrenly washed her hands and found her apron.

"Nothing? That's not like her."

"No," I agreed. "It's not."

"You gonna go track her down?"

"Once Holl is in, if she hasn't answered me by then."

Keeping my hands busy, I ran through the usual motions: checked our bank accounts, ran through advertising conversion, answered a dozen emails, placed orders for the cafe and then the bookstore. But anxiety was carving deeper and deeper into my psyche, making me shake inside my bones. This didn't feel right.

When my phone finally buzzed in my pocket, I about came out of my skin.

NOEL

Hey, I'm so sorry. I'm okay, but I was in an accident this morning. Didn't realize the meds would make me sleep so hard.

NAUSEA POOLED in my stomach as my heart plunged through it, throat aching, and my head suddenly spinning. She hadn't even called me. She was hurt, and she hadn't even called me. Swearing, I snagged my keys from where I'd set them on the desk and bolted for the front door.

She still didn't answer my phone call. What in the hell happened?

BREXLEY

Hey, I'm on my way! What's going on? What do you need?

"WREN!" I shouted over my shoulder. "I gotta go! You got Royal?"

"Yeah, babe, drive safe! Keep me posted."

I'm not even sure I answered her as I barreled into the blinding light of the Florida morning, door ringing behind me as my eyes watered, having very little to do with the sunshine.

"Dammit, Noel," I cursed as I slammed my phone in my pocket again. *Why can't she answer me?*

Was she actually okay, or was she putting on a brave face? As I booked it down the sidewalk, I spotted the zippy, red coupe across the street, the front door to the retail space wide open. Of all the times for the landlord to be there, of course it was now. It didn't matter. Nothing mattered except getting to my best friend.

In and out of my townhouse in about ninety seconds, I lunged for my car door, practically tearing the handle off when it didn't unlock like it was supposed to. Pulse slamming in my temples, I tried again, though it didn't budge.

What the fuck?

The fob clicked, but the car refused to chirp; the door stuck where it was. The fucking battery must have died. *Jesus, Mary, and Joseph.* I swallowed down the panic, bolting back inside and swapping my cute flats for worn tennis shoes before sprinting out the door.

NOEL'S APARTMENT was only a mile north of mine. Part of my routine was a five-mile run after work, which meant the quick sprint to her place was like a freaking warm-up. But when I stuttered to a stop outside her steps, jolting up to the front door, nobody answered. Sighing, I jumped off the porch and lifted the tiny emerald elephant out of her potted hydrangeas. After freeing the spare key, I climbed the steps again, willing my breathing to level out.

The townhouse was dark and smelled vaguely of old coffee.

"Noel?!" Silence was the only response. Fingers flying for my phone, I barked, "Noel?" Chloe, her little tabby cat, jingled down the stairs with a meow, and I bent to scratch her ears as the phone rang again. Finally, she answered, her voice soft.

"Brex?"

"Noel! Thank God. Where the hell are you?"

"Sarasota Memorial."

"What?" I balked, straightening. "Why? Are you okay? What happened?" About a million questions demanded answers, but I shoved them back down, aware that the four I'd rattled off were likely three too many. Pinching the bridge of my nose, I forced down a breath.

"I'm okay," she said softly, entirely unconvincing. "Look, I just want to get out of here, but they won't discharge me yet."

"The doctors want you to stay. Why? Noel, give me something here."

"I fractured my wrist and broke my clavicle. They were watching for a concussion."

I jammed my eyes closed, sliding down to sit on her cool tile floor as Chloe weaved between my legs. Noel was my entire world at this point. The one person I'd always been able to count on, who saw me for me and loved me, anyway. The idea of anything happening to her made a cold sweat coat my palms.

"Honestly, I just want to sleep in my own damn bed."

"Okay. I—uh, my car wouldn't start, but I'll find my way down, okay? I'll see you soon. I'm here now."

"At the hospital?" The confusion in her voice made me ache.

"No, sweetie, I'm at your house. I'll feed Chloe. She's fine. What do you need before I come to see you?"

"Brex, you don't have to do that."

"Listen here, twat, you gave me a freaking heart attack. Like hell am I not showing up after you got yourself in a car wreck." She gave a watery little laugh that felt like a blade to my chest. "Now, what do you need?"

TWENTY-TWO
RHYETT

"Mom, you're still in your prime. Stop that." Juniper Rhodes was many things, but old and haggard was certainly not one of them. She had it in her head that every piece of the homestead needed to be done with the same urgency as a fire evacuation. But the reality was, the woman wasn't even sixty, hiked every morning, did yoga three times a week, and was likely to outlive her caffeine-addicted work-a-holic children at this rate. She harrumphed.

"Easy to say when you're five thousand miles away, warm as fresh toast, while I'm shivering so violently, my muscles cramp."

I chuckled. Some things, it seemed, never changed. "Well, then get your ass down here. I'm sore for company."

"How are you doing, baby? You okay off on your own?"

"I'm fine, Mom." I'd be better if Brexley had reached back out. Aside from one or two-word replies to my vague 'how are you's', she had said nothing after I'd thrown my offer out there. My dreams had been one ongoing vivid vision of her perfect pussy, that round ass, bright smile, and a perfect palmful of breast since I'd touched her the first time. Remarkably enough, her colorful vocabulary, that husky laugh and frequent sass were too. Of course, I wasn't about to say any of that to my mother. "Swear it."

"I know you're fine—you're my resilient one, always have been. But you've always been the heart of this family, Rhyett. If you're homesick, we can have you on a flight the next day."

"I know, Mom." I rolled my eyes but, in a pathetic way, appreciated the sentiment. Being a grown-ass man didn't cancel out her over-bearing maternal instincts. "And you say that to all your kids."

"Because you're all at the heart of it, baby. But with you…you've always glued us together. Your dad and I have always known it, though having you gone has definitely reminded me to appreciate when we're all in one place."

"Thanks, miss you too. Hey—" I glanced at my watch, "—what in the hell are you up so early for?"

"Oh, the ice storm took down our power. Woke up freezing and had to go flip the breaker. Couldn't go back to sleep." Dammit. I hated being so far away. With Milo and Jameson out on the water, it suddenly felt imperative to make sure she was taken care of. Not that the woman hadn't been tackling life independently since her teenage years. Before I could offer Broderick in case of an issue, she asked, "So, how are things?"

From her perfect vintage porcelain farmhouse sink to the bronze fixtures and paint pallets, I walked her through everything that had been ordered and signed off on. Being a persistent jackass with boots on the ground, the contractors were having a much harder time brushing off her concerns when they tried to pull some shady shit.

"At this rate," I said after a forty-minute Q&A, rolling off the creaky RV mattress and heading down the three stairs into the kitchen. Little by little, I'd been transforming this space, too. Making it feel more hospitable and less temporary. "We'll be finished in time for winter, which means we can officially start planning Christmas on the beach."

Her joyous yelp earned a wince as I pulled the phone away from my ear. "Oh, I can't wait! Your dad will be so excited when he gets home."

"He on the water?"

"Just down in the harbor. They're cleaning tanks today."

"Good deal, good deal. Hey, look, Mom—"

"I've kept you too long. Oh, Rhy, I'm sorry!"

I chuckled, shaking my head as the espresso pod machine stopped blinking and started brewing. While I'd generally take the slimy aftertaste of a shot of wheatgrass over the bitter liquid, it was bound to be an all-hands-on-deck kind of week, and a triple shot with a generous pour of creamer was precisely what I needed. "No biggie, I just need to get some food in me before the contractor shows up, so I can get you here for Christmas."

"Go! Go! I apologize for keeping you."

"You're fine, Mom," I assured her, shaking my head. "I'll report back soon, alright?"

"Okay, yes, great! Thank you again, Rhy."

"Of course, ma."

"Hey, Rhy?"

"Yeah?"

"You take care of yourself down there, okay?"

"Always."

"Okay. Love you, son."

"Love you too. Now go drag Mav out of bed and get him to work." I loved the kid, but Maverick had a classic case of baby brother syndrome. There was always a rational justification that allowed him to shirk his fair share of household chores. With everyone but Alessandra out of the house, the six eldest had an intervention with our parents when we were all home last summer. Even Jeanne—who liked to baby *everyone*—called bullshit on the fact that Milo was busy handling domestic duties on the rare occasion he was off the water. They'd put his feet to the fire in the seven months since, and I was all for it. Like hell would the youngest Rhodes tarnish our reputation as some of the hardest workers on the island.

Mom snickered. "Sure thing. Snowed six inches last night; I'll have him shoveling before breakfast."

"Good. Talk soon." The machine finished right as the screen went to its wallpaper—a picture of my brothers and me crowded in for a tacky selfie on Mill Bay Beach back home. Despite our perpetual habit of reverting to boyhood antics when we were together, I missed the fuckers. Soon enough, we'd all be annoying each other senseless again.

A sip of the homemade Americano had me reaching for the cup of sugar on the counter. How anybody drank that shit black was beyond me. I'd just popped my bagel into the toaster when my phone lit up, buzzing as Brexley's name marched onto the screen.

I blew out a breath, a lick of surprise teasing my chest. By the third ring, I'd palmed the device and brought it to my ear with a, "Good morning, beautiful."

"Morning?" She attempted a laugh, but it was tinny and hollow. "Rhyett, it's eleven. Tell me I didn't just wake you."

"Nah, I'm up. Been chatting with my mom. You sound serious, what's wrong?"

"Why would you possibly assume something's wrong? You barely know me."

"Call it an instinct. Now you're being evasive. What's up?"

She took a long breath that sounded like a desperate reach to steady herself before answering. "Noel was in an accident."

"Are you okay?" Fuck, if something happened to her...

"Yeah, I wasn't with her."

"And Noel?"

"She's okay but a little banged up. I'm here at the hospital in Sarasota and need a ride home because my car wouldn't start this morning. Vallie is out of state, and Josie has her kids out on the water. I can't believe I'm ask—"

"Of course." I was already off of the banquet bench, moving back to the bedroom in the gooseneck.

"What?" Her voice went wispy, like sheer fabric in the wind.

"On my way—or I will be as soon as I find my pants—what do you need?"

"Rhyett, you don't—"

"Brexley. If you didn't need help, you wouldn't have asked for it. Once I'm dressed enough to not be shunned by society, I'll head your way. Which hospital?" She gave me the name and address, even Noel's room number, and I promised her I'd be there. Something uneasy settled in my gut before a very different sensation engulfed it.

She called *me*. While I wanted to take that as a moment of significance—that she'd call me when she needed something—that discomfort told me she didn't have anyone else she could count on in a time of need. My heart ached. She honestly didn't have any family she could depend on? Because the spring fling she'd known for a little over a week couldn't be her best option when shit hit the fan...right?

THERE WERE FEW THINGS, if any, that a Rhodes hated more than a hospital. If we were sick or hurt enough to land here, we'd already shaken hands with the Grim Reaper and could tell you what his breath smelled like. Hospitals were for the dying. For the people too blindsided by an injury, or too weak in fortitude to take care of their bodies in the first place. I had a pretty good poker face, but my anxiety spiked as the smell of antiseptic and the chatter of machines greeted me.

Maybe it was overstepping, but I'd already met Noel, and it felt rude to not at least offer her a smile and some flowers. Let her know I was grateful she was okay. If she was important to Brexley, that made her important to me. Although that also meant I had to survive the lobby, walk to the elevators, nine floors of fluorescents with an over-worked nurse who had haunted eyes, and the sterilization required to gain entrance to the wing.

Immediately stopped by a pretty brunette behind the desk—who looked a little less haggard than my friend from the elevator—wearing crisp, black scrubs. I offered her that smile Jeanne called my *lady killer*. It must have worked, because the woman's hard face relaxed, her throat working. A minute later, I was waved over to Noel's room, hesitating when I spotted a police officer leaning against the door frame.

As I approached, I cleared my throat, mostly so he knew I was a few steps behind him, and he rotated, his face solemn. Not good.

"Afternoon, officer. Everything alright?"

"Just getting a few more details," he said with a stiff, formal smile. I nodded, aware of the pinch between my brows as the tension settled there.

"Is it alright if I come in? I'm a friend of Noel's."

"Rhyett?" The sound of Brexley's voice, strained and hopeful, wrapped a rope around my ribs, squeezing until she slipped between the cop and the metal door frame. "Oh my God," she breathed, and to my surprise, hurled her arms around my neck, our bodies colliding. On instinct, I wrapped her up in a vice grip, tightening as I buried my face in her hair.

Breathing her in, I thought, *she called me.*

I kissed her cheek, setting her on her feet so I could get a clear shot of her eyes. Flicking between them, I got the reassurance I needed that she was okay. The shadows there made me straighten, shoulders pulling back as the officer smiled more sincerely this time, stepping aside to let us pass.

"Thanks for the information, Miss McShane. We'll be in touch." There was a second officer beside her bedside, and I did my best not to wince at the bruise marring the side of Noel's face. The second officer tapped a business card on the rolling table over her lap. "And I trust you'll do the same when you think of something."

When. I caught his verbiage and frowned, looking around the room and noting a woman at the foot of the bed who could be no one except for Noel's mother, the two of them practically cloned copies, just a few decades apart. Opposite the officer stood a man in a two-thousand dollar suit, his dark brow furrowed and arms crossed. A tie hung loosely around his neck, the top of his collar unbuttoned. Brexley's swallow was audible as she reached for my hand, guiding me to the head of the bed as the officer vacated the position.

I set the flowers on a side table before slipping from her hold to lean down and gently hug Noel, who giggled under her breath.

"Hey there, hotshot. I'm fine, I swear. They're making it a bigger deal than it is."

"Doesn't look not serious, Red. Brex seemed pretty rattled."

"Brex gets rattled if someone sneezes too close to me," she said, directing my eyes to the blonde hovering by my side. She grimaced but didn't argue. *Well, that's cute.*

"I'm sorry," the man across from us cut in. "I don't think we've had the pleasure of meeting."

Straightening, I extended a hand, "Rhyett Rhodes." His hair was still gelled meticulously into place, denim eyes flashing with a challenge nobody else seemed to sense. Given the situation, it should have been imperative to reassure him, but I didn't particularly care what conclusions he came to.

"Eric Connely," he said as he accepted. He shook like his diminutive stature was accompanied by a little dick, and his ego needed to compensate. Like it was a wrestling match. I fought back the bemused snort as he uselessly added, "Noel's *boyfriend.*"

"Nice to meet you," I said under a raised brow, surveying him a little closer. It wasn't. Everything about him spelled snake-oil salesman, and I quickly decided Noel could do better. Hell, any one of my brothers would be better for Red. Red...whose eyes were now on her lap, the dark bruise on her face and cast on her forearm tightening my chest.

"Well," he scoffed, adding some swagger to his posture like it might catch my attention. "I feel bad you drove out, but she needs her rest."

"Hmm, I'm just here to pick up Brex. I think we're feeding a cat, picking up some supplies, or something along those lines."

"I've got it covered. Sorry for your trouble."

Oh. Little man was definitely in the mood for a pissing contest with his chest puffed and his shoulders pulled back. I wanted to laugh but thought better of it for the girls' sake.

"No trouble at all. Brex," I said, turning to her, loving the way he bristled. "What can I get you? I'm happy to hang out as long as you need me to."

She looked like she was teetering on the edge of tears, so I reached down to thread our fingers together, giving her a reassuring squeeze. A raspy breath filled her ribs before she nodded. "I fed Chloe this morning, so she should be okay through dinner. You don't have to stay, Rhyett. We can go whenever. I appreciate the offer, though."

"Whatever you need, Ace."

"Told you he'd stick," Noel mumbled from the bed, cracking through Brexley's anxiety as laughter bubbled between her lips. Eric forced an unconvincing chuckle she ignored. "Thanks for coming, Hotshot."

"Anything you need, Red?"

She smiled at the moniker before her eyes flicked to Eric and then to the woman staring at her lap at the end of the bed. I reached out a hand.

"Noel's mother, I assume?"

She gave a breathy little laugh. "Frankie McShane. Thanks for looking after my girls, Rhyett."

"They were covered, Mrs. McShane," Eric said scornfully, feigning lightheartedness where there noticeably wasn't any.

"Yep," she responded before her eyes flicked back to mine. "Sure were."

AS WE LEFT the hospital an hour later, Brex slid her hand into mine as we passed the waving nurses at their station. My chest warmed, but my intuition was stuck in that room with Noel. "I really don't like that guy."

Every time I saw the man, I left feeling the imperative need for a shower. The girls and bartenders and college professors all fell at Eric's feet like they were in the presence of a titan. But not Rhyett. He'd taken one look at that rumpled, luxurious suit, and everything about his energy shifted into protector mode.

If Rhyett Rhodes had been sexy in a tank and trunks, he was fucking sinful in that muscle-hugging T. Broad shoulders pulled back as he studied the dynamic and made no moves to hide his distaste. The man already had my mind and hormones warring for dominance, and that protective, couldn't-care-less attitude he'd slid between Noel and Eric completely eradicated my resolve.

It wasn't until rubber met the blasted Skyway that I finally cleared my throat.

"Thank you, Rhyett."

"Anytime. Please don't hesitate to let me know if you need something."

"I mean...for Noel, too. For being so kind to her. For not letting Eric interrupt her." The greasy shitstick had been speaking for her since the moment I arrived. From the outside, he might have looked like the doting boyfriend. But from my eyes...he wasn't advocating *for her*, he was deciding things only she should be able to consent to—prescriptions, dosages, where her follow-up appointments would be held.

When I'd made to correct the pattern, he'd cut me off and asked the doctor to remove the distractions.

It was Rhyett's demanding presence and blunt, "She can speak for herself" that shut his mouth.

Leaving Noel felt counterintuitive, but as the doctors insisted on keeping her one night for observation, we didn't have much choice in the matter.

"She deserves better," he said bluntly. God, I *really* liked this man. More than one night and a first date could possibly warrant.

Irritation with her meddlesome boyfriend aside, my heart had run double time all day, my smart watch frequently reminding me to take a moment to breathe. The heart rate monitor had even gone off, prompting Rhyett to pull me onto his lap and run soothing circles across my hand with his thumb. I'd been so preoccupied with the reminder that he had shown up when I asked him to, that I hadn't taken a moment to breathe and realize the effect he had on my body.

He steadied me, just with his presence alone. And the reality was, he had come. When I had no one else to call, when Vallie burst into tears on the phone, and Josie frantically updated me that she still hadn't found a sitter, Rhyett had shown up. Fast enough that I knew he couldn't have been strictly road legal the whole way.

"Honestly, I think so too. Nobody else sees it that way. All they talk about is how amazing he is. How successful."

"Hmm," he grunted, a line appearing between his brows. "There are more important things." I wanted to ask what he was thinking but swallowed the words. We weren't at that stage of friendship, much less relationship...were we? My internal debate was unwarranted, however, when he spoke up on his own. "If she was a Rhodes, none of us would've let them leave on the first date."

That idea made me smile. The concept of Noel having six brothers watching her back. "Wish she'd had you here from the beginning, then. I was overruled."

"Do you trust your instincts, Brex?"

"For the most part."

"Good."

And then my golden boy went uncharacteristically silent. When we rolled into the auto parts store lot, he swiped the sticky note with the make and model of my car. He insisted we stop and then returned in equal silence, the battery in the back of his truck. We were in the heart of the city by the time he finally said, "What can I do for you tonight?"

Straight to the point. Specific. It should have felt ridiculous, but my heart warmed, my breathing steadying under his scrutiny as he followed the GPS to Noel's townhouse. This man had driven forty minutes to meet me in the hospital, stood up to her asshole boyfriend, insisted we pick up a battery for the car and escorted me to feed her cat and fill the water bowl.

"You've done enough."

"That wasn't the question."

I laughed, the sound raspy. Honesty. That's what everyone said it took to communicate in a relationship, right? What the hell did I want? Something inside me felt hollow, heavy with the what if's of the day. "Mind sticking around while I feed Chloe? I can walk if you have somewhere to be."

"Nowhere that can't wait for tomorrow." His expression softened as he pulled into the magically open parking space directly in front of her door.

"Do you always get princess parking, Hotshot?"

He chuckled. "*Princess* parking?"

"There is always—*always*—a Honda Civic here. I've never seen it leave. And magically, it's just gone? Why are you smiling?"

"The universe always gives us what we need. And I needed to take care of you and Noel as quickly as possible and get you home safe. It makes sense there was a nice spot."

"You're one of a kind, Mr. Rhodes."

He hopped out of the truck with a cheeky grin. "Don't you forget it."

BY THE TIME we made it back to my apartment, a bag full of clothes packed for Noel, I was emotionally and mentally exhausted. But as I opened my front door, he jerked his chin back towards the curb. "Which one's yours?"

"What?"

Fuck, that smile could melt steel. "Which Jeep is yours, Ace? I'll swap the battery out."

"Rhyett, I've got it." I'd made the mistake of blinking while I thought, opening my eyes to the hard blue wall of his chest. My eyes trailed up, following the subtle vein in his neck to his Adam's apple. I wanted to run my lips across it, trail my tongue up to that perfect coat of golden stubble. "I...can—"

He chuckled, breath warm on my face. "I know you *can* do it, but I would feel better if I knew you were taken care of before sundown —" was that insinuation in his tone? "—in case you get a second wind and head back down to Noel." He tapped my nose with a knuckle, grinning as he asked, "You okay there?"

"I—uh—yeah. I'm good. It's uh—" The more I babbled like an idiot, the broader his grin grew, and my heart stuttered forward in response. "—I drive the, uh, the black Jeep Wrangler hybrid."

"Keys?"

"Hmm?"

His chuckle demanded I peel my gaze from those full lips and bright teeth to focus on his eyes.

"I need the keys, Ace."

"Right, duh." I shook my head. *Oh. My. God. What is wrong with me?* Handing him the keys, I shook my head, turning for the townhouse. The man drove me to the precipice of stupidity with his kindness, and evidently, I'd just swan-dove right off the edge.

It only took two brain cells to rub together to know it was a day for a second pot of coffee. I'd chugged a few cups of the shitty hospital brew, wrinkling my nose all the while but grateful for something to do with my hands.

By the time I'd warmed up lasagna, and poured a mug and a cup of tea for Rhyett, he was knocking on the door frame before leaning into it. Shirtless. With an oil-streaked rag tossed haphazardly over his gorgeous shoulder. A thin coat of sweat glimmered over ink and tight muscles. My mouth filled with saliva as I traced the long line of his impeccable torso down to the defined v of his abs. A thin smattering of blonde hair trailed from the belt of his cargo shorts and for a heartbeat, I wondered what it would feel like against my fingers.

Rhyett cleared his throat, that self-satisfied smile rocking my world as much as that drool-worthy physique. "Can I come in?"

"Oh my word," I sputtered, nearly spilling my coffee before remembering it was in my hands. "Of course, please, come on in. I made you some tea—I didn't have anything but peppermint and some medicinal blends. But it's a combo I think is good." When had I ever been reduced to babbling in front of a beautiful man? Never. I had never been reduced to babbling. Except this man, his big, veiny hands dirty from working on my car, glistening from the Florida heat...

I cleared my throat, pulling out a chair, and unceremoniously plopped into it. "And I warmed up food. Just lunch, no biggie.

Consider it a tiny thank you for your troubles." *Oh my god, Brexley, stop talking.*

"If you give Italian as payment for simple tasks, go ahead and write me a list. You'll never get rid of me."

Careful what you wish for, Mr. Rhodes.

Just lunch turned into a second cup of tea and, eventually, a coffee sitting beside Brex on her couch. She was trying to convert me; I was pretty sure.

Noel was her equivalent to my Broderick. Her hell or high water, right-hand woman. And seeing her hurt—however temporary—was a personal affront for my little badass. When she'd finally exhausted her anxiety, shoulders relaxing as she leaned into the couch, I smiled, stroking my thumb over the place it rested on her thigh.

"I'm sorry, I've been talking forever. This probably isn't what you expected when you answered my call this morning."

"No expectations," I reassured. "Was just happy to hear from you. More so when I learned of the circumstances."

"More so?" she questioned, looking rightfully confused.

"That sounded different in my head. I just meant...that it meant a lot that you'd call me when you needed someone. That's all."

She bit that perfectly pink lower lip and before I could stop myself, I lifted a hand to free it. Her soft, plump skin and warm hitch of her breath against my fingers sent all my blood south, and I swore internally. Grazing along her cheekbone to cup the side of her face did nothing to alleviate the urgent ache wrapping around the base of my spine.

Eyes hooded with desire, she breathed my name like a plea, "Rhyett."

"Should I go?"

Something like panic flashed in her eyes, to my immense satisfaction. My palms were buzzing with the need to touch everything. To thread through that long blonde hair and wrap it around a fist. My cock gave a little jerk, the image intensifying the blood flow as I imagined those pouty pink lips wrapped around me. Self-control was a miraculous thing.

"Should I go?" I repeated, rubbing my thumb up and across her gentle cheekbone. My body screamed at the concept, aching to taste, touch, savor. She shook her head.

"Brexley, use your words, pretty girl."

"Stay," she whispered breathlessly. Her husky voice, heady with the desire sparking through my bloodstream, was enough to snap my restraints. It took all of two seconds to wrap my hands around her and pull her onto my lap. Brexley straddled me, sinking down over my crotch and gasping as she found me hard against her entrance. When her gaze found mine, it was hungry, urgent as she rocked over my cock, driving me crazy with that little shift of her hips. Her chin dropped, loose strands of long blonde hair falling into her face as her eyes slid closed, and I nearly lost it. Brexley was my own personal deity, and I wasn't sure what I'd done to earn this side of her, but it lit my chest on fire.

"Fuck, you're beautiful," I said, sliding my palms up, one halting to caress the side of her breast, the other wrapping around the back of her neck and pulling her to me. Her lips still tasted like basil and I smiled against them. Grinding my hips up against her, I ran my tongue between them, satisfaction pouring through me as she opened. There was nothing quite like that silent invitation. But it was her breathy little moan that fucking did me in. This woman could have whatever she wanted, but I needed a damn answer.

In an instant, I had her rotated onto the couch, taking in her trendy little getup. A black skirt that was cut way too short for her to be prancing around the city without me. Except in the moment...

I slipped my fingers up her inner thigh, relishing in the silky soft caress of her skin against my calloused palm. When I found her panties damp, I groaned, bowing my head to her shoulder as I began to rub against the sensitive nerves.

"Such a good girl," I whispered as she writhed against the touch, egging me on, pushing for more. Right as her thighs went taut, I slowed my movements and eased the pressure.

"Rhyett," she pleaded, and I smiled at the sound of my name on her lips. "*Rhyett*," she mewled again, arching into me as she begged for more.

"So close?" Her teeth caught that bottom lip as she nodded frantically, face pained, chest heaving. I smiled, leaning down to nip at her. "I need you to answer my question, Ace. I need you to tell me what this is, and then I'm going to make you come."

"Not. Fair."

"I never claimed I wouldn't play dirty. Tell me what you want, Brexley."

"You."

"Good start. But am I making you breakfast or leaving when this is done?"

"You—" She sucked down a breath as I applied a feather-light pressure through the damp fabric. Her thighs shook, and I smiled. "Not fair. I need you."

"Edging has its benefits. Do you trust me?"

Her baby blues went wide and I knew she remembered her question from the groves. She nodded.

"So, answer me, Brexley. I just want to know. What does this mean?"

"I don't know."

"What do you want it to mean?"

"Good company. You said we can just be..."

"Friends with benefits?"

Brex nodded as she writhed under my palm. "Is that...enough?"

"For now," I acquiesced. It wasn't. It wasn't nearly enough. However, if it were that or not having her at all, I'd take it. I could win her over; for some reason I didn't doubt that.

I lowered myself to my knees, sliding a hand behind her back to drop her zipper before peeling the leather lookalike from her skin. A tiny light blue scrap of fabric rested against her sex.

"So perfect," I said, slipping my fingers under the elastic and sliding them down her legs. Brexley was a damn vision, my hands aching as her head fell back against the couch, eyelids fluttering closed and soft lips parting. My fingers buzzed with the memory of pressing a thumb against them, the subtle give against my touch. A sliver of light showered over her skin—I'd laid her down in the direct line of golden, glorious Florida sun slicing past a gap in her curtains. I could never get enough of this. Of her. The woman was a siren, and I would willingly follow her to a watery grave if it meant getting a single taste. Lucky for me, it hadn't come to that.

"Let me see you, Brexley." She spread her legs wider as my hands scooped beneath her perfect ass, pulling her to the edge of the couch.

Fuck, I hadn't truly gotten to appreciate her before. She was perfect. I wasn't sure what I wanted first, her pretty lips or her glistening pussy.

Landing on the latter, I lowered to part her, dragging the flat of my tongue right up her slick center. She bucked, sucking down a breath as I licked again, this time focusing on her clit. Fucking Nirvana. "Your cunt is delicious, baby." My mouth against her seemed to unlock her, the soft whimper shooting straight to my balls.

"Oh fuck. Oh fuck, oh fuck, *oh fuck*." Her fingers threaded through my hair, the other hand wrapping in the knit blanket on the couch. "More, *more*, please."

My dark chuckle seemed to make her squirm harder, her mouth popping open as I happily complied.

I nipped and sucked, licked and kissed, but the moment I curled two fingers into her wet heat, she bowed off the couch, coming on my tongue. I drank her down as her body went tight, eyes rolling back, head lolling until I lost my view of that beautiful face. To have this little powerhouse come undone beneath my hands was a high no sane man would willingly come down from.

We might have been new in each other's lives, but Brexley was a brand of woman most men thought were myths. Her independence might have intimidated a lesser man, but I saw her resilience, her determination, her stubborn streak for the strengths they were.

Opening businesses wasn't for the faint of heart, and the fact that she and Noel had made it past the five-year mark with expansion on the horizon spoke volumes to the fierce female now submitting to the pleasure of my hands. All women were beautiful. But a badass boss had a different level of appeal. Equal parts brains and beauty, I smiled as she moaned her release, allowing me the privilege of gifting her that.

When Brexley's body went lax, I slowed my movements, sliding my fingers out only to leisurely drag my tongue up her center.

"That's my girl." Her haphazard nod made me chuckle, like she hadn't quite come back into her body yet. I needed more. Was desperate for it, balls aching, cock so thick I'd likely have a zipper imprint down the front. "Can I fuck you, beautiful girl?"

Her laugh was breathless. "Didn't you just?" She gasped for air, drawing a satisfied smile across my face.

"What did I say about using your words, Brexley?"

"Yes! Please, Rhyett, I need you."

"Good girl." I pulled out my wallet, opening the fresh condom from the inside pocket, and then thanked my lucky fucking stars that I'd thought to replace it after The Three Leaf.

"May I?" She breathed, reaching for it, chest still heaving as she came back into herself, her hooded eyes locked on my hand as I worked off my belt. Upon my nod of approval, she righted herself, licking her lips with a promise I didn't dare let myself make.

When Brexley freed my cock, immediately taking me into that pretty pink mouth, my restraint shattered. Warm and wet, she slicked over me like she already knew exactly what I needed. Adding her hand to the mix, she worked me until my crown hit the back of her throat. I made to stop her as tears lined her eyes, but she moaned and worked harder. *Fuck.*

"Jesus, Brexley," I breathed, restraint threatening to shake my legs as arousal gripped my spine. "You feel incredible." When she gagged, my balls tightened, and I would absolutely not allow that familiar ache to sever this heaven she'd pulled me into. "*Brex.*" It was a warning. She didn't heed it, drawing me deeper into her warmth. I needed to touch her. To discover every ridge and valley. She was getting me too fast. "Brex," I cautioned, fighting to keep my release in my balls. She took me clear to the back again, humming contentedly when her eyes started to water, a stray tear rolling down her cheek, and I groaned.

There wasn't anything in the world sexier than a woman who knew exactly what the fuck she wanted, except for the one who knew... and reached out to take it. I reached for her, drawing her upright and ignoring the desire demanding we finish what we started, even as the rubber rolled over the crown. I needed to see her.

In one smooth motion, I yanked her shirt up and over her head, groaning when her free breasts bounced. No bra. *Fuck me.* Brexley returned the favor, tossing mine to the ground beside the pile of discarded garments. She scraped her nails down my abs, smiling when I hissed.

"Wicked little thing," I smirked, coming down on her mouth as she lowered herself onto the couch, hands guiding me on top of her.

"Like you didn't see that coming."

When Brexley kissed me back, it was like igniting something deep in my soul. I was no stranger to lust, to primal hunger. Hell, women came to me to have a good time. Only, this was different. Deeper. I needed her. Not just for a release. I needed *her.*

"Brexley," I whispered, lining myself up. It wasn't the time for bold declarations, so I simply said, "You're perfect," and thrust home.

Pleasure didn't begin to describe the sensation that roared through my bloodstream. I'd meant the words. This woman, frantically searching for handholds against my skin, meeting my thrusts, was perfect for me. Fit me like a glove, her touch like fire in my veins, sparks bouncing every time we locked eyes. I moved faster, harder. A familiar tug built at the base of my spine as she moaned, muscles fluttering around me, body shaking beneath me. Everything she did made me want more of her. That should have terrified me. Should have fired off all those red flags that marked the gentlemanly path to the exit lane. Still, I'd never felt more at home, more wanted, more needed. Sweat dripped down my back by the time she detonated again, a cry of absolute ecstasy clawing up her throat. However, it was the sound of her voice crying out my name that took me over the edge on a roar.

TWENTY-FIVE
BREXLEY

Best. Sex. Ever. I'd told Noel the man had been the best I'd had, but that first night had been nothing—*nothing*—compared to the second. I still hadn't set him free on a damn bed. The couch had shown me enough.

Rhyett had carried me upstairs when my body had gone limp, wordlessly opening doors until he found my bedroom. I silently thanked myself for having the foresight to clean that morning. Not that I could take credit for it; it was a compulsion at this point. When he climbed into bed beside me, spooning our naked bodies together, something inside me liquified.

"So fucking beautiful," he whispered, his breath hot against my cheek. Goosebumps trailed away from the touchless caress, and I shivered as Rhyett nestled in against me. *Friends with benefits.* That's what I'd told him. But nothing about this embrace felt like friends, every inch of exposed skin squeezing together in a way that felt somehow more intimate than the sex...which had been...indescribable. Amazing. *Terrifying.* I'd been with partners, but never one who saw me, one who served me so intimately. Like my pleasure was a battle. His body was his weapon, deftly destroying everything else as he connected our souls. Other women talked about that spiritual rapture, but there'd never been a moment I'd come close. Not until Rhyett. Not until the man who undid me completely.

Still panting as his arms caged around me, I managed a feeble, "You're...incredible."

"Good, now get some rest, pretty girl."

I wasn't sure if I actually managed to nod or if it was just in my head, but the anxiety of the day seemed to hit a wall, my body letting down once he'd safely cocooned me in his arms, and I drifted into a contented, dreamless sleep.

THE SNICK of a door closing woke me up, fingers reaching for a body that wasn't there to find. Disappointment jolted me upright, only to collide with relief when I spotted Rhyett, shorts slung low on his hips, leaving that mouthwatering body mostly on display as he stood on my balcony with a phone to his ear. An alien combination of satisfaction and hope tangled in my chest.

I wanted him here. Hell, I couldn't remember the last time I'd wanted a man around after the orgasm faded. Groggily rubbing at my eyes before glancing at the bedside table, I spotted the time. I'd slept for well over an hour. He'd orgasmed me to sleep. In the middle of a workday.

Blinking and still a bit disoriented, I slid off the bed, wrapping the sheet around me and padding for the door. It was as the coffee pot filled, and I was yanking my shirt back over my head that a grinning Rhyett Rhodes descended the stairs.

"Afternoon, *Sleeping Beauty*."

"Hi."

Hi. Seriously? Had I forgotten how to speak around this man? Nerves entirely ruling, I tucked my hair behind my ear. I'd already smoothed down the chaos, but it still felt as disarrayed as the rest of my life today. Mainly to occupy my hands, I turned for the cabinets, pulling out two mugs and filling mine before lifting his in question.

"I could go for a cup, I suppose. You've got cream and sugar?"

"Ahh, yes," I said in mock disapproval. "My frilly coffee man." Rhyett's hard body pinned my hips to the counter before the last word left my tongue. His nose tickled my temple as he gently traced the side of my face, drawing a sigh from my lips, eyes slipping closed. His broad palm settled on my belly, pulling us tighter together as the other wrapped around me to run gentle fingers across my collarbone.

"Thank you for calling me today," he said softly, the words scraping over my skin as his erection pressed against me. "Not just for this—" he tightened his hold, "—but for thinking of me when you needed help."

Speechless, I just nodded against him, swallowing suddenly painfully audible. His presence, the weight of this connection, overwhelmed all my senses. I'd gotten rusty during my hiatus, and had somehow lost the ability to keep speaking and thinking through the sensations running rampant as they spun a hot spool in my belly, sending electricity up my limbs.

"Thank you for coming to help." Okay, good, I could form coherent words, even if they came out without gusto. But that was, at least, a complete sentence.

"Anytime, beautiful."

Drinks prepared adequately with cream and sugar, I turned to deliver his. "I need to go pick up Royal. Make sure the girls have the shop under control."

"They seem perfectly capable. You've trained them well."

"Eh, they came to me like that."

"They certainly don't seem to look at it that way."

Coffee still nearly hot enough to scald, I took a very tentative sip off the top. "What's that supposed to mean?"

God, his smile was beautiful. Everything about the man was gorgeous, magnetic, daring me to move forward. "Wren and Noel both adore you to high heaven."

"They're generous."

"They're honest."

"Well, thank you, then." We were all close, I knew that to my core, but I'd never had the opportunity of being a fly on the wall, either. "They've closed before, but they had advanced notice. I didn't just dump it on them."

"Would you like some company?"

How would I not? The man either didn't know or feigned innocence to his influence over me. "Don't you have things you have to take care of?"

Rhyett shrugged. "Of course, but it was a scary morning. I'm sure the house will be fine without me for a day. I wouldn't have offered it if I wasn't in the position to."

Somehow, I highly doubted that. Rhyett seemed like the kind of man who would do whatever he had to in pursuit of taking care of the people around him. Perhaps I was reading too much into what he'd done for me, though I didn't think so. "I've got it handled."

"I know, but that wasn't my question."

"Are you always this forward?"

That panty-melting smile broadened. "Are you always this evasive?"

"Answering my question with a question. I see how it is."

"I'm happy to help if I can. Would it be *helpful* for me to run Noel her bag?"

I shook my head, taking a long sip as I read the sincerity in his eyes. "No, thank you, Rhyett, but I've got it. If they're keeping her overnight, she'll be livid cooped up in that room. And I'd like to talk to her without Eric running interference. She didn't tell me much about what happened."

"Alright. Let's make sure your car starts up again, and then I'll get out of your hair."

Out of my hair. Like I wanted any part of this man away from any part of me. If Noel wasn't sitting in a stiff bed with broken bones, there was no way in hell I'd be going anywhere. I had enough faith in Wren and Holland to hold down the fort until we were back. It was only Royal that would still require my attention.

Rather than vocalizing any of that, I said, "Okay, yeah, thank you." *Idiot.* I was an idiot. What sane woman told a six-two, tattooed supermodel that she didn't need their assistance? Why yes, sir, actually could you kindly help me dust the cornices, and can you reach the shoe I threw onto the top shelf of my closet in a fit of temper? How about the air filters? You wanna check those, too? Help me vacuum my ceiling fans, preferably shirtless and covered in baby oil. Seriously, any other answer under God's blue sky would have been better.

Instead, I watched that smile vanish into his mug of coffee, laughing when he grimaced.

"Would you prefer a cup of tea?"

"At this rate, you'll convert me to the dark side." He palmed his blonde waves before checking his watch and sighing. "Well, I'm happy to reschedule if you think of anything, although I could catch this meeting at four-thirty in the meantime. This time of day—"

"You've got to get going," I supplied, already knowing the answer. "It's always rush hour up here."

"I'm only twenty minutes from the hospital. If either of you needs anything, please let me know."

"Thank you, Rhyett."

"One last thing," he said with a grin, snatching my keys off the counter and jingling them pointedly as he slid his coffee over with a pained looking expression. "I'll trade you."

"Really," I said, shaking my head, just determined to dig myself a grave deep enough that not even the coyotes could reach me. "You've done more than enough, I can do that."

"What kind of a gentleman would I be if I didn't ensure my handiwork?"

The man returned a few minutes later and happily slid my keys back to me before palming my hip and drawing me forward, everything in my body halting and redirecting to the place where his fingers slipped beneath the hem of my shirt. Sparks danced across my skin. His lips were tender this time, sweet with an unspoken farewell.

"See you soon, Ace."

I nodded, unable to suppress the smile from my face. When the door clicked behind Rhyett Rhodes, my heart twisted into a strange little knot as I pressed my back into the wood, hand still lingering on the cold metal handle.

Friends with benefits? Who was I kidding? I wanted to drag his perfect ass right back to Noel with me. Wanted to follow him home to his meetings so I could see what else that spectacular man could do.

Instead, I packed my belongings, as well as Noel's, and headed out the door to retrieve Royal. I'd just plugged my phone into my car when Rhyett's text buzzed through with an address. The next one a beat later.

Rhyett

In case you need anything south of the Skyway.

TWENTY-SIX
RHYETT

How's Brexley?

A little shaken up, but she's great.

You dog.

What the hell does that mean?

You know what you did.

What did Rhyett do?

Nothing J wouldn't have.

Rhyett, you know better than taking advantage of a
woman in a vulnerable situation.

Jesus El, who do you think you're talking to? I was a
perfect gentleman.

Just making sure you weren't an imposter. So…?

PAXTON

Hold up, the girl in the accident?

HADLEE

No, that's Brex's friend. Keep up Pax. Honestly.

AXEL

Can we focus here? Answer the question Rhy.

RHYETT

You're all ridiculous.

ALESSANDRA

Good lord, you guys. Some of us are working.

JAMESON

Rhy nailed that girl from the bar again.

LEIGHTON

Eew! TMI bro.

RHYETT

Fuck off J. Nobody is nailing anybody.

MAVERICK

Boring.

JAMESON

Bullshit, you called me like six hours ago.

FINN

Yeah, I call bull too, man.

MAVERICK

Six HOURS. No way. Let's be real guys… Rhy's a twenty-minute man.

RHYETT

Fuck off.

HADLEE

When you guys put your dicks away, I want to hear about Brexley.

With a huff, I tossed my phone onto the passenger seat. What was it about the sibling text thread that somehow reduced us all to teenagers? I mean, Mav was only eighteen, so the bastard got a pass. But the rest of the assholes needed to mind their damn business. We were grown men and women, for pity's sake. Business owners. Sought after public speakers. Hell, Paxton had his eyes on politics after his last football season wrapped up.

Add in a new candidate for *Team Rhodes,* and they all turned into feral adolescents.

I reached for the dial, turning up "Smokey Joe's La La" by Googie Rene. As the sun streamed in through the open windows, warming my skin, I honestly had no idea how Brexley could hate this bridge so much. Yeah, you had to slow down to a reasonable speed for the tolls, but the view was unparalleled. When the traffic slowed, I turned my face towards the sky. It might have been just shy of worship, yet after decades shrouded in mist and rain, it was damn near a spiritual experience getting to feel its warmth every day. Hell, even our house was concealed in pine and spruce, their stretching shadows keeping the windows shaded. Unless I was on the water or down at the beach, it was rare to bathe in Vitamin D like this. I almost begrudgingly accelerated when the jam finally broke.

City a blur, my heart grew heavy for Noel as I passed the exit for the hospital. Red was recognizably a standup human being, or Brex wouldn't have kept her around for the last two decades. Knowing she was only blocks away in some level of pain made my stomach tighten. I huffed, keeping my truck on the freeway despite the dispro-portionate attachment to the woman in that bed. I'd shelved my entire day of to-do's and now needed to make up for the detour. Not that I regretted a moment spent in the city with the girls. Not that it was physically possible to regret a decision that allowed me to soak up Brexley Snows.

Friends with benefits. With a five-six blonde with baby blue eyes and the body of a freaking Pilates instructor. This was every red-blooded man's wet dream. So, why did my chest tighten when the words intruded on my mind? That wasn't attraction talking. Attrac-tion took a back seat the moment she opened her body to me. Beyond that, a need for her had been planted in my chest. Women had always liked me—having a renowned captain for a father and a family big enough to single-handedly support all the small-town events had that effect on people. The genetics certainly didn't hurt. But they were always easy to love and let go.

Not Brexley. *Twice,* I'd had her wrapped around my cock, tight little body against my palms, and she had a vice-like grip on my thoughts. Chemistry I could wrangle. But this? I blew out a breath and turned up my music, hoping it would drown out the need to go back to her and allow me to focus on the real objective. Adjusting myself as my dick strained against the cargo shorts, I swore. I was lucky she was giving me anything—no point in taking that for granted and pining for more if she wasn't interested.

"Baby Let Me Take You" by The Detroit Emeralds came on next, and I groaned, setting my head on the rest as I swooped onto our exit, heading East towards the property. Okay. So that objective might be easier said than done.

THE BEAUTY of working with my hands in Florida was the complimentary detox. I was no stranger to sweat, but dear Lord, the heat and humidity certainly increased it. Embracing the challenge, courtesy of the elements and painful proximity to the equator, I heaved another shovel of earth into the wheelbarrow. Then I thanked my lucky stars the sun was setting. The only downside was the mosquitos. I'd been battling them since I'd arrived but had finally invested in some of those fancy candle torches that were supposed to help. They were burning in a little half-circle around my fifth wheel.

Mom had gotten so frustrated with the construction delays that she'd compromised her plans for the outdoor living areas, stating that she hadn't wanted them that much anyway.

Bullshit.

Juniper Rhodes loved few things more than Milo on the grill, her kids lounging around contentedly eating her signature potato salad and something good on the stereo. Eddy, our general contractor, had taken a glance at my sketches and grinned like a maniac. He couldn't add the project on without serious delays, but he got me all the lumber and stone at cost, and I was freaking pumped about it. Plus, I hadn't heard from Brexley except for a text last night letting me know Noel was being discharged and thanking me for my help again. To keep my brain off my evasive fling, I focused on my parents.

Nobody was perfect, but my parents had inspired me from the day I first drew breath. This might be their winter retreat for the next few years, but this would be their permanent oasis when they passed off the boat. And I'd be damned if it was anything less than idyllic. We'd grown up clipping pictures from magazines and pasting them on vision boards mom would pin up on the living room wall, only taking them down once they materialized. She could have single-handedly kept *Home And Garden* in business, which is why this particular challenge was my passion project. Ideally, I'd have the fire pit and seating in before they visited so we could all break it in together.

I pulled my glove off to peel the top off a blister when the sound of an engine jerked my head up. Back pocket now stuffed full of gloves, sweat still pouring down my chest, I spotted the iconic nose of a black Jeep Wrangler and grinned, shaking my head.

"Well, if you're not just full of surprises."

TWENTY-SEVEN
BREXLEY

In order to convince Noel to take the time she needed to heal, I'd had to slap on my best extrovert face with a broad smile and doe-eyes. She'd cackled yet relented, promising to video chat again later and reassuring me that she was fine and healing. Her amusement turned into a sly snicker as she stared daggers at me.

"So, how's Rhyett?"

"How should I know?" I retorted, about to devise some pathetic excuse when she cut me off.

"Just accustomed to befriending blowfish, then?" My face had just hijacked the muscles, scowl slipping into place, when she gave a breathy cackle, stretching out her good arm to jab a sore spot on my neck. "He attack you when you got home? You've got kiss tattoos on your neck and shoulder, dummy."

Heat rushed up through my cheeks as my eyes fell to my lap. For some reason, the idea that Rhyett had marked me while he fucked me senseless didn't make my skin crawl like it ought to. Some primitive part of me kind of...liked it.

THANKS TO HOLLAND AND WRENLY, the place was still running smoothly. We'd done well, hiring the two of them. Both thanks to Noel's impeccable instincts when it came to people. My systems had been easy enough for them to get the hang of, and this trial—as terrifying as it was—was the first affirmation that we'd done it right. Someday we could walk away from operations in exchange for a new adventure, and The Cracked Corset would keep sailing without us.

A strange kind of anticipation twisted in my stomach as the bell rang. My mouth about fell open as what could only be described as a trio of models stepped in the door. All impossibly tall, the women held themselves with an unnerving air of authority. The first had precisely curled brunette hair down to her waist, her bright eyes scanning the space before she ran her long, pale fingers down the line of books, smiling with familiarity in her eyes before she plucked one from a shelf. The two behind were undoubtedly sisters, both so blonde their pin-straight hair was nearly white: one all angles and one soft-looking with muscled curves. The latter tossed her long hair over her shoulder as she sashayed into the space.

I felt every woman's self-image take a twenty-point hit at the exact moment mine did. Where was Noel when I needed her? Noel was blind to the unfairly attractive—she had a saint's ability to love everyone and befriend them in an instant.

Wrenly blew out a breath as two men stepped in behind them, one scowling and the other entertained. They were equally beautiful. It was nauseating.

"This is the absolute definition of bi-panic," Wrenly muttered, nearly fumbling the French press she was putting away. I laughed, shaking my head and returning to running inventory on sugar packets and honey containers beneath the counter, hoping Holland would bail us out. I was still busying myself with numbers when a throat cleared. The tall brunette. Of course. Her posse had taken over two tables in the corner. This was not what I was built for. This was Noel's forte. But I swallowed my nerves and lifted my head to march for the counter.

"Find everything okay?"

"Ahh, not quite, but we got what we came for."

"Oh," I said, nearly choking on my own spit as I looked up at her. "Anything I can help you find?"

"I doubt it," she said softly, sliding her stack of books across the counter. Examining titles as I scanned them through the system, I smiled.

"Great taste," I complimented as the final code rang in.

"Thanks, my sisters pick well."

After she inserted her card and the receipt printed, I forced that trained smile on my face and met her impossibly green eyes. "Thank you so much for coming in! Hope you have a great day."

"Thanks for the great selection. You too!"

She was the kind of woman I wanted to hate, though I couldn't since her voice's warmth was somehow reassuring. We exchanged pleasant smiles before she turned back for her family, the dark-haired man with a permanent scowl holding the door for them all. Then the shop was quiet, a few patrons noting their exit before returning to their books and pastries.

By the end of the day, the countless faces had all blended together, a colorful haze of comings and goings, round after round of conversation smooshing into the next. It was official. Noel was an angel. I would take twelve hours in my dark little cubby over plastering a smile on my face and forcing conversation any day. At one point, I'd looked up to see a tall blonde guy hesitate by our door, and my heart leapt, only to settle into a pool of disappointment. I blew out a pained sigh.

"What?" Wren asked, concern etched between her brows as she set down two mugs.

"Nothing," I said back, sliding her the cinnamon before wiping the back of my hand over my brow. She placed her stencil and sprinkled the foam with spice. Wrenly smirked over at me before flashing a smile at the two blondes waiting on beverages.

"Riiiight," she said, drawing it out as the door clanged behind them. Holland rounded the corner and collapsed into the chair closest to the bar with a sigh.

"I miss Noel."

"Same," I muttered.

"Why did that feel like four days' worth of work?"

"Does she always field that many people?" Wrenly barked, blinking and rubbing at her temples.

"Sales weren't any higher than usual, so I guess so?" I sucked down air right as the phone rang. A glance at the clock on the wall told me we were officially wrapped up. Thank God.

To Holland, I said, "Quick, lock the door before more show up." She laughed but jumped to comply as I reached for the phone. "The Cracked Corset, this is Brexley. How can I help you?"

"Oh, thank God, you made it," Noel said on a sigh. Whether she was mocking the nerves or actually battling anxiety, I couldn't tell.

"Kind of. It's official, you're eligible for sainthood."

"Please heal fast!" Holland added as my dog came meandering around the corner, looking glum.

"All the girls agree, Royal included."

She giggled softly. "Well, it's nice to be missed. How'd it go today?"

"I hate people."

She chuckled, and then I heard her sharp intake of breath. "Not fair. You can't make me laugh, it hurts too much."

"Ooof, I'm sorry. You need anything? The girls and I stayed on top of side work today. I can bring dinner?"

"Uhh, I'm not sure..."

"It's honestly no trouble."

"I think Eric is on his way back."

"That's fine. I'll get stuff for him too." Asshole. "I really don't mind."

"He'll probably want the house to himself."

Scowling, I cleared my throat. "Oh, okay. That makes sense." No, it didn't. She needed her support group. "I'll come by tomorrow after the lunch rush."

"Okay," she said, perking up. "I'd like that. So...? Have you heard from Rhyett?"

I laughed, blood warming my cheeks. She'd gotten the full debrief when I'd taken her the duffel bag full of belongings. "He texted me this morning, but I haven't responded."

"And why the hell not?" I could practically hear her glowering at me as I pinned the phone between my shoulder and ear, wiping down the counter. A nervous laugh bubbled up my chest.

"I don't know, Noel. I lose control around him."

"And?"

"*And* I hate that. We don't need the distraction. We have enough going on right now, and if I'm ever going to write my own book, I can't afford anything else."

"Listen real clearly here, Brex. So help me, if you don't go after that man, I'm beating you senseless when I'm out of this bed."

"I don't think your doctor would approve of the violence."

"The cast doubles as a bludgeoning instrument."

I gave a breathy laugh, my hand hesitating against the damp rag as the girls both retreated to the back to fetch bags.

"I told him I just want to be friends with benefits."

"But you really want him." There was no trace of question in her tone.

"It would never work. Benefits is the best-case scenario."

"So go cash that in, you dummy. If you still feel like making googly eyes, you can talk to him later."

"He's an hour away."

"Stop making excuses and go do something that brings you joy. Preferably start with Rhyett. Then move on to telling him how you feel."

I looked up to the ceiling, like a greater power could bail me out, but laughed despite myself.

"Stop rolling your eyes at me."

"I am not rolling my eyes."

"She is too!" Holland tattled as she came out with her purse strap around her shoulder.

"Go get your man, or I'm coming in to work tomorrow."

"Oh please," I scoffed, tossing the dirty rag into the bleach bucket. "You are not. You need to heal."

"I do. Which means you'd be a real asshole if you make me peel myself off this bed and away from my *A Court Of Mist And Fury* re-read."

I smiled, intending to come back with something jaunty but failing to form the words. Noel filled in the gaps when the beat between us took a second longer than warranted.

"You do deserve to feel good. You are too good for him, not the other way around. And that man is fucking crazy about you. I've seen it myself. Go get him, Brex."

NOT EXPECTING the nerves to turn to ice in my belly, I made my way to the address he'd sent me, anxiety building rather than dispersing. When I crawled down the little dirt road, rounding the corner to reveal one hell of a house being erected and the cutest damn fifth wheel you've ever seen, complete with lights, tiki torches, and two patio chairs perched below the awning, my breath stalled out entirely.

Rhyett Rhodes stood, bare to his waist, skin glistening with a day's hard work. A white shirt lay over one of the patio chairs, and black work gloves peeked out of his back pocket. Every inch of glorious muscle was on display, rippling as he straightened to flash me that bright grin and hook his shovel over his shoulders, resting his hands to either side. My mouth popped open when I stepped out of my jeep. I wanted to trace the v of his abs with my tongue.

"My Sweet Lord" by George Harrison was playing over his speakers, that bright grin turning knowingly.

"Well," he drawled happily. I heard Royal's tags clink together as she jumped out of the Jeep behind me. But my eyes dropped to Rhyett's stack of obliques, tracking the sweat trailing down them. "If you're not just full of surprises."

"Brexley Snows, as I live and breathe." I greeted her with wide open arms, not that I could in good conscience hug her as filthy as I was, coated in sweat and grime.

The woman's grin was infectious, but I didn't miss the nerves in her eyes.

"You all good, Ace?"

She nodded, timidly walking in my direction as Royal bounded on by, bypassing her and barking to a sandy halt by my feet. She immediately demanded pets with a wet nose pressed into my palm. Brexley's amused eyes tracked the interaction as she shook her head.

"Traitor," she muttered as Royal's tongue lolled out contentedly. The desire to go to her was so demanding, that it took all my focus to hold my position by the pup's side.

"All good, Brex? Nothing new with Noel, I trust."

"All good, just, you know, in your neck of the woods. So, thought I'd swing by to say hello. I was worried you were just up here all alone."

A chorus of crickets kicked up somewhere in the distance, and I became painfully aware I was standing here stinking to high heaven. Hands aching. Muscles throbbing. But all I wanted to do was scoop her up and kiss her breathless. Brexley tucked her fingers in her pockets, hooking her thumbs around the outside. I hadn't actually realized how dark it had gotten until her headlights cut across the lawn.

Mirroring her position, I stuffed my hands in my pockets,

wincing internally at the sting of fresh blisters. "Well, I'm touched. My neck of the woods, huh?"

She took a leisurely step forward, twisting her hips and seeming contemplative. The flicker of the nearest torch cast dancing shadows across her face. Playing in her long blonde hair. Fuck, she was stunning.

"You burying evidence out here or something?"

"Nah, we'd just feed it to the pigs."

"Obviously."

"What do you take me for, an amateur?"

"My mistake," she said, her smile teasing the corner of her lips, raising her hands in mock defense. She wore form-fitting black shorts, miles of tan legs leading to stylish ankle boots, and a light blue button-up that cinched at the elbows and tied at the waist. It was nearly the color of her eyes and dipped low enough to show off her generous cleavage. My palms tingled, a need igniting with one look at those sinful little curves. Fuck, I could remember what those perfect handfuls felt like. My gaze dipped lower, mouth-watering as arousal gripped the base of my spine. The tangy memory of her cunt on my tongue had me growing hard in a heartbeat. I jerked my eyes up to her face, trying to focus.

If she'd driven an hour to see me, it was highly unlikely it was just for my dick. As much as I'd like to feel her slide onto it, lean down and suck a rosy nipple—

"But for real, whatcha working on?"

Jesus, Rhyett, get a hold of yourself. I cleared my throat. "Covered floating wood patio, hot tub surround, grill station combo."

Brexley's nervous laugh was a balm to my panic. "Hold up, say that again."

"I'm not a man of many words, so let me show you. Come in?" I jerked my head towards the trailer. "Humble beginnings, but they're all mine." Honestly, the rig was as nice as any apartment I'd lived in. However, people who didn't grow up in my family, or who didn't grow up traveling incessantly, tended to fall into old stereotypes. We'd been called every slur in the book, our favorite being trailer trash, of course. Little did Judgy McJudgersons know that Milo's net worth was likely triple what most men his age would make in a life-time. It was the experience they wanted for their kids. The feeling of the wind on our faces and pavement below rolling tires. The freedom of an open road as it rushed towards a pale blue sky, the sun beating on our skin through the windows and calling every city we parked in our home. We'd grown up with the blessings of a consistent place to return to, and learned history in real time as we clocked miles on our vehicles. Embraced minimalism so often on the boat that this little rig felt spacious, even to me now. It was a blessing to be expanding that vision, bringing my mother's dreams to long-fought-for fruition.

That knowledge didn't stop me from needing to check my ego as this bombshell's gaze flicked back to the camper. Resonating with our family was a bit make-or-break for anyone poking around. It was a pretty quick yay or nay in the dating department. Brexley's warm eyes landed back on my face, only friendly nerves and curiosity coloring her cheeks.

"I'd like that. I brought you a trailer-warming gift!" Her exclamation was accompanied by an eager twist as she pulled her messenger bag around the side. Pulled out a bottle of red. "I figure a bottle takes about three hours to finish, in the right company."

TWO NIGHTS WITH THE WOMAN, and I had been reduced to a pubescent boy hiding in the shower, debating on taking the edge off in case she was wanting. I assumed she was wanting. She'd set the terms of our little arrangement and then showed up unannounced an hour after sundown. That's what friends with benefits did when they had needs to fill, right? I couldn't have been sure because I'd never done the whole long-term friends with benefits thing. The few women I'd fooled around with whom I'd already been well acquainted had gone about their merry lives after a handful of orgasms.

Nobody had ever come back before.

Just Brexley.

Ducking beneath the shower stream again, I did a good ol' sniff test, making sure I no longer smelled like the hogs, then jumped out to towel off. Trying to slow my brain down, I slipped into gray sweatpants and turned to the mirror as I ran my fingers through my hair and took a steadying breath.

She looked exquisite. My mind's eye had photographed her perfectly, elegant fingers wrapped around the base of her glass, the stem settled between them. It was pink and glittery, yet the plastic margarita cup somehow didn't detract from the overall wow factor of Brexley Snows standing in my kitchen looking at my sketches.

She'd laughed when I pulled it out of the cabinet, her raised brows all I needed to supply, "Mom's fiftieth birthday was margarita themed."

"Whatever you need to tell yourself, Mr. Rhodes." That breathy, amused voice had been on a loop in my head since.

With a lungful of courage, I ventured out past the sliding door that clunked into place behind me. Everything was loud in RV life. Everything. The rollers on the door, the magnet that caught it at the end. The creak of the stairs. With her here, I was suddenly painfully aware of all the otherwise inconsequential noises.

Brexley had since abandoned her pink cup to the Formica island and was bracing her jaw on an open palm. Her eyes flicked up to me when the second step creaked, and she gulped.

"Rhyett. I don't know what to say. These are incredible."

I shrugged. "They're just rough sketches."

"These are *really* good," she repeated, emphasizing her point before returning to the sheet in front of her. Almost begrudgingly, she mumbled, "Like *professional* good."

"Well, thanks." Trying not to peacock at her praise, I ran my palm over my stubble. Watched her study as I stepped around the counter. I scooped up my wine, settling my hand on her low back and peering over her shoulder. My hum of approval earned her attention, and I smiled, leaning forward to tap the idyllic sketch. "That one is for back home." Brex craned her neck to look up at me, lips parting softly. Her attention made it infinitely harder to stay focused, but I continued, "We need a nice park downtown, a little gazebo for shade and events. It would make it look like a postcard down there."

"So thoughtful," she breathed against my lips, her gaze tracing mine before she cleared her throat with a shake of her head. Refocused on the task at hand, she turned over to a new page and I did my best not to wince. Despite my best efforts, I could be sentimental, although this story wasn't necessarily mine to tell. Brexley's breath came in a long, sympathetic drag, and she leaned into me as she looked at the little lion sketched into stone.

"That one, uh—that was for my nephew's memorial."

Horrorstruck baby blues glanced back up to me, her mouth popping open. "Oh, Rhyett, I'm sorry I shouldn't have kept looking. I didn't mean to snoop on something so—"

Her fingers had started shaking against the edge of the page and I reached out, smoothing my palm over her hand and hooking my fingers through hers.

"You're fine," I soothed. "It was a long time ago. Jeanne was twenty-two when she and Lincoln lost him during labor. It was horrible for all of us. But the worst part was the way it destroyed the two of them. They split up that year." Wrapping my other arm around her, I grazed his name with my finger where the Celtic knot met the edge of the braid. An old pang of grief tightened my chest. Jeanne had come to me to design his memorial stone, and there wasn't a chance in hell I was saying no. It had taken two tries to get the stone right, but I was still grateful we'd done it.

"Emmerson," she whispered, leaning her face against mine and giving my hand a little squeeze.

"He would've been a teenager by now."

Her swallow was audible as I turned the page to the next drawing. This one was a promise.

"A farmhouse?" Her tone lifted a touch as she narrowed her eyes. It was the American Dream brought to life—a two-story white farmhouse with blue shutters and a wraparound porch to watch the storms. I'd always known I'd land somewhere with thunderstorms worth soaking in.

"That one's my favorite," I admitted.

"You love apple pie too, don't you?"

"What kind of a question is that?" I teased, nipping at her neck. She smiled, tucking her chin into her shoulder as I growled, "Who doesn't?"

Rhyett Rhodes was a family man. I mean, I'd known it, but standing in his immaculate trailer, the walls custom-painted white, hand-crafted trim edging, and designer lights hanging above the island, I saw the evidence everywhere. He'd taken a classy fifth wheel and upgraded it until it felt like a home. The damn thing would make the cast of *Fixer Upper* proud, right down to shiplap accents. His love for his siblings and parents was scattered across the fridge in sloppily displayed photos of those blinding white smiles. From the hand-drawn design for Emmerson's headstone to his plans for an all-American farmhouse that an architect would weep over, Rhyett screamed husband material. Not hookup hottie.

"How in the hell hasn't a leggy little model scooped you up and put a ring on it?" Refusing to crane my neck any further, I twisted around until we were chest to chest. Rhyett leaned back to accommodate the adjustment, setting his wine on the counter so he could wrap an arm around my back, the other coming to cup my face. God, what was it about him that sent me spilling over all my edges?

Those steel blue eyes flicked between mine as he lowered precariously into the I'm-about-to-lose-control radius. Some backwards instinct froze my ability to inhale, like it was his *scent* that was dangerous, not the imminent proximity of a beautiful man with a knack for unraveling my resolve in a wink and a smile. Rhyett ran his tongue over his lips, and my heart sped, my mouth going dry as my clit gave a needy throb of protest. *Focus, Brex, you want to get to know him.*

"Why don't you tell me, Ace? I'm a package deal."

My eyes dropped for a beat as he skimmed my cheekbone with those warm lips. *Not the package he's talking about.* Forcing enough air into my lungs to speak was a mistake. Silence was safer. Because, dammit, his scent *was* dangerous. A subtle earthy spice and something distinctly male. Mouthwatering, all the same. My words came out in the same tenor as Marilyn Monroe's version of *Happy Birthday Mr. President.*

"Your—the—you mean your family?" *Idiot. Breathy, horny idiot.* I cleared my throat, willing the blood flow to direct to my brain cells if any were left. "You think you haven't gotten married because of your family?" *Oh, thank God, I can still form a sentence.*

Ass pressed into the faux-stone counter, his warm palm against my back, two hundred pounds of shirtless fisherman at my front, and the heat of his exhale across my face, I was well and truly stranded. He chuckled, as his fortified gaze traced my face, my lips, before he decided to grant me some small clemency and put distance between us. Rhyett snatched his wine off the counter, wrapping his long fingers around the neck of the bottle and dragging it along, retreating to the leather couch.

"We can be a lot. And my family means more to me than anything in the world. Trying to come into a complicated family dynamic can be intimidating, and none of us have been willing to compromise our relationships to prioritize new ones."

"None of you are married?" There. My tone was almost normal. More Brex, less bimbo. I followed him into the tiny living room, sitting crisscrossed on the cushion beside him.

"Jeanne, technically. But they separated so long ago, so we never see either of them anymore."

"That must be hard."

"It is." His admission hit me in the chest, cooling down the inferno in my belly for a moment. "It's what they needed at the time. They couldn't figure out grief together. Who knows. But as for me, I want the real thing, or nothing serious. Not sure there's a good in-between."

"The real thing?"

He sipped his wine, contemplating before saying, "Like...my parents. They have that one-in-a-million, soulmate kind of connection. Not like they don't argue—believe me, they did their share—however, they found the one person worth arguing with and fighting for, you know? I figure if I can't create that kind of intimacy, I'm better off just having fun and living life."

My parents' unwelcome faces marched into my mind. They were nothing but a hot mess, and their mess became mine as I grew up. The few memories engraved in my mind with them both were filled with screaming matches and broken cabinets, mugs chucked into the drywall, and, eventually, my father's stone face as he stared over our property, presumably wondering when enough was enough. In retrospect, the day she'd leveled him with a cast iron probably should have been it. Two less-compatible humans had likely never attempted to cohabitate in the same space. I hadn't realized I was scowling until he ran a warm thumb between my brows like he could smooth away the frustration. "That would be nice," I admitted.

"This Feeling" by The Alabama Shakes came on over the speakers as I raised the flamboyant pink cup to my lips.

"Eclectic playlist, I like it."

"Thanks. I love music—it's one of those soul-deep connectors between people." He set the bottle down on a mid-century modern side table, intention darkening his eyes as he watched me. "Magic, really," he said softly, extending a hand. When I set aside my glass and accepted, Rhyett stood, guiding me with him until our bodies were flush against one another.

His bare chest warmed my palms as he wrapped me up, leading me into a simple swaying rotation as he inhaled against my hair. Heat poured through my low belly, head spinning as Rhyett asked, "Why are you here, Brex?" His grip tightened on my waist, like he was reassuring me that he wanted me where I was. "Not that I'm not absolutely thrilled, but I don't suppose you were just craving a margarita-sized glass of red in a trailer."

Silence settled beyond the music, and I just leaned into his hard warmth as we rocked back and forth, cheek to cheek. Rhyett allowed it. Gave me the time to attempt to arrange my thoughts into coherent words. Articulating emotions wasn't necessarily my strong suit. An unfortunate hazard of a dumpster fire family, most likely with my father to blame. When Dad didn't know how to deal, he just checked out. Put his energy into work. Except *Rhyett*...a man like Rhyett deserved an honest to god attempt.

"I thought that maybe...this was worth feeling out. That you... that I should feel you out."

"I think you've felt me twice and came back for more."

I laughed, pinching his exquisite back. Which was nearly impossible, as the man was some sort of carving. What in the hell did they do out on the water? "That wasn't half bad either."

"Half bad," he scoffed as we rotated again, his hands sliding over my back, down to my ass. The moment that warm palm tightened, my heart jumped up in my chest, immediately making me want more. "So. Friends with benefits, getting to know each other?"

"Maybe?"

Warm palms gave my backside a firm squeeze, and I sighed, trying to fight my libido as it slammed through my body, pooling an insatiable heat between my thighs. When he shifted so that our lips skimmed across each other, everything in me threatened to melt. He was electric; the tension between us was an instant inferno.

"Are you expecting me to seek out other women's company while we get to know each other?" His stubble was rough against my cheek as he shifted towards my ear. "Or is this friendship of ours exclusive?" He nipped my lobe with his teeth before pressing warm kisses to my neck. Mixing arousal with logic was never an advisable cocktail, even as his scent encompassed me, overwhelming my need to touch and be touched.

My swallow practically ached as we rocked together. This was too fast. We were talking about real shit too fast. *The question* was too fast.

Nonetheless, then I thought about beautiful Vallie and Josie ogling him the moment he walked in, thought of how smitten the pretty waitress had been when he blatantly only had eyes for me, and my chest constricted until it was painful, nausea simmering in my gut.

His lips slanted as he ran soothing lines up my arms. "Not gonna lie, Brex, I see that fear. That challenge in your eyes, and I want to rise to it. Let go, baby. Let this be whatever it's meant to be, and I can show you what surrender feels like." He slipped his fingers under the hem of my shirt, rough palms agonizingly warm against my skin. "I promise you won't regret it. You just gotta tell me where that head of yours is at."

God, the man was too good with his words. It's like he saw right to the center of my flighty heart and didn't hesitate to aim and release his shot. Not about to tell him what to do, I whispered, "As long as we're doing this—whatever this is—it's only you."

"Good," he said, tone lethally soft. "Because I have no intention of sharing. You're already it for me, Brex. I might have lost my damn mind, but all it took was that first night."

Fucking A. If Rhyett's arms hadn't been around me, those words entwined with the claiming kiss he pressed to my mouth would've taken my knees out of commission. He stopped for a moment to speak against my lips. "If you give me a chance to earn more of you, I'll fight like hell for it. This is a start."

When he ceased our rotation, Rhyett moved for my legs, hoisting me up and around his waist as our desire collided. I locked my feet against his low back. Giving in, perhaps, but I couldn't stop myself. I must have skimmed over the part in my self-help book that warns against hot Alaskans and their ceaseless powers of seduction, because my ability to resist Rhyett Rhodes was seemingly nonexistent. More troublesome, perhaps, was the fact that I didn't want to.

Sweet but needy, his mouth softly coaxed some deep-buried part of my soul back to life as he teased and tasted me into a furious frenzy. His iron fingers tightened on my thighs when I traced his lower lip with my tongue, shifting to explore his mouth as he raised it to meet mine. My satisfied moan earned a rumble in his chest that was suspiciously like a growl, and we were moving.

With urgent reverence, Rhyett carried me up the steps and down the short hallway, turning sideways to squeeze us through the door-frame to the little bedroom. All but tossing me onto the big mattress, he was quick to follow, with his rough palms scraping down my sides to peel the shorts off. I bucked my hips up for him, relishing the feel of his hands on my thighs as they branded the flesh.

Stubble rough against my belly, Rhyett buried his face against it, pressing kisses along the line of black lace before deftly hooking his fingers below the fabric. On instinct, I raised a knee to stabilize myself, but he rocked against it, swollen cock twitching with the stimulus.

"What do you want?" I gasped, remembering the hard, slick feel of him in my throat. The satisfied expression on his face before he forced me to stop.

"Just you," he said on a harsh exhale. *Oh.* The man was good. My nails scraped along the hard planes of his back as he settled between my legs, rocking his hips as a hand scooped beneath my shirt.

"Good answer."

THIRTY

RHYETT

Brexley's bravado drew a hiss from between my teeth when she plunged her hand beneath my shorts, right where my leaking cock was straining against the zipper. She moaned as her thumb traced the slick crown, her eyes fluttering shut as she prayed my name.

"Rhyett."

"Fuck," I grunted, muscles straining as I fought for control over the suffocating desire to taste and claim. She rubbed taunting circles around my head, my legs giving a defiant shake. This woman could play me like a damn fiddle. And we were just getting started. "I need you, baby."

"Please," she begged. I nodded, stretching across her to where my condoms were stashed below the built-in table. Thank God for good foresight. I groaned as she kept working me, her movements elongating, becoming nearly agonizing as I fought the need to spill against her palm.

"Brex, baby, if you don't stop, there won't be much I can do for you."

She laughed, the sound wicked and panting. "You'll get creative," she teased, her hooded eyes flashing with sly satisfaction. *Jesus.* "Come on, Rhyett, show me what you've got."

I huffed a laugh, moving to pin her hands together and up, capturing her mouth in the process—*fuck*, what I would give to immortalize that sound. My other hand jerked my button open and zipper down, freeing my erection. Hell, it was impressive, even to me. The drive for her was nearly suffocating. Brex's soft lips popped open, her baby blues softening into bright little doe eyes.

"Stay here," I said, lacing the command with warning as I moved to slide on the condom. She did, dark lashes fluttering as I re-pinned her arms above her head. "That's my girl," I encouraged, dragging the tip of my cock over her wet pussy. A needy shudder rocked through her frame. "Fuck, baby, you're soaked." Repeating the motion with a groan, I spread her desire to her clit, swirling, teasing, loving the way she bucked for me.

There'd never been a woman I wanted to please as badly as Brexley Snows. Each husky moan. Each twitch of hungry muscles and throb of her needy cunt had me fighting some primal need to cover her in cum. More. She deserved more. There would be times to paint her in my need for her, but this wasn't one of them.

Breathlessly, she nodded, lifting her chin so that I could take her mouth. Each rock of my hips teased her entrance, heavy cock so thick it was starting to ache.

"Please," she breathed against me. I nodded, sliding home, setting a steady pace until her body fluttered around me. Slowly, I drug myself away from her entrance, fighting the pulsing in my balls. "Rhyett," she protested. With a smile, I lowered a hand between us to tease at her clit, relishing the way her body arched below my touch. The way those blues locked on mine, her teeth pinching that pert lower lip. As her thighs constricted on my sides, I smiled, halting the movement. She moaned, bucking against me, needing more and seeking friction. But she wasn't about to steal this from herself. I intended to serve her a release so shattering she never forgot it.

"Don't you come yet, Brexley. Not until I say so."

"What?" she balked, indignant rage simmering in the depth of her gaze.

"You heard me. Trust me."

"But—"

I cut off her protest with a bruising kiss, relishing in the give and take, in the way she opened for me. Releasing her wrists, I pulled her up with me, sucking a hard, rosy nipple between my lips. Deeper. She whined, arching into me, dropping her head back, and praying my name. "Baby girl, it's cute you think you're in control here." She was. She could have asked about anything of me, and I would have greedily complied. However, there was a challenge in Brexley that needed to be met. "Let me show you what it's like to be completely at my mercy."

Lining myself up, I paused, circling that button that would make her detonate. When she nodded, air filling her lungs in short little pants, I smiled. She'd play with me.

"Turn over," I demanded as I dropped my cock and guided her onto her hands and knees. "Perfect. You're so perfect." My fingers trailed down her spine, the opposite hand gripping her hip, sliding down that perky, round ass until I sheathed two fingers in her wet heat.

"Rhyett," Brexley mewled again. The woman owned me. Each movement. Each heady breath. Each moan. She wrapped her claim tighter around my soul with every rock of her hips, every plea for more. There was pleasure, and there was...this. This *yielding*. This shattering beneath my hands as I took her pleasure.

Running my finger through her soaked entrance and up, I hedged around that perfect, tight, forbidden place, smiling as she whimpered and arched into me. "Has anyone ever taken you here?"

"No," she cried out, her legs shaking beneath her. My smile broadened. Thank fuck. We'd collided too late in life to claim many firsts, but that was undoubtedly one of them. I ran a finger around that virgin hole, cock twitching. The idea of earning that right was enough to push me over the brink of madness. Some carnal, primal need—to take her, claim her, show her what she was missing—filled my veins.

"So much to show you, beautiful."

"Rhyett!" It was a plea, that needy edge sharpening. That was an experience for a different time, when she trusted me completely. When I knew her body better than my own. Moving my hand away, I gave her a soft smack on the ass, her gasp coming out hard as I traded my fingers for my swollen cock.

She was so. Damn. Tight. And the sound she made as I fed my cock deeper into her center inch by inch. Fuck, what I would give to hear that moan every day. To watch her respond beneath me. To feel our bodies and souls connect in this feral, desperate bliss.

My pace was punishing as need transcended sense. Hands grazing over her back, her smooth, soft belly, I whispered, "Come, Brexley. Be my good girl, and come on my cock." She gave that ball-tightening little whimper again. The one that made my heart lurch, dick along with it. "Come on, Brexley," I breathed, snaking my hand between her legs to stimulate her clit as I demanded, "Now."

She did. Rapture. Complete and total ecstasy as her body

clamped around me, and I fought to keep my pace, fought to see it through and gritted my teeth as my own release tore from me.

Brexley collapsed onto the mattress, burying her face in my pillows with a contented little sigh. I came down, wrapping my arms around her and pulling our sweat-slicked bodies together. Caging her against my chest and thanking the entire freaking universe when she nuzzled me back.

Brexley Snows was mine. She just didn't know it yet.

"GOOD MORNING, HOTSHOT." Her voice was husky with the newness of dawn, fingers tiptoeing across my bicep, down my shoulder. I hummed into her warm, soft touch. Snatching her hand in mine, I brought her fingers to my mouth, pressing kisses across her knuckles.

"Morning, beautiful."

A breathy little laugh left a feather-light caress across my cheek. "Your voice is sexy in the morning, handsome."

"You stayed," I said, grinning as I opened my eyes. The best part of my little RV bedroom was how the light poured in from both sides. The picture windows were illuminating her mussed hair in vivid backlight.

"I did. You're a cuddler."

I chuckled, soaking her in. "Guilty." Her makeup had rubbed off, all but a smudge of mascara vaguely reminiscent of the early 2000s music scene. Her usually pin-straight blonde hair was tangled and swept to one side. She was perfect. Tracing the dimple on her chin, the flat of her lip, an aching kind of warmth filled my chest. There was attraction, and there was...this. This compulsive desire to take care of her. To lift her problems away, to protect and serve and show her everything the world could offer her. I ran my palm down her hair, smoothing out a bit of the chaos before cupping her cheek. Her entire, beautiful face fit against my hand. Leaned up for a kiss. She met me halfway, dragging my lip between her teeth.

"Mmm," I hummed contentedly. Moved my hands for her still bare torso, groaning when I cupped a breast to find her nipple peaked. With cold or want, I wasn't sure yet. Perhaps both?

"As fucking fantastic as you feel, I have to go to work, Hotshot."

"No," I protested. "Hang out. I promise I'll keep you occupied." Wrapping her up in my arms, I pulled her down against me. Warm, delicate hands settled beneath my shoulder and over my chest. Brexley smelled like coffee and sugar, like... "You smell like a marshmallow."

"You *like*?"

"I want to cover you in chocolate and taste every inch."

"Dangerous," she said before pressing a kiss to my chest. "I want to stay here forever. Right here, in this moment."

"Do it," I suggested, memorizing each swell of her body beneath my calloused fingers. "I'll second the motion."

"If Noel wasn't out of commission."

I closed my eyes, inhaling that sugary scent and kicking myself for not bringing her up first. "I know," I said. "Does she need anything?"

"I don't think your particular expertise will be of any use, Mr. Rhodes."

"Hey now," I protested. "How do you know I'm not a shaman?"

"I think it would've come up last night."

"You know what they say about people who assume."

"We're all privy to the healing powers of a handful of orgasms, but we decided this is *exclusive*, remember?"

My cheeks were aching before I realized I'd smiled in response. Thank fuck for that. The exclusive part and the glowing, undeniable feminine satisfaction. "A handful, huh?"

"Don't get cocky, Mr. Rhodes."

"Punny."

"Oh no, you're *one of those*." Her eyes fell to the floor as she shook her head, a breathy little laugh escaping and wrapping right the hell around my chest. Everything about this woman felt like a tether to life.

"Guilty. So. What's on the agenda?"

"Wrenly and Holland are opening, but I'll close it down with them. We're celebrating St. Patrick's Day with a lucky *blind date with a book*."

"Sounds kinda genius. I'd love to see the shop all greened out. I'll be in your neck of the woods tonight. Alright if I stop by?"

"I think I'll require it."

"Good." I squeezed her tighter before resuming my steady trail over her bare arm. "In the meantime, can I make you breakfast?"

My wicked little thing nipped at the tender skin between my chest and shoulder. "I thought I'd just eat *you*."

THIRTY-ONE
BREXLEY

The blind date table sold out before closing, which, all in all, was a freaking miracle in the ROI department, and if Noel had been here, we'd be singing obnoxiously off-key. A better portion of the evening had been spent convincing myself that I did not, in fact, need to call her to do just that. But it wasn't just a record sales day that had me aching to hear her voice. Noel and I had shared everything since we were kids, and the giddy bliss that had Wrenly, Holland, and all our baristas side eyeing me was bound to burst out of me the moment I heard her voice.

Rhyett Rhodes had turned me into a bumbling idiot after orgasming me stupid. While he'd assembled his out-of-use French press to brew me coffee, I'd wandered around his temporary four hundred square feet, which felt homier than my apartment did after years. His story was everywhere in snapshots and Polaroids, cards from his mother—who looked way too enthusiastic for her age, the only sign of her years gathered in an elegant bouquet of happy lines beside her eyes—and pieces she'd sent him from home.

"They look...happy?" I'd asked as he poured the boiling water over the grounds, my fingers longingly tracing the frame on the wall as an old ache reared its ugly head. I'd flown solo for enough years to recognize the sour taste of jealousy on my tongue, the hollowness it planted deep in my belly where hunger would be. He'd chuckled, but everything about the relaxed state of his expression and hold of his shoulders told me I was peering into a glass house.

"They're a hot mess. But yeah. It's their mess, you know?"

Telling that twisted sensation in my gut to take a hike, I studied the image. A couple who could only be Juniper and Milo—Rhyett's parents—were dressed to the nines, and he was spinning her around a dance floor, her long salt and pepper hair fanned out around the same megawatt smile I saw on her son. Milo watched her like she'd hung the stars, a quiet kind of satisfaction on his lips.

"He looks tall," I noted. "Is he taller than you?"

"Six-four. Jameson hit it, but the rest of us leveled off an inch or two early." Rhyett pulled two mugs from the cabinet, turning for creamer before he poured his own cup of water for tea. Turkey bacon —because the real stuff was shit for you, according to the shirtless hunk in front of me—and a potato, veggie, and egg scramble sizzled on cast iron skillets behind him. A man that could cook, fish, and build successful ventures repeatedly? What in the hell was a woman supposed to do?

"Did you always want to own businesses?"

"Pretty much. I mean, when we were kids, all of us boys thought we would conquer the sea like Milo and Grandpa, but..." he shook his head. "I prefer smiling faces to freezing my ass off and taking big risks. Dad got lucky with Mom, you know? When I find my person, I want to be with her full-time, not part-time." He shut the tea drawer, moving smoothly for a spoon and golden nectar. "How about you? You always think you'd own a bookstore?"

I weighed the words briefly before admitting, "No, actually. I wanted to be an author."

Rhyett's abrupt halt of movement indicated a shock equivalent to telling him the sky was green. Brow furrowed, he slowly squeezed a string of honey into his cup, nodding his head.

"So, why aren't you?" He finally asked.

"Eh," I said on a shrug. "Who's got the time?"

"Well, all of the names on your shelves, for starters."

"I just...I'm a numbers girl. I don't think I've got the guts to put myself out there like that. You spend months—maybe years—pouring your heart and soul, sleepless nights, and plenty of tears into your art, only for some ninny with a megaphone to bash it online from their parents' basement, where their personal dreams went to die. I know enough authors to see how much it hurts to filet yourself open like that. I'm not sure I have the strength for that."

"Yeah, but it's like you said. They're standing on bloated opin- ions without ever having put themselves out there for critique. What about the readers who would *love* your work? Who would see themselves in your characters? Is the opinion of a handful of naysayers really worth...letting your own dreams die in a basement?"

"I don't have a basement," I quipped beneath lowered lashes, shifting on my feet flirtatiously as my stomach did somersaults in an attempt to avoid absorbing his words.

"Literary cafes work just as well. What did you want to write about?"

As I watched him strain the French press and pass me my cup, I realized I couldn't remember the last time someone had asked me that. I mean, Noel, but she already knew every plot line I'd thought of over the last several decades. We sometimes used the names of the fictitious friends as examples, although there wasn't a single beat of their lives printed in ink.

"I guess I needed validation when I was younger, you know? The books I loved all had some triumphant, romanticized found family. Or a group of people brought together by circumstances—room-mates, that kind of thing—like *Friends* or *New Girl*. I always thought I'd tell a story about unlikely people brought together when they needed each other." I shrugged. "But then I grew up."

"What did growing up do?"

"Reinforced that those stories aren't real. Neither are the princes who came in to save the heroines."

"What about a heroine who saves herself?"

I narrowed my eyes at my machismo-loving lover but only found sincerity in those steel blue eyes. "Been done before."

"Not by you," he pointed out, stirring his mug absentmindedly.

"No," I agreed. "Not by me."

"So...what would it look like if you wanted to start writing again?"

I licked my lips to suppress the smile that threatened them. "How do you know I wrote before?"

A solitary brow arch spelled nothing but trouble. *Knowing* trouble. My façade collapsed like a house of cards, a grin fighting the straight line of my lips as I admitted, "Okay, yes, I wrote before."

"When did you stop?"

When did I stop? I gingerly sipped my coffee and ignored the surprise that flitted across his expression, long ago having developed scald calluses on my mouth.

I...hadn't thought about that. *When* the dream died didn't seem nearly as pivotal as the fact that it was six feet under. Or roasted into ashes that had long-since blown away to dance with the leaves of an eternal-summer breeze. Another tastebud-searing sip did absolutely nothing to pull it to the surface, but Rhyett didn't interrupt. He slurped loudly on his tea and turned to stir the scramble as my chest constricted, my throat along with it like I'd been stung by a bee and needed a Benadryl.

When did I...stop writing? My temples began to throb, my heart picking up as my clumsy mental fingers thumbed through files buried in enough dust to knit a fucking blanket. Maybe *when* wasn't as important as *what. What had I last written?*

"Noel and I had a story about a girl struck by lightning and her journey developing powers afterwards."

"Like *The Flash?*"

"Probably partially inspired by it. Noel is a superhero dork. But our girl had been a brainiac before, and the storm enhanced her intelligence, making her hyper-observant. And then, in the climax, she developed electrokinesis."

Rhyett was smiling softly as he rotated to dish our plates. "How old were you?"

"I'm not entirely sure, maybe...fourteen?"

"Did Noel keep writing?"

"A bit," I admitted sheepishly. "She won a few competitions and published some short stories in magazines. Her manuscripts might be collecting a whole ecosystem of dust bunnies, but at least she wrote them. I just...stopped."

He nodded as if he'd expected the answer. "When did your dad stop coming home?"

I blinked. Once. Twice. My lips parted as I realized what he'd so deftly figured out. Eyes stabbing through the RV counter into my past—the grandeur of our last empty family house, the unanswered calls, the notes for holidays, and the rotating door of agency-loyal nannies—as what he'd just insinuated struck home like a punch to the gut.

"Your dad didn't break you, Brexley. He did the best he could with what he knew. But you've made one hell of a name for yourself in a big ass pond. Sometimes it's easy to feel like life happens to us. Only, what if it happens *for* us?"

"You're saying I was abandoned on purpose?"

"Nah. I'm saying, what if only you can write your lightning girl saving herself, because you've already done it?"

Royal chose that precise moment to unceremoniously belch as she stretched out by the front door, her need for her morning adventure more pressing than the fact that this man who'd known me for less than a month had seen more of my soul than people who'd watched me survive all the ups and downs in real-time.

Hours later, as we walked through all the closing work in the shop, my mind spun with that old story. It sounded too Young Adult to bring it into my own demographic. Having dedicated my life to curating shelves full of smut so women had a safe space to explore their own sexuality and live a thousand adventures from the security of their slippers, it felt a little counterintuitive to go back to my old stomping grounds. Yet, stuffed in that closet we called an office, I sat down with pen and paper and outlined the damn thing. Brought it up to speed. Played with the idea of aging up the characters so adults could have an adventure too.

And it sounded damn good.

THIRTY-TWO
RHYETT

I wasn't surprised to see the light on at the bookstore when I arrived with the last of the paint prep supplies. What I was surprised to find was Brexley on the floor of her office, Royal so lazily sprawled out that she just lolled her head in my direction. Evidently, I'd lost my novelty pretty damn fast.

"Hey," I said softly, but it was a fight not to laugh as her hand flew to her chest.

"Jesus," she blew out on a tense breath, shaking her head.

"No, ma'am. Rhyett Rhodes." I chuckled as she rolled her eyes, returning to where she'd dropped her pen. Leaning on the doorframe, bracing my arm as I tried to peek over her shoulder, I asked, "Whatcha doing?"

"It could work," she breathed, eyes round and a little bloodshot, her blonde locks a little too close to sex hair for my comfort, as though she'd run her hands through it compulsively while she worked. "You were right."

"Always."

Her pointed glare only brought on warmth to my chest.

"I outlined it."

"What?"

The intensity on her face drew me into the tiny cubby. Knelt beside her. Royal immediately demanded her good girl tax, tail wagging when I complied. Brexley seemed not to notice, her entire demeanor pointing to being wildly out of this world. If I didn't know better, I'd have thought she was high.

"The book, I outlined the whole thing. Made a cast list with character traits. They're all still in there." She didn't look up as she tapped the pen against her temple.

"Damn," I breathed, rocking back to settle on my ass beside her. She held up a handful of loose-leaf pages, some corners already dog-eared, others tabbed. I spotted patches of highlights and an outline worksheet. Where the hell had she gotten all of that so quickly? When I reached for the worksheets, she smacked my knuckles with her pen, eyes hardening to daggers before looking back at the page she'd been filling in when I arrived.

A little more than amused, I peeked around her again. Drunk Brexley had been adorable. Boss Brexley was a little bit intimidating. Bedroom Brex was downright sexier than sin. Men had happily *died* for less. The image of her eyes watering as she sucked me deeper into her throat was permanently embossed in my brain.

But focused Brexley? She was instantly my favorite. Humidified flyaway frizz gave her an air of wildness, vs. her usual polished, purposely presented persona. Focus carved two lines between her brows, her pout revealing that flat spot on her bottom lip. The stain had long since rubbed off on her mug; it was just that natural pale pink. I ached to run my thumb along the length but wasn't brave or stupid enough to attempt it.

The scratch of her pen over paper filled the small space. Royal settled her head on my lap, then rolled over for scratches. I took the unguarded moment to study my girl. Her space. Brexley's desk was precisely organized, filing cabinets on either end acting as the base for the topper. The mug containing a cacophony of colored pens read, *'just one more chapter'*. Only two photographs adorned the surface—both of her and Noel, one with Royal happily between them. Family. That was her family.

Found family, she'd called it. No wonder she loved that theme in her stories.

A stack of books was neatly organized in the corner, each with a sticky note adhered to the spine with 'yes', 'no', or 'Noel' scrawled in tight handwriting. I had a feeling everything Brexley did was firm and precise. The shop's affinity for floral arrangements and potted plants had spilled into her space, and I wondered if that was her touch or Noel's. Deep purple blooms—the same tropical kind we had on the property—sat in a little fishbowl in the corner.

For what was essentially a closet conversion, she'd made it functional, neat, and tidy. As much as I'd prefer to watch her work or snoop around her space, when ten minutes passed and then twenty, I sucked down air, leaned over to kiss her cheek, and extricated myself from a now sleeping pup. Who the hell was I to interrupt her while she was in the zone?

"I'll be back in a few minutes, alright?"

"Um, yeah, I–I think I'm almost done." She winced, forcing her eyes up to me. "It's all kind of just pouring out, you know? I want to see you, though." Even as the words left her lips, her eyes went a bit glossy. She drummed her pen against her knee, glancing back down to the scattered sheets of paper. Elora would call this a divine download, and she'd kick my ass for interrupting in the first place. That thought, combined with the comically adorable scrunch of her nose, made me chuckle.

"I won't be far," I promised. "Just outside, unloading the truck."

"I'm sorry, Rhyett, I just..."

"Hey," I lowered my gaze to meet hers as it flicked from the sheets to me, a flush creeping up her skin. "I'm not going anywhere. Take your time."

"Are you sure?"

I smiled, nodding. "You're on a roll, Ace. Keep it rolling."

"Okay," she said on a harsh exhale, shoulders relaxing as she dropped her focus back to her work.

On my way out, I noticed the red light of the coffee pot still glowed brightly in the dusk light and thick shadows. I chuckled, wandering behind the counter to find a mug, and poured the remaining serving into it. Took it back to her.

"Did you know the coffee pot was still on?"

"Uh-huh, drank it."

"Dra—you *drank* it? Like the whole thing?"

"Yup."

"Trying to test the full capacity of your heart, or is this an experiment in cortisol tolerance?"

"Gotta stay fo-cused." She disjointed the syllables as her eyes narrowed and her fingers resumed a frantic scrawl across the paper. Chuckling, I shook my head, admiring the determination in the set of her jaw. Fuck, she was cute.

"Alright, baby. You focus. I'm going to get my work done across the street. When you come out of lightning girl's head, come get me. I'll take you two home."

"Hmmm."

Not entirely convinced she'd actually registered what I said, I set the coffee down beside her and kissed the top of her head before moving for the door. Did she have any idea how deeply her claws had sunk into me? Not even my high school sweetheart had acquired the death grip this woman had on my heart. And we'd been on again, off again, for years until I thought better of the dating game. For the last decade and a half, I'd kept thinking better of it. At least until I'd watched this little blonde sink darts in a board like she'd been born with them in between her delicate fingers.

I didn't particularly care for leaving her there alone with an unlocked front door, but I supposed if I left mine open, I'd hear any commotion, thanks to Royal. Did she always linger with the front door unlocked? I'd have to remedy that.

The speakeasy was moving along at that tantalizingly glacial pace all renovations did. Things continuously had to look worse every day before they started to improve. Demolition had been a satisfying—though messy—process, but it was mostly complete, thank all that was holy. In place of total chaos was a beautiful blank slate. Drywall had been hung, patched, mudded and textured on the new frames. Plumbing and electric had wrapped up on schedule for the first time in history.

Clem had been over the moon excited to see the restored floors in what was beginning to look like a lounge. "You got vision, kid," she said on the tail end of a whistle, raising a hand to cover her mouth as she surveyed all the progress. "Is that a record player?"

"You know it," I'd quipped back. "Only way to get it right for the atmosphere."

"Don't you go pulling more people into my damn state, young man."

I chuckled, shaking my head. "I solemnly swear to target locals."

"Good," she said, rotating to take in all the details. It was a strangely satisfying stamp of approval to tuck in my back pocket for less productive days. She'd swung by with a little crate of strawberries the next day but didn't bother to hide her snooping eyes as she popped in to deliver them. Her garden, it seemed, was benefiting from her offloading this fiasco to me. Which I thought was wise until I rolled back in this late, exhaustion in my bones.

Glancing back across the street, I decided that my paranoia was irrational and that Brexley was perfectly safe forty yards from my open glass door. So I put on a hat, connected to my speaker, and queued up my work playlist. Nostalgia ate at my heels when Paul McCartney's "Calico Skies" came on first. Humming along to the familiar tune, I pried open the paint bucket. Mixed it until my hand threatened to rebel and filled the fresh tray.

The first patch of drywall confirmed what I already knew—the deep charcoal against the exposed brick walls would look fucking incredible. Clem's original spill had encouraged the idea, the color pallets reversing between the cigar room and the main bar. She would be freaking tickled if I could send her a progress report with the brand-new painted walls before I left tonight.

Confidence and determination lit a fire beneath me as I put my head down and got to work. Only the ache of my forearm and the tremble in my hand told me how long I'd been rolling and pouring layer after layer into that tray when Brexley's presence snagged my attention from the project. I turned to find her face disgruntled, mouth parted in something like disdain.

"Figures," she said, shaking her head. "Knew it was some out-of-state investor."

I grimaced, raising a hand to flip my ball cap backwards. "Noel didn't tell you I was the asshole across the street?"

The tight mess of her lips told me I'd hit the nail on the head. Of course, Noel and I had parted ways only about twelve hours before her accident. I should have assumed, but like an idiot, I didn't.

"I'm trying really hard not to be mad."

"Well, that's good. What would that help?"

"Nothing. But I can't change what I feel."

"Which is?"

"There's always a catch."

That sounded menacing. I set the paint roller down on the tray, wiping my hands on the work denim her eyes were scanning over. I took a few steps forward, relieved when she didn't retreat.

Looking for clarification so I didn't assume she was being entirely illogical, I asked, "Catch?"

"Best sex of your life, but it costs you your dream space. Yeah. That's about right."

Well, that felt like shit. "Come on, don't look at it like that."

"How am I supposed to look at it, Rhyett? Do you know how long I looked at this building? Do you know how many emails I sent?"

"Can't it mean something good that her assistant answered my call? Like we were meant to be in each other's lives? I didn't know you had your heart set on it when I took it. I swear."

"I just–"

When she cut herself off, gaze dropping to her feet, I hooked a finger under her chin, pulling her back up to me. "Just, what, Brexley?"

"Why is there always a catch?" She shook her head. "Nevermind, it sounds stupid, even in my head."

"Your emotions aren't stupid, Ace. Tell me what you're thinking."

She blew a harsh breath through her nose, chewing over her words for a beat before admitting, "Why does everything good in life come with a price? You're...*look*, Rhyett, I don't want to say something I'm going to regret. I know this isn't your fault. I just. Fuck. I had this whole vision of how we'd expand The Cracked Corset. Of where everything would go. Of the events we could host–bigger authors–and bigger signings would mean better press." Her jaw tightened, and she shook her head. "Better press would mean more exposure. More online orders. More growth." She huffed, blinking at me when I wouldn't let her go. "And this place is perfect, and the only spot within walking distance to expand. But, it didn't seem to matter how many messages I sent. She never answered. I guess... Everything worth having comes with a sacrifice."

"Is that how you look at this? At *us*?" I kept my tone level, hoping she could see how badly I wanted to understand.

"Please don't get me wrong, if it came down to choosing between you and the building, it would be you. But it pisses me off that the universe can't just let something go my way without taking something else off the table." She changed her voice, mimicking a television announcer. "*Dream man, or dream business, the clock is ticking, Brexley Snows.*"

I chuckled, tucking a loose strand of hair behind her ear. "You let the gameshow host pick?"

"Clock ran out of time. Had to select a random door."

"For what it's worth, I'm sorry."

She sucked down a breath, eyes softening, the clench of her jaw easing. "I guess...when it comes down to it, *I'm not.*"

"Well. That means a lot. I do intend to make it worth your while."

"For the rest of your life, Rhodes."

I chuckled, pressing a kiss to her forehead. "Thank you for sharing. I know you haven't always felt comfortable doing that. Was that difficult to get out?"

"A little," she admitted, swallowing hard.

"Just because you can see the logic, doesn't mean you should undermine the emotion, baby. It's okay to feel let down, even when you don't want to be."

The stern set of her jaw softened as she tongued a molar, nodding forlornly.

"Hey," I said, closing the distance and wrapping my arms around her back. "I'm sorry you were disappointed. Let's look at the bright side. Once my parents move down, I'll be right across the street."

A hint of a smile tugged at the corner of her lips. "What you're saying is there's a decent chance I'll get to sneak at least one look at your ass every day."

"I'll buy emo-boy pants, just for you."

She breathed a laugh, her expression softening as her palms fluttered up and settled on my chest. "That might sweeten the deal a bit."

"See? Silver linings, baby."

"But not in here," she snarked, wrinkling her nose. "It would ruin the color palette."

"I'll stick to bronze, I think."

"A man with excellent taste. Are you sure you're straight?"

"Very funny," I said, tightening my grip and pulling her against my hips to grind my hard cock against her belly.

Her slender throat bobbed, lips parting a beat before she breathed, "Ahh, I see."

"I don't think you need to worry."

"I wouldn't say that. We have a serious problem."

"And what's that?" She wasn't still mad about the building, right? She wouldn't hold a grudge like that—

"You have paint on your face."

"No, I don't," I said with a confidence I didn't entirely feel, leaning back and loosening my hold to feel around my skin. Which was precisely when she lifted her hands from where they'd settled on my work shirt and smeared wet charcoal across my cheeks, shrieking as I lunged for her.

I squealed like a stuck freaking pig when Rhyett chased after me, spinning out of reach and bolting down the hallway as I laughed maniacally. Those long arms snagged me around the waist, pulling a yelp up my lungs a beat before he shoved me up against the wall, caging me in as his lips taunted mine in a featherlight caress, a playful nip, and a torturous retreat when I made to kiss him.

Rhyett's kickass speaker swapped to Eric Clapton singing "Wonderful Tonight," making the whole situation feel a bit like a damn movie. My breath hitched with realization, eyes sliding shut as I dropped my head to the drywall.

"Eric Clapton, George Harrison. *Of course*. I should have known it was you over here, playing my music at *all hours* of the night."

"*Your* music?" he balked. "I think you mean *my* music."

"You're right," I snipped back, putting my hand on my hip as I popped it and leveled him with a glare. "My bad. I forgot you're geriatric."

The way his tongue ran over a canine gave me the distinct impression that I was about to be devoured by a very smug wolf. "Oh, that's how we're gonna play? I'll show you geriatric." Before I could ask any questions, he flipped me over his shoulder, clapping me right on the ass as he marched us another few feet down the hall, kicking a door open with his booted foot.

What was it about a man in well-worn work boots that just instantly soaked my panties? Although maybe that had been the smack to my backside as he growled at me.

The moment the door latched behind us, Rhyett dumped me on my feet, trouble written over every inch of his face. Eyes lit with humor and lust as he caged me between his arms. It only took one look at my painted handprints down his face and neck to send me into a fit of laughter. The man's smile only broadened, and then he pinned my hips to the door, leaning down and smearing his face up the side of my neck.

"Eww! Ahhrg!" Shoving my hands against his chest didn't budge him a single freaking inch, but his laughter on my artery tightened that spring begging to release in my core. Heat flushed my skin, despite the sticky, damp layer he'd just spread over me. "Rhyett—"

The protest was cut short by his lips slamming against mine. The chemical odor of paint overwhelmed his mouthwatering scent, but it didn't matter as he pressed me against the wall, a hand coming to grip my jaw as the other tugged at the hem of my shorts.

"Oh God," I breathed as his thick fingers found the edge of my panties beneath the denim. "Rhyett." His name sliced between us, only stoking his resolve as he ground into me.

"Talk to me, baby."

"I need you inside me."

"Should have thought about that before you started a fight you can't finish." His words made me gasp, gaping at him like a fish before his laugh vibrated inside my mouth, lips finding mine as his tongue swept in, tasting, teasing. Erection hard against my belly, Rhyett ground into me again. His fingers tugged my panties aside. Some distant part of my brain recognized that paint wouldn't likely be my friend down there, but when he removed them, I had to fight back a groan. Maybe he thought it through, too, because he started to work me through the thin fabric, growling when he found the soaked spot between my lips.

"Fuck, Brex."

"Yes, please."

When Rhyett dropped to his knees in front of me, he took my shorts with him, ripping a gasp up my throat before bringing his lips down on me. His rough stubble stung against the sensitive skin, although the sensation was then eclipsed by the heat of his mouth over my sex.

"Dammit, Brexley. Your pussy is so fucking perfect."

Responding would've required he stop touching me long enough to recombobulate the heat, need, and pleasure into something articulate. But Rhyett kept moving, leaving me entirely discombobulated. There would be no bobulating. No—

"Oh fuck," I gritted between my teeth. "*Oh, Rhyett.*"

He practically purred as he worked me, and in the next moment, had me hoisted up in his arms, his mouth on mine. I could taste myself on his lips, his tongue. It was wrong and wonderful and strange and delicious all at once. It was different this time. He was primal. Needy. His hands were a little rougher as he shifted me in his arms to drop his pants. Everything about him screamed urgent.

"Fuck," he muttered, eyes jamming closed as he leaned my weight into the door.

"That didn't sound like the good kind."

"It's not," he said on a groan.

"You don't have a condom."

His eyes were still sealed shut; lips pressed together like he was cursing the day he'd been born. He shook his head.

"I just tested, and everything was clear," I reminded him. I'd told him that first night, but reiterating it seemed prudent. "And I'm about to start my cycle. You're as safe as you can get shy of—"

Rhyett cut my words off with a shake of his head, disbelief and hunger warring in his eyes. "I've never been with someone like that. Fuck, Brex, I wouldn't ask you—"

"You're not asking, Rhyett," I cut him off, needing this. Needing *him*. "I'm telling you. I want you. Just us. Please?"

"Fuck," he growled, connecting our foreheads as he leaned me against the door. "Are you sure?"

Flicking his nose with mine, I urged him to look at me. When he did, his eyes were pained, the solemn edge making me laugh breathlessly.

"Rhyett, Hotshot, I'm sure. I wouldn't offer if I wasn't. And I haven't...ever, either." The admission cut me raw. Never before had I felt inexperienced, but that truth settled between us like dynamite, his eyes flaring as they rotated between my own. The lack of hesitation was all the confirmation he required, because Rhyett snaked a hand between us, groaning as he positioned himself over my slick center before rubbing his cock over my clit. My legs threatened to buckle, pleasure coiling as he repeated the motion in long, agonizing drags.

"Fuck, baby," he breathed, notching his dick right at my center, just enough of a tease to make me crazy, my teeth gritting. I pulled against his back, desperate for him to move, to fill me. Foreheads still connected, I felt his focus before our gazes locked, and his apprehension melted into anticipation. "Just you, baby. Only ever you."

There wasn't time to respond as Rhyett finally thrust up in one smooth motion. My spine arched, head smacking into the door. I'd feel it later, but, for now—

"*Ho-ly* fuck." His two-syllable *holy* accurately summarized the culmination of my thoughts as well. All I could manage was to nod. Pitifully. If he noticed it, it was a freaking miracle. When I shifted my hips, needing the friction, he shook his head, holding me more forcefully in place, as though he knew exactly how hard to press before it became painful.

"Give me—give me a second."

I huffed a laugh against him, our chests heaving together like waves meeting the shore. "You feel—" The air and ability to verbalize both whooshed out of me all at once as he slowly dragged his slick cock out of me before his smooth thrust stole any remaining sense from my brain. Too good—this was too good to be real. When Rhyett kissed me this time, it was like he returned the breath to my lungs. I was so used to him stealing it away, a thief in the night, that it took me a moment to register the way my heart was sailing. The man had woken me up. He didn't even know it. Had no way to register that every movement, every thrust seemed to connect us deeper. And not just in the way his crown was hitting my G-spot. In a way that fucking terrified me. Because for the first time in my life, I couldn't imagine letting anyone else touch me like Rhyett Rhodes was claiming me now.

Pace nearly punishing, Rhyett drew cries of pleasure up my throat, his lips parted, a look of complete consternation on his face.

"Come on, pretty girl. Give it to me. Come for me, baby." Each phrase was punctuated with weighted breath. The desire lacing each exhale was enough to push me over the edge. "Come, baby. I'm *buried* in you right now. Just us. Come for me so I can feel you soak my dick, Brexley." Sweat pricked on my arms, down my back, right as a bead slid down his forehead. Panting, sucking down air, I begged him to give me what he wanted.

"More, Rhyett. I need—"

His increased intensity severed the request. With each thrust, he bound us tighter. Wound me to him in a way I couldn't even contemplate as the oxygen was knocked from me. This wasn't supposed to happen. I wasn't looking for someone I wanted to do life with. Bad boss bitches didn't need a man to complete them. But oh my god, *this* man.

"You're the only one, Brex. No other woman knows what my cock feels like bare. No other woman has drenched me in her cum. Come on, Ace. Give it to me."

His steely blue eyes flashed up to me when I inhaled, a quick draw of air before I moaned, my center winding tighter than I even knew possible. A wave of pleasure barreled down mercilessly.

"Come, Brexley. Now, baby."

That did it. Right there. He didn't just knock me over the edge, he shoved me off the cliff. Pleasure exploded through me, the release ripping from my body. Vaguely I heard his mouth pouring praise, words like *perfect*, words like *mine* and *beautiful* and *more*.

I was drowning in an agony of desire and pleasure that so nearly bordered on pain, so intimately intertwined with relief. Rhyett groaned as he thrust home, as deep as he could go as he hit the back of me. It was the way he threw his head back, mouth parted soundlessly, that told me he'd cum inside me.

Dating in your mid-twenties felt a lot like watching reruns of a shitty sitcom—the same shit in a new package. Except Rhyett had just taken and given me a first I'd never so much as thought of with anyone else. And as he shakily lowered me to my feet, my useless legs buckling and pouring my body into his strong arms, I realized how deeply grateful I was that it had been him to take that final *first*.

THIRTY-FOUR
RHYETT

"I thought that retrievers were supposed to...*retrieve*," I said, stifling a smile. Royal had discovered a comical love of the rabbits that ran free throughout the property, treating them like orphans rather than prey. Brexley was gaping, a furrow between her golden brows, as her loyal companion rolled in the grass between three rodent friends before curling up with them.

"What in the fuck kind of dog is that?" she balked, blinking pointedly at our momentary distraction. I lost my battle with laughter.

A quick meal later, we'd since christened every solid surface in the trailer. My favorite moment was when we finally made it back to my bed, and she collapsed, satiated at last. That sleepy, satisfied curl of her lips was enough to send a man to his grave happy.

The subsequent cuddles, coos, and caresses? The icing on the fucking cake. Tracing the pale curve of her tight ass, I hummed contentedly. I'd never experienced this kind of connection with sex. One where I just couldn't get enough. Couldn't touch, feel, or taste adequate amounts of flesh. A tiny whimper sounded in her chest, making my raw cock jerk to attention. *Holy fuck, down boy*.

Admittedly, her ass looked fucking delectable. Bare breasts pale in the moonlight, Brexley's lean form spilled across my mattress. Golden hair askew in a halo around her face. The woman even slept temptingly.

Royal whined softly, like she had sporadically since we drug her inside, away from the bunnies.

"Freaking weirdo," I grumbled, shaking my head. She whined again before crawling under the bed. It was dark enough under there for her to feel denned in, so that was something, at least. What in the hell kind of dog befriended rabbits?

Snuggling in tighter around Brexley's sleeping form, I ran feather-light touches up and down her side. The ensuing purr was priceless. I fell asleep connecting the angles on her body.

———

THE SMELL of coffee greeted me. Along with the rhythmic tapping of keys, I noted with no shortage of intrigue. She was writing. *Actually writing.* She'd been stuck in a pit of frustration for days as we rotated between her place and mine. The evasive 'flow state', she called it. The lines between her brows were back, as was the complex set of her jaw, yet it was the speed at which her fingers moved that made me smile the widest. I scrubbed a palm over my face before moving to the kitchen island, pouring myself the remainder of the coffee from the French press and turning to make more.

"Morning, Ace."

"Morning, Hotshot." Baby blues flitted to me and then back to her screen. Managing to sip on the black cup of coffee without gagging, I wandered to her side, peering at the words hammering out stroke by stroke. A brief hesitation caught my attention before she typed, *Rhyett Rhodes, you freaking snoop, you are mouthwatering with those gray sweats slung around your hips.*

I burst out laughing, shimmying said sweats a bit lower, hoping to draw her attention away from the electronic device. "Slung around my hips, huh?"

"That's how a writer would say it."

"Then that's how you shall say it." She took a heartbeat to lean into my chest before returning to her frantic tapping. "So," I hedged, "how's it going?"

"One. Never interrupt a writer mid-flow. Two." She sighed. I was still learning her noises, her levels of contentment. But at least to me, it sounded good. "It's going really well, surprisingly. It's like all the things I've wanted to say in the last ten years were just filed and waiting."

"Good. Sounds like you're writing away."

"Rhyett, I've been up since five. And I've penned ten-thousand words."

"I'm a little hung up on the first part, Ace." I tapped my phone on the counter beside us and scowled. "You've been up for three and a half hours without waking me?"

"It just started pouring out." She turned her palms up to the ceiling as if to tell me she didn't understand how.

"I take it ten-thousand is a lot?"

"Seeing as I've not attempted more than a few hundred since high school? Hell yeah."

"Well, good. I'll go back to not bothering you, then. You going into the shop?"

She grimaced, setting her hands in her lap. "I should. I know I should."

"But...?"

"Wren offered to open."

"The point of hiring staff is to stop working *in* your business so you can work *on* it."

"Which means...?"

"Take a break. Jesus, play hooky for a week. You've obviously earned it."

"I have, haven't I?" She nodded defiantly. "What's on your docket today?" She asked, sipping her coffee.

"Subs in and out all day at both locations. Priority is this place, obviously. And I want to finish the outdoor living space before the family arrives." We'd affectionately been referring to the built-in hangout as 'the deck'. It made sense despite the fact that we were building so much more into it. Brex had adjusted my sketches last week, adding a bench seat and a white wall for projecting movies. It was a damn good idea. Honestly, it left me a little perplexed as to how the hell I hadn't come up with it myself.

"Did the bar's stove come in?" she said out of the corner of her mouth, eyes beginning to track words on the page.

"Not yet." The stove was a beauty. Top fucking tier. My chef back home would donate an organ for it. But these demographics would actually earn me my money back. Taste for kickass cuisine was abundant in the city. And I'd be damned if we didn't have the prime appetizers in a twenty-minute radius. Bite-sized bliss and the best booze money could buy. That was the mission. "They said between noon and six tomorrow."

Something dangerous flashed in her eyes, familiar hunger sliding beneath the innocent baby blues as she scooted her chair back. I'd never felt so wanted as I had in these weeks beside Brexley. Her work ethic rivaled a Rhodes, but we didn't let the endless task list come between us. Somehow our stolen moments became all the more precious. The words hadn't even left her mouth and I knew what she was thinking, her scheme written over the expectation set on her petite features.

"So, you're saying you're here today?"

Running my tongue over a canine and my mind through the list of to-dos, ultimately ruling they could wait, I set my coffee down and swiftly closed the gap. When I grabbed the back of her chair, Brexley's breath hitched in her throat, and I couldn't help but smile as the sound sent a jolt down my spine. Eyes locked on hers, I leaned her back, nudging her knees apart as I stepped between her thighs. The determined lift of her chin did a pretty good job of concealing her nerves. Fuck, I needed to play poker with this woman. She'd clean house. Only the tight hold of her belly and those shallow little breaths showed her nerves. Slowly, I lowered my face to hers, dropping my voice.

"Tell me what you have in mind, and I'll make it a reality, Ace."

The moment her teeth grazed that lower lip, my cock jerked to attention, a smile on my face as her delicate hands raked up my chest before scraping down my stomach.

"Careful what you wish for, Rhyett Rhodes."

THIRTY-FIVE
RHYETT

Brexley had this way of winding dangerous promises into a taunting tone that drew pricks along my flesh. Her blonde hair was wound up into a clip, leaving the long, tan line of her neck bared to me. I threaded my fingers into the loose updo and tilted her head back as my lips caressed her slender throat. She swallowed audibly, the shift against my lips enough to send me spiraling if I wasn't already. This woman had me wrapped so tightly around her delicate fingers, her sharp mind, and her decadent body, and she didn't even know it.

Or, perhaps, she did. Perhaps that was the danger in her tone. An intrinsic knowing that should she speak it, I would so willingly comply.

"If you don't tell me, I'll have to use my imagination, Ace." My teeth against the sensitive skin above her artery sent goosebumps in a wave down her body. Her shiver sent a flood right to my dick. There was something about being able to affect her so quickly, so profoundly. "You've spent your life locked away reading those filthy books of yours." She tasted fresh, clean, save for the hint of sweat. I wanted to lick every inch of her. "Tell me about them." I nipped at the soft spot between her neck and shoulder, quickly soothing it with my lips. "There has to be a scene you've just been dying to try out."

There was something so fucking satisfying about the sharp intake of breath before Brexley's moan. Something that sent control wayside as I pulled her from her seat, whipped us to the counter, and lifted her onto the surface of the island.

"Tell me what you thought about to get yourself off at night."

This gasp tickled my stubbled jaw. She tightened her legs around my waist. "Tell me what the men in your books do that keep you all so rapt."

"I can't think with you this close," she whispered. I could tell she'd meant for the words to have gusto, but they'd come out breathless, which brought me some fucked up kind of satisfaction. She wasn't rattled arguing with my contractors when I'd sent her to sign for an installation and they'd brought the wrong damn thing. Or running her shop or facing life head-on by herself. But she trembled against me here, my mouth on her neck, hips pressed to hers, hand in her hair as hers roamed the length of my back.

"*A scene*, Brexley." I sucked harder this time, relishing her rapid breaths. Stopping just shy of leaving a mark, I moved up to her jaw, fingers tightening as I angled her face for easy access. "I just need one to start."

She nodded, chest rising and falling against mine. "Okay. Yes. *God, Rhyett*, yes." My fingers hedged the hem of her shirt, sliding across her smooth belly, and the woman nearly growled. "Fuck. Baby, slow down, you're driving me—never mind, don't stop. Please don't ever fucking stop."

Chuckling, I slid my palms up until they rested just below her breasts. "Was he blonde, like me?"

"One of them," she said, the words soft and a little high-pitched. Nerves, arousal, embarrassment, or some shaken cocktail of the three. I blinked, leaning back to study her face as it pinked. *Oh.* This was too good.

"*One* of them, like one of the books? Or one of them, like *one of the men in the scene?*"

"You're not allowed to judge book club."

"Hell, baby, I'm not allowed to judge, period. I'm no saint—" Her slender fingers severed my words. Her ensuing scowl buried them forever.

"Listen, Hotshot. I don't want to think about you with anybody else."

"Deal." Kissing Brexley was like a fucking head rush. My body pricked with sensation anywhere she touched. Heart pounding, dick so hard it was painful. "Now. Tell me what the blonde one did."

"Well, there was a summer fling and a very handsome best friend."

Two things happened simultaneously. My cock jerked at the idea of watching someone I trusted touch my woman. Of sharing *her*.

Naturally, my mind filled in the blanks, dropping Jameson and then Broderick into the equation. Two: my rage boiled until it seared my skin. The desire to bust my best friends' fingers one at a time eclipsed the cruel fantasy. *Not even for Jameson or Broderick.* There wasn't a world in the universe where I'd be okay watching another man's hands on her hips or lips on her skin. Not a world where I could watch someone else's dick—

"Story time's over," I growled, scooping her up and taking her to my bed. *My* bed. Not Broderick. Not Jameson's. *Mine.* Her satisfied trill of laughter curbed the primal male need to fight, claim, and protect, but only enough to see reason.

This could be used to my advantage. This was a book she'd likely read more than once, a scene she'd no doubt carefully selected because it haunted her waking hours. When I slipped my fingers higher, I found her lace panties damp. She was fucking soaked for me —or the combination of me and this idea in her head—and like hell would I not take advantage of that.

Begrudgingly, I snarled, "What happened next?"

As I laid her down on my plush mattress, Brexley vividly described her favorite erotic fantasy. It came out in desperate pants that sent blood straight to my dick. Like I could even get any harder. *Jesus.* "The blonde—" she said, gasping as I nipped at the sensitive skin above her shoulder. "She was *in love* with the blonde."

"Good taste."

Breathlessly, she giggled, tossing her head back as I nipped my way up her neck. Chest rising and falling in desperate reaches for air, she set the scene. "They were in...the mountains."

"Like, a cabin?" I asked, ducking down to suck a rosy nipple between my lips, and relishing in the way she lost her words, hand rushing to cup the back of my head, pulling me tighter to her breast. When I ceased my sucking, she gasped down air, catching on to the prompt and fumbling for the details.

"*Outside*—they were outside."

This woman would be my undoing. *Holy shit.* What straight, red-blooded man didn't at least fantasize a time or two about fucking their woman somewhere forbidden? I gave her nipple a slow, decadent pull, twirling my tongue around the tip.

"Her boyfriend started while his friend *watched.* He slipped off her panties—" a desperate inhalation broke the words apart as I rewarded her with another hard suck. "And slipped his fingers...*inside*—but she was watching the second man."

While agonizing territorial instinct and arousal battled for control, I tugged my clothes off, then slipped hers away. I moved down her body, palms desperate to touch and feel and claim. Peeling her lace panties off with my teeth, I pinned her to the mattress with one hand planted between her breasts.

By the time I had access, her clit was a swollen button of need. The instant I lapped up her drenched slit, Brexley bucked against me, little whimpers hitting my system like a shot of whiskey. Heat burst in my belly, wrapping around my spine as I added fingers to the equation, slipping them into her tight center.

"You taste incredible, Ace." Brexley rode my hand like she'd been begging for my presence between her legs, and I feasted until her back bowed, those perfect, pale breasts arching into the air, her head falling back as her muscles spasmed. When her words failed, I froze, earning an impatient groan as I forced her to continue with the pleasure promised in telling the tale.

"He couldn't stand watching any longer, so he moved in, caressing her neck, her breasts. When they kissed, it was—like...*fireworks*," she fought the words out between desperate little whimpers and gulps of air. "They drove each other *crazy*...enemies to *lovers*... but they wanted...each other the whole time."

Brexley's words cut off as my free palm found her perky tit, giving it a light squeeze as she writhed beneath me. My mouth moved up to hers, taking the kiss with all the drive I was attempting to keep contained in my body. There wasn't a muscle left that wasn't tense with need to fuck her senseless. To show her I was all she'd ever need. To ring pleasure from her body like nobody else could. But this game...it was worth seeing through to the end. So I kissed her like the man in her fantasy. Kissed her like she wasn't mine to take, but I was about to do it anyway.

"What happened next?" I demanded, fighting to control my breathing and trailing my lips over her chest as she caught her breath. She had the cutest little birthmark beneath the tattoo on her collarbone, the soft pigmentation catching my attention as I kissed my way across her skin. Brexley squirmed beneath me, seeking the release I'd just robbed from her. Cruel, perhaps, but when we finally fell over that edge—hopefully, *together*—it would be fucking magnificent. When I planted my leg between hers, she ground against it, desperate for that friction. I chuckled, demanding, "Finish it, Ace."

"*Rhyett*," she moaned, my cock twitching in response. 'Painful' was an understatement, all the blood in my body was congregating in the angry purple head of it. I fisted my dick, trying to release some of the pressure as I waited for her to continue.

"Where's the blonde, baby?"

She breathed, "Pressed against her back."

"Is she laying down or—"

"*Kneeling*. They put her on her knees."

"Good girl. Where were his hands, Ace?"

"Waist," she panted, adding, "ass."

"Mmmm, I like that," I said, my grip on control slipping through my fingers as I chuckled darkly, allowing my palms to glide over her body before sliding away, rising to kneel.

"*Baby*," she protested, the desperate haze of lust in her voice an intoxicating reward for this play of ours.

"Come here, Ace."

Chest heaving, sparkling blue eyes hooded with desire, she reluctantly raised herself up and into my arms. Once she was steady, I turned her toward the headboard. Wrapping around her from behind, I braced one arm across her waist, and pulled her up and into my torso, shifting my other hand to rub over the side of her ass.

"And his friend?"

"Kissing her, hands on her chest—" She groaned as my front hand transitioned in favor of a steady rotation between her breasts. "He—"

"*What, Ace?* What does he do?" I prompted when she came up short.

"Eiffel tower."

"What?" I said, chuckling at whatever code word she'd thrown out that I was unaware of. So much for being the older, more experienced one of the two of us. What the hell did she read in those books?

"She sucks him...while the other fucks her from behind."

"*Oh*." God damn, the visual was intense. How a man could be equally consumed by lust and rage, I would never be able to understand. But I kept playing, releasing my hold and setting a palm between her shoulders to guide her onto her hands and knees. This time, I didn't hesitate to slide my throbbing dick up and into her soaked center, rewarded with her cry of pleasure as she bowed forward onto the bed. I might not be able to rail her like two men, but I could damn well show her she didn't need them.

"Were they gentle?" I rasped, voice ragged as my restraint cracked, muscles trembling with the need to *move*. She shook her head, frantic as she arched her ass into me. Holding back my need to spill inside her, I finally started to roll my hips. Cock rock hard, I fucked into her tight, wet center, relishing as her walls clenched around me. Sliding my hand across her neck to her throat, I traced the line of her lips before pressing two fingers to the seam.

"Suck," I ordered. The demand sent a tremor through her body, threatening to milk my orgasm right out of me. But she did. She turned her face, giving me the perfect view as her pink lips wrapped around my fingers, eyes sliding closed as she sucked deep. Riding her hard, our bodies made obscene, wet noises as my balls slapped against her, and I fought back the release barreling down my spine. Right as her body tightened around mine, that telltale flex of her walls gave me just enough time to pull free, slipping my fingers from her mouth simultaneously.

This moan was frustrated, her protest punctuated by my name. "*Rhyett*, please."

"Is that how they finished her, baby? Just like that?"

Panting, she shook her head.

"I didn't think so. Finish the story, Ace."

"He...*the friend...*"

"Yes?"

"He fucks her from the front."

Blood pounding in my ears, my cock jerked, pre-cum gleaming on the tip. I slid my palm down the length, wiping it away as I demanded, "And the blonde?"

"He—" she cut herself off, turning to glance at me, but slamming her eyes shut when I started to drag my cock out of her, shifting back with tantalizing slowness.

"What, baby? What does he do?"

"He—"

I chuckled when she cut herself off again, her skin flushing pink. Curling over her, I pressed a kiss to her temple as she fought for oxygen. "Behind these closed doors, there's no shame in *anything* that you want. Do you understand me?" When she nodded, I gave a demanding thrust, relishing in her answering whimper. I would do anything for this woman. *Be* anything for her. "Answer me, Brex."

"He takes her ass."

God damn. Jaw clenching, I looked up to the ceiling, trying with every ounce of self-control not to release hot streams of cum over her shaking thighs. Clearing my throat, hands struggling to stay steady as I ran them over the muscles of her back, I asked, "And you like that?"

"Maybe someday," she said tentatively. I nodded, though her eyes were closed and she wouldn't see it.

"Start slow?" I asked. Her contented hum was enough. "Don't move," I ordered, reluctantly shifting away from her. Loose strands of Brexley's silky blonde hair fell across her face as she bowed her head into her hands, panting against the bed as I reached for my dresser drawer. Returning with a bottle of oil, I poured out a generous amount, smiling when her breath hitched as my fingers caressed that tight, forbidden place. Pulling away, I gave her ass a gentle smack a beat before sheathing my cock in her sweet center, seating myself in one thrust.

"Tell me if this feels good." Setting a slow pace, despite the protests of my throbbing dick, I gently massaged her ass before slowly applying just enough pressure to that perfect virgin hole to see if she liked it. Brexley's moan was accompanied by an encouraging arch of her back. Gently thrusting, I dared to hedge further, slipping just the tip of my thumb into that tight ring of muscle. When she gasped, I asked, "Am I hurting you?" Brexley vehemently shook her head, stray golden locks shifting off her shoulders. "Is that *good*?" Her nod was all I needed, grabbing her hip with my free hand and setting a steady pace. "Good, baby. I'll do whatever I can to make all those visions a reality, Brex. All you gotta do is ask." She nodded, moaning as I picked up my pace, shifting in a steady rhythm, devouring the sounds her pleasure poured between her lips. This time, when her walls clamped around me, I leaned into the pressure.

Brexley's orgasm wasn't her usual release. It was like the combination of our game and the new, forbidden sensations *detonated* her. Keeping my pace, I drug out the orgasm, cursing as my muscles threatened to cramp, and she just *kept coming*. Only when she fell onto the bed did I allow myself to fuck her until my own release washed through me.

It still wasn't enough.

THIRTY-SIX

BREXLEY

Rough palm melded against mine, Rhyett took a long step forward to pull open the door of The Cracked Corset. No matter how present or distant my mind was, he always beat me to them. Some sort of ancient chivalry still alive and well within Mr. Rhodes. Royal pranced right on in, as though the gesture had been intended for her. She happily sat for pets from Holland and accepted her treats before trotting away for the office.

"Good morning, ladies! How's it going?" There were morning people, and then there was Rhyett Rhodes. I loved the silence of the city before it was bustling, but the man had some intensely bizarre intrinsic love of starting a new day, and that enthusiasm bled into his voice.

Holland and Wren exchanged long glances across the coffee bar, knowing amusement written all over their expressions as they both looked at our dangling joined hands.

"You tell me," Wren quipped, grinning at Rhyett.

"Fantastic, thanks very much." He leaned down to kiss the top of my head. "You're looking particularly beautiful today, Wren."

If blushes could light fires, Wrenly would have ignited right then and there. It was an effort not to chuckle as she dropped her eyes to the espresso machine before thanking him and asking, "The usual, Rhyett?"

"Yes, ma'am," he said, returning Wren's unabashed smile. "To go, please, Wren."

"You got it."

"Hey Hotshot! How've you been?" The sound of Noel's voice was a balm to my bleeding heart. The big dummy was balancing a laptop on her good arm, the other still stuck in the sling tight to her stomach.

"Noel! What are you doing here?" Reproach laced my tone, but I moved for her with a disproportionate level of enthusiasm. It gave me away, dammit.

"So help me God, if I have to stay in that room for one more minute."

Rhyett, having retained more sense than me through the relentless wave of orgasms we'd delivered each other, rushed to her, scooping the computer away and pulling her to his side for a gentle hug.

"Come on, Red. You have to behave so you can be back out here working your magic."

"Did you tell her the cast of *Twilight* wandered in here?" Wren asked tauntingly.

"What?!" Noel balked, turning my way.

"Well, not literally. We were just blessed with above-average genetics painting the canvas this week."

"Dammit," she muttered, following Rhyett's lead to the cushioned corner booth.

"Rhy, drink's up."

Something about the familiar tune to Wren's voice around his nickname sent a jolt through my system, head snapping up as Rhyett —blessedly oblivious—sauntered over to scoop his paper cup off the pickup station. The girls had refreshed the flowers this morning. Books were beautifully lined up on the wall, the counter clear, and mugs in perfect formation behind them. The noise from the kitchen told me the morning had been busy enough to generate an Everest-sized pile of dishes for Manny and Ben in the back. The shop was perfect. And my not-boyfriend, more mutually exclusive lover, had been in enough times to have a regular order and a nickname with my staff.

Like seas colliding, warmth and terror clashed in my belly, refusing to mix in equal measures of stubbornness. Warmth grappled for victory as he leaned over the counter, complimenting my lead barista's new thigh tattoo of a floral-wreathed lion. Terror was quick to suck the sensation into the undertow the moment she grinned back at him, leaning on her forearms to tell him the story behind the ink and the artist.

"He fits, Brex." Noel's voice was soft enough that it was just for me, but my stomach squirmed just the same. He didn't need to inflate the ideas already expanding in his perfect, big, fat, idealistic head. But she wasn't wrong. He did fit. And he made me smile, laugh, relax, and come. *A lot.* It was like his own personal mission to see me satisfied both day and night. When the man had pulled me up to dance in his arms in his little, tiny house on wheels, I thought my heart would implode. And the little cynic who lived–proudly displayed on the mantle in my brain–informed me it wouldn't last. *Couldn't* last. The honeymoon phase never did.

A quieter voice...the one I'd stashed behind the potted plants gathering dust in the corner, said that sometimes people just fit. They stick. And keep on sticking. I'd never intended to find a man that stuck. Letting him into my life and climbing into his bed might have been a colossal mistake. However, if Rhyett Rhodes was a mistake...he was my best one to date.

***

"IT WAS GOOD; IT WAS FUN," Josie said with a shrug. Her dark curls had been swept back into a braid down the length of her spine. Perfect, frizzy ringlets framed either side of her face as she reached for another book and slid it into the corresponding sleeve. The first waves of the season's signature Florida heat were challenging even our most practiced techniques and most expensive selections of curl creams and hair sprays.

"I hear a 'but' somewhere in there," Noel commented, rotating her mug in little circles with her finger. Josie squirmed, wrinkling her nose as she sealed another bubble envelope.

"*But*...he has no lips."

"What?" I balked, barking a laugh.

"Skinny little white guy lips," she snickered. "Like. He's cute, funny, and so smart. I find him super sexy despite being blonde and my freaking height." The repeated shrug of her left shoulder revealed her hesitance on the last part of that statement. "We have so much fun laughing and playing, and for a hot minute on Saturday, I even entertained introducing him to the kids. But when he kisses, I just...I can't find his lips." When we all burst out laughing, a tinge of pink climbed into her terra-cotta complexion. Contrary to her cute, funny, lipless date, Josie had been blessed with the full lips bestowed on little girl's fashion dolls. She bit down on the lower one before throwing her head back on a groan. "Why's it gotta be so damn hard to find it all? Like, I just want the whole package again, you know?"

Josie and Blaze shared a romance novel-worthy love that made my eyes burn if I thought about it. Childhood best friends who danced around their feelings until they shared a comical first kiss playing *Seven Minutes In Heaven*. Blaze was the cool kid in love with the theater girl, but he didn't hesitate to pick Josie over his brainless jock buddies. We blamed him for her obsessive love of football. When Blaze returned from his first deployment as a hometown hero, he and Josie rekindled their love, married a year later, and welcomed Gemma not long after that. Tragically, Blaze died in the line of duty when their son was just a newborn, leaving Jos with a framed, folded flag where a husband should be. Two years later, we were all glad she was dating, but there was no way to avoid comparing her prospects to the man who still held her heart.

"I mean," Noel shrugged, breaking the silence that settled whenever we thought about Blaze. She reached for a stack of books, earning a smack on the hand in the process. She scowled at Josie's retreating fingers before sighing and leaning back to baby her arm, like she should have been doing all day. "How's he in bed?"

"Like we've gotten that far," Josie countered, swiping the book off the top of the stack Noel had been reaching for. "The suck-o part is, if I look past the whole kissing his teeth part, I think he'd be really, really good with the kids."

"Never know. He could make up for it with his equipment," Noel said with a coy wink.

"Or his fingers," I offered hopefully.

"But I don't want to end up with somebody I can't enjoy making out with on a Friday night, you know?" We all sighed simultaneously, glowering at the stack of books to be shipped in front of us. Noel and I had a ritual of tackling this task together every Saturday, and Josie showing up unannounced and uninvited just affirmed all my prior assumptions about her epic character. Vallie had been texting her moral support all evening, stuck in meetings back-to-back due to some international time difference.

Noel glanced at her phone as it vibrated for the dozenth time, rolling her eyes before reaching for it with her good hand.

"Yeah?" she said, voice clipped. "I'm fine. No, I'm fine. I'm at the shop...Helping Brex, I told you that. No, it's shipment day, so I'm not just leaving her here..." Her glower made me shift in my seat before deciding to go grab us refills. Carafe in hand, I returned to a still scowling Noel. "I'll be home on time, I promise. We'll be fine...Fine, I'll have Rhyett walk us back. Will that work?"

When I canted my head, brow furrowed, she put the phone on mute and whispered, "Eric," before hitting the microphone button again. I drew in a long breath, not liking the way my chest tightened as I poured us all a warmup.

"Rhyett is the definition of a perfect gentleman and head over heels for Brex. I think you're fine."

Beginning to feel like a blowfish as I fought to contain my opinions, I released the air from my puffed-up cheeks on a long exhale, turning to return the coffee pot to an eager-looking Wrenly. She was just about out for the night, the bar spotless and pristinely organized, as always.

When I came back, Noel had managed to extricate herself from the conversation and was pursing her lips as she handed a now-silent Josie a book off the stack.

"Everything okay?"

"Yeah, he's just—ever since the accident, he's been extra overbearing. Protective, that kind of stuff. But me being out of the house is seemingly a criminal offense."

Josie and I locked eyes for a beat, and I saw the same flicker of concern in her that was riddling mine. Speaking for us both, I hedged, "Is everything okay between the two of you, Noel? Things were...tense at the hospital. Even Rhyett picked up on it."

"We're fine. Just a rough patch," she said, waving me off and snatching another novel to pass my direction as if she was any closer in proximity than I was to the stack between us. "Anyways, how is Mr. Hotshot? Still your northern dream boat?" She turned to Josie, adding, "He got Brex writing again. Did she tell you? Twenty-thousand words and counting."

Personally, I hated to be pressed on issues I wasn't ready to talk about. Still, something was eating at me, the ability to form a coherent sentence suddenly vanishing as I slid another book into an envelope.

"Damn, I love that. And he's got great lips," Josie noted, dark eyes flicking my way. "Why can't Jake have a mouth like Rhyett? I'd be all over him if there were just...more of him to kiss."

I laughed, trying to get back into the casual rhythm we'd had before being interrupted. My thoughts drifted to said mouth, the feel of him ravaging my skin, feasting on my sex like I was his freaking dessert. Need pulsed between my legs, and I crossed one over the other. Embarrassed that my swallow was audible, I said, "God, and he knows how to use them. It's never been this good for me. You'll find someone worth kissing, Jos. Maybe Jake could get some filler?"

Her amused cackle warmed the air between the three of us, humor seeming to loosen the tight hold of Noel's shoulders, her face relaxing. "That would be the day."

"Not a terrible idea," Noel said, swaggering back into her seat as a smile played in the corners of her mouth. "Never know, he might be open to it. You're a hell of a catch to miss out on over a few hundred bucks and some pokes."

"But for real, what in the hell is going on with you?" Josie pressed. "Rhyett looked ready to devour you when he came by for lunch."

I rolled my eyes, tossing my hair over a shoulder. "That was Manny's ham on rye, don't get confused."

THIRTY-SEVEN

RHYETT

Albert Einstein allegedly claimed, *"Any man that can drive safely while kissing a pretty girl is simply not giving the kiss the attention it deserves."*

That wasn't the end of the limitation, in my humble opinion. I gritted my teeth, cursing under my breath as Brexley's slick mouth bobbed up and down on my cock, having pried open my zipper to gain access. She'd commented on the dark tint of my windows on a few occasions, and had I known this would be the result of answering her question about peeping toms, I would've done it sooner.

Fingers wrapped around my shaft, lips swollen with the effort, she tugged on that thread wrapped around my spine. My balls jumped with that familiar ache as I groaned.

"Holy fuck," I breathed, watching yet another car zip around us before I could jerk the truck off the freeway onto the ramp and down towards the beach. I tightened my hold on her hair, wishing my other hand was free to roam.

"Oh fuck, Brex, you've got me, baby." If her satisfied moan hadn't been the end of it, the way she opened her throat as she slid down next was. "How do you *even*—" Then I was coming down her throat in hot spurts that made my legs shake. My bombshell lapped up every freaking ounce.

Swearing at the intensity of an adrenaline-fueled orgasm, I left an ungodly amount of room between the nose of my pickup and the car in front of us. I looked like a nervous teenager just learning to drive. Which was fitting, as that was likely the last time a girl had sucked me off sitting in the middle of a bench seat.

Brexley slipped her lips over the crown with a satisfied little *pop*. Then swirled her tongue over the slit like she was afraid to waste a drop, as she grinned at me. *Jesus.*

Wiping her lips, she leaned back in her seat, shifting to make the buckle more comfortable. She'd swapped to a dark pink lip stain a few weeks back, and I was still amazed when she came up just as polished looking as she'd been when she'd gone down. Well, save for where my fingers had gripped her silky blonde hair. That would need straightening. Her smile sent fire through my belly.

"You are fucking amazing, baby."

"I know," she said, mostly teasing as she batted her lashes at me.

"My little temptress."

As I turned into the parking lot, that statement earned a full-fledged grin, like I'd just let her in on the most tantalizing secret. Which brought me to—

"Why are there so many cars here?" She scowled at the expansive lot. "I hate tourist traps."

"I know. This one is worth it, I promise."

"Sure it is," she teased, running her fingers through her long hair and straightening in her seat. "That's what they all say."

"I mean it. Come on, baby, you gotta trust me on this one."

Brex put her hands up defensively, rolling her eyes but shifting in her seat like a kid on Christmas morning. She'd never been to the beaches south of the Skyway. Which was ridiculous since she'd lived an hour away from the best beach in the country her entire life. Fixing that was imperative. When I found a spot big enough for the long bed, I threw her in park, reaching over the bench seat to grab our beach bag.

"It's busy," she noted with a scowl, watching the colorful herd of people buzz in and out of the main entrance like rainbow ants.

"Yup. You'll see why in a second."

"You better make this up to me."

My laugh earned that adorable lip-bite thing she did when she didn't want to admit she was having fun. But with them still swollen from rubbing across my shaft, the desire to run my fingers over them was even higher than usual. Clearing my throat and trying not to pitch a tent before we made it to the water, I jerked my head towards the buzzing entrance.

"Come on, Ace, I'll carry you in."

"Like hell," she mumbled, shaking her head. I raised a brow, about to say *what are you going to do about it?* But the image of her thrown over my shoulder with a palm smacking her ass must have been just as vivid to her as it was to me, because she edged sideways, a playful smirk on her face a heartbeat before she leapt for me. I snatched her around the waist, earning an elated trill of laughter as I spun her around, bringing her up to kiss. I turned around so she could climb up for a piggyback ride and refused to laugh when she sighed as she complied. Wrapped around my back, her long, lean arms tangled around my neck, and I smiled.

The sun was shining, a pure blue sky stretching infinitely in every direction. My girl was happily draped over my back like a little koala. A koala about to set foot on the softest sand I'd seen anywhere on the planet.

"It's so *white*," she noted when we edged the end of the sidewalk, where hundreds of yards of fluffy, pure sand devoured it.

"Stunning, isn't it?"

"Blinding," she countered begrudgingly. I laughed and handed her my Ray Bans, blinking in an attempt to aid my eyes as they adjusted. "Woah," she breathed, peeking at the expanse of the beach through polarized lenses.

Teal and aqua water splashed against the purest white sand in the world, the white caps breathtaking. Every color imaginable adorned the beach in kaleidoscope umbrellas and bright blue tents, blankets strewn about to stake a claim on the good spots. Families played in the waves for a good fifty yards past the shore, the water only breaking against their knees. Beyond the break, jet skis kicked up fountains of water. Laughter, the squeal of happy kids, and warring boomboxes battled for airtime, but it was the kind of chaos that left you smiling.

"Life's Too Short" by Two Friends and Fitz blasted over a speaker, the man in charge busy at a grill beneath a blue box tent anchored into the sand. His dreads were adorned with orange beads that popped against his dark complexion. He grinned as his wife wrapped her arms around him from behind, kissing his shoulder and laying her head down as they swayed to the music. Perfect duplicates of each of them ran around, kicking a ball. The girl in neon pink and the boy in electric blue.

A few yards over, the round belly of a sunburnt ginger man—a tourist, no doubt—stuck up above his kids' messy sand-carved turtle. A laughing woman in a blush hijab and flowing, patterned white and blue outfit clutched a diaper in hand, chasing her cackling, naked toddler in a circle around a hand-scraped moat. Her older boy yelped not to step on his castle.

Chuckling, I reached down and pulled Brexley's flip-flops from her feet before wiggling her off my back and turning to watch her reaction. As her feet connected with the flour-soft surface, her pink lips popped open, eyes rounding before she laughed a breathless, you-told-me-so chuckle.

Feeling spectacularly smug, I said, "Welcome to the south side of the bridge, Ace."

"Okay," she breathed, closing her eyes as she wiggled deeper into the sand. "You didn't *completely* oversell it."

"Hah!" I threw my arms up in the air like I'd scored a touch-down, wishing Noel had been here in time to validate the words. "Did anybody hear that?" Her eyes went wide, mouth popping open as pink crept into her cheeks. "Somebody?!" I begged, laughing as she hopped up, trying to cover my mouth with delicate fingers. I snatched her wrists in one hand, turning my face to the side. "Come on, say it again. I need to record it."

Two of the husbands nearest me, including our unofficial DJ, flashed me knowing smiles before averting their eyes.

"Come on, Ace. You won't believe the water."

***

"SHE'S ALMOST DONE," I bragged to Noel, who sat propped in her chair. She was free of the sling, but her black cast was still harsh against her pale skin. Concealed in the shade of her umbrella, she grinned at Brexley.

"I always told you you could do it."

Brexley rolled her eyes, then tracked my movements as I threw another ball for Josie's youngest, a two-year-old boy named Kyler. He squealed in delight, toddling after it at full speed. He had his mother's warm complexion, but sun-bleached blonde hair, making him the perfect Florida poster child. His giggles and insistence on playing with a Tampa Bay ball only solidified the image.

My heart gave a little ache as I spotted her with their friend, Vallie, walking back towards us with a giggling Gemma in tow. In true sibling fashion, Gemma looked nothing like her baby brother, save for their little button noses. She had her mama's dark hair and their dad's fair skin and green eyes, with a grin that would be agonizing to say no to.

Good luck, Josie.

"It just kind of...all came flooding back, when Rhyett started asking questions."

"Sure, it did," Noel sighed, fanning herself with a pamphlet. "I'm just chopped liver; I see how it is."

"Yelling *four-k a day* like a writing drill sergeant wasn't particularly effective," Brex remarked teasingly. Noel threw her head back, clutching her chest like she'd been mortally wounded.

"Phew," Vallie said as she collapsed into the shaded sand beside Noel. "Summer is on its way, isn't it?"

"It's not even April," Brex complained, scowling up at the sky like the sunshine and the perfect eighty-degree day had personally affronted her. I laughed, shaking my head as Gemma threw herself around my leg.

"Mr. Ryan, Mr. Ryan—"

"Rhyett, baby. Rhy-ett," Josie corrected, accepting Brexley's outstretched water bottle and drinking greedily.

"Rhyett, can I have a hotdog like what you and Aunt Brex had?"

I grimaced, peering up at Josie, who shrugged in permanent resignation. Single moms were superheroes. She mouthed, "Fine with me," and bent to grab her purse from the beach bag, but I waved her off.

"My treat," I offered. The woman sighed as she collapsed into the sand.

"You *so* don't have to do that," she protested, but I could see the smile on her lips.

"I know," I reassured. "Anything for these cuties!" I growled the last words like a monster, scooping Gemma up onto my shoulder as she squealed before snatching Kyler into my arm like a football. His laughter was enough to make my chest ache. Growing up in a big family, I'd assumed we'd all have our own brood of children by now. An old aching longing settled in my belly, pulling my focus back to Brexley, whose eyes were heavily trained on the three of us. Would she want that? A noisy house full of laughter and bickering and chaos, but so much love we didn't know what to do with it.

I slapped on a smile and locked on Josie. "Does mama want to come, or are we off to see a man about some hot dogs?"

"By all means," she said on a long breath that transformed into a yawn.

"Hang on tight, pumpkins," I warned, jostling them as we rotated towards the community center.

"We're not pumpkins," Gemma piped up, giggling and patting my head reproachfully. Brexley's grin was the last image in my mind before we headed off the beach.

THIRTY-EIGHT

BREXLEY

"If you don't steal his last name, I might," Vallie sighed, laying her head on my shoulder. Her braids scratched against sensitive, satisfied, sunburnt skin. I couldn't remember the last time I'd been at the beach long enough to burn. If Rhyett's full lips and perfect smile hadn't wooed the girls into complacency, his immediate love of Josie's kids would've.

"Watch out, Wrenly, you've got competition," Noel muttered, chuckling when Vallie shot her a glare. She'd yet to make a move, and I was beginning to think we'd have to conspire as a group to make it happen. Josie's voice tugged me back to the topic at hand.

"He was born to be a father, Brex." She sighed, watching as he ran serpentine patterns across the sand, with both kids giggling hysterically.

"He'd be great," I agreed, sighing as Kyler's squeal of delight faded behind the constant noise of the beach. Radios fighting for attention, kids crying, vendors barking order numbers in the distance, the omnipresent crash of waves. Tourist season was so tightly packed you could barely breathe here.

But I had to give it to Rhyett; the sand was powder fine, and his assortment of picnic supplies had been happily devoured. First by us, and then by the kids. That clear blue water was the perfect temperature for swimming in the spring.

"How has nobody on that island scooped him off the market?" Vallie demanded, not bothering to lift her head. I had a feeling she'd closed her eyes, the long week wearing us all down.

"Beats me," I admitted, stomach squirming at the idea of anyone else touching him. Those gorgeous muscles and full lips. The perfect, solid half-moon of an ass. Nope, I didn't like that visual one bit.

"Genes like that, you'd think somebody would've sought him out for a litter of little gremlins, if nothing else," Josie said, taking a long drag off our last remaining water bottle before passing it back. My chest ached. Because she was right. And for the first time in my life, I...I wanted that. Forcing a laugh, I occupied my mouth with the water straw.

"Maybe I should call Jake back. He's such a good guy. I just wish I had more...I don't know, just *more*. But watching Rhyett with them...they deserve a good man in their lives."

"And you deserve someone who does more than stand in for pictures and show up when convenient. Someone you actually want to drag to bed. Don't be ridiculous."

I don't think I was alone in how my stomach flipped at Noel's uncharacteristically clipped tone.

"Uh, yeah, I know," Josie said, vocal cords tiptoeing along the looming ledge of tears.

"So, stop compromising for less than you're worth. It's annoying."

"Noel," I cautioned, reaching out for Josie's hand as her face lost its color. "What was that?"

"I'm sorry, I'm just—it's fucking hot and I'm hungry. Plus, Eric's been texting me all day, hounding me to get home, so I'll just go." She rocketed to her feet, wincing. "Sorry, Josie, it's not you, honestly. Fuck. I'm an asshole. I love you guys."

As she marched off without another word, the three of us swapped worried glances, Vallie sitting up and lifting her hand to shield her eyes as she tracked Noel's retreat. She was rocking a magenta bikini against her rich sepia skin, delicate gold necklaces sinking between generous cleavage.

"Uh...what was that?" She looked to me for an explanation, but I could only shake my head. I should go after her. Figure it out.

"I think...I think she's having problems with Eric." I hedged, nervously tiptoeing the line between honesty and unsubstantiated gossip.

"Should I go after her?" Josie offered, her eyes still heavy. "I didn't mean to—"

"It's not you, Jos," I reassured her. "Noel adores you. I'll go talk to her." Except when I jumped from my seat to head back, I locked eyes with Rhyett, his hands full of little red cardboard food containers. Two beaming kids running ahead of him. The image knocked the wind out of me. The man was picture freaking perfect.

"Mama, mama! They had fries!"

"Rite ga' us fwies!" Kyler sang happily, wiggling like he had a tail to wag. The hero of the hour dispersed his loot, before he came up shy, looking in a full circle, brow furrowing.

"Where's Noel?"

"I'M sorry you didn't catch her." Rhyett was quiet after I told him about Noel's little outburst. Of all people, Josie was the last one that needed any attitude from anyone. Especially not someone she leaned on as much as Noel.

"She'll talk to me when she's ready."

"Yeah," he agreed as he turned us onto their road. "You hungry, baby?"

I blew out a breath, patting my belly and earning a laugh when I distended it until I looked pregnant.

"Still full?"

"You let us feast all day." The yawn snuck up on me and I stretched contentedly. Hours of sunshine had soaked into my body, making my joints loose and my eyes sleepy.

"Good lord, the kids can eat."

I laughed, nodding. "Yeah, tell me about it. I watched them for a weekend over the winter so Josie could go to a conference. It's like the whole day revolves around mealtimes, snack times, and in-between-snacks snacks."

"That never stops with boys, just so you're aware."

"I'll be sure to warn Josie."

"Mom always said we about ate them out of house and home."

"With twelve?!" I teased, grinning. It still sounded outlandish to me. A dozen kids. A dozen mouths to feed. I had no idea how they'd done it. "No kidding."

"She's a drama queen."

"And I know how much six boys can put down in an hour."

"I've got a random question for you," he stated as he turned around and backed up until his tailgate nearly kissed the front of the fifth wheel.

"Hmm?"

"When you're done with your book, will you publish it?"

I blew out a long breath, eyes suddenly too heavy to have this conversation. "The truth is...I hadn't thought about it in so long, I'm not sure. I'd like that. But I don't know the first thing about querying."

"That's where you get an agent?"

"Try to, yeah."

"Ahh," Rhyett said, nodding thoughtfully. "Anything I can do to facilitate the research?"

Eyes wide, I rotated in my seat as he threw the truck in park. "You want to...help me find a publisher?"

"Hell yeah," he said, that heartbreaker's smile reminding me I was already in so much deeper than I'd ever meant to be. Shifting my gaze from the heartthrob in front of me, to the progress on the property, I let my thoughts wander as my heart scaled the walls of my throat.

The Rhodes home was fully erected now, the future landscape beds carved out and windows installed. Green grass was coloring in the expanse of the once mostly muddy ground. Rhyett's beautiful deck was finished, save for the boxes of lights sitting on the edge of the hot tub surround. He'd stained it a few days back, giving it that shiny finished look I just knew his mother would love.

He loved her, and his sisters too. Rhyett seemed to possess a sincere love for his entire, enormous family. When I was little, my father had once told me to watch how a man treated the women in his life when it came time to select suitors. He'd been right: you could tell a lot about a man by studying his interactions with sisters and cousins and the respect, or lack thereof, for his mother. I didn't need to see Rhyett with them to know how deeply he cared for them.

The evidence was everywhere. Him uprooting his life to come oversee the erection of a project thousands of miles away, in the magazine-worthy design of a backyard space big enough to accommodate them all. He'd even thought ahead to summer and engineered a way to screen in the space so the bugs didn't eat them alive. His face lit up when he talked about his sisters. Hell, I knew some of their favorite colors, their dietary preferences, their college majors. And I'd yet to see one of them, digitally or physically.

Don't even get me started on the sex—I couldn't keep up with the man, his need to feast on my body more than I could bear some nights. Is over-orgasming a thing? Because if it is, Rhyett certainly served it in heaps, leaving me breathless, a little lightheaded, and a bit dumb. He could get me to agree to just about anything in that post-coitus bliss.

Compared to my chaotic upbringing, his steady presence was so alien, I wasn't sure how to describe it. Rhyett kept his hands busy—an achiever like me. But he knew how to prioritize his time to make me feel seen and read me like a book. Saw me in a way nobody else ever did. Right down to the overwhelm of thinking about publishing. It should be comforting. But something in his rock-solid permanence scared me. Watching him play with Kyler and Gemma made my chest tighten, expectation bickering with my inner bitch, who screamed that it was all too good to be real.

"Yeah," I breathed, turning back to his sincere eyes. Hell, he'd even had the sense to just let me think, staring off into space. Just his steadily stroking hand settling on my thigh to let me know he was there. "I think...I think you'd be good at that." He cut off my reply by bringing his mouth to mine. One soft kiss, and my head was spinning, all fear of the future amputated by his touch, his scent, the way he consumed all of me. And once again, I was lost in Rhyett Rhodes.

THIRTY-NINE

RHYETT

Before I'd had time to question it, weeks bled into a month. The hour wedged between us had been traded for laughter and blow jobs and slipping my fingers under her skirt to find her soaked and waiting. Long days of labor punctuated by the delicate feminine scent of desire in the cab. Enough to drive even the best man to the brink of madness. My favorite days were the ones when Brexley would jump into my truck with the latest pages she'd penned in hand. She'd read me some of it. The pieces she said I'd inspired. No woman had ever put me in a book before. Even if it was just pieces of me. I mean, no one that I knew of anyways. I winced at the thought of my earlier years flitting from fling to fling.

The heat of Florida spring had darkened my skin, now a rich caramel tan to rival Brexley's. Hell, even Noel's skin was kissed with it, her freckles out in full force. She was cute as hell, and some profoundly male part of me wondered if I could dissuade her from her weasel of a boyfriend into the arms of someone closer to being worthy. My younger brother, Axel, or maybe our cousin, Jake? Maybe it was knowing she was biased towards *Team Rhyett,* although I didn't think so. Her cast had come off last week, and the girls invited me along for celebratory drinks. I sneakily snatched the bill before any of the sharp-witted, self-made millennial women could object. 'The girls,' I'd learned, received my offers to pay for things with the same enthusiasm as buying a timeshare in Antarctica. My stealth mode paid off, although Josie's glare matched Noel's tone as she told me they'd get mine next time.

Windows down, music blasting, Brex started to sing along to "She's Always A Woman" by Billy Joel. I grinned, loving the fact that she turned her face into that Florida sun she was so determined to loathe. She had a terrible voice. I mean, sometimes it was nice, in the way a mother's voice is nice as she hums melodies to get her baby to sleep. This song was mellow enough that she'd fool someone who didn't know better. But in general, she reached for notes out of range and fell flat more often than not. I fucking loved it. Because she was free to be herself in that truck cab. With me. Free to be silly and imperfect and to...well...*sing*. I might have been reading too much into it, but I doubted Brexley had ever sung for anyone. It wasn't in her nature.

But she sang for me.

We parked in the shade beneath the copse of trees beside the trailer, then made our way around to the now graveled path to the front door. Royal lazily lifted her head from where she basked in the late evening sun. The so-called retriever was unwilling to abandon her rabbits. Honestly, I wasn't entirely convinced she was actually a dog.

Brexley was spending most of her evenings camped out on the Rhodes property. Hell, she'd helped me hang the patio lights last month. Was my right-hand lady while we installed fencing all weekend to pen in the soon-to-arrive cattle she'd dubbed Hank and Frankie.

"You can't name your food," I protested, wiping sweat from my forehead. She just glared at me, swiping between the photos of the first two animals secured for the property.

"Hank." She showed me the Angus I'd hand-selected myself. "Frankie." His hopeful first mate. Bemused, I shook my head as sweat stung my eyes. Working beside Brexley was like outrunning one of the billowing storm clouds that blew in here. You knew your time was limited. Beautiful fury on the horizon. She'd lasted twenty-five minutes after my sopping shirt hit the dirt before she was in my arms. Devouring her mouth, I dropped the shovel, exchanging it for my girl. She was up and around my waist in a heartbeat, kissing back as fiercely as she took it. The contractors brought our union to a halt with their catcalls and applause. I flipped them the bird, earning a chorus of laughter as she found her feet.

"You're mine when they leave," she promised, cupping my erection through the denim. I groaned, fighting the desire to grind into her open palm. I could give a shit less about ears too close. I wanted her...lusty, naughty, right here and now. Brexley shook her head like my intentions were plastered over my face.

"Get to work!" I barked over her shoulder. More laughter mingled through the chaos of construction.

THE FAMILIAR TAP of her keyboard caught my attention as I stepped out of the shower. It had become a comforting reassurance over the last few weeks, her ceaseless work towards that long-buried dream like a balm after long days. Dry and dressed, I'd just finished tidying my stubble line when I realized it had gone silent.

"Brex? Baby?" Silence answered my call. "Brex?" When she still didn't respond, my heart sprinted from zero to jackhammer in half a second. Popping through the pocket doorway, I saw an empty living room and whipped my head to the bedroom.

Empty.

Breathing kicking up, I danced down the stairs, peripheral vision halting my feet before logic could catch up. She was sitting out on the deck, staring back at the property with a focus on her face. I hustled down the steps of the trailer, stepping onto the smooth, warm wood surface with bare feet. Her attention had shifted, now seemingly preoccupied with the erratic movements of a courageous little lizard as he came to assess the newcomers.

Cautiously, I hedged, "Brex?" When her eyes turned to me, brimming with emotion, I rushed to her side and pulled her against me. When she buried her watery eyes against my shoulder, I prompted, "Baby, what happened?"

She hoisted the laptop off the cushion beside her, swallowing audibly. "I did it."

RHYETT

Brexley finished her book yesterday.

JAMESON

Too bad she didn't finish you.

RHYETT

Watch your mouth, asshole.

ELORA

James, ew.

Rhyett! That's amazing. How's she feel about it?

RHYETT

She's been pretty emotional. Ordered a printed copy
to edit with.

HADLEE

So exciting! Does she think she'll publish?

RHYETT

We're navigating everything one step at a time.

PAXTON

We're?

RHYETT

That's what I said.

PAXTON

I know. There's a 'we're'?

RHYETT

Oh. Uh, yeah. I think there is.

ELORA

Good relationships are built on clear communication,
Rhyett. Are you communicating?

JAMESON

Fuck off, Dr. Phil. He's got this.

LEIGHTON

El is right. Have you tossed around the g-word and the
b-word?

MAVERICK

Gorgonzola and bacon

RHYETT

Jesus

MAVERICK

What? I'm hungry. Ordering pizza.

ALESSANDRA

Okay, I caught up. Congratulations Brexley. I can't
wait to read it. Maverick. Dear God, are you always
hungry? James. WTF. *barfing emoji*

AXEL

So. There's a WE?

. . .

I LEFT Axel's message on read, forehead aching from how deeply it had furrowed. Brex had headed into the city for work this morning with a sappy smile on her face. Euphoria was the closest word the English language had to her energy as she headed to work to tell Noel. Rubbing my forehead, I looked up at the house, the comforting rhythm of a hammer against wood beckoning me forward. Between the property and the bar, my life had been a consecutive cacophony of chaos. Sawdust and paint ribbons peeled off my boots. Brex brought a radiant glow to the cracks of time between. Stolen kisses, and shared cups of sugar-laden coffee, quickies when the last contractors left, or we retreated to her townhouse.

My boots scuffed across the concrete front walk. Electric saws buzzed, hammers cracked against their targets, men barked amongst themselves, a boombox blaring somewhere upstairs. I smiled. The boat was its own song, but something about an active project site was a symphony. The challenge of contractors weaving around each other was music to my fucking ears.

"Afternoon Ed!" A heartbeat later, the man materialized. White beard and weathered skin from years in the sun, Ed and his happy beer belly meandered around the corner.

"Afternoon, Mr. Rhodes. I need you to sign off on the master tub and the powder room sinks today. Double check the brickwork out front, or forever hold your peace."

"Sounds good, Ed. How's the granite?"

"Looking good, kid. Come on in. I'll give you the progress report."

"YOU THINK THINGS ARE THAT SERIOUS?" The disbelief in Broderick's tone wasn't entirely unexpected, but it still made me pause. Perhaps I was leaving too much unsaid between Brexley and me. But everything in my gut felt so...sure. In her. In us. In the way she made me feel. In how she looked on my property or draped across my bed.

"She might be it for me."

"Excuse-fucking-me?"

I laughed, making my way through the crowd, snaking between vendors and tourists alike. The walk was bustling with more people than should physically be able to fit on it, but the energy was electric, addicting and invigorating. Life. It was an overwhelming abundance of life. I freaking loved it.

"I mean it, man." The low whistle on the opposite end of the phone brought a smile to my face. "Is that too soon? Are there rules I'm missing?"

"Fuck me, like I know? My track record looks about like yours."

I blew out a long breath, trying to hide my wince. "How are things, by the way?"

"We broke up," he said, his tone giving nothing away.

"Ah man, I'm sorry."

"No, you're not." He chuckled knowingly.

"No," I admitted sheepishly. "I'm not. She wasn't good enough for you."

"You say that like I've earned anybody putting up with my ass indefinitely."

"Only an idiot wouldn't see what you have to offer."

"Are you propositioning me?" he teased. That was good. He wasn't too bent outta shape about it.

"You'll have to take that up with Brexley."

"I have a feeling you'll be otherwise engaged."

"Yeah," I breathed, drifting off as I spotted her through the throngs of people.

"Oh man, you found her."

"Hmm?"

His rumble of a laugh rattled the phone. "Go get her, man."

"Yeah," I breathed, eyes tracing up and down the lines of my girl. "Yeah, okay. We'll talk later?"

"You got it." The line dropped, and I slid my phone away.

The sight of Brexley Snows in a dress the color of Alaskan forget-me-nots, her blonde hair brushing the tight curve of her ass as she leaned onto the railing of the pier, was enough to make a man lose his mind. She'd invited me into the city to watch a spring festival consisting entirely of maritime merriment—her words, not mine.

"It's exactly the kind of dopey small-town thing you love," she explained. "They bring ships in from all over the world—some date back to the eighteen hundreds. Big white sails like pirate ships. You'll love it."

She was right. I did. After twenty years on the water, the history of the vessels was unbelievable. Although not nearly as surreal as the dainty dream leaning on the metal rail of the pier to watch them, balanced precariously on her tiptoes, one foot kicked in the air. I'd rather not think about the fact that every man around had a view of her perfect perky ass in that dress, so I focused instead on the fact that she was grinning as a ship sailed by. My heart did that thing where it suddenly developed two left feet, stumbling forward. They were as glorious as she'd said they would be. But she dwarfed them with her beauty tenfold.

Unable to keep the smile from my face, I caged her against the rail, setting a hand beside each of hers and pressing my hips to her ass. Suddenly, her position on the rail was totally excusable since she fit me better than a freaking glove. Brex whipped her face around, meeting my mouth as I lowered to take her in a kiss, threading my fingers into her hair a heartbeat later. I couldn't pull her close enough. Couldn't tighten my grip enough. Couldn't *get enough.*

"Hey, beautiful," I breathed, loving that I'd stolen the air from her.

Finally, she sucked down a breath. "Hey, Hotshot." She turned her face back to the water, studying the countless boats as they casually drifted down the bay. "Beautiful, isn't it?"

"Yeah," I agreed, keeping my eyes locked on her profile, memorizing her face. The sharp line of her nose. Full pout of her lips. "Beautiful."

Perfect mouth parted, Brexley turned to find me staring. *I'm in love with you.* I wanted to say it. Wanted to declare that I'd found my person to anyone within radius to hear it. But the odds of that being received and not scaring the daylights out of her was slim to none. Brexley would have to say it first. Have to finalize this thing between us. Or she'd spook. Even though the look in her eyes told me she already knew it too. Tonight was expertly crafted, partly due to my willingness to collaborate with Noel and Josie, who'd helped me put everything in place.

All I could do was follow the plan and hope it was enough.

FORTY

BREXLEY

Rhyett had evasively told me he had a plan for after the parade and our walk through the peaked white tents of the festival. The city had been flooded with vendors and artists, all bustling through the makeshift market celebrating stunning displays of ships of every size, age, and shape. Sails as colorful as the patrons on the promenade whipped in the wind, boats softly bobbing in the water. Eighty-three degrees and breezy, the perfect Florida day for thousands of tourists to suck the marrow out of our people in exchange for fuller tills for our businesses. A worthwhile trade? To be determined.

Trying not to think about the sweat cascading down my body, pooling in my palm where it was pressed into Rhyett's big hand, I followed him through the crowd as the sun set beyond the bay. Warm strips of orange and strawberry red settled over the horizon, spotted with cotton clouds promising a spring rain sometime tonight.

What had at one point been a silky, blown-out hairstyle was now a stringy, frizzy mess, inflated by the humidity like a static cloud. The moment we got wherever we were going, I'd have to sneak away and smooth it back into a braid or a bun at the nape of my neck. Something, *anything* to get it off my skin, where it had been plastered by the sticky substance someone at one point deemed 'air'. That was a blatant lie, but who cared now?

Rhyett's sunbeam of a smile caught my attention, drawing my thoughts of sticky skin to a very different variety. Naturally, he was grinning at a vendor, a beat before she waltzed forward to grasp his hand with a familiarity only Rhyett could inspire in a stranger. A busty middle-aged blonde in an impeccable dress with petite black heels.

"Do you two know each other?" I asked, despite my passionate belief that they did not.

"Nope!" Ahh, there it was. Couldn't take the man anywhere without him finding friends. Seriously, we'd gone to the farmers market, and he'd filled his phone with contacts like he'd arrived to collect people rather than produce. "We just spoke over the phone. Debbie, this is Brexley. Brex, meet Debbie."

Accepting the woman's shake, I did my best to mime a smile, trying not to suffocate in the crowd of bustling bodies. It wasn't even summer yet—a thought that had me internally groaning. "Nice to meet you."

"The pleasure is all mine. Now, if you two will follow me," she said, motioning with some secret implication behind her.

I tugged on Rhyett's hand, dropping my voice. "We're following a stranger through a festival *why...?*"

"Come on, Ace." Okay, sometimes the smile was just obnoxious. How the fuck was I supposed to say no to *that*? Had the bay not been overflowing with boats, I might have fancied a swim over either of their company. Regardless of my need to strip the sticky sweat from my skin, I followed in his wake, cursing the grin that would make me do anything shy of prancing in front of a crowd in my skivvies.

"Rhyett," I hissed under my breath as he all but dragged me, zig-zagging between bodies in various degrees of celebration or exhaustion. Screaming children were melting onto the pavement—rightly so—while musicians played loudly across the packed promenade. "What are we doing?"

"Come on, Ace," he repeated simply, squeezing my fingers.

"I am coming," I said back, a bit louder than intended. Rhyett smirked back at me, somehow glorious in the thin sheen of sweat across his golden skin, whereas I felt like a drowned rat. The heat in his eyes told me I was in trouble.

"Not yet, you're not."

Oh fuck, that was louder than strictly necessary. Eyes singed my skin everywhere. While that was probably just crowd anxiety, I couldn't help the way my flesh tingled with the buzz of activity. When Rhyett stopped, he did it so suddenly I nearly slammed into his broad back. But then he turned, pressing a kiss to my forehead and motioning me to follow Debbie, the stranger, onto...*oh my God.*

She had just walked up a gangplank on what could only be

described as a ship from *Pirates of The Caribbean.* My mouth fell open as I watched Debbie's black kitten heels vanish onto the boat's bright deck.

"Rhyett," I whispered, like my confusion was somehow top secret. "What on Earth is going on?"

"Go find out, beautiful," he said simply, jerking his chin towards the plank. I narrowed my eyes, a tangle of fear and thrill in my chest. Was this a boat tour? What was happening? Opting to trust him, I sucked down a breath and walked up the ramp, resisting the screaming urge to throw my arms out like wings for balance.

"I've got you, baby." Rhyett's voice skimmed along my ear, tickling my neck. Like he saw the fear in my body as I eyed the splashing waves below us and wanted to reassure me. His hand came to hover at my low back, sending warmth and a jolt of confidence through my belly.

When we reached the top of the plank, he moved up beside me, except I was too preoccupied with trying to make sense of what I was seeing. The deck had been strung with bright bulb lights overhead, swaying gently in the breeze, and with twinkle lights up the masts and across the rails. The tables were scattered across the space, with white linen cloths and crystal wine glasses, a single red rose bejeweling each vase in the center.

"Welcome to our dinner cruise," Debbie said proudly, motioning to the tables. "You can take your pick, Mr. Rhodes."

"Thanks, Debbie, everything looks amazing." Rhyett nodded politely before pulling me to the front of the boat. *Gaping.* I was still gaping. When he pulled the black chair out for me to sit, a nervous laugh broke free.

"Oh, you're good," I said conspiratorially. "Nicely done, sir."

"I thought some distance from the crowd would be more your speed."

"You're not wrong."

"That's close enough to being right for me."

I laughed, shaking my head and running my fingers through my hair, wishing I'd had a second to refresh for him. When the waiter arrived with ice water and a chilled bottle of house champagne, I held it together long enough to cover my mouth and try not to hyperventilate.

His laughter was warmer than the last rays of sunshine peeking through the clouds on the horizon. "Is that good panic, or I'm a despicable bastard that needs to get you off the damn boat panic?"

"Good," I breathed. "I've never been on a pirate ship," I squeaked, staring up at the enormous, billowing black sails.

"What do you think?"

"So far, so good. I like how soft the bobbing is, hopefully it won't ruin dinner. It's so...big." His arched brow had me rolling my eyes. "The boat, smartass."

"Oh good, I was going to say—*decorum*, Brexley." He reached for the champagne, pouring us each a flute.

"Har har har." I shook my head. "What is all this, Rhyett?" I gestured to our beautiful surroundings.

"Your birthday dinner."

That brought me up short, breath halting as my lips popped open. "It's not my birthday," I said softly.

"No. But it was, and you didn't even bother to tell me."

"I prefer it that way."

"What way?"

"Quiet. We didn't really do birthdays."

"Didn't *do* birthdays?" he balked, like that was the most horrifying thing he'd ever heard. I shrugged.

"They just aren't a big deal in my family. My mom was gone and my dad was working and neither had time to arrange anything."

"Well. That's fucked up," he said bluntly. I laughed. Rhyett was many things, but subtle definitely wasn't one of them. "I'd like to remedy that, beautiful. If you'll let me. Don't keep that stuff from me —you deserve to be pampered."

It was suddenly immensely difficult to swallow. "How'd you pull this off?"

"Looked to see what kind of activities were tied to the festival."

"And landed on a dinner cruise?"

"Among a few others."

"Others?!" I demanded, reaching for the chilled water, and thanking high heaven when my skin made contact with the slick surface. I could have taken a bath in that. Another couple followed Debbie onto the deck, right as the musicians arrived beside the instruments propped in the corner. When they sat down to play, I returned to my too-sexy-for-his-own-good date. I wanted to sneak away and rip that sharp button-up off his hard chest so I could taste him. Sketch his abs with the tip of my tongue. Have him buried in me. If I hadn't been so damn hungry, the desire to steal away would've ruined all his big plans.

Rhyett's eyes darkened, and he shook his head before taking a sip from the crystal flute. "Keep looking at me like that, Brexley Snows, and we'll have a problem."

"*Decorum*, Mr. Rhodes," I teased, swapping my water for bubbles.

"You look beautiful tonight, baby. I know I told you, but, God. Sometimes I need to pinch myself."

My laugh escaped before I could contain it. "Oh, now I know you're just trying to get lucky. I'm a sweaty mess."

"Kind of how I like you most. Soaking wet."

"Naughty," I said, running my teeth across my lip.

"I'll show you naughty."

"Big words for a man stranded on a boat deck."

Rhyett's jaw popped open for a beat before he tongued at a molar, shaking his head. When he went to sip his champagne, it was on the tail end of a very long breath. "I can get creative. Don't tempt me, baby." Rhyett leaned forward, bracing his elbows on the table and spinning the flute on its base. "Trust me when I tell you I've already pictured you bent over the railing. Clutching the spindles for dear life while I do a little railing of my own." My mouth suddenly went dry, heart in my throat as my core clenched. So, I turned to trusty alcohol to buy me some brain cells. Only, he wasn't even done. "As a matter of fact, I can picture the look on your face if I tugged you over to my side. I could slip right under that little blue dress, Ace. Nobody could see what my hands were doing to you beneath the tablecloth. I have an excellent poker face. Do you?"

I squirmed in my seat, enamored with the hunger in his eyes as wet heat pooled between my thighs. "That...that should not turn me on."

He chuckled. "But it does."

Glass empty, I nodded, trying my best to swallow as he grabbed the champagne and refilled mine.

"Good," he said confidently. "Because it isn't our location holding me back."

"No?" It was supposed to be strong. Supposed to be a challenge, but it came out eagerly. A headiness settled between us as terror and arousal wrapped around me, pushing my heart rate as desire pooled between my legs. Frantically, my gaze darted around, ensuring no one was within earshot.

"I want to hear you scream my name," he said, casually running fingers up my arm. The man's face said we could have been discussing the ship, but I didn't miss his satisfied smirk as goosebumps speckled my skin. He leaned forward until our cheeks met, his words hot against my ear. "Want to feel you tremble beneath me as I fill you with cum and know that you're mine." His low voice and smooth touch hardened my nipples to needy peaks against the dress. What I would have given to be home, to have him suck them into his mouth. "I want you to think that through until I get you off...this damned boat," he added, quirking his brow. The waiter returned then, salads in his hand with an assortment of dressing. I stared out at the water a little too intently, wishing I could control the flush in my cheeks and neck. I was burning alive. And for once in my life, it wasn't the fault of the freaking Florida sun. He'd been outshone by an Alaskan entrepreneur with a smile just as radiant.

"Fuck," I gasped as the server stepped out of earshot.

"Soon, baby," Rhyett promised darkly.

How could he have swagger holding still? It made literally no sense, but he did, braced against the table. The next courses were a blur—all impeccable selections of soup with sourdough, steak with seasonal veggies, and a New York cheesecake a woman would murder for during certain weeks of the month. They might as well have been properly portioned pools of sawdust for how much atten-tion I gave them. My mouth was watering, but it was for the memory of his cock and the promise in his words. All the while, Rhyett ran agonizing lines up and down my leg beneath the table, fingers just tracing the crease where my thigh met my hip before retreating. His endless teasing was driving me mad.

I felt nothing but relief when we made our way off the deck and back to the ferry to Rhyett's car. Nothing but relief as his truck lights flashed when he pressed the button on the fob. Because tonight, after an evening enjoying fine dining and an unbeatable atmosphere, I got to go home and enjoy Rhyett Rhodes.

"I think…you drained out…all my brain cells."

Sweat rolled down my arms as I hit the bed on a breathless laugh. "That's…a distinct possibility," I panted in a lust-filled haze.

"Can't…feel my legs…everything is tingling."

"Good, maybe you'll sleep."

Brexley's hand limply landed on my chest. When I turned to look at her, her eyes were mostly lidded, like she couldn't quite summon the energy to open them.

"What was that?"

"Too tired…to hit you."

"Five orgasms, and that's how you thank me?"

"Shhhh," she hissed. "I'm delightful."

The distinct sensation of muscle fatigue fought my attempt at a smile. Was it possible to over-smile? Smile overdose? If that was a thing, Brexley had made me achieve it. Hell, I didn't think I could get hard again if I fucking tried. She'd drained me dry, and to my immense satisfaction, it seemed like I'd done the same to her.

When my skin had cooled, I rolled over on my side, dragging her back against me. Her satisfied hum was a balm my soul never knew it needed. Paired with her perky little ass wiggling back against my still naked groin, I was in the kind of heaven men only dream of.

"Goodnight, Ace."

"Hmnm."

I exhaled a light chuckle, nuzzling tighter against her as we melted into the pillow-top mattress, her neck draped over my bicep and belly rising and falling in relaxed little swells beneath the opposite arm. This was what serenity felt like. The quiet moments stolen away from the hustle of the city and the grind of work. The breaths between orders and inventory.

Speakeasy a few weeks from being up and running, the estate on its heels, and Brex's novel in the second round of edits with Noel, life felt like it was barreling on forward. I lived for the quiet reprieve these days.

For the caress of her exhale tickling the hair across my arm. The goosebumps that lined her tan skin when she came on my hand. The breath before a moan and the demand it held over my body. Or the rich sound of her gasp as she wrote and thought of something genius. Brexley brought a bright flame to life, the kind that warmed a space and made it feel like home—a home I could see welcoming children in, raising them up to be incredible Rhodes. For the first time in my life, I could imagine what that future would look like. What it would look like *with her*. And the best part was I'd never expected to find that. Certainly not here.

When her body finally liquified into sleep in my arms, I nuzzled against her neck and breathed, "I love you, Brexley Snows."

THE METALLIC CLANG of the aluminum door slamming shut jerked me from a dead sleep, sending me jackknifing off the mattress. I'd been down here for enough time to know it took a good deal of effort to slam the damn thing.

"I'm armed!" I bellowed, lunging across Brexley for the gun safe by our bed, and barreling out of our room, gun trained on the floor as adrenaline rushed through my veins. Sleep still blurring my vision, I ran down the three stairs, cursing as a familiar cacophony filled my ears.

"Keep your pants on, big guy!"

"Jesus, Jameson," I growled as I ambled around the corner, rubbing at the crick in my neck from jolting upright and cursing my nosy siblings with their impromptu arrival. Because where one went, the others would *inevitably* follow.

Blinking bleary eyes, I meandered into the tight kitchen, entirely unsurprised to see every available seat filled. Standard Rhodes protocol: invade, occupy, improve, move on, usually leaving some inevitable piece of clothing behind. Jameson was standing over the stove, a stack of Rhodes' family buttermilk pancakes towering precariously on the island behind him. His dark hair was a touch longer than when I'd left, beard in its usual unkempt state. Elora was typing away at the long tabletop I'd installed along the back of the rig, legs crisscrossed in the scoop seat bar stool, with bulky headphones punctuating her short, golden-brown hair. Entirely oblivious to the fact that they'd just scared the daylights out of me. I turned my attention back to the prick at the stove.

"Trying to get yourself killed?"

"And here I thought a pancake breakfast would be a nice way to wake up." My asshole of a brother turned to face me, his chest bare except for the towel tossed over his shoulder. I attempted to blink the sleep away as his eyes widened, head canting. Jameson's fuzzy face twisted into the most irritatingly arrogant smirk, pointedly scanning me from head to toe.

"Maybe you're a little...too excited to see me." Jameson's brow arch, that said I-have-dirt-on-Rhyett, was the point at which I realized what was so fucking funny. The air conditioner came to life just in time for the cold to brush over my *still-naked* ass.

"Jesus. Fuck," I growled, dropping a hand from my pistol to cover my morning wood. A particularly vivid dream about Brexley had been so rudely interrupted.

"I thought I told you to keep your pants on," he jabbed as I turned around. Alice was curled up against the sofa with a book in her lap, long, dark locks swept back into a braid. She didn't bother to look up from her reading, wordlessly hoisting a pillow into the air, which I snatched to cover myself with.

Royal was sprawled out beside her, belly up and head pressed against the side of her thigh. Mav, humming under his breath, sat on the opposite side of the couch, scrolling on his phone, blessedly oblivious. The singing was an omnipresent habit he'd picked up somewhere between first and second grade and never gotten rid of. His brown curls stuck out from under the cap he had on backwards.

"Thanks, Alice," I grumbled, lumbering back to my bedroom as Jameson burst into maniacal laughter.

I returned the gun to the safe, cursing the jackass as my girl stirred awake to the sound of his resounding humor.

"'S happening?" Brex mumbled, blinking into the gloom of the trailer's master, long legs stretching out towards the window as she stretched and rotated to her side.

"Nothing, baby, go back to sleep." I tossed the sheets more

securely across her mouthwatering, naked body. I'd had plans for our morning, and my siblings in my kitchen certainly weren't part of it.

I jerked on my sweats, snatching my shirt from the floor. With one last glance as her eyes drifted shut, I closed the door with a click.

"You're out of milk," Jameson's voice trailed back as someone started the stereo. Jack Johnson's "Better Together" started over the trailer speakers. The front door creaked open again, and I made a mental note to pick up some W-D-40 from the hardware store.

"Have you seen the bunnies?!" Hadlee. My little sister's voice greeted me a moment before she came bounding in the door with a grin stretching her face. Hads was the smallest of my sisters, clocking in around five foot three and a hundred and ten pounds if she was soaking wet and wearing a winter jacket. She made up for her size with an attitude big enough to make boat captains squirm. Underneath the sass was a heart of gold. Conveniently, the same color as her long, wavy hair.

Her smile twisted into a knowing, mischievous smirk when she spotted me. The same one she constantly plastered on when she was up to no good. We'd called her Hurricane Hadlee as a toddler, due to her supreme ability to remove every single jar, piece of Tupperware, pot, pan, and wooden spoon in the kitchen within thirty seconds or less. The smile only reinforced the moniker.

"Rhy! This place is amazing!" She slammed into me with the force of a linebacker, and I laughed as I caught her, hoisting her off the ground. Petite arms snaked around my neck. "You didn't tell me we have *bunnies!*"

"All of Florida seems to have bunnies, Hads."

"*So cute.*" She smacked a wet kiss on my cheek, and I laughed, lowering her to the ground to wipe my face. "You look good, Rhy. Happy. Sleepy. Want some tea?"

"Uh, yeah, thanks."

"I brought a new chai blend. You're gonna love it. It's on the counter."

I poured myself a cup of Hadlee's tea from the French press, emptying it to make coffee for Brex, who would undoubtedly not sleep long with this level of energy in our tiny space. Camera in hand, laptop tucked beneath her arm, Hadlee reappeared from the small middle room I used as an office, making a beeline to the bar stool beside Elora.

"How's the blog?" I asked, as she passed by.

"Busy!" She chirped happily. "I've got two shoots and about a week's worth of road posts to catch up on." Hadlee's passion for travel had entangled effortlessly with a knack for capturing authentic portraits and weaving stories with words. Her travel blog had built up through college and took off in the last year, complete with advertising deals and sponsors sending her free boots, tents, and tools that made life on the road a bit easier. She lived for the adventure.

"Good, sis. Good." I focused on my tea as Jameson slid another pancake onto the castle of breakfast carbs. If Jameson was in charge, there'd be enough sugar in there to satisfy a small herd of horses. He didn't bother to vocalize as he turned back to the stove, his inked chest already sweaty, shirt tucked in a back pocket. We were just missing Jeanne, Paxton, Axel, Finn, the twins, and our parents. Parents, who I assumed were up examining the new house or peppering Ed with this morning's edition of twenty questions. *Good luck, Ed.* Flicking my eyes to the bedroom, where I swore I'd heard a creak of floorboards, I looked back with a scowl on my face.

"Clothe yourself, jackass."

"Oil splatter, asshole."

Rolling my eyes, I poured the coffee grounds into the French press as the kettle whistled. "Because oil burns are better than stains?"

"It's fucking hot here, okay. Milo is crazy, letting that woman drag his ass into the third circle of hell. This level's penance? The creatures of *Jumanji.*"

"You've been here for what, an hour?" I said, laughing. Absolutely sure I'd heard a shift in the bedroom this time, I poured the water and turned for a mug.

"I swear to God, I saw a mosquito the size of my palm this morning. Those little lizard things are fucking everywhere."

"They're adorable," Hadlee crooned, not bothering to look up from her work.

"Tell me that when you're foaming from the mouth, Hads. I'm going to have nightmares about them crawling over me."

"Has anyone reminded you you're a freaking baby?" Elora piped up, glaring at Jameson as he flopped another pancake onto the pile. "They're lizards, not rabid rats."

Five minutes surrounded in their chaos, and my cheeks already hurt from smiling. "Seriously though? When the hell did you get in? You're like locusts."

"You know what it's like getting anywhere from that godforsaken rock," Alice grumbled. Flying in and out of a remote island prone to thick fog and rain was a bit like playing roulette. Some days you could leave, some you couldn't without any idea of which one your tickets were booked on. From there, it was usually two, three, or four connections to get anywhere in the lower forty-eight. Red eyes were a give-in. Overnight layovers, even more so.

"Bright and early, with no sleep in between?" I insinuated, earning a wink from Alice before she refocused on her book.

I'd just plated a stack of pancakes with peanut butter and maple syrup when the master opened. Brex wore my t-shirt and not much else, her hair disheveled. I swooped up to her in a heartbeat, abandoning breakfast on the way.

"Good morning, beautiful," I said, scooping her up for a morning kiss and loving the hum of contentment before she went stiff, peering over my shoulder. I didn't have to look to know everyone had halted to survey the newcomer. "The Rhodes have descended," I murmured apologetically.

"I—uh—see that," she said, lowering onto flat feet and flitting into the bathroom where she frantically combed fingers through her blonde waves. A throat cleared behind me, and I peered back to see Mav and Jameson holding up ten fingers with satisfied expressions carved on their faces. These fucking guys. Slight relief that Axel had stayed behind, and Finn was too busy being Finn to add to their stupidity. I mimed slicing my throat while glowering down at them and barely holding back a laugh as they both darted back to their respective places. How much of her could they have possibly peeked around my bulky fucking frame? The hallway was only like two feet wide.

"I'll, um, just get dressed if that's cool?" Brex grimaced at her reflection, splashing cold water on her face.

"Of course, baby, I've got breakfast for you. Do you want to come meet everyone or get a cup of coffee down first?"

"In a space this small?" she balked quietly. "I think I'd better get it over with, don't you?"

"They might burst through the bedroom door if you don't," I admitted. Something like a smile played at the edge of her nervous lips.

FORTY-TWO
BREXLEY

BREXLEY

The Rhodes are in town today. Girls' night tonight?

VALLIE

I'm in.

JOSIE

Let me confirm with the sitter, and I'll get right back to you guys.

NOEL

Hey, I'm sorry. I've got to pass.

BREXLEY

What?

NOEL

Eric wants time together.

VALLIE

Eric gets you all week. Come out with us.

NOEL

Sorry guys.

JOSIE

I'm out too, sorry.

VALLIE

That's okay. Brex, raincheck? We can shoot for next week.

"Nah, nah, nah, horses first," Alessandra insisted, tossing her braid over a shoulder. The Rhodes siblings looked like they'd been put through a clone machine with minimal input for changes. Alessandra—Alice—was the darkest in coloring, her olive skin complimented by dark hair. But her features were so similar to her siblings, all of whom possessed varying versions of those steely blue eyes I loved on Rhyett. They'd all gathered around the island before dividing to conquer different things. Rhyett had placed the Formica sink cover, extending the countertop so they could sprawl out the remaining plans for the homestead.

"What's the point in living on land like this if we don't have horses?"

"How are you going to monetize *horses*, Alice? We need to focus on the steps that generate income first and add on the frivolous things afterwards."

"Frivolous?" she squeaked, rolling her eyes at Jameson, who was still working on his third plate of pancakes. Jameson was the closest in coloring to his debate partner. His coffee-brown hair was a finger's width longer than Rhyett's and tossed in that devil-may-care kind of rugged appeal women went crazy for. He shrugged as though his prior statement was enough information. The man had yet to put on his shirt.

"How are horses frivolous, but a dirt bike course is on par?" Alice demanded, spearing another bite of pancake with disproportionate ferocity. I wasn't sure what the platter of food had done to offend her, but it was indeed paying the price.

"Do you know what people pay to go dirt biking for a day?"

"Do you know what people pay to get horseback lessons?"

My eyes continuously flicked back to Rhyett; he was draped against the sofa behind me, rubbing a thumb between his eyes in equal parts amusement and irritation as the debates continued.

"The ROI will be higher on the bikes. They're easier to get into. Don't require the maintenance of livestock."

"Because no dirt bike requires maintenance," Alice snarled back, shaking her head. "You think you're so clever, don't you?"

"Well, someone had to get the brains of the family."

"Oh fuck off, like dirt movers are cheap."

"No," Rhyett sighed behind me. "They're not. But neither are horses, Alice. As it is, we're still on track for chickens, goats, and hogs first. We've got a few cattle lined up. They're the easiest animals to start making some money with—eggs, chicks, pork, milk and eventually, beef. The garden was fully framed last week, and the first round of seeds went in on Monday. Crops start next year."

Jameson waved his arm like he was presenting Rhyett to a game show crowd. "See. *Sense.*"

"He doesn't like your idea either, dumbass."

"He—"

Jameson's retort was cut off by the creak and slam of the front door as Elora and Hadlee made their way back inside, shifting the trailer beneath their onboarding.

"Have you guys seen the deck Rhy built us?!" If Alice was the baby of the bunch, Hadlee was the designated ray of sunshine. Everything she said or did seemed to come through in a burst of light. Enthusiasm, embodied. "It's immaculate. Mom's gonna flip if Daddy can't get her out of that damn house."

"She discovered *the stove*, Rhy," Elora said with significance, as though that explained everything.

"Poor Ed," Rhyett said with a chuckle.

"Poor Ed," the siblings echoed. I laughed, turning up to look at Rhyett's crooked grin as he shook his head. I'd have to ask about that story at a different time.

"Should we show them all the house? Go save Ed from Juniper?" He asked, eyes only for me. Rhyett had a way of focusing on me no matter how much chaos consumed the oxygen around us. From the festival of ships to a trailer full of energetic siblings, he made me feel like the world rose and fell at my feet. It was unnerving. It was comforting. Some blended combination of the two made my stomach do violent somersaults.

I nodded, sliding off his lap and reaching for him as he rose. Hand in hand, we led the way back outside.

WHILE THE PROGRESS had been elegantly apparent from the front of the house, it was almost startling within. Another month and Ed's crew would be down to the very final touches. A thin layer of dust still coated every surface, stray fragments of blue painter's tape crunching underfoot as did the occasional nail. Though overall, the walls no longer felt like a skeleton, but the beginnings of a genuine home. The empty tile floors, however, echoed every footfall, every squeal of delight as the girls soaked up esthetic or satisfied curses as the men inspected the handiwork.

Maverick, the youngest of the brood, had a set of Bluetooth headphones in his ears that evidently muffled everything the rest of us could hear, his throaty voice quietly singing "Mr. Blue Sky" by Electric Light Orchestra as he followed behind us.

"This needs to be larger," a woman's voice carried to us from what could only have been the kitchen. "At least another foot, if we're going to have room for everyone. There's absolutely no way we'll all fit. And what happens when they get married? Have kids? I need a space for grandkids here, Ed. We can't just separate half the family like a cramped mausoleum, here. The weirdos don't get dumped outside the family crypt."

"Mom, you're not torturing Ed, are you?" Rhyett called as we rounded the kitchen corner. The room was positively radiant with natural light, an enormous picture window across from the counter filling the entire space with a warm yellow glow.

"Rhyett," Juniper crooned, handing her husband her bag and throwing herself around her son, who gave my hand a squeeze before releasing it to return her enthusiasm. "Baby, how are you? God, we miss you up there, sweetie. Are things good? How's the bar coming along? Oh! Ed, you know my son? This is Rhyett."

Ed, who proudly displayed his weekend beer-with-buddies habit in the form of a little pot belly, and too much color in his cheeks, chuckled, evidently still in good spirits after the endless interrogation of his morning. Rhyett rolled his eyes, but there was a deep kind of fondness around them as he squeezed her back to his chest.

"Yes, Mom, Ed is acquainted with the man living on site."

"Right, right, of course. I'm not sure where my brain is at today. There's so much to do—to see! Are you okay? How's it been down here on your own? How's Brexley?"

I straightened at my name, eyes flicking up to Rhyett's as his smile broadened. "I'm good, just like I told you on the phone the last dozen times." He snaked his arms away from an enthusiastic Juniper so that he could reach out and tug me in tighter. "Mom, this is Brexley Snows. Brex, baby, meet my mom, Juniper. And my dad, Milo."

Milo was a striking silver fox, traces of dark hair still peppered through his impressive head of waves. He was a visceral cross between his boys—equal parts Rhyett and Jameson, with a hint of Maverick, like he'd only passed along pieces to each of them. He was the bestower of those steel blue eyes they all shared. I'd just noticed he had the dual cheek dimples Maverick boasted when he stepped forward, prompting me to accept his hand. Where I expected a shake, he pulled me in for a great big bear hug.

"Brexley, we've heard so much about you. So nice to finally meet in person."

Extricating myself as politely as possible, I gave Rhyett a little clasp, hoping for some kind of reassurance. Jameson snickered behind me, and the weight of so many eyes made my skin heat.

"You're from around here?" Juniper asked, leaning around Rhyett's chest to see my face while he kept an arm around her, hand firmly clamped onto her shoulder like he was anchoring her in place. It took all my restraint not to laugh.

"Uh, yeah, I'm born and raised in Tampa."

"Amazing! It always sounds wild until I realize my kids can say the same about the island. Different, somehow, knowing that they're all over the place more often than not."

"Hard to keep track," Milo offered, leaning back against the counter as he slid his hands into his front pockets. Ed, clipboard still in hand, seized the momentary distraction as an escape route, shrugging his shoulders as if apologizing for abandoning me in my time of need. "They bounce around from place to place, always seeing new things."

"You must be so proud of your kids," I said, scrambling for something to say. "So many people are so afraid to venture out on their own that they stay in a five-block radius their whole lives."

"Tragic statistic, that," Milo agreed solemnly as Juniper raised her hand, bracelets clinking together as she threaded her fingers through Rhyett's other hand.

"I'm not sure how people live that way, so cooped up all the time. I couldn't do it. I love Mistyvale, although it's too damn small to stay there your whole life."

"But people do."

"A coward dies a thousand deaths," Rhyett said, the slant to his beautiful mouth telling me there was a family link here. When they all finished in unison, my eyes widened.

"But a hero dies only once."

"What was that?" I asked, cautiously tiptoeing on the edge of the family line.

"Shakespeare, dear," Juniper said, smiling. The woman was more like her son than Milo, I decided. Her constant smile, the flash of mischief in her green eyes.

"*Cowards die many times before their deaths; The valiant never taste of death but once.* Technically, that's what he wrote," Elora corrected as she slid onto the newly installed white quartz counters beside her dad. "Something of a family motto."

"Take chances, embrace justified risks, live big, and fail fast," Milo said, as though by memory. My head was starting to swim with overwhelm. It seemed fake, this familiar, jovial connection between them all. What kind of family swapped Shakespeare quotes like casual trivia?

"Fail fast?" I asked.

"Failure is the lone inevitable thing other than death. Those at the top of any industry simply saw each perceived failure as a stepping stone, a lesson, to get them where they needed to go. We don't treat it like public education does. We encourage it. Get in the game. Play hard. Give it all you got. If you're going to fail, fail fast, and dust yourself off. Get steady on your feet. Repeat until victory."

I narrowed my eyes, stifling the accompanying scoff. "Am I on *Punk'd?*"

A giggling Hadlee stood beside me, looping her arm under mine and tugging me back towards the hallway in a guided retreat. I knew I liked her. "Come on, I can show you my ideas for the study, and you can get out of this fiasco for a minute before they start singing."

The fire popped and skittered, Hadlee and Maverick's laughter carrying over the quiet flicker of flames against the finished copper fire pit. They were playing a round of corn hole beside the deck, where the rest of us lounged. Dusk had long since settled, the low flicker of the patio lights illuminating the space and adding an addictive glow to Brexley's eyes as she quietly observed the chaos.

"I love the lights. Great pick, Ace."

"Mmm," she purred, leaning back into my chest. "Thanks, I think they're nice."

"You've been exceptionally quiet this evening. You okay?" I hugged her tighter for emphasis. She had been lost in thought most of the night and entirely silent as we all watched some old-time movie with Audrey Hepburn in it.

"Yeah, I'm just...observing."

"We can be a little overwhelming to take in."

"It's...different. That's all. I'm not used to this kind of dynamic."

"Good different?"

"Just...different," she said simply. "I understand better why you're so protective of your time and relationships with them. An alien concept to me, but they all love you."

"I'm a lovable guy," I teased, tightening my thighs against her hips where she was sprawled between them. Deciding she'd likely appreciate a change in subject, I asked, "Did you ever get Royal to come out from under the porch?"

She laughed. "The big dummy is happily sleeping with a litter of bunnies. I think they're confused about who their mama is."

Actually, that thought had some merit to it. "You think she took in some orphans?"

"I mean, she would." She ran her palms over her face. "Leave it to my dog to adopt a bunch of rabbits."

"I want to say that's a first, but I can't actually verify that." The woman on screen yelped, the sound system loud enough that she startled against me. Alice was painting Elora's toenails. Jameson, Juniper, and Milo were contentedly watching from inside the hot tub, clinking glass bottles of beer as they watched us conspiratorially from their place on the patio.

"Uh oh, we've been spotted."

"Spotted?" She asked. So innocent. So adorable. So naive.

"The parents and brother are conspiring, and I think we're the subject."

"Conspiring *how?*" she said, lowering to her best imitation of a top-secret agent voice.

"I think they like you."

"Impossible. They don't know me."

"I mean...I remember being pretty fond of each other the first day we met, too." Christ, had that only been two months ago? It felt infinitely longer and fractionally shorter simultaneously. Cicadas started chittering somewhere in the shrubs, the cry of a bat echoing above us.

"That's not the same, and I don't think they're proposing a group event." Brexley's blush was practically palpable. She shimmied farther under the blanket, reverting her gaze back to the movie on the screen.

"Certainly not." Based on the cheeky look on my brother's face, I assumed they were conspiring more along the line of wedding bells, but I sure as shit wasn't going to say that to Brexley. "But they're up to something. Never trust a Rhodes. Have I told you about our prank wars growing up?"

"Don't let him spin this shit," Elora said, shooting a glare in my direction as Alice laughed. "Rhyett was the king of the prank wars."

"Honestly, how we never destroyed the house, I'll never know."

"What kind of pranks?" Brexley hedged, her tone equal parts cautious and intrigued, baby blues narrowed as she craned to look up at me. The bench seats we'd built were the perfect freaking size. Just big enough for me to stretch my legs out and give her plenty of space to curl into the crook of my side. It did little in the way of skepticism, however.

"Name it, we did it," Alice quipped. "Plastic wrap on the toilets—"

"Plastic wrap across doorways, like a spider's web," Elora added.

"Covering the stairwell in cups of water so nobody could get up or down without running handfuls of cups to the bathroom."

"Swapping bedrooms while people were out for the day. That was Rhyett's favorite."

"Swapping bedrooms?" she chirped, her focus on me hardening.

"The whole damn thing," Alice said, rolling her eyes as Elora blew on the fresh polish.

"I mean. We left the beds," I interjected. "Just swapped comforters."

"Just," Elora scoffed, dipping the brush into the sticky, bright red liquid.

"All our clothes—"

"Trophies."

"—books, posters—"

"Shoe collections."

"Journals, craft supplies, beading kits."

"All of it," Elora finished with a huff, leaning back to admire her handiwork. When Brexley raised her eyebrows, looking to me for an explanation, I merely shrugged.

"Island life gets boring," I said by way of justification. It was true. "If we weren't working or out on the water, doing chores or schoolwork, we were at the library or getting into trouble out on the road."

"That means at the gathering spot at the end of the main road through town, for reference. Rhy forgets not everyone grew up on the island. You should come up, by the way!"

"To Alaska? I mean, I've always wanted to see it. It's supposed to be beautiful."

"It is. Honestly, I'm so sick of being stateside. I nearly cried when I booked my ticket home," Elora said wistfully.

"You headed back already?" I asked, a smile snaking through my tone. Hadlee and Finn were the only ones of us that seemed content to be gone for long stretches of time. Everyone else wandered on back more often than not.

"Portland is not my jam. Neither was Seattle. I miss the local flavor, the consistency, the bankers that know my name and who my family is. There's something about going home." Elora sighed, turning to plant her feet on the hardwood. "I'm famished. You have snacks worth stealing?"

"Oh, me too," Alice said, nearly flying to her feet.

"Help yourself," I said, motioning to the trailer. Royal had finally emerged from the rabbit den and perked up as the girls headed towards the promise of kibble and treats.

"Brex, you wanna join?" Elora tossed over her shoulder. My girl looked to me on reflex before rushing to follow.

"Yeah, thanks. I could go for a brownie."

I cleared my throat. "*Alice.*" Grey-blue eyes twinkled with amusement under the string of lights as she smothered her knowing smile. "Should Brex trust your baking?" Alessandra was the most rebellious of my sisters, always giving the guys a run for their money in the department of questionable behavior. When Alaska legalized marijuana, she'd taken up baking, eventually opening The Happy Pastry, and selling edibles every weekend at the farmer's market during the summers. She flashed me a cheeky grin, tossing her braid over a shoulder without answering as she ascended the steps. Brex was gaping at me, her eyes alight with equal surprise and mischief.

"Brex," I warned as she followed Alice's lead into the RV. "Start with a half," I insisted, shaking my head. Brexley's answering grin was punctuated with a raised, mocking brow. The front door slammed closed right as Jameson arrived beside me, sluicing water down his frame to pool onto the hardwood.

"Well," he said, grinning. "This should be fun."

"AMATEUR HOUR UP IN HERE," I teased, nudging the coffee across the counter. Brexley had made the unfortunate mistake of attempting to keep up with a Rhodes last night, matching Alice drink for drink. Between that and the highly suspect baked goods now residing in my freezer, she'd ended her evening with her head in the bushes and my hands wrapped in her hair—not in a fun way. Her groan of misery made me chuckle. I was constantly laughing these days.

"Come on, trust me, drink this." I slid over Elora's patent-worthy hangover elixir. She'd left it in preparation for Jameson and Hadlee, but Brex got priority in my books. The other idiots knew what they were getting into when they started.

"What in the hell happened last night?" She raised as far as her elbows, palms permanently pressed against her eyes. Good Lord, where to start? She'd probably like to know she'd robbed them all blind and had Jameson fuming mad by the third round of poker, aptly living up to her nickname. But for the sake of her self-image, I should likely not share that she'd also sung karaoke with my sisters, tripped off the deck and fallen on her ass in the bushes, laughing so hard it took both Jameson and I to get her upright. I'd keep it simple and summarize.

"You went toe-to-toe with Alice Rhodes. Rookie mistake."

"You could've warned me."

"I tried," I insisted, hands up in self-defense. "You didn't listen."

"I know how to hold my liquor."

"Clearly," Jameson drawled, wincing at the streaming window light as he slid into the stool beside her. Her responding middle finger reminded me exactly why I loved this woman.

I loved this woman. That phrase had casually battered my skull like the inside of a pinball machine, lighting up the neurons every time it rattled around. It resonated. I loved Brexley Snows. Even as she drug her hands across a hungover face, scowling at the sunlight. Lucky for her, the shop was closed on Sundays. Otherwise, I would've had to peel her out of bed hours earlier.

"Come on, Ace, down the hatch."

Distrust was written over every inch of her, from the deep angle of her brows to the dip of her chin and curl of her shoulders. Still unenthusiastic, she snatched the elixir off the counter and threw it back like a shot. Spluttering and coughing, she glared in my direction and slammed the glass back down with equal enthusiasm.

"Jesus, Mary, and Joseph—" The ensuing string of colorful curses had Jameson spitting his coffee back into his mug, nearly choking on his laughter. "What in the fuck was that?!"

"Surefire cure," Hadlee said calmly, attempting to hide the humor at Brexley's expense, although it lingered in the corners of her mouth. "Elora came up with that shit years ago. Give it an hour, max, and you'll be right as rain."

"Hell of a mouth there, Brex," my brother muttered as he finally got ahold of himself. "You'd make most sailors blush. You'll fit right in." He dropped his head back and laughed when she threw up both middle fingers this time.

"Was that *ginger?*"

"Partially," I acquiesced. "Cayenne, and I'm not sure what else."

"Why was it green?"

"Nutritional value."

"Fuck."

There was no swallowing my laugh at that, but I hoped to make up for it as I slid over a buttermilk pancake, greasy taco, and scoop of mac-n-cheese.

"What the hell is that?"

"*My* hangover elixir," Jameson answered, smirking back at her. "But I'm impressed you survived Elora's."

"Dammit," she grumbled, begrudgingly reaching over to wrap her palms around the plate, dragging it across the counter.

SURE ENOUGH, between Jameson's cure and Elora's, the three of them were on their feet and ready to go in time to pile in the SUV with Juniper and Milo. Much like the property, my bar was in the finishing touches of remodeling, and everyone *oohed* and *awed* at proper intervals. The contractors were, gratefully, absent as my parents examined and evaluated every inch of handiwork.

The Rhodes were nothing if not detail-oriented perfectionists.

Their chatter wasn't enough for me to miss as Brexley snaked her way through the bodies until she could flit down the back hallway, vanishing from the commotion.

I exhaled hard as the door snicked shut behind me, leaning into the wall and jamming my eyes closed. It was the hangover, I told myself. Except the overwhelming feeling crept into my chest yesterday the moment I woke up to a trailer packed full of Rhodes siblings. There was a reason I lived alone. My bandwidth for people was only so big. It was why Noel handled that side of our business.

Speaking of...the text had just fired off, updating her on the craziness, when the door cracked open and Rhyett slipped in.

"Hey," he said softly. "You alright?"

Nodding, I said, "Yeah, just taking a second to catch my breath."

"Sorry. They can be a lot," he admitted, his eyes full of knowing. "But they love as big as they bother."

"They're great, Rhyett." They were. Juniper had given me a ginger chew in the car rather than supplying any kind of motherly scolding for our adolescent drinking spree. Milo had happily reported facts about landmarks, wildlife, and bird species that I hadn't learned in a lifetime of my living here. Elora and Hadlee had helped me evaluate the bookshop's online presence and provided enough free feedback to last a year, helping me strategize for our mission of scaling it. Jameson's snark was endearing in the way brothers were often endearing. It was just... "I'm just not used to having people around that, you know, give a shit...care about what's going on in your life. I mean, the girls *are* my family."

He seemed to grapple for a minute, like words had tiptoed to the edge of his tongue only to retreat to the recess of his mind. Closing the gap between us, Rhyett reached down and took both my hands in his, bowing his head to rest his forehead on mine.

"They like you," he said at last. "That's a big deal. Believe me when I tell you if the Rhodes don't approve of someone, they're quick to make it known."

That, I could see. As level headed as Elora seemed, I had a sneaking suspicion she had a tongue you never wanted to be on the sharp end of. Although Hadlee's disproportionate amount of sunshine alluded to the same thing. Was Rhyett the actual anchor in the family?

"I like them."

"Good. That means a lot to me, baby."

"I know."

"Whatever this is...I'm a package deal, you know?"

"You told me."

"Any regrets?" He dragged his nose over the tip of mine, back and forth, in soft little bunny kisses that made my throat constrict. Like I could think clearly when he was touching me. His breath was hot on my parted mouth.

"None so far."

"Good." When Rhyett's lips came down on mine, they were laced with unmistakable need. The hard ridge of his erection against my belly stole my breath away. He reached one hand back to flip the deadbolt to the bathroom and sent my heart in a frantic sprint, my core tightening on instinct. "God, Brex, you have no idea what you do to me."

"Rhyett, they're all out there."

"Yeah," he breathed, evidently uninhibited. His mouth was warm and sweet against mine, hands rough with desire as they scraped the length of my body, coming to rest below my breasts. One roamed down to flip the button on my jean shorts, dropping the zipper in the next movement. I gasped as he slipped a hand in and cupped my sex, quick to flick the fabric of my panties aside and run his fingers between my lips, teasing my entrance. The heat of his palm against my clit had me grinding against him a few breaths later, his taste heavy on my tongue, lips locked.

"Rhyett," I breathed again, this time not entirely sure what I wanted from him. We should stop. But I didn't *want* to. I wanted him. Insatiable, this need, this fire between us.

"We'll be quiet," he supplied simply, sliding a finger around the rim of me before dipping inside, sending my heart into my throat and spine arching into his other hand, now gripping my low back. "Quick," he promised as he curled his finger, hitting that spot that made my toes curl on command. "I can't wait, baby. I'm dying to feel you."

My nod was all he needed. In heartbeats, he had his fly down, hard cock free, and was backing me towards the vanity. Rhyett's fingers roughly tugged at the denim and my shorts hit the floor. I'd barely stepped out of them in time for him to start moving me up onto the counter.

It was different, this fever, than the first time he'd taken me. This was carnal, yet there was also something more profound than how his body moved into me. His hand scooped up a leg and hooked it against the sink to give him access, mouth devouring mine. Demand laced his kisses, almost like he'd die if he couldn't have me. Whether I wanted to admit it to myself or not, Rhyett was breathing life into me with every touch, every caress. It didn't take long for my body to respond, heating, pulsing, pulling forward in silent demand as desire pooled between my legs.

"There's my girl," he whispered as his relentless fingers slid out, gliding my wetness up to circle my clit. "My good girl."

"Oh God," I breathed, writhing beneath him as pleasure sent my legs trembling. *More.* Less. I wasn't sure which, but my body ground against his touch of its own accord. "Oh God, *oh God–*"

Rhyett's palm silenced my moan, his face splitting into the cockiest smile as his fingers worked me ruthlessly. Right as I thought he'd take me over the edge, he pressed his palm to my clit and then slid his thick fingers through my slit, two of them finding my entrance and shoving inside again, his thumb settling over that bundle of nerves.

"Shhhh, baby," he cooed, that delicious male arrogance dripping from his voice as lust-hooded eyes trained on my face. He knew exactly where he had me. Rhyett's hold across my mouth tightened as he mercilessly curled into my G-spot. My entire body convulsed, muscles clamping down around him, legs shaking where they were spread on the vanity. His cock gradually thickened and hung heavy between his thighs, making my mouth water with anticipation as he drove pleasure from my core. *Good God, this man.* Arousal slick on his fingers, he moved back to my clit, rubbing and rotating until my head fell back, mouth parting against his palm on my lips. I nipped against his flesh, earning the most satisfying groan in response.

Rhyett eased the hold, trading that possessive pressure for a quick kiss before he brought his fingers back to trace my lower lip.

"Suck, baby," he whispered, dipping his finger into my mouth. I did. God, I did. His murmured praise would have been enough on its own but combining them with the way those fingers moved against my walls, the curve of his palm firmly pressed against my clit, and I detonated around him. Sucking him deeper into my mouth, my muscles all clenched, toes curling, release soaking his fingers and slipping down my ass. "Fuck," he breathed. "*Fuuuck*, baby."

As my body tapped out, turning liquid, head lolling back, Rhyett breathed a triumphant little laugh, the kind that was buried in his chest, looping his arms under mine to support me. Both slick with sweat, he gave me a moment to catch my breath, face laid against his slick shoulder, before tugging me forward, his fingers digging into my ass. "Come here."

I did. Hell, I rushed my limp limbs to comply. The man could have told me to do a headstand, and while it likely would end poorly, I would have done my best. Rhyett coasted both hands up and down my sides as he crushed his lips to mine, allowing me a moment to find my feet before leisurely pulling apart like we had all the time in the world.

He rotated me, gliding a palm up my back to bend me over the counter. Bracing my hands to either side of the sink, I looked up into the newly installed gold mirror, which sat against the rough brick, and my breath caught in my chest. Holy fuck, the man was beautiful. The emotion-laden glint in his eyes seemed to reflect the sentiment as they traced my face in the glass. He slid that flat palm up to scoop up my hair, twisting it into a fist that forced my eyes up. His smile was all lust-fueled satisfaction. Lips parting once, twice, I felt like he was about to say something, but he sealed them shut as he wrapped his other hand around his cock, giving it a long, hard stroke.

Rhyett slipped it up the length of my slit before tapping my ass, sending my breath out in a woosh, nerves butterflying in my belly. The ensuing chuckle sent blood rushing up my cheeks. "Not here, baby," he reassured me. "Not that I don't want you." He dragged the crown around the rim of my asshole, smirk broadening in the reflection as my body shuddered. "Believe me, you're more tempting than I could describe. A different time—a different place. I just need your wet cunt today, okay?"

My gasping nod was all he gave me time for. In one synchronized shift, he released my hair to grab my jaw, turning me over a shoulder. When he thrust home, he brought his lips down hard to swallow my moan, and a piece of my very being melded into his fingers, drifting away from my body as though I'd gifted it to him. As Rhyett set the brutal pace of a starving man, a part of him seemed to embed in my very soul. Marking. Claiming.

"Fuck, you're beautiful, baby. Your body should be illegal. So fucking gorgeous." His graveled words brought unexpected tears to my eyes, the endearing look on his face not helping. I slammed my eyes closed again, trying not to completely freak him out as he pounded into my pussy relentlessly.

Mine.

This man was mine. And I'd never meant to be his, but as he gritted his teeth with the effort, beads of sweat glimmering on his brow, eyes locking in the mirror before I lost control and slid mine shut, I saw it there. The declaration. The possession.

I belonged to Rhyett Rhodes.

My body knew it as it sang with pleasure, my legs fighting the numbness that tingled through as release tore from both of us, his calloused hand clamping down over my mouth again to keep me from crying out his name. Always his name.

When hot ropes of Rhyett's orgasm spilled inside me, he all but collapsed against my frame, pulling me flush against him, our bodies still joined, and breath tangling as we reveled in ecstasy.

"You're perfect," he panted against me, the words wrapping tighter around the claim I felt in my marrow.

RHYETT MADE no attempt at subtlety as he boldly led me back down the long hallway, having helped me straighten up after our second soul-demolishing bathroom tryst. Heart pounding against my skin, I attempted to plaster on a poker face, but it took approximately half a breath for Jameson's steel eyes to lock on mine, bearded cheek lifting with an all-knowing smirk. Tattooed biceps flexing beneath the white of his t-shirt, he glanced to Rhyett, who must have scowled because his brother just slid his hands into his pockets before heading for the door.

"He knows," I breathed, embarrassment flushing my cheeks.

"Good," Rhyett said simply. "It's good to be very clear with Jameson; never leave any room for confusion."

"And what are we being clear about, exactly?"

"That you're mine, baby. Strictly off limits. You can read about whatever you want, but there's nobody I love enough to ever let them touch you."

His words triggered something primal inside me. The feminist in me wanted to protest, but the fear and outrage only made it as far as the back of my throat, because I couldn't even argue with him. He spoke the truth, and that's what terrified me.

Inhaling was still about as easy as bathing a feral cat when we caught up with Milo and Juniper at the cafe beside the bookstore.

They'd already ordered appetizers by the time we settled in our seats. Jameson had hung back to tell us where they'd all gone, though he hadn't said a word and simply led the way when we emerged.

A PLATTER of bruschetta and a round of tableside guacamole later, Juniper and Rhyett were debating the deep complexities of selecting the proper fridge for the industry-worthy kitchen they'd designed together.

"I think that will work fine. I just think the smart fridges are so fancy," Juniper said happily, draining the last of her mojito. "I'm so scatterbrained that a shelf updating my shopping list isn't the worst idea in the world."

"Creepy is more like it," Milo muttered under his breath. He'd been relatively neutral in the entire debate, but the subtle quirks of his lips had me thinking he was team-Rhyett the whole time and unwilling to get in the middle of it.

"Are we still doing the pool?" Hadlee said, absentmindedly tapping away on her phone, as she had been for the duration of the great fridge debacle of the twenty-first century.

"Next spring, Had," Rhyett said simply, but Jameson wasn't having it.

"Maybe if you got off the internet and actually listened, you would've heard that the first time." Jameson snipped. Hadlee didn't miss a beat.

"Maybe if you weren't such a dick, I'd take you out to dinner courtesy of the five-figure deal I just closed."

Milo's fork froze mid-air with a bite of whatever he'd ordered in some spicy-looking red sauce, while Juniper's hit the table with a thud before she gasped. Elora smirked knowingly at her brother right as Rhyett erupted in a whoop.

"Nicely done, Had!" He reached over my head to offer her a high-five, and I laughed when it turned into a hair ruffle. *Brothers.* Not that I knew from personal experience, but it seemed a very big brother thing for him to do. Her trill of laughter was cut off by the explosion of questions that circled the table. Hadlee gave us the down-low on the travel magazine that had hired her for freelance work with a pretty price tag, four weeks' worth of free hotels throughout the country, and compensation for airfare or mileage.

That was one way to see the country.

Something like jealousy sat bitter on my tongue. Not jealousy of Hadlee, per se, but rather just a bitter twist that I hadn't thought to do something so courageously ambitious. Here she was, years younger than me, and hitting the gas full throttle. I could learn from that level of tenacity. Someone like that would grow the bookstore faster than I'd ever dreamed.

"Oh," Juniper squeaked, throat bobbing as she pressed both middle fingers into her tear ducts like she could forcibly contain the pride brimming in her eyes. "One baby is coming home after years away, starting a personal coaching business all by herself." That had to be Elora. "Another about to take over as boat captain. Hadlee landing five-figure travel deals. And Rhyett finally found someone who loves him. I just couldn't be more grateful."

My stomach dropped, my mind retaining enough sense to worry that the blood in my face had gone with it. Rhyett just laughed.

"You act like I'm a sixty-year-old bachelor, Mom."

"Oh shush, just let a mother be happy."

"I'm not saying don't be happy, just don't act like I'm on my deathbed. I'm in my prime, over here..." His words trailed off into the suddenly deafening buzz that had invaded my ears. Nausea swam circles in my stomach. She wasn't...wrong. She wasn't wrong at all, in fact.

I was in love with Rhyett Rhodes.

I was in love with the man who was supposed to be a one-night stand. Fuck, I had fallen for someone a decade older than me, someone wonderful and ambitious and successful. Who prioritized my pleasure like a fucking currency who—

I chugged my water, setting it down with a clink, disoriented when it did nothing to quench the desert in my mouth. Looking around for our server and coming up empty, I snatched Rhyett's next. Vaguely, I knew he'd glanced in my direction as I stole it, but I couldn't look up at him, my ears still too full of cotton to hear the conversation.

Rhyett wasn't just better than I'd ever dreamed of. So was his family. It was beyond me, but somehow this rag-tag group of siblings genuinely loved each other. Sarcastic quips and subtle digs might have been an art form, but it was obvious even to my untrained, bitter eyes that they actually gave a shit at a deep level. Maybe the missing half of them were total pricks, but I didn't think so. They were kind and welcoming and easy to be around. Perhaps a little huggy for my taste, but at least it came from a good place.

There wasn't a world in the universe where I knew how to *do* that, *be* that for someone. Let alone fourteen someone's. And, oh God, if we had kids...

"I'm not feeling well," I said softly, not sure if anyone but Rhyett heard me over whatever exchange was playing up and down the seats like a light-up piano. My napkin settled where my ass had just been as I stepped around the chair. I was too busy trying not to puke to pay them any mind. "Please excuse me."

Maybe Rhyett said something, but I certainly didn't hear it as I made a beeline for the bookstore.

"She alright?" Jameson asked for what must have been the dozenth time. Of all my family members, my closest brother was the last one I would've guessed would take to her so quickly. Brex had locked herself in The Cracked Corset's bathroom and told me she thought last night caught up with her when I'd tracked her down after a good twenty minutes. But the words came out strangled. I wasn't buying it, but Jameson didn't need to know that.

"Just not feeling well. I'll take her home."

"You sure, man? We don't mind hanging back."

"Yeah, it's alright. I've got her, thanks though."

"Alright, I'll get rid of them for you." Jameson shot me a knowing smile before strolling towards the front door. He could be a real prick if somebody deserved it, was absolutely the devil's advocate, but also a pretty solid brother. He would likely drag my nosy family off somewhere else so that I could give Brexley a clear retreat. I followed him to the front door so I could bolt the lock. Laughed as he waved off the vultures, pointing back towards the SUV.

Thank you, Jameson.

"Baby, you okay?" She didn't answer, my stomach twisting as the silence filled the space. Tentatively, I pushed the bathroom door open. "Brex."

"Here," she croaked. Gently, I pushed the stall open, finding my girl in a heap on the floor, her knees tucked up to her chest and mascara making a mess of those perfect cheeks. There was only one situation where streaked mascara was acceptable and this sure as shit wasn't it.

"Baby," I said reproachfully, shifting into the stall and joining her on the floor. "What's going on, beautiful?" I wiped the tear streaks off her cheeks, smudging away the dark flakes again when her little chin dimple quivered.

"I'm having a breakdown. You have *six* sisters. Don't you know what a breakdown looks like by now?"

"Why are we having a breakdown?"

"We?" She whispered, obviously fighting the tightness in her throat.

"Obviously. If you're having a breakdown, I'm doing it with you. If it affects you, it's my problem. Now, who am I killing, or what am I fixing?"

She sputtered in tears, choking on a laugh and wiping her face, "I must be PMSing."

"Especially if you're PMSing. Nobody messes with my girl when her hormones are already out to get her. Was it Jameson? Somebody online?"

"This wasn't supposed to happen, Rhyett."

I quirked my head, dread tightening its grip on my windpipe. "What wasn't supposed to happen, baby?"

"This. Us. I wasn't supposed to love you."

If hearts could stop and restart, mine certainly did in that moment. Stuttering back into motion, my lips twisted sideways. "You love me?"

A fresh wave of tears coursed down her face, but she managed to nod as her teeth worried that lower lip. "Don't look so smug, you jackass."

Truthfully, I hadn't realized I was looking smug, but I did my best to shift my face into a more neutral position. "I love you too, Brexley Snows."

Something like a sob shuddered through her, and I couldn't help but chuckle, lowering my forehead to hers and resting my chin on her braced arms.

"Don't say that," she mumbled, "don't."

"Baby, why wouldn't I say that? I've just been waiting for you to say it first."

"Because we weren't supposed to. This wasn't supposed to happen. I thought I would get you out of my system."

"By getting me into it?"

"Don't be funny."

"Sorry, that's my default setting. I'll be duller."

"I mean it," she protested. "We're just not right for each other."

I raised a speculative brow. "Ace, what do you mean?"

She rolled her eyes. "I mean, *this*." She gestured between us. "We're not supposed to be together."

"Says *who*?" I scoffed. "The universe? Fate? Sorry, babe, but I'm pretty sure they don't get a say in who I love."

"It's not that simple."

Leaning in and lowering my voice, I shook my head. "Well. It is for me. I love you, Brexley Snows. Simple as that."

Her eyes went round, tears lining the rim. "Stop it, Rhyett. You're making me feel things."

"Oh no, not emotions," I teased with mock horror before chuckling. "Anything but that." She didn't retreat when I moved to wrap around her, thanking all that was holy as her frame fit right against my side.

"Rhy, you're born to be a father, and I don't even know if I want kids."

"I'm in no rush. And at my age, it's actually not a make or break for me."

"I get overwhelmed if my houseplants make noise when the air conditioner comes on, and you literally thrive in chaos."

"Unavoidable hazard of being in a big family."

"Right. But I didn't grow up with eleven siblings vying for attention. There was just me. I don't know how to handle the noise, the opinions, the constant ribbing."

"That's mostly Jameson and Maverick. You'll like Paxton and Axel. If Finn ever holds still long enough to meet him, he's a big ol' softie. The girls only dish it back; they don't start it."

"You know what I'm saying," she said, sniffling.

"Baby, my family already loves you. You won them over the moment you showed up and again when you flipped off Jameson. They like a girl that can hold her own."

"They don't even know me. Hell, you don't even know me."

"I wouldn't exactly say that," I teased, repeating one of our first conversations.

"I just...I think I need a break from the crazy. I need some time to process."

"Okay, we'll stay at your place tonight. Let my family invade the RV in full force."

"No, Rhyett. I need some time away from you."

"Brex—"

"No. I mean it. It's not fair, and I can't think when you smile at me or touch me or—" She cut herself off when I gently ran a palm up her calf, hoping to soothe her, but earning a fierce scowl instead. "See?" she gritted, snaking out of my arms and rising to her feet. "I can't think when I'm with you. I just need—space!"

I got to my feet, refusing to just let her run off without talking through shit first. Closing the gap, I reached over to cup her silky face, forcing her to look at me. "Okay, just...let me walk you home, so I know you're safe. Take a breather tonight, and we can talk in the morning. I know you're scared, baby. But don't fight this thing between us. Whatever it is. Just, let go. I promised you won't regret it, and I mean that."

With a furrow between her brow, she nodded.

"Okay," I said, keeping my voice level as I stroked her hair. The walk to her place was made in agonizing silence. My heart ached. A dull throb formed in my temples. Brex's energy was akin to a lightning storm, my instincts all telling me I was about to get hit with a bolt. As I walked her to her door, she swore, slapping a palm to her head.

"Royal!" she lamented. "Royal is at your place."

"She's fine," I assured her, waving her off. "You can come down as soon as you feel up to it. I've got her."

"Rhyett, I don't know if I'll be up for anything tonight. I should just pick her up."

"Come on down with me?"

Brexley shook her head, throat bobbing. "I don't think being in a small space is conducive with the whole 'thinking things through' thing." It took considerable effort not to chuckle at her air quotes.

I gingerly tucked a strand of silky blonde hair behind her ear. "Look, Ace. I've got her. Take a breather. Seven people in an RV is a lot for anyone. She's not hurting anything. Take a bubble bath and a night to breathe. Give yourself time to clear your head."

She opened her mouth and closed it twice before softly saying, "Yeah, okay. If you're sure."

"Positive." I meant it. But the bonus was she had to come face me once she'd cooled off for a minute.

"Then it's a plan. I'll see you in the morning, okay?" I leaned down and kissed her forehead, wishing for her lips, for the feel of her against me. But overwhelm seemed to seep from her in waves. I could give her a moment without any Rhodes to catch her breath. Her stiff silence and rigid posture spoke volumes more than I was prepared to acknowledge.

THE RIDESHARE HOME was one of the longest in my life, the infinite bridge feeling suddenly every bit as obnoxious as she'd always said it was. Something angry was trying to claw its way to the aching spot in my gut. Anger at myself mostly, for falling for a woman who had blatantly not wanted anything legitimate. But also anger at my family for shoving her over the edge. Brexley deserved the fucking world. Nonetheless, I was the first to admit I should have been more upfront with her.

Moping in an unflattering pool of self-pity, it took the driver slamming on the brakes for me to finally look out the front window. My heart took a nosedive as I flew out of the car. *No.* Phone in my hand, I bolted for the house. The driver yelled after me, but there was no turning back.

FORTY-SIX

BREXLEY

The sound of a car out front had me peering down through the blinds like a crazy neighborhood busybody. To my absolute horror, it was an idling rideshare. Bright decal lit up in the back window as Rhyett slowly stood from my front porch stairs and climbed into the sedan.

Oh my God. He'd just been *sitting outside* alone, waiting for a driver? Where the hell were all the Rhodes? They'd just left him in the city to look after me? Oh god, my irrational meltdown was about to cost him a fortune in mileage fees.

By the time the front door smacked against the drywall and my feet were on the sidewalk, the car was gone. I was left feeling like the biggest jackass. I'd been so overwhelmed in my own emotions, I hadn't even thought through the implications of just sending him off like that. Palming my face, I slid my phone out of my back pocket.

BREXLEY

Can you talk?

NOEL

Give me a second.

A SECOND PASSED. About ninety more did as well. But then, like the angel she was, Noel's face appeared on my screen.

"Brex? What's wrong? Why do you look like you saw someone run over a box of puppies?"

"Jesus," I said, recoiling from the mental image.

"Well, that's about as grim as your face."

I squinted at the screen, the curtain of clothing to either side of her. "Are you in your closet?"

"Eric's feeling territorial. Promised him an uninterrupted movie night, but hoes before bros, man." The laugh bubbled up despite myself. At least until she scowled, demanding, "Now, tell me what the hell is going on."

My face ached as it fell. "I think I have to stop sleeping with Rhyett."

"Because you're fertile?"

"What?"

Noel deadpanned, explaining, "Well, I mean, that's the only reason I wouldn't let him do whatever he wanted to me, if I were you."

"Oh my God."

"Am I wrong? He's fucking gorgeous. And he's crazy about you. Why the sudden celibacy? Some sort of—"

Throat thick, I cut her off. "I'm not good enough for this family, Noel. They're the freaking *Brady Bunch*. Except, bigger."

"Oh, bullshit," she barked, rebounding quickly from my less-than-polite intervention.

"You don't get it. They're all these crazy high achievers."

Noel ran her fingers through red curls, expression hardening in a way that was entirely disproportionate with the joviality she maintained in her tone. "And you're a badass bitch that owns her own business with her super adorable, super brilliant best friend that you should always listen to, and you pull in six fucking figures all by yourself. I think you have achieved pretty high results yourself, don't you?"

"They're all so symbiotic. Besides, I don't want to let off the gas, you know? It's why I wasn't supposed to be fooling around with anybody." That statement tasted like battery acid. It had stopped being about the sex not long after it started. "My Dad pulled high six-figures, but he was never home. I don't want to put him through—"

Noel scoffed, disbelief in her tone as she interrupted. "Ugh, Brex. You are not your dad, or your deadbeat freaking mom." Even though she was right, I couldn't help wincing. Either not noticing or caring, Noel continued, "You're amazing. And Rhyett is amazing. And maybe we can learn some tricks from each other—he's a business owner too, or did you forget that part?" When I made to protest, she shook her head, snapping, "You're doing it again."

"What?"

"The beat-up Brexley routine. You *are* good enough. He's amazing. You both deserve each other, and you've waited long enough to be happy. So go be happy." She blinked pointedly, like what she was saying was freaking common sense.

"It's not that simple."

A knock sounded and had her glowering at what I assumed was her bathroom door. "Just a second! No, I'm just going to the bathroom and jumping through the shower. Promise." She rolled her eyes at whatever the response was before tossing open the glass shower door and turning on the faucet. Her eyes flicked back to me. "Look. I bought a few minutes, but I gotta keep this quick."

I scowled down at my screen, demanding, "Everything okay?"

"We're talking about your trainwreck, not mine."

"Things have seemed a little...tense, lately."

"Yeah," she muttered, waving me off. "Focus. Seriously, listen to me. How long have I known you?"

"Since we were little kids, why—"

"More like since we were still shitting our pants. And in that time, I've never—not once—seen you as happy as you've been the last few months with Rhyett. For the love of all that's holy, do not throw this away because of some bullshit dysmorphic idea that you're not good enough, or deserving enough, or *whatever* enough. You are. And you deserve a family that will love you senselessly. If Rhyett-the-walking-sunbeam is any indication of the love in that household, I think the universe is finally compensating for the—*I said one minute!! Jesus Christ*—shit hand you were dealt."

Making a mental note to call her back in the morning to check on her own domestic bullshit, I nodded, fighting back tears. "Love you too," I whispered.

"Listen, Linda. I love you more than anyone else on this planet. Save for maybe a saint or something. However, if you fuck this up to punish yourself for your shitty parents, I'll kill you myself."

I huffed a laugh, sliding into my shoes and snatching my keys off the counter.

"Now, go get your man before he thinks you don't love him."

"I told him that."

Her hazel eyes flew wide, something like fear hidden there. "That you don't love him?"

"No. That I do."

Noel's shoulders relaxed, her breath coming out in a woosh. "Good. Now go show him."

Swallowing thickly, arguing with the stinging in my eyes, I reached for a pathetic attempt at humor. "Dirty," I said through a sniffle. She laughed even though it wasn't funny. That's why I loved her. She just got me. Always had.

"Alright, I expect an update at work tomorrow."

"Yeah, I'm going after him."

"That's my girl." Eric said something through the door that had her huffing and rolling her eyes, and then she blew me a kiss a second before the screen went dark.

I may have broken more than a handful of traffic laws in my effort to catch up to Rhyett on the way down to the south side of the bridge and out to the rural stretch of town. My mind spun in furious circles between Rhyett's staggering patience and Noel's too-kind words. Between how welcoming his siblings had already all been and how painfully awkward I'd felt under their praise.

The haunting memory of a hollow home with two absent parents seemed to taunt me, eyes burning as I remembered dinners alone and unreturned phone calls. Dad had tried. In his own way, perhaps, but he had at least tried. At least I still got the occasional 'thinking of you' text and a call on Christmas from wherever he was flying from.

None of that prepared me for a family that loved as big as the Rhodes did. They knew each other inside and out and had each other's backs. And there was something in Juniper's eyes when Hadlee announced her latest deal that stuck a spear in my heart, because if I was actually fucking honest with myself, I wanted someone to feel that way about me if I ever achieved anything worth noting.

If an agent rang my phone right now to offer me representation, it would be Rhyett I'd want to call. *Rhyett* I'd want to celebrate with. *Idiot.* I prayed I hadn't pushed him away, prayed to a god who'd forgotten my name that he'd forgive my brief mid-life crisis and give me the opportunity to learn how to do this.

Every thought tumbled out of my head into a messy heap at my feet as I rounded the corner to see the blinding red and white strobe and scream of firetrucks turning onto Rhodes Road.

"Oh my God." I turned the music down as panic bleated through my veins. There were three trucks kicking up dust ahead of me, sirens silencing them as they hit the dirt. Beyond them, the entire house was lit orange, smoke billowing into the evening sky as dusk became darkness.

No.

I didn't have a chance for the why's or the how's since my eyes hopped from Rhyett's trailer to the rideshare I'd seen earlier. The back passenger door flung open and the driver braced outside with a cell to his ear.

The thing they never tell you about an unmanaged blaze is that it's loud. Ears full of a deadly, crackling roar, my gaze flicked from the firefighters leaping into motion to the driver on the phone, and then back to the house. It was somewhere in the back, yet the glow assaulted every window downstairs—the kitchen? Where was Rhyett? He wasn't talking to the firefighters, and there was no way he'd retreated into the RV to watch through tinted panes.

"Rhyett?" I yelled, looking around as dread settled in my stomach. The responders were shouting orders, flying into motion while the driver and I were frozen in place. "Rhyett?" I called again, my brain finally locating the control panel for my feet and hurtling us towards the rig. Something ached as I snatched the handle, throwing the door open.

"Rhyett?!" I repeated as I flew inside, already knowing he wasn't there. Having cleared the tiny space, I jumped back outside as the rental SUV screeched onto the dirt lane, not even fully stopped before Jameson, Milo, and Maverick were all out of the vehicle.

Absently, numbly, I moved towards the building, horror gripping my throat as the chaos unfolded. I was flung back into my body when a little gray rabbit sprinted across my path to the house. A little gray rabbit that nearly caused me to faceplant.

Mind grappling with why that tugged on my consciousness, I stumbled a step forward, battling the icy terror that little rabbit planted in my path.

Royal.

FORTY-SEVEN

RHYETT

No government organization on the planet could assemble quite as fast as the Rhodes family during a crisis. It was that reason and that reason alone that had stolen twenty seconds from my response time to send an alert to Jameson after I'd shouted for the driver to call 911.

Basilio. Basilio, the first-generation Cuban immigrant whose name meant *royal.* He'd told me in the car while I was trying not to spiral, and some fucked up part of my brain chose to not only remember it now but had connected it to the reason I was in the least intelligent pinch of my life.

Royal.

Brexley's fucking rabbit-adopting dog was yelping as I sprinted for the house, aiming to turn off the gas line. The deepest part of my mind had heard her the moment the car door opened. And like the enormous idiot I was, I'd decided to save her. Not just because I firmly believed that dogs are too damn good for us and we could never deserve them, but because this dumbass dog was the closest thing to family Brexley had outside of Noel.

Which led me here. With my big ass shoulders wedged between fallen two-by-fours, filtering air through my shirt as I tucked as close to the mud-covered earth as I could. Vaguely, my mind registered the fire ants fleeing as quickly as colonially possible, some still bothering to take chunks of me with them for the road. Not only was I pinned, but I'd been reduced to insect fast food. Fucking fantastic.

"Royal," I hissed again, swearing as she whined and shifted, refusing to budge. "Come on baby girl! Come on, we gotta get out of here. Your mama will never forgive me if something happens to you." A prolonged, indignant cry somewhere between a whimper and a hound dog left her mouth. She moved towards me, though my brief relief was cut off when she shuffled right back.

"God damn it, Royal! Come on. Come. Come, girl."

Under ordinary circumstances, those were my favorite words to utter. The fucked-up coping mechanism that was dark humor crawled up my spine as I focused on my surroundings. Was that my subconscious deciding we'd very likely die here? Fuck. Not a great sign when your brain starts cracking jokes, especially when the adrenaline should be sharpening everything.

"Come!" I demanded, slapping the ground only for her to whine again, digging in fierce, tiny pulls into the dirt like she was trying to yank something out of the earth. That's when I spotted it—a baby rabbit. The damn dog was about to kill us both trying to save a baby rabbit. I'd assumed she was stuck down here, unable to get out, but no, she was playing superhero to a rodent. "So fucking help me, if you get me killed, I'm coming back to haunt you forever." Coughing, rotating and twisting, shimmying and breathing, I managed to wiggle out of the pinch point, glancing over my shoulder as the fire truck lights finally flashed across the lawn. *Thank fuck.*

Army crawling through the mud, aware of more headlights sweeping under the deck, I worked my way over to her, growling when the rabbit retreated deeper in the direction of the foundation of the house. The thing kicked and squealed when I clamped down around the back of its neck, lifting the wood it had wrestled under away to set it free. The instant the damn bunny bolted, Royal released her tense muscles and started belly crawling back to where I'd come from.

"Are you fucking kidding me?" I snarled. My pulse was hammering against my temples, lungs starting to protest the proximity to the fire. I hacked out a wheezy cough, tucking my shirt back over my nose.

In the world's stupidest rescue to date, we both made our way towards the flashing lights, wincing or whining when the house behind us groaned. Slithering along, cursing my own stupidity, my eyes spotted her jeep beside the rideshare. Brexley. *My Brexley.* She'd come after me and arrived at my family's dream house in flames, with me in the mud below the back porch with her crazy ass dog. We had to get the fuck out of here before things escalated. Because I had to hold her. I had to tell her what she meant to me.

Royal slipped under the deck, immediately spinning back to stick her nose under the wood lattice almost like she was waiting for me. "Crazy girl," I muttered, lowering myself deeper into the dirt and shimmying back under the border.

Before she could do something else to get us roasted alive, I scooped up Royal and started to distance us from the house. *The house.* I'd panicked about what had been an almost complete family estate, but the oily dread had been swallowed by fear when I'd remembered this damn ball of muddy fluff.

Muddy fluff that was currently frantically licking the grime off my face like she was aware she'd almost gotten us both killed. "So help me, you better fetch beers from the fridge for the rest of your life," I muttered, adjusting her damp furry frame in my arms. She just licked me faster, earning a laugh that turned into a coughing fit. The Rhodes family championship belt for World's Biggest Dumbass officially went to me. I'd always sworn it would be Maverick.

"Okay, okay," I said, wincing as I leaned away from her sloppy kisses, overtaken by another coughing fit as we made our way across the yard. "Yes, I love you too, you rabbit savior."

There was a deafening crack from behind us, followed by the shattering of glass. I winced. So much for a family oasis.

FORTY-EIGHT
BREXLEY

Jameson had wanted to go after Rhyett, halted by the insistence of his mother and the firefighters. The next concern was the proximity of the rig. Dying to do something with their hands, they'd flown into action. Hadlee and Elora had bolted into the fifth wheel to move things out of the way and pull in slides. Jameson hooked up Rhyett's truck with Alice's quick help, dropping the rig onto the hitch. Juniper was immediately on the driver's phone talking to local authorities while Milo followed strict instructions from the responders and led them to the gas shut-off. I silently thanked Rhyett for taking the time to point out so many details on the tour.

All the while, I stood frozen, feeling useless as everyone moved around me. I didn't realize when tears started pouring down my face. Didn't realize my breath was all but stalling out in my chest. Didn't even notice when I started shaking. It wasn't until the telltale creak of the rig moving that I realized I'd turned to stone. But it was Elora's soft hand against my back that finally snapped me into the present.

"He'll get her."

He'll get her. Her big brother had very likely gone after my dumb freaking dog instead of doing the rational thing and staying the hell away from the danger. And she thought I was worried for Royal. I mean, yes, I was terrified for my dog, but it was Rhyett who had me ready to puke into the grass. When something inside the house cracked with a pop that rang in my ears, glass shattering a moment later, we all winced. Juniper wandered to my side, her round eyes on the dream home they'd all been looking forward to sharing for the winter. But it was her son's name she whispered as her fingers hovered over her lips.

"There they are," Jameson said as he jogged up to my side, the rumble of the truck still purring behind us, where he'd pulled the rig out of range without blocking the entrance for more emergency personnel. The trucks were parked at three different points, the men already at work to extinguish the damn thing. But he was pointing towards the corner of the house, still fully intact, where the porch was perched, so cheerily oblivious to the dire circumstances.

My heart leapt into my throat, and before anybody could tell me otherwise, I was sprinting for his outline against the house. Rhyett saw me coming, bending down to set Royal on her feet, where she promptly bolted across the green until she nearly collided with my shins, jumping and pawing at me like I'd been the idiot that got into danger. Her frantic yips were punctuated with a vertical leap as she nipped, kissed, and nudged me. However, it was the caress of Rhyett's eyes that held my focus until he was safely out of range of any danger. Wordlessly, he scooped me into his muddy arms as Royal continued her love assault, and we nearly fell over in the process.

"What were you thinking?" I demanded, my voice cracking on a suppressed sob. "Dammit, Rhyett," I muttered between kisses. His hands were somehow everywhere, cradling my face, sliding down my neck, squeezing the cage of my ribs. Like he was checking to make sure I was real and tangible and in one piece. Once they found my ass, I became acutely aware my own had roamed in much the same manner. Refusing to be swept down the river of lust, I slammed my palms into his chest, anger fueling the motion, though it did absolutely nothing to move the man claiming my mouth in a violent, primal collision.

My breath was a gasp as I pushed against him again, repeating, "*What* were you thinking?!"

That damn chuckle wound through my rib cage until it constricted when he coughed, turning his face so he didn't hack into mine. His fingers threaded into my hair, pulling my head against his chest. The prickles of eyes skimming up my spine told me the whole family was watching. I didn't care. Couldn't bring myself to peel away as the steady, rapid thud of his heartbeat hammered in my ear, soothing my panic.

"Baby," he finally rasped, petting down the length of my hair to where it rested against my low back. "When are you going to get it through your head?"

"What?" I blubbered, now full-on ugly crying into his shirt.

"There's nothing I wouldn't do to make you happy. Even chasing your dumbass dog into a rabbit den about to ignite. I mean, she's a little whacky, but she's family." *Dammit.* The tears ratcheted up to a downpour. "I love you, Brexley Snows."

"So stupid," I said on a sob, wiping my face on his filthy shirt. "So, so stupid. Don't you ever—*ever*—do something like that again," I demanded, punctuating each 'ever' with a solid smack against the unyielding planes of his chest.

"I'm okay, baby. So is Royal. Totally worth it."

"No," I said, my voice cracking. "Not okay."

"Baby, we're right here."

"What if something happened to you?!"

"Nothing's going to happen to me. Baby, will you look at me?" His warm, gritty palms came to rest against my face as the hiss of water on flames grew. Sirens grew closer as the Rhodes family and two firefighters descended on Rhyett. I shook my head, smiling as his chuckle rumbled against my face. "Why not?"

"Because I love you, you big idiot."

One week ago, the project I'd come here for caught fire. A gas line leak, although we still weren't sure how it ignited. The entire structure was totaled, much to the livid dismay of our insurance company and every member of the family alike. There were few things Juniper Rhodes hated more than hospitals, but red tape was undoubtedly one of them. And she'd had to deal with both in the last seven days.

"How are you all so calm?" Brexley asked one morning, a bit staggered. I'd simply shrugged.

"Priorities, baby. Once you've got the priorities in place, anything outside them doesn't necessarily matter. The house was empty, and everyone's safe. The insurance is going to cover the rebuild. We can't change it, so might as well let it go." The truth was, our family had faced enough trials, enough losses, that we'd stopped sweating the small stuff ages ago. She'd looked a bit dazed, but then kissed the breath out of me, which I took as a good sign.

With a looming demolition and delays on the final pieces of the bar's renovation, I felt helplessly stuck sitting on my hands. The first responders had fussed and scolded as they examined me, but even as Royal sat curled at my feet, I didn't really give a shit. Weird and a little dumb, but she was a lover. She'd refused to leave my side in the following days, like she was somehow aware of the pinch she'd put us both in.

Feet in the sand, I watched the enormous, fluffy, billowing white clouds of an impending thunderstorm crawling towards the stretch of the coast. According to Brexley, they'd become a daily occurrence in no time. Warm waves crashed against my sticky skin, and I breathed in the sunshine and humidity as the horizon turned pink with approaching nightfall. I felt the zing of her focus before the subtle slide of sandy footsteps was audible. The crash of the gulf swallowed the sound of her approach. Brexley. My Brexley.

"That the last of it?" she asked as she looped her arms around my bicep, leaning her head on top.

"Yeah, no point now in sticking around. You sure you can take the time?"

"I can write anywhere," Brexley assured me, giving the muscle a friendly little pinch that had me thinking about her deft fingers on other places. In the week since the fire, Brexley received not one but two offers for representation from her top pick agents. The odds were insurmountable, and both had incredible traction when landing record-setting deals. It seemed my little entrepreneur had missed her calling after all. "And Holland and Wrenly have proven they're both worth their salt. The shift leads are great. We've set ourselves up well for a trip."

"You're going to love Mistyvale." I smiled at the thought of her getting to take in the emerald island. The towering green mountains and purple flowers, hanging curtains of moss. She was going to lose it.

"I can't promise I'll want to come back?"

I laughed, turning to press a kiss to her head. "You saying I'll be on my own for snowbird season at the bar this year?"

"Mmmm, we'll see. Elora makes it sound like heaven."

"Damn. I was thinking of getting a bigger place in the city. Somewhere with a guest bed and designated room for your books."

"I don't think that's your best idea," she said softly as the sun sank below the horizon and the crowd clapped in celebration of another beautiful curtain falling on the world's stage.

"No?"

"Mmm, I was thinking of something quieter for inspiration."

"Like, Mistyvale quiet or like..."

"Why don't we get a place south of the Skyway?"

"Sounds great, Kara, thank you." Rhyett slipped his phone into a back pocket, a grin permanently etched in his face. "She found one," he said smugly, coming to plant kisses down my neck. Kara was the real estate agent that Juniper and Milo used to find their property, and she'd located a rental five minutes from it, so we could spread out a little more than piling into the RV. This way, he could oversee the second attempt at a building job.

"I'm still so sorry you guys are going through this," I said for what was likely the hundredth time. Rhyett nipped at the sensitive skin of my neck.

"Not anybody's fault, Ace. Honest mistake. Everyone's safe, and honestly, Ed did a shoddy job on that back deck. It'll give him the chance to do it right."

"You're incorrigible," I laughed, squeezing his arm and pulling him back towards the parking lot so we could beat the crowd before they were all sitting idle in the road. With one last big breath, he followed me back to the car. When Rhyett started the truck, the cab filled with "If We Were Vampires" by Jason Isbell and The 400 Unit, the lyrics immediately bringing tears to my eyes. The engine rumbled to life as he threaded our fingers together, my eyes staying trained on Rhyett's beautiful profile as we drove over the Skyway for what was likely the last time for a few months as the insurance people worked everything out.

ROYAL HAD REPLACED a doormat sometime during the twenty minutes we spent making store-bought fettuccine Alfredo. She didn't bother to shift as the wave of red splashed into my glass, or as the next filled Rhyett's. Nor did she budge when we sat down at the table. We'd worn her out dragging her on morning runs and trips to the dog beach on Rhyett's side of the bridge.

Louis Armstrong's "A Kiss to Build A Dream On" came on over my record player as we settled in for dinner, our little routine already familiar. We ran through our plans for the trip to Alaska, and then Rhyett grilled me on my research into the agent I'd selected, ensuring there weren't any holes in my confidence.

He'd been mid-explanation about the next phase for the bar when his phone buzzed, Elora's name on the text bubble. Overall, Rhyett wasn't quick to grab his cell, although it was almost a reflex when there was a 'Rhodes' on screen. He'd missed them all the moment we'd dropped them at the airport, and I could tell his excitement for our trip was more about getting time together than it was about showing me the island.

He chuckled, turning the phone my way to share the grinning face of Elora beside a man with glowing, warm umber skin, a nervous smile, and deep brown eyes that looked just shy of pain. Her text read, *'look who I ran into today.'* Rhyett fired back *'always fun seeing old friends. Don't give him too hard a time, okay, El?'*

"That's our Broderick," he said, grinning. "Those two have had a friendly rivalry going since we were all kids. It's kinda ridiculous." I glanced back to Broderick's undeniably nervous face and laughed. He had to see the truth in that picture...didn't he?

"*Rivals*, huh?" I asked skeptically.

"Broderick was the yearbook editor, so El had to be editor and director of artistic design. He set records as swim team captain, so she upped the ante when she landed the role. Broderick was student body president, so when Elora was a senior, she had to win with ten more votes. He got Valedictorian with a four-point-oh, so she took college and AP classes and took the title with a four-point-five."

"Four-point-five?" I demanded, eyes widening as I twirled more pasta onto my fork, Alfredo sauce slapping the edge of the plate, a splatter hitting the table.

"She loves terrorizing him. It's kinda priceless. And since his two best friends were me and Jameson, there was no escaping her."

I swiped up the drops of sauce with a finger, popping it in my mouth.

The heat of his focus caught my attention as his explanations wandered off. "Now, that's just not fair."

"I'm eating," I protested.

"Well, you eat sexy."

"It's not a hot dog, Rhodes. Keep your pants on."

He laughed into his wine glass, shaking his head. Royal suddenly rolled off the mat, an ear flopped backwards as she quirked her head at the door.

"You expecting company?" Rhyett asked, glass hovering halfway to the table. I shook my head, but we were both on our feet before the knock sounded. Royal's enthusiastic tail told me she knew who was on the other side before we did.

The whoosh of air ruffled my hair when I threw it open, finding a familiar back and mess of red curls.

"Noel?" I asked, the skepticism thick in my voice. When she turned around, my glass fell to the concrete step, shattering on impact and sending maroon liquid everywhere. Her lip was split, downcast eyes glued to her feet, with a fresh bruise blooming across her cheekbone. "Noel!?" I barked, lunging forward, but she shook her head, holding up a trembling hand.

"Is Rhyett home?" she asked in a quavering voice, still not meeting my eyes. I nodded as Rhyett elbowed into the door frame and leapt out in the same motion, shoulders back, head swiveling as he looked for the threat before setting his hand on her back and ushering her inside. Once we had her sitting on the sofa, the mess on the stoop temporarily forgotten, she cleared her throat, finally lifting her red-rimmed eyes to my boyfriend's face. He sucked in a breath even though he held his tongue.

When Noel spoke, she was quiet but firm. "I need your help."

THANK YOU FOR READING!

WANT MORE RHYETT AND BREX? I have a bonus epilogue for you!

You can snag your copy here: https://dl.bookfunnel.com/caxren7vkp

. . .

WHAT COMES NEXT? Are you ready for Noel and Jameson's story? You can read *Brewing Temptation* now.

E-Book pre-order: https://a.co/d/89jzKFM

Signed paperbacks are available on my shop. https://870b9b.myshopify.com/

YOUR REVIEWS MATTER! (Seriously. Thank you from the bottom of my heart.) If you loved Rhyett and Brexley's story, we are SO appreciative for every single rating and review!

YOU CAN LEAVE your review on Goodreads here now: https://www.goodreads.com/book/show/168283789-south-of-the-skyway

You can post reviews on Amazon here: https://a.co/d/joodilp

ACKNOWLEDGEMENTS

To my amazing readers! Whether you found me through Grayshell, or you're new to my world, thank you so much for making this dream a reality. You're the real deal.

My amazing Alpha readers, Kate and Halaia: thank you so much for believing in me, for jumping in to a brand new genre and brand new world, and making this readable.

Lili, Halaia, Kate, Darian and Mel: Thank you for the laughs, your friendships, and comical inspiration for Brexley and Noel's endless shenanigans. There are so many pieces of you guys in here.

My hubby: for having my back, speaking life into this series, and keeping me fed+hydrated when I vanish into story land.

Heather! Woman. You are my life line. I don't even want to imagine what it would look like trying to navigate this wild world without you!

Shannon! Thank you so much for taking my babbling and making a gorgeous set of covers for my babies! They're perfection.

All of my indie author friends—there is no world where I could have done this without you guys. Thank you from the bottom of my heart for all of your help and encouragement. Love you guys forever xoxo

ABOUT THE AUTHOR

Sydne Barnett is a lover of spunky, badass heroines, and heroes that embrace their wild. She's an avid reader, never turns down a good cup of coffee, loves hiking with her hubby, and lives for finding their next adventure.

If she's not writing, you can probably find her behind her camera, swimming, or curled up with a homemade pastry, watching Friends, HYMYM, or Gilmore Girls.

Raised in the Treasure Valley, Idaho, Sydne has a love for one-light towns, and winding backroads, but refusing to ignore her soul's call for adventure, she hit the road with her family, and now they call the world their home.

Let's connect!

Reader's Group: https://www.facebook.com/groups/grayshellbabes

Tiktok: https://www.tiktok.com/@barnettbooktalk

Instagram: https://www.instagram.com/barnettbooktalk/

Newsletter: https://shorturl.at/acJSZ

Patreon: https://www.patreon.com/GrayshellUnhinged

Also in *Nomadic Rhodes*

Brewing Temptation (Book 2)
Finding A Way Back Home, (Book 3)

Romantic High Fantasy as S.J. Barnett

Commanding Flame And Shield (Grayshell Rising, Book One)
Commanding Earth And Shadow (Grayshell Rising, Book Two)